# SCIPIO'S END

BOOK SIX OF THE
SCIPIO AFRICANUS SAGA

MARTIN TESSMER

## Dedication

*To all my faithful readers.*

*Thanks for pursuing Scipio's quest with me*

# *ACKNOWLEDGMENTS*

Among 20th and 21st century historians, I am primarily indebted to Professor Richard Gabriel for his informative and readable *Scipio Africanus: Rome's Greatest General,* and *Ancient Arms and Armies of Antiquity*. H. Liddell Hart's *Scipio Africanus: Greater Than Napoleon* provided many valuable insights into Scipio the general and Scipio the man. John Peddle's *Hannibal's War* helped flesh out the personality, tactics, and motivations of Hannibal the Great. Nigel Bagnall's *The Punic Wars* provided confirmatory evidence for information I drew from Gabriel, Livy, Polybius, Mommsen, and others. Thanks to you all.

Among classic historians, I owe a deep debt of gratitude to Titus Livius (Livy) for *Hannibal's War: Books 21-30* (translated by J.C. Yardley) and Polybius for *The Histories* (translated by Robin Waterfield). Cassius Dio's *Roman History* provided additional details and confirmed some of Livy's and Polybius' assertions. Appian, Dodge, and Mommsen, thanks to you all for the many tidbits and corrections your works provided.

Cato the Elder's *De Agri Cultura* and Plutarch's *Roman Lives* provided insight into Cato and the Gracchi, central figures of Western History.

I must give a tip of the hat to Wikipedia. Wikimedia, and the scores of websites about the people and countries of 200 BCE. The Total War Center and Forum Romanum were excellent sources of information, commentary, and argument. The scholarship of our 21st century digital community is exacting and generous.

Susan Sernau, my copy editor, has been a continuing source of guidance and inspiration. Susan, I am deeply indebted to you.

# CREDITS

- Cover design by pro_ebookcovers at Fiverr.com.
- Battle maps by Martin Tessmer.
- Terrain maps by Martin Tessmer.
- Gallic Warrior drawing provided by Deposit Photos.
- Scipio Africanus coin photo provided by Bode Museum.
- Thracian Warrior drawing provided by Wikimedia Commons, courtesy of Dariusz T. Wielec.
- Antiochus III photo provided by Wikimedia Commons, courtesy of Auguste Girandon.
- Thermopylae Pass photo provided by Wikimedia, courtesy of Ronny Siegel.
- Hannibal the Great photo provided by Martin Tessmer.
- Gladiatrix photo by provided by Wikimedia Commons, courtesy of Casevar.
- Roman quinquereme drawing provided by Wikimedia Commons, courtesy of Lutatius.
- Cataphract image provided by Wikimedia Commons, courtesy of Zereshk.

- Battle of Magnesia image provided by Pinterest, source unknown.
- Cato the Elder image provided by Wikimedia Commons, courtesy of Carlo Brogi
- Hannibal Barca image provided by Wikimedia Commons, courtesy of Sebastian Slodtz.
- Scipio Africanus image provided by Wikimedia Commons, courtesy of Peter Paul Rubens.
- Cornelia Africana photo provided by Martin Tessmer.
- Tiberius and Gaius Gracchus photo provided by Martin Tessmer.

# *A NOTE ON HISTORICAL ACCURACY*

*Scipio's End* is a dramatization of the actual events surrounding Publius Cornelius Scipio's military and political activities after his conquest of Carthage, as recorded by Livy, Polybius, Gabriel, Appian, Mommsen, Bagnall, and Beard.

This is a work of historical fiction, meaning it weaves together elements of fiction and historical record. It is not a history textbook.

The book's major characters, places, events, battles, and timelines are matters of record, meaning they are noted by at least one of our acknowledged historians. Footnotes are included in the text to document its historical aspects. I have included numerous quotes of the characters' actual words, as described by Livy and Polybius, with a source footnote at the end of the quote.

The story's Hellenic Party and Latin Party names were created to capture the enmity between a Roman faction favoring a more "decadent" Hellenic lifestyle and the Roman agrarian traditionalists who disparaged them. Scipio and Cato were notable examples of Hellenic and Latin attitudes, respectively.

"He seems to have taken the best elements from Greece and Rome, and to have blended them—refining the crudeness and narrowness of early Republican Rome without diminishing its virility.

Yet it was this very influence as an apostle of civilization and of the humanities that earned him the bitter animosity, as it stimulated the fear, of Romans of the old school. Cato and his kind might have forgiven his military success and self-confidence, but nothing but his downfall could atone for his crime in introducing Greek customs, philosophy, and literature."

Basil H. Liddell-Hart. *Scipio Africanus: Greater than Napoleon*. Cambridge, MA: Perseus Books. 1926, pp. 273-74.

# TABLE OF CONTENTS

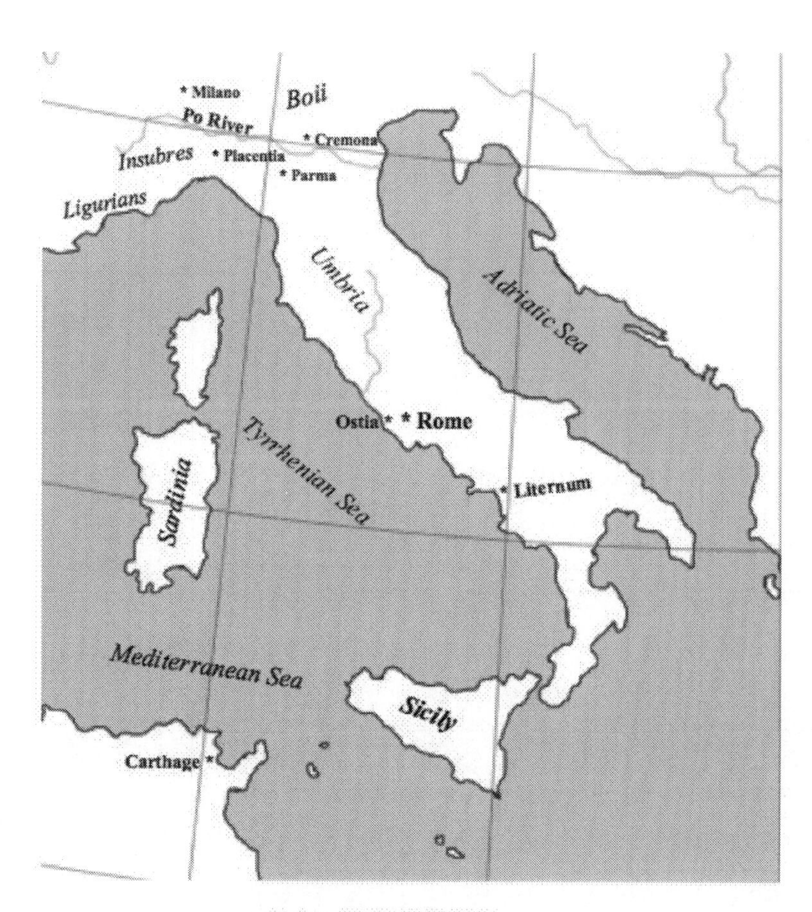


**Italia 194-189 BCE**

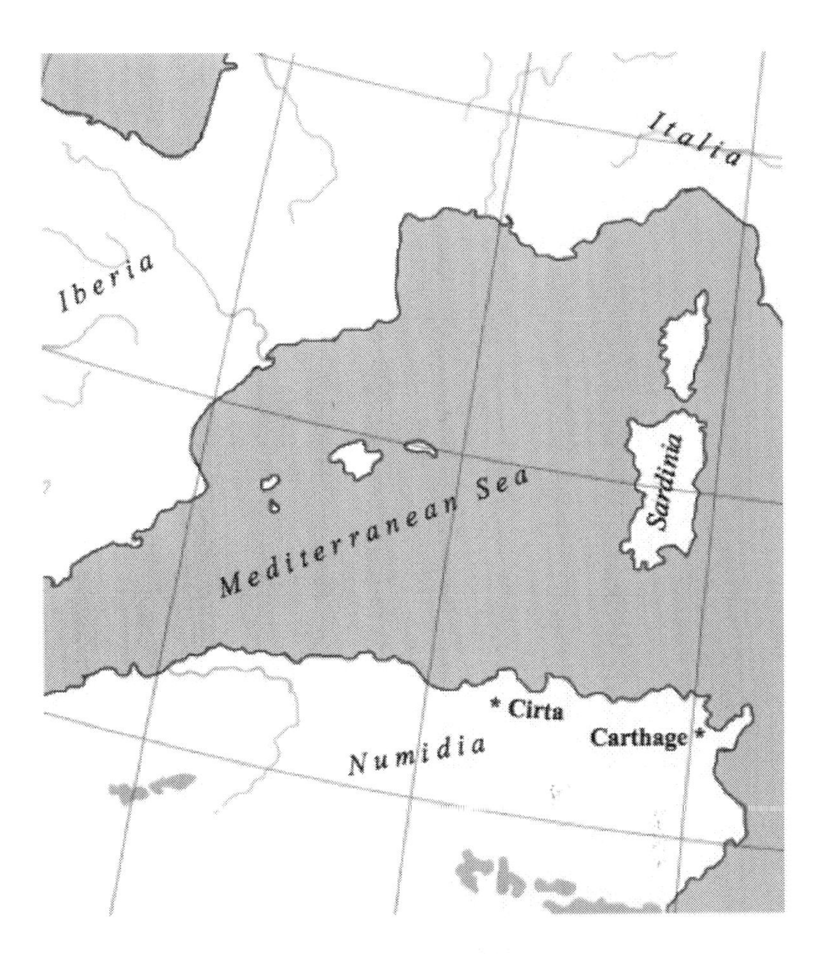


North Africa and Iberia

194-189 BCE

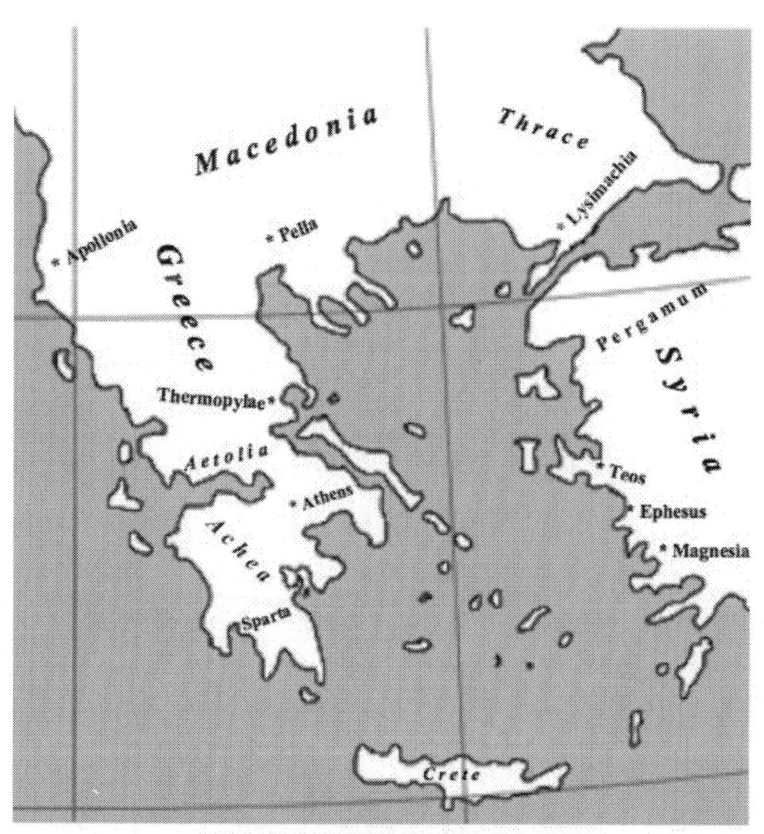


**Greece, Macedonia, and Asia Minor**

**194-189 BCE**

# I. A DAY IN A LIFE

PO RIVER VALLEY, NORTH ITALIA, 194 BCE. The goshawk's cries shrill through the somnolent Roman camp. Perched atop the sturdy camp palisade, the chicken-sized predator cocks his copper eye at the far wall across the camp, watching his mate hop across the serried stakes.

The slate blue hawk shrieks again, posing a question. *Is there prey?* The female spreads her wings and coasts toward the Alps' foothills to the north, seeking better game. With a ruffled shrug of his feathers, the goshawk arcs into the lemon sky, pursuing his life mate.

*Jupiter's cock, what are those birds screeching about?* Fabian Procius pokes his head out from his rough wool blanket, rubbing the sleep from his eyes. The veteran legionnaire pushes himself to a sitting position and studies his seven dozing tentmates, listening to their snores and mutters. He sniffs disdainfully. *Look at them. It's almost dawn and they're as still as stones. They'd better get up and get ready for the march. It's going to be a long one today.*

Fabian sits up and rubs the small of his back. *Panacea,*[i] *help me, I feel so stiff today!* He grins. *You have thirty years on you now, boy. You feel stiff every day.*

The soldier grasps his grey wool tunic and hobnailed sandals. He crawls out from his contubernium, the eight-man tent he shares with his fellow foot soldiers. Fabian stands in the middle of the fifty-foot wide path between the tent rows, stretching back his arms. He wraps his linen subligaculum about his naked loins, pinning the top strip into the waistband.

After a tug to ensure his underwear is secure, Fabian begins his morning calisthenics.[ii] He dances through the dozens of squats, jumps, and pushups that are his daily routine, moving smoothly from one exercise to another. Fabian finishes with a series of boulder lifts, using a large river rock he'd placed near the tent flap. Minutes later he flips the rock down, his body covered with a fine sheen of sweat. *There! Now I'm awake!*

After a visit to the latrine ditch near the west wall, Fabian treads toward the open gates of the eastern portal, following the horses and mules that are being herded out to graze. He exits the gates and veers away from the animals, stopping by a bush-lined feeder stream. He glances down the waterway and then back at the camp. *No one's here. Got a bit of privacy for a while.*

Shedding his loincloth, Fabian laves himself in the stream's snowmelt waters, hooting with each handful he splashes onto himself. He dries himself with the brown cape he plundered from the Gallic fort his army destroyed last week, admiring the vivid blue squares embroidered on its border. *I wash this up, it'll make a fine gift for the wife.*

A chill wind wafts across his body and he scrambles back into his clothes. He gazes at the cloud-clawing Alps that loom north of him, already wearing their white caps of January snow. *Going to be crisp today. Good marching weather!*

A Roman patrol emerges from the foothills across the plain, their bronze helmets winking at the hazed morning sun. Fabian smiles. *The exploradores are out early. I won't have to worry about a sneak attack.* The legionnaire bends over and peers into a streamside pool of water, studying his reflection. He rubs the top of his head. *I've got to get the camp barber to shave my head again. Don't look as old when I'm bald.*

A half-mile upstream, three pairs of ice-blue eyes peer out from the scrub oak surrounding the creek. The eyes watch Fabian bathing in the stream. When Fabian rises to leave, the eyes turn to the herdsmen leading the camp horses and mules into the tallest patches of grass.

"They have let their animals out early today, brothers," says one pair of eyes. "That means they're going to break camp."

"Aye, and we know where they'll be going," replies another.

"Let's get back to the horses," the third orders. "We have to prepare a fitting welcome for them." The bushes rustle, and the eyes disappear.

His toilet complete, Fabian walks briskly back to camp. He grins at the sound of the buccina blaring out the wake-up call. *The horns will get those lazy bastards up and running. Hope my tent mates have got the cookfire going.* He enters the eastern portal, waving at the four sentries atop the guard towers. Fabius smiles with satisfaction when he nears his tent. Two of his men are stoking a flickering pyramid of twigs and branches.

"Where have you been?" asks a doe-eyed youth, poking the fire with a pine branch.

"Nowhere special, Tree," says Fabian.

Standing almost six feet tall, young Cassius has been nicknamed "Tree" by his tentmates, an appellation that he bears with good humor. He grins slyly. "Been visiting the town prostitutes? A final poke before we go?"

"I've been preparing for the march," Fabian replies stiffly. "You're a young man. you should get up earlier. Get in a workout before the day starts! That's what Marcus Silenus used to do. Do you remember him from school? He was the greatest legionnaire of all."

"Yes he did, but he was crazy!" The willowy boy replies. "And I hear that bastard son of his, Marcus Aemilius, is just as insane! Marching six hours a day is more than enough for me!"

Fabian reaches over and squeezes Cassius' bicep in his hoary palm. "You should be so crazy! Just look at you. You're a hastati and you can barely hold your shield for half an hour."

Cassius shrugs. "I only need to hold it that long. Then the principes move up and replace us," He turns back to the fire.

*He's as bad as my boy back home!* Fabian crawls inside the tent and grabs his sarcina by its cross pole, pulling it outside with him. He scrabbles inside the leather pack until he finds his grain pouch and cooking pot. The legionnaire throws two handfuls of farro wheat into the pot, followed by a pinch of his salt allotment. He pours in some water from his waterskin and stirs it with a stick.

Soon, Fabian's porridge is energetically bubbling. "Time to sweeten the pot," he says, plopping in three of the dried pears that were part of this month's food allotment. He pulls the pot off the fire, grabs his wide pewter spoon, and shovels down his breakfast. *Wish I had some of that Parma cheese to go with this, it was fantastic! Shouldn't have swapped it for that wineskin of Falernian.*

The buccina sound the call for the march. Fabian strolls over to the camp wall and pries two saplings from it, hefting them in his hands. *These two won't be too hard to carry. Wish the consul would tow them in a wagon. But no, we have to carry them because Scipio Africanus made his men do it! As if he could ever be another Scipio!*

Fabian runs his calloused thumb across one sapling's knobby bark, tweaking his forefinger on its sharpened end. *Hmm. We could jam a spearhead on these and make emergency spears out of them.*

He jabs the stake at an imaginary enemy, then jams its butt end into the ground, angling it forward. *We could stick a spike on the other end and dig them into the ground, make a spear wall in no time. I'll tell my cousin Cato about this, he's a big man in Rome.*

Fabian fingers the stake, thinking. He shakes his head. *No, Cato doesn't like new ideas. Scipio Africanus, that's the one! He's always dreaming up new formations and weapons.*

The soldier heads back to his tent, his two stakes bouncing upon his shoulder. He returns by the Via Principalis, the hundred-foot-wide street that divides the officers' tents from the legionnaires' quarters. As he turns left toward his own tent, he watches the men of the second legion dismantle the consul's and tribunes' tents. He sees Consul Tiberius Sempronius standing in front of the workers, already clad in his gleaming bronze battle armor.

Fabian frowns at the lanky young consul. *Just our luck to get him instead of Scipio. Why's our best general sitting in Rome while we get a rawboned pup? Only reason he got elected was his father fought with Scipio.*[iii] *That Senate is as crazy as Furor!*

The first cohort of the second legion marches past Fabian, flowing out through the main gate. As a member of the second legion's ninth cohort, Fabian knows he has a half hour before he will march out with his fellows. *Still have time to sharpen my sword.*

Cassius trots over, his eyes wide with concern "Look out, old Quintus is looking for you, and it's not to give you a wreath!"

Fabian sees a blood red helmet crest bobbing above the top of his tent. He sighs. *You leave camp for a few minutes, and they act like you joined the Boii!* He marches toward the block-bodied centurion, his shoulders tense with anticipation. Quintus stands waiting, slapping his short sword in his palm.

"Where have you been? You are the decanus for your tent, you should be getting your men ready to leave. And what do you do? You traipse out the gates to go masturbate by the bushes!"

Young Cassius chuckles, covering his grin with his long slender fingers. As a frequent target of the gravelly centurion, Tree is delighted to see Quintus berating someone else.

"I just wanted to clean up before we left," Fabian declares. "Wanted to look good for the march."

"Clean up? Look good? This is a campaign, not a wedding! Better you were bathed in the blood of our enemies, then you'd look more presentable!"

He points his gladius toward the main gates. "Take your men to quaestor's tent, he needs help loading the pay wagons. Then get back here and get ready to march!"

"I hear and obey," Fabian replies. *You fly-specked pig-butt!*

An hour and a half later, the last of the six-mile army column marches out from the disassembled camp. The Umbrian riders flank the scores of baggage wagons that bring up the rear, their eyes scanning the foothills that ring the vast Po Valley. The North Italia allies study every bush and tree around them. The Umbrians have fought the Gauls for over a century. They know that the wily barbarians may strike at any time, as sudden and furious as an alpine storm.

The army marches southwest toward the Milano garrison, the jagged Alps rearing high in the distance. Tiberius Sempronius rides in the army vanguard, nervously scanning the rolling green hills that encircle them. For the tenth time that morning, the young general sends a scouting patrol out to comb the hillsides. An hour later, his patrol leader returns with the same message as the other scouts: no signs of enemy activity.

The young consul grins. “That is welcome news, Pontius. Perhaps General Flaccus has pacified the region, after last year’s victory over Dorulatus.[iv]”

“You mean Marcus Valerius Flaccus? I heard he spent most of the battle in his tent,” the grizzled scout replies. “But he was the man in charge, so I guess he gets credit for the victory.” The scout leader chuckles. “Maybe that explains why he didn’t get a triumph for his victory, although Cato got one for Iberia.”[v]

“I know nothing about that,” the young consul sniffs. “I only know that Dorulatus is dead, and the Insubres have retreated to their mountain territories.”

“Ah, but the Boii, they are the ones we should worry about,” Pontius replies. “They’ve got those three crazy brothers leading them. All they do is loot and burn.”

“Why worry about the Boii? They are far to the southeast of us. Let the next consul worry about them.”

At midday the army enters the wide plains of the Ticinus River Valley, an area dotted with farms and wheat fields. Fabian notices a thin rope of black smoke trailing above the distant foothills to the right of him. He waves over Pontius.

"Go see where that smoke is coming from. Get back here as soon as you can." As Pontius gallops off, Sempronius calls over the legates of the second and fourth legions.

"We will take our rest here," he tells them. "Turn the animals loose to graze." The buccinae sound the call for the army's midday break. The legionnaires drop their packs and sprawl out upon the flood plain, grateful for a rest after four hours of marching.[vi]

Fabian pulls off his domed helmet and stretches out upon the side of the road, resting his head on his sarcina. He chews on a handful of boiled fava beans from last night's dinner, feeling at peace with the world.

As he gazes at the drifting clouds, Fabian dreams of the Iberian farm he hopes to own when his two-year service expires next month. *General Scipio said there are still plots available at the colonies he founded there,*[vii] *ones with good water and fertile ground. I'm going to petition for one when I get back, get away from Rome's stinking masses. Must be over a million people there now, if you count all the cursed slaves who are taking our farm jobs. Won't have to worry about that in Iberia!*

The horns blare the order to reform. Fabian pushes himself upright and strolls over to his cohort, rubbing the back of his neck. The army drovers herd the pack animals back from their grazing spots. The soldiers return to their columns, and the army marches on.

Consul Sempronius removes his helmet and wipes his brow. *Vulcan's balls, it's hot for a winter day. You'd think we were marching into Africa!* He shades his brow with his hand, looking for his overdue scouting party.

Minutes later, he sees three dots moving toward him. The dots grow larger, and the outline of three riders appear. *There they are! What took them so long?*

The consul notices that one of the riders is slumped forward in his saddle. *What in Hades…?* He sees the other two scouts' eyes are large with alarm.

The lead scout pulls up in front of Sempronius. "General, the outpost is burning!" he blurts, as the other two riders draw up behind him.

The slumped figure slides sideways off the horse and thumps onto the ground, trailing the blood-streaked ropes that were tied around his body.

Sempronius dismounts and bends over the motionless figure. Pontius' glassy eyes stare up at him.

"What happened?" Sempronius says.

"The Gauls are attacking the outpost!" one scout declares. "They're trying to burn down its walls!" He looks at Pontius' corpse. His lower lip trembles. "Pontius took a spear in the back. He told us to leave him, but we just couldn't do it."

"Get Pontius into a wagon," Sempronius says. "We'll burn him later." He motions over his two legion commanders. "The Milano outpost is under siege. We march to it, double time."

The horns echo down the miles-long column, and the infantry picks up their pace. The Roman and allied cavalry fan out to the sides of the soldiers, combing the countryside for potential attackers.

Sempronius rides at the front of the column, flanked by his praetorian guard. His eyes follow the smoke column that twists into the cloud-streaked sky, watching it darken from gray to black. His heart quickens. *They're out there waiting for us, somewhere. My first battle is coming. Praise Jupiter I have so many veterans with me.*

A half mile behind Sempronius, Fabian marches in the middle of his cohort, glancing anxiously at the low lying hills surrounding him. "Something's up," he says to young Cassius, who marches next to him. "We're in a big hurry to go nowhere."

"Are we going to fight?" Cassius asks, nervously clenching his sword belt.

Fabian eyes the smoke column. "I'd get ready. But don't worry. Just remember what we say: keep your place in line and you'll be fine."

A scout races in toward Sempronius, his horse lathered with effort. The equite vaults from his mount and trots over to the general. "What is it?" Sempronius barks.

The equite juts out his quaking right hand in a salute. "Gauls, thousands of Gauls. It's the Boii, and the Insubres. I can tell by their standards."

The young consul swallows. *Be calm, the men are watching you.* "How many did you say?"

"Thousands, General. Tens of thousands. Over by the outpost."

"And the outpost?"

The scout shakes his bowed head. "I pray it was quick for them."

Sempronius waves over the legates of his two legions. "The outpost is gone. The Gauls are waiting for us near the end of the valley. We will pitch camp at its mouth and prepare for them. Go tell the allied commanders."

An hour later, the vanguard passes through a dense forest and enters the widespread Milano Valley. Sempronius raises his right hand. The army halts. He peers over his horse's neck, taking in the grim spectacle before him.

Thousands of tall armored men line the wide grassy plain. They stand with their five-foot oblong shields planted into the ground in front of them. The shields on Sempronius' right bear a boar rampant on a powder blue background, the mark of the Boii nation. The left side clans hold the light green shields of the Insubres, a pair of crossed axes testifying to their warlike spirit.

The remains of the Milano outpost lie a spear's throw behind the barbarians. Four mounds of smoldering logs bespeak the fate of the stout walls that once guarded its legionnaires. Scores of naked corpses sprawl outside the ruins, dragged from the fires so that they could be safely plundered.

Anger flares inside Sempronius, burning away his anxiety. *Gods help me, I will give you men revenge.*

A train of bare-chested warriors march out from the outpost remains. Each carries a Roman javelin on his shoulders. A blood-stained satchel dangles from each of the pila, bulging roundly with its contents. The forty men march past their compatriots. They halt in front of the three Boii brothers who lead the army.

Boiorix, Sudarix and Tarbos are burly, bare-chested warriors clad in the blue plaid pants of the Boii nation. Their conical helmets all sport curved bull's horns, with Boiorix's gold horns longer and brighter than his brothers' silver ones.

Boiorix nods at the spear carriers. "Put them in a nice, straight line," he says, grinning. "The Romans like things neat and orderly."

The men march another dozen paces from the front of their lines. They stop, spaced an arm's length from each other. "Go on, show them!" Boiorix shouts. The Gauls lay the satchels at their feet and shove their spears' butt ends deep into the ground. They reach into the satchels.

Each man pulls out a severed Roman head. Grasping the heads by the ears, they stab them onto the spearheads, twisting them down until they are firmly fastened.

"Open their mouths and eyes," Boiorix commands. "I want the Romans to see the flies crawling in and out." His minions finish their grisly task and march back to their clans.

The Romans watch their compatriots' heads being mounted, aghast with horror. "Pigs!" screams one legionnaire. "Gods damn you to fire!" bellows another. Dozens fling their pila at the Gauls. The javelins land far short of their distant mark.

The barbarians laugh. Dozens pull down their pants and bare their backsides to the Romans, hooting their derision.

"Enough!" Sempronius shouts, fighting to keep his voice steady. "Keep your discipline! They will pay for this soon enough!"

Sempronius looks to his left, watching the sun creep down toward the pyramidal alpine peaks. *Too late to move anywhere. We'll have to build our camp here. Right in front of that horror.* He turns to his legates.

"Britannicus, Caduceus, I need you to get the first four cohorts into a defensive formation. Use the allies, too. The rest of our men will build the camp."

"But the wagons haven't brought up our tents yet," Caduceus replies. "We always start with..."

Sempronius whirls on him, his face blood red. "Don't worry about the fucking tents, we have to get our walls up!" The legates spin on their heels and march away.

The Roman and allied infantrymen tread onto the plain and form a battle line. The arriving soldiers set to work digging a deep trench around the camp perimeter, their pack mattocks biting deep into the rich river bottomland. They pile the dirt into a three-foot palisade and plant their stakes—and those of the men guarding them—into the earthen mound. The Gauls watch the Romans, shouting insults and jokes.

The sun begins to set. Boiorix raises his sword over his head. "Let's get our men into camp," He tells his brothers. Boiorix stalks back to the enormous ring of wagons and baggage that forms the Gauls' rude camp. The Gauls eagerly follow, bored with watching the industrious Romans.

Late that night, the Romans finish their camp. The weary legionnaires file through the twin gates and pitch their tents in the rows outlined by small wooden stakes. Most of the men are too tired to cook dinner.

They content themselves with whatever dried cheese and fruit they can find in their packs.

Fabian sprawls on the pathway in front of his tent, grasping the last of his dried biscuits. He douses the buccelatum with olive oil and bites through its leathery crust, chewing laboriously. *Better than nothing—but not by much.*

"There go Britannicus and Caduceus," a nearby standard-bearer comments. "Something's up for sure."

Fabian watches the two commanders push into Sempronius' tent, their faces grim. "They're having a war meeting. We're going to fight those big bastards tomorrow, sure as old Sol rises to light the day."

He looks back at his tent. A smile tugs at the corners of his mouth. *Might as well splurge. Who knows if I'll be here tomorrow night?*

The veteran crawls back inside his tent. Cassius snores next to his sleeping blanket, curled into a fetal ball. *Get your rest for tomorrow, boy. You young ones have more energy, but you don't know how to use it. A half hour on the front and you'll be ready to drop.*

Fabian reaches inside his pack and retrieves a hand-sized package wrapped in waxed papyrus. He crawls out of the tent.

The decurion sits cross-legged on the pathway and carefully unwraps his package. A small block of dried Parma bacon lies inside it, marbled with veins of dark red pork. Fabian bends over and inhales its smoky aroma. *Ah, gods! Women should make a perfume of this—they'd be irresistible.* He chomps into a corner of the block and slowly chews it, letting the taste linger on his tongue. Two more bites and half the block is gone.

Fabian hefts the remainder in his hand. *Should I eat it? Be a waste to save it if I die tomorrow. But if I live, how will I celebrate?* He takes another bite. *Wish General Scipio was here. He'd get us out of this scrape.*

Fabian fingers the last of his bacon. *You're a Roman,* he admonishes himself. *Show some willpower.* The decurion rewraps his treasure. After a final, lingering, sniff, Fabian crawls inside the tent and stuffs the remainder into the bottom of his pack. He wraps himself inside his camp blanket, ready for sleep.

*Got to keep my wits about me tomorrow. I've got Portia waiting for me. And that farm in Iberia. And bacon after the battle.*

While Fabian drifts off, Consul Sempronius concludes a war meeting with his legates and senior tribunes. The officers encircle a Po Valley map stretched across the consul's oak plank table, studying the wooden figurines that designate the two sides' forces of infantry and cavalry.

"So it's decided," Sempronius says. "We will remain in camp and reinforce our defenses. I will send a message to my fellow consul, Scipio Africanus, requesting he take his army up here as soon as possible."[viii]

The tribunes glance at one another, shuffling uneasily. Britannicus steps nearer to Sempronius. "We are to hide inside our walls?" the gray-haired patrician says evenly. "After what they did to our men?"

Sempronius' green eyes flash with irritation. "That is the wise thing to do. There may be forty thousand of them out there, fighting on their home land. I'm not interested in a revenge fight. I want to ensure their total destruction. To wipe them out. We can best do that by combining our forces. Is that understood?"

Brash Caduceus breaks the ensuing silence. The older man raises his one remaining hand. "I will say this," the legate replies. "If you want to beat wily Boiorix and his brothers, Scipio's your man. I've fought alongside him in Iberia, when he conquered the Three Generals. He'd outsmart Minerva herself!"

Several of the tribunes chuckle, grateful for a break in the tension. Britannicus stares at the tent wall, his lips pressed into lines of frustrated anger.

"I believe you are right," Sempronius says, "and yet he languishes in Rome, doing nothing. That is why I am sending messengers within the hour, requesting his aid.[ix] We will see what the Senate has to say about this."

ROME, 194 BCE. The rooster crows his challenge to the morning sun, strutting along the pebbled walkway in the Scipio manse's garden. He charges at a peacock who strays too close to him, pecking at its wings.

The shimmering green bird unleashes one of its unearthly, wailing cries. It scrabbles into the sage and basil bushes that cluster beneath the roses. The rooster preens, strutting along the walk. He crows a warning to any who would challenge him.

Inside the town house, the household begins to stir. Eighty-year-old Rufus rises from his sleeping pallet near the kitchen entry. He pokes a finger into the small blanketed form next to him.

"Get up Little Rufus, it's time to bake the bread." The gaunt old man stretches out his knobby hands, waiting for his grandson to join him. The little boy pulls his blanket over his head.

"Don't want to," the child mumbles. "Go 'way."

Rufus gently nudges the boy with a sandaled foot. "Come on now, we have duties."

"Don't care," comes the reply.

*He's as stubborn as his father was,* Rufus fumes. *Told him not to join that slave legion. But no, he had to go and get himself killed fighting the Carthaginians. Thank the gods the Scipios let us stay here as freemen, or we'd be begging on the Aventine.*

"Today is a special day for the Master," the elder Rufus says. "There will be moon cakes!"

A gray eye peeps at him from a corner of the blanket. "Moon cakes?"

"Yes! Sweet, sweet yellow cake, with icing fit for the gods! I made them myself."

The spindly little boy pushes himself up from his straw mat, rubbing his eyes.

"That's better," Rufus says. The old man hobbles toward the small kitchen in the rear of the house. He strikes stone to iron and kindles the tinder in the clay oven's semicircular mouth. When the branches flare, he tosses in two handfuls of charcoal.

"Go on, now. Prepare the bread," he says to his sleepy helper.

Little Rufus reaches into an amphora as tall as he is. He doles out two cupfuls of emmer grain into a pottery bowl. His grandfather tosses in the salt, olive oil, and water. "Mix it."

The boy squats on the cobbled kitchen floor, the bowl nestled between his legs. He stirs the mix with a marble pestle, circling it one way, and then another. The mix becomes a glue-like, sepia dough.

Rufus dips his hands in olive oil. He scoops out handfuls of the mix and pats them into round, flat cakes. The elder slides his knife across the top, neatly dividing each cake into eight portions. He places two loaves on his oak paddle and eases them into the mouth of the clay oven, leaving them to bake on a rack above its glowing coals.

"We have to hurry," he says, "the pater familias will be up by now."

Rufus need not have worried. Scipio Africanus still lies abed, his eyelids flickering with the tumult of the dream inside him. The same dream he has had thrice this week.

*His best friend Laelius and his brother Lucius stand in the field of battle, their purple consul's capes draped around their glittering bronze armor. They shout and gesture at each other, arguing over who is to lead the army.*

*Thousands of Antiochus' Syrians flood down the hills and jaunt toward the immobile legions, his murderous scythed chariots trundling in front of his army. The two commanders ignore the Syrian hordes, screaming at each other as their doom approaches.*

*"I deserve it!" Laelius declares. "I've led men through a dozen*

*battles!"*

*"My brother and I share the same blood," Lucius counters. "I am born to conquer!"*

*The Syrians close upon the immobile front lines. They hurl their spears. Hundreds of Romans fall like statues, spears jutting from their torsos. The survivors do not move.*

*Scipio watches the slaughter, his heart in his throat. "They are attacking!" he screams. "Do something!"*

*The two turn and stare at him, their faces flush with anger. "Tell us, Brother," Lucius says. "Who's in charge? What should we do?"*

*The chariots chop into the Romans, flinging limbs from their butchering wheels. Scipio flaps his arms helplessly. "I can't!" he yells. "They won't let me!"*

Scipio vaults upright on this sleeping pallet, his heart hammering in his ears. *That cursed dream again. Gods above, what is that supposed to mean?*

He holds his right hand in front of him. *At least the shakes haven't come upon me. I can't look ill in front of the Senate. Too much at stake today.*

"Well, the great general has finally risen from his throne."

Amelia strolls into the bedroom. Her auburn hair cascades to the shoulders of a wispy silk tunic that matches her emerald eyes. At forty years old, the wife of Scipio has become a beautiful, dignified matron, blessed with a ripe, full figure. She strolls toward Scipio's beside. A mischievous smile plays about her lips.

"Here, I fixed you something to break your fast. You can have it in bed."

Scipio blinks sleepily. "Break my fast in bed? A novel idea, though I doubt it will catch on."

"Well, today is a special day, as well you know," Amelia replies. "It's your dies natalis, your forty-second birth day! I have prepared a special breakfast for it!"

Scipio smirks. "I am not sure I want to be reminded it's my forty-second, but I could use some food. What did you fix me?"

"Olive oil."

"Oil? You're giving me oil for breakfast?"

"It's more like olive oil for your dessert."

Amelia snaps her fingers. A handsome young woman appears in the bedroom doorway. She carries a shallow brass bowl, its sides etched with figures of satyrs chasing half-naked nymphs.

Amelia takes the bowl from the woman and lays it next to the sleeping pallet. "Do you like the design, Husband? I bought it at Market Street last week, especially for your breakfast."

Scipio props himself on his elbows. "I don't understand any of this. I should get ready for the Senate meeting." He starts to rise, but a firm hand pushes him back.

"Lie still. You may be First Speaker of Rome, but it's time for you to be quiet. And enjoy."

She motions to the slave. The willowy young woman shrugs off her dark blue tunic. It slides down her tawny body and pools at her feet, leaving her nude. The slave walks over and stands next to Scipio's bedside, her face impassive.

Scipio looks inquisitively at his wife.

Amelia steps next to the woman. She runs her hands down the slave's body, smiling at her husband. "No, she's not your present. Well, not all of it. Magita is here to, shall we say, inspire you. I rented her from the Capitoline brothel."

"She is a wonder," Scipio says, tearing his eyes away from Magita.

"But you are even more beautiful!"

Amelia chuckles. "Well played, but you can save your flattery for the Senate! Besides, I paid her more for her skills than her appearance." She turns to the slave. "Proceed, Magita."

Magita pulls the linen sheet from Scipio's naked body. She runs her long, tapered fingers down his chest and across his abdomen, lingering on his nether region.

Magita arches an eyebrow. "Hmm. I see you do not require much encouragement, Dominus. But let me continue."

The courtesan dips her hands into the bowl of oil. She rubs her palms together, her carmine nails flashing with light. She bends over Scipio. Her hands cup him, gently twisting and stroking.

When Scipio's moans turn to gasps, Amelia steps between them. "Cease, or I will not be able to give him the rest of my present."

Magita reaches for the cotton towel next to the basin and wipes her hands. She slips her tunic over her head. With a slight nod to Amelia, she strolls out the doorway, smiling to herself.

"You've had dessert; now for the main course." Amelia reaches under her gown and tugs twice. A white linen scrap crumples between her feet.

Amelia climbs onto the pallet and straddles her husband. She lowers herself upon him, her green gown pooling around his hips. She undulates slowly, her hands splayed upon his stomach. Her cries comingle with his moans. They shudder together.

She slides off and lays beside him, stroking his sweaty face. "There, now you can go to the Senate! But take a few minutes for your birth day celebration in the atrium. Publius and Cornelia made some presents for you."

Scipio chuckles. "Another silver pin from Cornelia? And a wood carving from Publius?"

Amelia reaches down and tweaks his nose. "Just try to act surprised, Consul. Publius made one of Nike. I told him you buried the one I once gave you, at our retirement home in Liternum. He rushed over to Rufus and begged him to help make a new one for you."

She grins. "It looks more like a pigeon than the goddess of victory, so I thought I should tell you what it is."

"Best you did," Scipio says. "He does not take criticism lightly—at least not from me! He only listens to his Uncle Laelius."

Amelia taps his forehead. "Don't pout. He wants to seem perfect in your eyes. Do you know what it's like, being the son of the greatest general in Rome?"

Scipio's eyes darken. "I surely do. My father was the most powerful general in Rome, along with your father. He's the one who yoked me to this career of war and politics, making me promise to defend Rome forever."

Amelia strokes his shoulder. "Which you would never do to Publius," she says, a question in her voice.

Scipio's mouth tightens. "He shall choose his own path. That much I can give him."

"Do not be surprised if he follows you, anyway, though he might end up an admiral instead of a general!"

"He does love the sea," Scipio replies. "Maybe too much. He spends a lot of time on it."

Scipio brightens. "He is a good son, though. Much older than his ten years. And little Cornelia, she has your spirit. She is willful but caring. Always wants to do the right thing, even when it is to her detriment. Fortuna has blessed us."

Amelia rolls her eyes. "Would she were less beautiful. She has already become a challenge! I happened upon Tiberius Gracchus, that handsome young priest, at the temple of Jupiter. Can you believe it, he wants to marry her when she gets older! He says the gods came to him in a vision, told him they would sire the greatest Romans of all!" She shakes her head. "All the women in Rome, and still he seeks her!"

Scipio's face darkens. "She's what, two years old? He'd better keep his distance, or I'll slit his throat!"

Amelia laughs. "His morals are irreproachable, he is the chief priest of Rome! I told him that we will consider his proposal—later."

"Good, I have enough worries with the Senate. Today I have to plead my case to go to Syria. Those powder butts don't understand the threat that Antiochus poses. They are truly a pain in the ass."

He grins slyly. "In truth, I could use some treatment there!"

Amelia shoves him. "You have had enough massages for one day! Get up and go see the children."

"No more dessert?" he says, feigning disappointment. "No more main course?"

"You are now a man of golden years. You have to learn to pace yourself." She grins impishly. "Besides, every evening dinner should have a main course, don't you agree?"

"Oh, wholeheartedly!" he chirps, rising from the bed.

A half hour later, Scipio strolls into the family atrium, clad in a consul's purple-bordered toga. Amelia sits on a low-slung couch, facing a table lined with cakes shaped like crescent moons. Each honey-covered cake holds a flickering beeswax candle, turning the yellow icing into moonglow.[x] Publius and Cornelia sit next to Amelia, squirming to get at the treats.

A handsome, broad-shouldered man sits on the adjoining couch, smiling at the children's impatience. His smoothly muscled arm is curled about the waist of a svelte brunette woman with sea-blue eyes. She cradles their infant son in her sinewy, blade-scarred arms.

Scipio's face splits into a wide grin. He spreads out his arms. "Laelius! Prima! I am overjoyed you could attend!"

Prima hands the baby to Laelius and rises from the couch. Moving with the fluid grace of a trained fighter, the gladiatrix strides over and hugs Scipio firmly, kissing him lingeringly on each check. "May Jupiter bless your dies natalis. Just look at you, so regal-looking!"

"Ah, but I am the prettier one," Laelius says, running his fingers through his thick black curls. "All those weighty decisions have made you as gray as Senectus, though the god of old age is balder—but not by much!"

Prima wrinkles her nose at Scipio. "Ignore him; jealousy warps his tongue. You know he wants to be a consul, too."

"I *will* be a consul," Laelius blurts. "I'm a commoner, an orphan, and a war hero. I'll be the people's choice!"

"Then maybe I can be the patrician's choice," comes a voice from the doorway. A slender version of Scipio sidles into the atrium. He hurries to the moon cakes and pops one into his mouth.

"Your brother hasn't had one yet, Lucius," says Amelia. He flushes.

"Apologies," he stammers. "He should have first pick—as always."

"It's all right, Lucius. You can have mine. I have to get to the Senate chambers. And you have to be there, too, *Senator*."

"I'll go, I'll go!" Lucius replies peevishly. "Just not yet. I don't need to be there for all those sacrifices and prayers."

"You do if you want to be a praetor, and then a consul." Scipio retorts. He waves his hand toward Publius and Cornelia. "Go ahead. You get two each."

The children spring to the table and grab moon cakes in each hand, blowing out the candles. Publius grins at his father, his lips glistening with icing.

"Uncle Laelius is taking me sailing today!" Publius declares, crumbs dribbling from his mouth.

Scipio feigns amazement. "Again? I swear to Neptune, we might as well move down to Ostia, so you can live on the docks!" Scipio grabs a moon cake and bends over to kiss Amelia, "Until tonight, Carissima. I will look forward to the main course."

"It will be a special dish, I assure you," Amelia purrs. "Lots of spice."

"I can't wait to taste it," he replies, pacing toward the vestibule.

"Am I missing something?" Laelius says to Prima. "What are they having for dinner?"

"Nothing that you haven't had," Prima replies.

Scipio pauses at the family lararium in the vestibule. He bows to the wax death masks that encircle the small wooden altar, his eyes fixed on the one of his father Publius.

"I renew my vow to you, honored father. I promise to always protect Rome from harm, from all threats within and without." He shakes his head. "Especially against that backward-looking Latin Party!"

Scipio lays a moon cake on the top of the altar, placing it among the clay figurines of his family. He dips his hand into the incense bowl and scatters its contents over a shard of glowing charcoal in the altar's bronze brazier. The spicy smoke wafts into his nostrils. He bows his head.

"Gratitude, my birth genius, for watching over me this year. I humbly ask that you guide and guard me during the next."[xi] He looks at the figurines. "Protect my family through day and through night."

His worship complete, Rome's greatest general tromps through the manse's open front doors, ready for his battle with the Senate. Rufus stands in the cobbled street, holding a gray stallion by its rope bridle. Scipio clambers onto the horse, wincing at the stabs of pain in his lower back.

Scipio puts heels to his horse and trots slowly toward the Forum, his mind spinning with plans. *I've got to get them to approve a campaign against Antiochus. He could be organizing an invasion of Greece while we sit and argue about whether to keep our troops there*!

He glances over at the neighborhood's open air school. A dozen tunic-clad children sit on several small benches, busily scratching notes into their wax tablets. An elderly man paces back and forth in front of them, waggling his forefinger as he speaks.

Scipio listens to the students' bright chatter. He watches them wave their hands, eager to answer their tutor. He smiles wistfully. I *should have become a teacher, I wouldn't have to spend my life planning a war against an enemy half a world away from me. Father, cursed, beloved, Father, I still carry the burden of my promise to you.*

LYSIMACHIA, THRACE. Two men sit at the head of the thirty-foot marble slab that serves as a meeting table. A dozen Syrian commanders sit hushed before them.

The first is a hawk-faced man of middle age, his long arms as lean and tough as a raptor's claws. A black silk robe drapes down his angular shoulders, its borders filigreed with the same charging lions that decorate his crown. He slumps sideways in his tall chair, lost in thought. The Syrian commanders watch him expectantly, knowing his silence will be short.

"We are plagued with enemies!" King Antiochus fumes. "Flamininus' legions are blocking my way to central Greece. And the Thracians, they are too stupid to know when they're beat! They harass our armies every step of the way. Philip of Macedonia, who knows if he is friend or foe!"

He rubs the space between his eyebrows, squinting with frustration. "We're a year behind in my plan. The conquest of Greece and Italia seems like an unattainable goal."

The officers stare at each other, dismayed and disappointed. They had dreamed of becoming governors of Sparta, Athens, and Rome.

A heavyset older man lumbers from his seat at the middle of the table. "The Army of a Hundred Nations has over a hundred thousand men now, with more joining every day. If we collect them all here, we would be an unstoppable force. We could be in northern Greece within a fortnight!"

Antiochus sniffs. "And leave our homeland open to attacks from our enemies in Pergamum? Or from the Aetolians? I think not." The king's words set the officers to bickering about stratagems.

The man sitting next to the King Antiochus rises, and all fall silent. He is a tall, stately, man. His curled hair and beard are gray, but he bears the rock-muscled body of a lifelong warrior, his posture that of a man used to unquestioned command. His green eye burns with unquenched determination.

"I have come here, at Antiochus' request, to act as his advisor. And now I will advise. I would not worry about the Aetolians. Yes, they are allied to Rome, but it is an alliance of convenience. They resent the Romans, and think Rome does not give them credit for their mutual victories. Give them a reason to change sides, and they will do it."

"And what would that reason be, Hannibal?" asks Antiochus. The Carthaginian smiles.

"Power. Give them the power to conquer central Greece, and they will readily join us. Promise them enough provinces, and they will bend a knee to you." He chuckles. "They are not trustworthy, but they are ambitious. I trust ambition more than trust."

A slim, black-haired youth rises from his place near the head of the table. "May I speak now?" he says, scowling.

"Go ahead, Seleucus," Antiochus dourly replies. "You have always had your mother's need to express yourself." His comments provoke muted laughs from the officers.

Seleucus blushes, but he continues.

"What about Scipio Africanus, Father? "I have heard that he wants to bring an army over here and drive you back to Syria!"

The officers look anxiously at Antiochus, their dreams of conquest replaced by fears of destruction. Seleucus' eyes gleam with satisfaction, knowing his words have had their desired effect.

Seleucus takes a deep breath. "Syria is already a mighty nation, with riches beyond compare. We should forget about conquering Greece, and make a treaty with Rome. If we become one of their amici, no one would ever threaten us."

Hannibal winces at Seleucus' words. *This fool will cost me my last chance for revenge.* He nods toward the king.

"Perhaps your son is right," Hannibal says, his voice edged with sarcasm. "Perhaps the Romans will let you keep your ancestral lands, if agree to their conditions."

"What did you say?" Antiochus sputters. "They will *let* me keep my lands? No one *lets* me keep anything, I take what I want! And I want the territories that were taken from my father, Seleucus the Second![xii] I don't want to make peace with Rome. I am the champion of Greek freedom against Roman domination!"[xiii]

A burly, dark-skinned man pushes up from the head of the table, his face dark with anger. "My brother Seleucus is a fool. Have you not seen Rome take over Iberia, and do the same to Carthage? If we do not take Greece they will do it for us, and then cross the sea to our homeland! Strike them now, before Scipio arrives!"

Hannibal rubs his eyes. *Baal's balls, young Antiochus is as crazy as his father. The Syrians are not ready to take on Flamininus' veterans.*

The Carthaginian legend shakes his head. "As one who has oft defeated the Romans in battle, I say we must better train our men before we engage them."

"Ignore him, he is not of our family," Antiochus the Younger growls. "We can move on Flamininus now, and remove any future threat."

"Right now, Flaminius is the best ally we could have," Hannibal replies. "Though Scipio was his mentor, Flamininus disagrees with him about foreign occupation. He wants to take his men back home, to allay Greece's fears of Roman domination. Leave Flamininus alone, and he will leave."

"No, we strike now!" Antiochus the Younger blurts.

His father frowns at him. "Sit down," Antiochus says quietly.

"Winter is still upon the land," Hannibal says. "For now, secure your control of Thrace, but do not advance any farther. If you pose no threat to Greece major, Flamininus will see no reason to remain."

"So we exchange one threat for a worse one?" King Antiochus says, "Scipio will come here if Flamininus leaves!" He shakes his head. "I would rather face the student than the master."

"My spies tell me a different story," Hannibal replies. "Scipio would like to increase Rome's presence here, but the Latin Party will prevent that. In just a few months, Scipio will not be a problem. Wait and see, my king. Wait and see."

The king sighs. "So many opinions! Very well, Hannibal. I will wait a few months, until spring comes and the Romans stir from their winter quarters. Then we will see what happens with Flamininus—and Scipio."

Hannibal resumes his seat. He glances over at Antiochus' two sons. Seleucus sits in a slump, staring glassily into his lap. Antiochus the Younger leans on the table top, his hands clasped in front of him. He scowls at Hannibal.

*That one bears watching*, Hannibal decides. *He may become more obstacle than ally*. Hannibal grins at the young commander. He raises his middle finger and stabs it at him.

SENATE CHAMBERS, ROME. Scipio stands on the stone tile floor of the Curia Hostilia, pleading his case before the three hundred senators sitting on its semicircular stone benches. He paces back and forth, his eyes boring into the senator's faces.

"Antiochus is gathering strength. His Army of a Hundred Nations has invaded Thrace, and is moving into Greece." He slaps his fist into his palm. "We have to stop him now, before he crosses into Macedonia!"

Senators Cato and Flaccus sit in the front row to his right, surrounded by their Latin Party followers. Flaccus leans to Cato's ear. "We can't let Scipio do battle with Antiochus. If he wins, the Hellenics would hold power for a hundred years! We've got to send Scipio to Gaul."

"Antiochus is a greater threat than the Gauls," Cato mutters, his eyes fixed on Scipio.

"But Scipio is the greatest threat," Flaccus whispers. "If he defeats the Syrians, you will see your worst nightmare come true. Our country will lose its purity, its austerity. We'll become just like the weak-willed Greeks, whiling time and money on artistic pursuits. Do not oppose me on this!"

Cato glares at Flaccus but he says nothing. Flaccus rises from his seat. He steps onto the Senate floor. "Will you yield the floor to me, Consul?"

"Speak your piece, Flaccus." Scipio says. He sits in one of the two consular chairs that flank the Senate Elder's stool.

The tall storklike, patrician moves to Scipio's spot. He extends his right index finger toward the ceiling, striking an orator's pose. "Honored Senators, Scipio makes overmuch of this situation. Yes, we must protect our Greek possessions, but—"

"But they are our allies, not our possessions," Scipio interjects. Flaccus flushes. Several Hellenic senators chuckle at his discomfiture.

"Yes, we must protect Greece," Flaccus continues, "But we do not need to send our best general there. Our Aetolian allies have massed a considerable army. King Philip of Macedonia, whom we so recently defeated, he has a treaty with us. He will not allow the Syrians to cross into his kingdom. Antiochus would be a fool to war with either of them."

Flaccus spreads his arms. "And if the Syrian does go to war with them, his depleted army would be easy prey for General Flamininus and his men. No, my colleagues, Gaul is where Scipio is needed. Let him join his fellow consul." Flaccus stalks back to his seat, amid scattered shouts of agreement. He crosses his arms and smirks insolently at Scipio.

Scipio resumes his place on the floor. "Yes, the Aetolians and Macedonians are powerful opponents. But whose opponents will they be? The Aetolians still complain that they were not given due credit when we conquered Philip at Cynoscephalae.[xiv] And Philip, we all know he serves his own interests. Either of them could easily join Antiochus."

"Flamininus is still there with his legions, Scipio," interjects a senator.

Scipio waves away the comment. "He is a fine general, but he would be overwhelmed. And he does not want to be there. He thinks we should pull our troops out of Greece, and let our amici fend for themselves."

He shakes his head. "That they could not do. The Syrians would take them all and become more powerful than ever." He eyes the Senators. "Then they would move on us."

Flaccus digs his elbow into Cato's ribs. "Get up and say something!" he hisses. "Do you want those Hellenics spending tax money on libraries and museums? Bringing in Greek doctors?"

The stocky little farmer shoves Flaccus sideways. He rises from his seat, turning to face the senators sitting above him.

"Why are we even discussing this? Scipio indulges in impossible scenarios, in speculations of what would happen in Greece. But *we* know what is really happening."

Cato walks over to Cyprian, the Senate Leader. He extends his hand to the aged man. "May I have the letter?" he asks. The elder hands him a goatskin scroll. Cato brandishes it at the senators.

"This is the letter from Consul Sempronius, which came to us yesterday. He asks that Scipio join him as soon as possible, because he is besieged by a vast army of Boii and Insubres."

Scipio winces at Cato's words. *Gods damn it! I should never have backed that puff Sempronius, regardless of the money he brought to the campaign.*

Flaccus senses a change in the Senate's mood. He pushes himself up from his place. "General Sempronius is in danger! The Gauls are going to invade Italia! We cannot allow this!"

Scipio whirls upon Flaccus. "Had you not hastened back here after your little victory up there, perhaps there would be no rebellion to quell!" *And perhaps you'd have gotten that triumph you so dearly wanted. But no, you had to rush back to oppose my election. Fool, you have been bit by your own dog.*

Cato grits his teeth. He stands up and spreads his arms. "You know I am a good soldier, Senators. I quelled the Iberian revolt, and returned with a mountain of plunder. I tell you now, as a proven general, that General Scipio must go to Gaul."

The Cyprian totters up from his chair. The eighty-year-old booms his oak staff upon the floor. All fall silent.

"You three have made your arguments. Is there anyone else who would speak?"

Lucius starts to rise. Dozens of senators turn to look at him.

Scipio gapes at the sight. *That's it, brother, show some spine!*

"I, ah…my father Publius once said…" Lucius flushes with embarrassment. He eases back down and looks at the floor.

"I hear no one else, so I call the vote." The elder points at a twelve-foot statue of a blindfolded goddess holding a set of scales. "Those in favor of Scipio taking his consular army to Syria, step over to the statue of Jusititia." He swings his arm to the opposite side of the floor. "Those who favor Scipio joining Sempronius in Gaul, go stand by Jupiter."

The senators step down the benches and walk toward one of the two statues. Scipio watches expectantly, his fists clenched. Minutes later, his face falls.

Cyprian booms his staff. "It is decided. Scipio Africanus is to join Sempronius in Gaul." He looks at Scipio. "You are to take your two legions and the two of our allies. For your army, you will be given—" He pauses when Scipio springs up from his chair.

"Save your breath. I know what I'll be given, and I know what I'm supposed to do with it. By the gods, I have done this enough times before!" Scipio strides from the chambers, his back stiff as a shield.

"I am off to marshal my troops," he flings over his shoulder. "We set out for Milano on the next full moon."

A grin splits Flaccus face. He rises and cups his hands to his mouth. "Come back here, Consul, this meeting is not yet over!"

"Shut up and sit down," Cato mutters glumly, his face in his hands.

Scipio gallops through Market Street, scattering the street's vendors and shoppers. The people's shouted curses fall on deaf ears—his mind is already on Gaul.

*I will be there, Sempronius. You had best have a damn good reason for ruining my plans.*

*Gallic Warriors*

# II. INITIATION

MILANO, PO VALLEY, 194 BCE. Sempronius and a tower guard stare at the thousands of Gauls lined across the plain. “This is the second day they’ve stood out there,” the consul says. “What do you think they’re waiting for?” His eyes grow large. “Do you think they’re getting more men?”

“I don’t know, General,” the guard replies testily. “Looks like they’ve got plenty enough as it is.”

“Well, they are waiting for something. I just wish I knew what it was.” The consul throws up his hands. “This is so frustrating! We can’t just hide in here like mice, it will dispirit the men. I’m going to put our men out into battle formation. We need a display of force.”

“Whatever you say,” the stout older man says. *Why is this pup complaining to me? He should be talking to his legates.*

“What I say is action. Now.” The youthful consul clatters down the tower stairs, his chin set with determination. Soon, the camp horns sound the call to formation.

On the far side of the stream-lined plain, Boiorix stands in front of his infantry, his two brothers at his side. They watch as ten thousand legionnaires march out from the main gates.

“Ah, the mouse roars,” says Boiorix.

“I hope they attack us,” Sudarix says, fingering his twin-bladed axe. “Old Skullcleaver needs some exercise!”

As the Gauls look on, the second and fourth legions arrange themselves into precisely-spaced squares of five hundred men. The Umbrian legions follow them out the gates, assuming the same formation. Twenty thousand men face the Gallic camp.

Boiorix's youngest brother stirs restlessly, his slim fingers closed about his belt axe.

"Are they going to attack, Boiorix?" he says eagerly.

The chief grimaces. "No, Tarbos, they are just out there as a gesture of defiance." He shakes his head, his twin braids flapping against his gold neck torus. "A pity they've come out at all. Our men felt like they were hiding from us."[xv]

"The men are restless from inaction," declares barrel-chested Sudarix. "They long for glory—and plunder."

"Let's go after them!" Tarbos urges. "It'll be easier to fight them outside their camp."

Boiorix turns around and studies the Alps. He notes the darkening skies about its saw-toothed peaks. His eyes gleam with excitement.

"The weather will be changing tonight," he says to his brothers. "Tomorrow will be the day I've been waiting for."

"I never understand you," Tarbos says. "The day for what?"

"The day the clouds come to earth," the chieftain replies, grinning mysteriously.

At dawn the next morning, a tribune shakes Sempronius from his slumber. The general cocks a sleepy eye at his officer. "What is it?" he murmurs. "Are we under attack?"

"I think not, but you should see this."

Clad in his knee-length sleeping tunic, Sempronius steps out from his tent—and steps into a thick wet mist. "Fog!" he mutters. "This must have come in last night."

Sempronius marches toward the front gates, following the tribune's fog-shadowed outline. The two officers clamber up the tower ladder and peer toward the Gallic camp.

All they see is a soupy cloud of mist. They hear the jangle of a Roman patrol riding past the gates, its leader shouting directions so his men can find him. But they cannot see anyone, or anything.

"What do the scouts tell us?" Sempronius asks.

"The early patrols reported that they heard movement in the Gallic camp, sounds of many men stirring about. But they cannot say any more than that. Too hard to see."

*Shit!* "Get the men ready. We have to prepare for anything." The tribune clambers down the tower. Soon, the camp horns sound the call to arms.

Sempronius strides back to his tent, cursing the weather gods. *Why now? Scipio is still days from arriving.* As his attendant straps him into his bronze cuirass, he hears the faint call of a ram's horn. The call is quickly echoed by a dozen of its fellows. The consul's heart leaps. *They're coming!*

With trembling fingers, Sempronius straps on his helmet and his sword belt. He dashes for the front ramparts. Hundreds of half-naked legionnaires run past him, a sword or spear their only armament.

The consul clambers up the tower. He stares into the fog, searching shadowy outlines of enemies. His two legates soon join him.

"What a cloak of shit this is! This is an Olympian fucking mess!" says stern, gray-haired Britannicus.

"We won't see them until they're on top of us," Caduceus says. The tall young legate frowns. "We'll need line discipline more than ever for this fight."

"Who in Hades offended the gods, that they would do this to us?" Britannicus continues. "You know they're going to attack. I think that Boiorix has been waiting for the fog to come in." He snorts. "He is smart for a Gaul."

"This could work to our advantage, Consul," Caduceus replies. "They can't charge into the cohort gaps like they usually do, if they can't see them. We just have to fight with discipline. Tell our men to fight the man in front of them and forget about everything else." He grins. "One thing we know, the Boii and Insubres are not disciplined. If you can withstand their initial surges, they grow bored and give up."

Sempronius nods. "We can use that stratagem, if we can get out of camp to repel them. We have to get our legions out there before they break through our walls."

"Then we had best act quickly, because they won't—"

The Gallic horns interrupt Britannicus, louder and closer than before. Straining his ears, Sempronius hears a tumultuous sound, as if surf were rolling into a seashore. The rumbling becomes more distinct, and he recognizes it. It is the sound of thousands of voices combined into one gigantic, constant roar, backdropped by the clanking of shields and armor.

"Prepare for battle!" Sempronius shouts to his legates. "Put the light infantry on the ramparts. Get the cavalrymen up there, too, they're no use on horses. The second legion will go through the front gates, and fourth follows them. Allies to the rear portal."

The legates dash down the stairs. Minutes later, thousands of soldiers swarm about the camp, rushing to their assigned defenses. The equites tether their horses and scramble up the ramparts. They line up along the mile-long walkway that borders the eight-foot walls, their short swords bared for any who try to scale it.

The light infantrymen follow the equites up the stairs, lugging fistfuls of javelins. The young soldiers station themselves among the cavalrymen, holding their small round shields over their throats. The velites and equites look toward their guard tower's faint outline, waiting for the signal that the Gauls are within striking distance.

The enemies' roars grow louder, their voices drowning out the Roman officers' commands. A ragged line of shadowy shapes appears along the camp front.

"Loose!" the tower guard screams.

Hundreds of javelins whistle over the rampart, disappearing into the drizzly fog. Screams of agony erupt, followed by a return volley of thick Gallic spears. The Romans fling another round of pila, provoking more cries. The rams' horns sound again. The roar of enemy voices grows deafening.

The Boii and Insubres burst into view. Thousands of tall, brown-haired men run headlong toward the camp ramparts, ignoring the javelins that plunge down upon them. The Gauls attack with their naked longswords in their fists, holding their oblong shields high to ward off the fog-shrouded spears.

Many of the Roman pila find their mark, and scores of Gauls fall. Their compatriots trip over the shadowed bodies. leaving their backs exposed to the pila. Dozens more fall, but the Gauls do not relent.

Boiorix leads the charge, his two brothers running alongside him. "Insubres to the rear gates!" he shouts to his chieftains. "Boii to the main! Pass it on!"

A javelin thunks into his raised shield. *Easy, there,* he tells himself. *If you get killed they'll all fall apart.* He pauses to let his men surge past him.

The Gallic horde surrounds the Roman walls. They flow across the plain and clamber up to the staked walls. The Boii lay down scores of tree-limb ladders. They scramble to the top of the walls, shoving their blades into the Romans stationed along the walkways. The velites jab the back with their spears, striking down dozens. The equites dash back and forth along the walkway, stabbing into any hands or heads that appear between the fog-shrouded stakes.

"Bring up the ram," Boiorix shouts.

Ten heavily armored Gauls break through the front line, cradling a thick pine tree. They surge toward the main gates, heedless of the spears plunging down on them. One falls sideways, screaming as he clutches at the javelin jutting from his kneecap. Another crumples wordlessly onto the earth, his dimmed eye staring at the spear in his other socket. Undeterred, the ramsmen bash the tree against the gates, yelling triumphantly as the timbers bow inward.

The Gauls sense the gates will break soon. They bunch up about the front gate, making a roof with their shields. The Boii watch the rammers prepare their next charge.

"Come on, you curs, give it a lick!" bellows a stout older Gaul, his flaming red beard a beacon in the fog. The Gauls back up and boom the tree against the gates. They hear the sound of splintering timbers.

"One more time!" the leader yells. The Gauls trot backward and prepare for the final charge.

Inside the gates, the second legion has massed about the entryway. Fabian stands in the fourth row of soldiers, watching the camp gates splinter. He turns to his friend, young Cassius.

"Those lunatics will break in here soon. We're going to fight hand to hand, no way around it. Just remember what our centurion told us. Keep your head about you, or you'll lose it."

He barks a grim laugh. "I have to. Portia would kill me if I died over here!"

Fabian hears a trickling sound, and looks over to his right. Cassius stands there, his eyes glassy with fear. A yellow stream runs down his leg.

"Easy, son. Don't let fear slow your arm." Fabian says.

The tall boy glances sideways at him. "Easy words for you to speak," he quavers. "You're not the one that's scared."

Fabian shrugs. "It serves no purpose. Attend my words, I've fought these savages before. That's a mob out there, not an army. All muscle and guts, no organization. Just keep your place next to me, and I'll see you through this."

Cassius' eyes stare from the shadows inside his domed helmet. His mouth tightens into the rictus of a smile. He nods jerkily, too terrified to speak.

Britannicus rides in behind Fabian's line, his scarred face as calm as if he were going for a holiday ride. "When they haul back to make another charge with that ram, take the bars off the gates. Fling them open as soon as the ram gets ready to hit." He points up to one of the flanking guard towers. "The centurion will give you the signal."

Minutes later, six legionnaires quietly slide the bars from the gates. They grab the iron handles that hold the bars in place, looking up at the centurion standing in the tower.

The centurion peers down into the mist, his hand above his head. He chops down his hand. "Now!"

The Romans jerk open the gates. The battering ram plunges into foggy space. The rammers stumble into the camp, running into a gauntlet of the Romans.

"At them!" Legate Britannicus shouts.

The front line hastati swarm over the rammers, stabbing into every exposed place. The ram falls to the earth and rolls to the side, draped with the rammers' corpses. The hastati reform and wait, their blades poised to kill.

The Gauls see the ram disappear into the mist, but they hear no sound of a crash. They look at each other, confused.

"The gates are open, you idiots. Attack!" screams the red-bearded Gaul. His order comes too late.

Marching six abreast, the men of the second legion stride out through the open gates. They draw their swords, brace their shields, and march straight into the charging Boii. Stabbing methodically with each step they take, the hastati thresh through the first line of Gauls, driving the barbarians from the entryway.

"Get back at them!" screams Boiorix, but his voice is drowned in the din of clashing swords. The Gauls retreat farther from the gates, leaving a wide swath of open space in front of them.

The second legion's rear cohorts march out to fill the gap, lining up along the front wall. The velites and equites continue their onslaught from the ramparts. They fling their javelins over the heads of their ground troops, rejoicing in the screams that tell them they have found their mark.

Boiorix's face purples with frustrated rage. He turns to Sudarix and Tarbos.

"Tell the chieftains to spread the word. If we break into the camp we will have a three-day feast. The men can have all the plunder they can grab. Everything!"

The chieftains trot back to their men. An excited murmur spreads through the ranks of the Boii and the Insubres, punctuated with cheers. "That will get them going," Boiorix tells Tarbos.

The Gauls surge forward with renewed vigor. They swarm in as a tightly packed mob, jostling each other in their eagerness to reap their plunder. The battle becomes a clash of shield against shield, and body against body.[xvi]

Grunting and cursing, the densely packed Gauls batter their shields at the steadfast Romans. The front-line hastati patiently stab at the enemies' exposed arms and legs, bloodying their limbs. Still the Boii rage on, hammering at the Romans. Slowly, step by step, the legionnaires retreat.

Sempronius rides along the gap between the hastati and the principes, his fear lost in his urgency to rally his troops. "Get some fresh troops to the front," he tells Britannicus. "We've got to get the rest of the fourth legion out past the gate!"

"It will be done," replies Britannicus. He gallops to the front lines.

"Principes to the front," Britannicus yells to his senior tribunes. "Tell the men not to worry about what is going on around them, they just have to kill the man in front of them."

At a signal from the tribunes, the centurions blow their attack whistles. The elite principes edge up between the hastati. They spread their shields in front of the weary legionnaires, offering them a safe withdrawal. The hastati retreat between the gaps and line up in front of the senior triarii, waiting for orders to return to the front.

Calm and practiced, the principes cut down hundreds of the rampaging Boii. They step over the bodies of the fallen, pausing only to administer a killing stab to any who show signs of life. The front line Gauls retreat, pushing their own men backwards.

Boiorix grimaces at what he sees. *I should have bribed the Ligurians to join us. They wouldn't take this shit from the Romans.* He pulls his two brothers next to his face so he can be heard over the din. "Get those fucking cowards back into the battle! Tell the chieftains to use the Ox Driver on them."

Minutes later, the clans' chieftains shove their way to the back of the two front lines. Each carries a wrist-thick spear. Grasping the neck of their spears with both hands, the chieftains beat upon the backs of their warriors,[xvii] screaming for them to push forward. The terrified Boii ram frantically against the Romans, heedless of their stabs and slices. The battle again becomes a stalemate. The Roman attack whistles blow. The hastati step forward to refresh the principes.

First Tribune Quintus Victorius marches up with them, his face flaming with anger. *The men are losing their will to fight,* he decides. *I'll give them something to fight for!*

He jostles his way to his legion's standard bearer, a muscular giant with a wolf's pelt draped across his back. "Trexis, give me our standard!" he barks, reaching for a six-foot pole that sports a silver boar's head atop it.

The signifer jerks back the standard. "No! I swore to guard this with my life!" he splutters.

Victorius takes a deep breath and blows it out. "Apologies for what I must do," the diminutive centurion says. He reaches into his belt pouch. "Here. Take this."

Victorius jerks his hand from his pouch. He springs upon the standard bearer and delivers a crunching blow to his chin, his fist encased in wooden boxing knuckles. Trexis' eyes roll up in his head. His knees collapse.

Quintus reaches under the signifer's massive shoulders and eases him to the ground. "Protect this man," he yells to two stunned principes. The tribune grabs the standard and races to the front.

Quintus rears back and hurls the standard into the Gallic lines.[xviii] The standard's spearhead thunks into the ground behind the front line of the Boii. The delighted barbarians grab the boar's head pole and bob it over their heads, hooting and laughing at the astounded Romans.

"They have our standard!" Fabian cries to Cassius. "The bastards have taken our honor!"

"Let's go get it!" Quintus Victorius screams. He blows the whistle for a full-scale attack.

Fabian and Cassius stride forward with their linemates, heedless of the thick swarm of Gauls in front of them. Ducking, stabbing, and slashing, the men of the second legion cut their way deep into Gallic center. They swing their scuta sideways, battering away the barbarians' long shields, and thrust their short swords into the Boii's exposed torsos. Within minutes, a mound of dead are piled about the blond-haired Gaul holding the standard. The legionnaires rush at him, screaming like madmen. The Gaul drops the pole and flees.

On the left flank of the battle line, fourth legion tribune Gaius Atinius watches the second legion storm over the Gauls. He purses his lips with dismay—and shame. *Charon take me, I should have thought of that!*

Atinius dashes over and wrenches his legion's silver eagle from its stunned signifer. He dashes into the vertical gap between the two legions, the standard bearer chasing after him.

Running forward like a javelin thrower, he hurls the standard straight into the faces of the Boii.[xix] The fourth legion surges forward to retrieve their standard, beating back the Gauls. Minutes later, they triumphantly wave their standard above their heads. Having broken the Gauls' ranks, the Romans press their advantage.

The Boii retreat slowly from the camp, battling the Romans with each step they take. The ram's horns sound, and the chieftains repeat their Ox Driver tactics. The Gauls surge forward again.

With the Gauls' retreat from the Roman camp walls, the rest of the legionnaires march out and extend the battle line, preventing the legions from being surrounded. The battle now rages along a mile wide arc, with neither side giving quarter.

The sun rises high. The fog dissipates under its burning rays. The day grows hot and humid. The Boii's hours of frenzied attacks begin to take their toll—on themselves. They hold their shields low. Their shield-splitting blows lose their force. Their reflexes slow.[xx]

Riding behind the front lines, Sempronius pauses to remove his helmet and wipe his brow. *Vulcan's balls, it's getting hot out here*! He looks at the sweat pooled in his palm. *If I am sweating just from riding this horse, those big bastards must be soaked with it.* He calls over his two legates.

"Old Sol has joined us as an ally," he says, referring to the sun god. "Maintain a steady onslaught. Don't worry about breaking through their lines, just don't let them break into ours. Refresh the front lines constantly."

Fighting with the measured energy of disciplined troops, the Romans advance, step by step. Their murderous thrusts pierce opponents who previously blocked them. Hundreds of Gauls fall to the men of the second and fourth. The Gallic horns sound, and the Gauls withdraw to regroup.

Sempronius senses that he is on the cusp of victory. He summons his two legates. Britannicus rides over to join his consul. Gaius Atinius, the fourth's senior tribune, trots in on foot.

"How are the allies doing?" Sempronius asks Britannicus.

"They are holding their own. They are working to drive the Gauls from the rear gates."

Sempronius scowls at Atinius. "Where is Caduceus? Go get your legate!"

"An ax split his head," Atinius replies, his voice quavering. "He died before we could get him to the rear."

Sempronius bows his head. "May Charon guide him to the underworld."

He grasps Britannicus' and Atinius' shoulders. "Caduceus' death cannot delay us, this is our moment! Bring up the rearmost cohorts, they are our freshest troops. Double-time them into the Gauls. Bring the velites in behind them. Do not relent!"

The two commanders disappear. Twenty minutes later, each legions' seventh, eighth, ninth, and tenth cohorts march to the front, sturdy fighters who have yet to raise a sword against the enemy.

"They're attacking again," Boiorix yells to his chieftains. "Get out there and kill them!" The weary warriors sally forth to meet the legionnaires, tramping past the bodies of their fallen comrades.

The Roman attack whistles blow, and the cohorts halt. Clouds of spears fly out from behind them, cascading upon the advancing Gauls. Scores of them fall and stumble, pierced by the rain of javelins. Hundreds join them when the next two volleys descend.

"Charge them, curse you!" Boiorix yells.

A scream erupts next to his shoulder. He sees his brother Tarbos staring beseechingly at him. A spear dangles from Tarbos' intestines, dark blood flowing down its shaft. He crumples to his knees.

"Tarbos!" Boiorix grabs his brother by the shoulders and drags him back behind the battle lines, all thought of conquest gone. *I should have made him wear a mail shirt!*

Sudarix stumbles along behind Boiorix, weeping unabashedly. "You'll be fine, little brother, you'll be fine! We just need to get a poultice on you." Sudarix looks at Boiorix, a question in his eyes. The chief shakes his head.

The brothers strap Tarbos into a horse travois and tow him back toward camp. "Vercix, take over for me," Boiorix tells a chieftain. "I will return shortly."

The Boii see their leaders depart. "They're running back to camp!" shouts a chieftain, and others take up the call. Many of the veteran warriors steel themselves for a final battle with the Romans, ignoring Boiorix's departure. Many more look longingly back toward their camp.

The Roman whistles sound again. The fresh cohorts resume their rapid charge into the Gauls. They cross the space between them and thresh into the disorganized Boii. Moving in unison, they push the barbarians so close together that they cannot raise their long swords to strike back, leaving them vulnerable to the Romans' dagger-like thrusts.

Scores of Boii drop their weapons and dash for camp. They are soon followed by hundreds more. Then thousands.

The Insubres at the rear gates see the Boii retreating. They abandon their fight with the allies and run for their home base, pursued by the Umbrian cavalry and foot soldiers.

Sempronius watches the Gauls stampede across the plain, leaving thousands of bodies in their wake. His heart swells with pride. *I have my first victory! Rome will give me a triumph!*

He rides into the center of the second legion. "Victory is within your grasp!" he shouts repeatedly, riding across the rows of hastati in the front. He gallops to the fourth legion and repeats his call. The soldiers respond with cheers.

"We have them!" shouts Britannicus, excited by the consul's words. The impetuous young velites dash out from the rear ranks, hurling their spears into the backs of the fleeing Boii and Insubres. They dash after the fleeing Gauls, followed by the hastati and principes.

Inflamed with their desire for revenge, the disciplined legionnaires turn into vengeful killers. They scatter across the battlefield, stabbing down any of the fallen who show signs of life.

Cassius and Fabian watch the men in front of them hurtle out in pursuit. "Come on, let's get them!" Cassius yells. He dashes away.

"Wait, damn it, keep your place in line," Fabian yells. But Cassius is already fading from sight. "Stupid boy!" Fabian mutters. He takes a deep breath and runs after him.

The Roman army spreads across the battlefield, flowing toward the enemy camp. Sempronius watches them, his elation replaced with dismay. *The cohorts are breaking apart. We are more like a mob than an army.*

The consul puts heels to his stallion. He races toward Boiorix's camp, running from one tribune to another. "Get your men back into formation and return to camp!" he screams.

Across the battlefield, the cornicen sound the call to reorganize. Soon, the scattered Roman pursuers reform and march back toward camp—except for the cohorts of the second legion. Four thousand men dash onward, heedless of the men withdrawing behind them.

Thousands of Boii and Insubres pour through their camp's entryway, dragging along their wounded. Inside his command tent, Boiorix rises from Tarbos' corpse. He wipes the tears from his eyes and pulls a weeping Sudarix from the floor.

"Come on, brother. We have to organize our men. And get our revenge."

The two walk to the camp's gateless opening, watching their men clamber over the wagons and tree trunks that form the camp walls. He strides outside of the entryway and studies the oncoming Romans.

Boiorix notices that thousands of Romans are marching back to camp, save for a wide swath of legionnaires continuing the pursuit. His breath quickens. “Get the men ready to attack,” he says to Sudarix, his eyes never leaving the oncoming Romans.

His brother blinks. “But our men are still coming into camp.”

“I don’t care if they’re fucking crawling in here! Mass them up for a counterattack!” His eyes grow feral. “This battle is not yet over.”

Fabian nears the front of the Gallic camp, gasping for breath from his run. “Cassius, get back here with me!” He yells. He sees the boy charging in with the pursuing legionnaires, throwing spears and rocks at the fleeing Gauls. *Gods damn him, he can’t hear me! I ought to throw a spear into his back.*

Fabian hears the rams’ horns sound inside the Gallic camp. His stomach churns with the realization that the Gauls are sounding a counterattack.

The decurion watches in horror as ten thousand warriors trot out from the camp gateway, led by a golden-horned chieftain who grips a hand axe in each fist. A silver-horned warrior runs next to him, his long sword at the ready. Fabian sees the edges of the Gallic wave fan out toward the flanks of the scattered legionnaires, initiating a deadly encirclement.

*I’ve got to get him out of there!* Fabian throws down his weighty shield and runs toward Cassius. “Get back here!” he screams.

Too late, the pursuing Romans realize they are outnumbered. They reverse course and start to flee from the enemy camp. But the Gauls are already closing in upon their flanks.

The Gauls sense that revenge and slaughter are theirs. They sprint toward the retreating Romans, crying the names of their fallen clansmen.

The Roman tribunes see that retreat will only expose them to slaughter. They draw their men into rude battle lines and face the crazed onslaught, their faces grim with the knowledge of their chances.

Boiorix is the first to reach the wayward cohorts. Screaming demonically, he crashes into the centurion who faces him. "For Tarbos!" he screams, swirling his hand axes over his head.

The chieftain loops his left hand axe toward the Roman's stomach. When the centurion moves his shield to block it, Boiorix springs into the air and chops his other axe into the Roman's helmet, delving it into his skull. Before the centurion hits the ground, Boiorix is chopping into a nearby hastati's knees, mad with his lust for revenge.

The hastati falls. Boiorix steps over the moaning Roman, seeking further prey. He sees a tall youth staring at him, his eyes glassy with fear. *Time to skin that rabbit.* Boiorix cocks his twin axes in front of his chest. He stalks forward.

"Cassius!" Fabian screams. With the last of his energy, Fabian rams through the legionnaires in front of him and arrives at Cassius' side.

"Run, Cassius! Get back to camp!" He shoves Cassius backward. Fabian grabs a fallen scutum and surges toward Boiorix, his eyes searching for an attack spot.

The Boii chieftain swoops his left axe at Fabian's foot, aiming a crippling blow. Fabian blocks the blow with his shield's iron rim. Boiorix loops his right axe toward Fabian's head, and Fabian clangs his sword blade against it.

The decurion shoves his shield into the chief's bronze breastplate, knocking him onto his back. Fabian steps in for the kill. Boiorix rises to a sitting position and grabs his axes.

Fabian jabs his sword through the straps of the Boii's calf-high sandal, slashing deep into his ankle. The chieftain bellows with pain, but he manages to push himself unsteadily to his feet. He lunges forward, aiming a killing axe blow at Fabian's head.

Boiorix's injured foot crumples under him. He crashes sideways onto the ground. Quick as a striking snake, Fabian dives upon him, his sword arm ready.

Fabian feels a blinding pain in his lower back. He sees a gory swordpoint protruding from his lower stomach, sliding out through him as if it were alive.

Sudarix stands behind Fabian, gripping his long sword in both hands. He yanks the blade out and stabs at Fabian's head, but the legionnaire has already fallen onto his stomach.

Boiorix scrabbles forward on his hands and knees. "Roman pig!" he growls. He raises his right arm and arcs down his axe.

There is a bony, wet crunch. Fabian's head rolls away from his twitching body. The eyes blink once, twice, and then turn glassy.

The Gallic chief tries to push himself upright, but he falls sideways. "I'm worthless, Sudarix. Get me out of here." His brother places his shoulder under Boiorix's arm and shuffles him back toward camp.

"Aaaagh!" screams a voice behind them. The two turn to see a willowy young Roman charging toward them, his sword raised to strike.

"Apologies," Sudarix says. He drops his brother and yanks his long sword from his chest scabbard. The Gallic warrior crouches down and grasps his blade with both hands, seeking one telling blow.

Tears streaming down his downy cheeks, Cassius leaps upon Sudarix. He thrusts his bossed shield into the Gaul, seeking to batter him to the ground. Sudarix steps to his left, shoves out his foot, and scoops Cassius' foot from under him. Cassius falls onto his back.

Sudarix is instantly upon him. He chops his blade into the underside of Cassius' right knee, severing his hamstring. "You should have stayed with your mother, boy!"

He slices deeply into the young soldier's groin. Sudarix watches the bright arterial blood spout from Cassius' crotch. He grins.

The Boii chieftain stalks away from the moaning youth. He pulls his brother from the ground. "He'll bleed out soon enough," Sudarix tells him. Let's get you back to camp."

Wailing with pain, Cassius grabs his dagger and saws a strip off the edge of his tunic. With trembling hands he wraps the bandage about his upper thigh, hoping to stanch the wound. He sees the gray bandage darken, then overflow with blood. Recognition dawns in his eyes.

Cassius crawls to his friend's head. He reaches out and strokes Fabian's muddied curls. "I'm sorry. Oh, I'm so sorry," he cries.

With the last of his strength, Cassius reaches out with his fingertips. He gently closes Fabian's sightless eyes. "Safe passage," he murmurs, stretching out next to him. Cassius shivers, shakes, and moves no more.

Back near his camp, Sempronius races up and down the battle plain, shouting at his men to return to their base. "Don't look for your cohort, run!" he shouts. When he nears the Gallic camp, he yanks his horse to a halt, horrified at what unfolds before him.

The Gauls have encircled the wayward cohorts. They march forward slowly, inexorably, battering thousands of Romans into each other. The legionnaires fight back, but they are soon jammed tightly together. Spears fly out from the Gallic rear lines, and hundreds fall. The Gauls rush into the breaches, hewing down all about them. Soon, all that remains of the proud cohorts is an island of defiant foot soldiers, determined to die fighting.

The rams' horns blow a final charge. Twenty thousand Gauls surge forward. The Romans disappear beneath them.

Sempronius watches from a hillock. As the Boii and Insubres envelop the last of his men, he leans from his horse and vomits, tears dripping from his eyes. The young patrician turns his horse from the final screams and trots aimlessly back to camp, his mind dulled with horror and shame. He rides through the open gateway and dismounts in front of his tent.

"Call an officer's meeting for the third watch," he mumbles to his attendant, his voice distant. "I am not to be disturbed until then."

Sempronius pushes the tent flaps aside and strides to his sleeping pallet. He throws himself face down upon it, his armor clinking about him. He buries his face in his arms. His body convulses, wracked with stifled sobs.

The consul raises his head. He gazes at the terracotta figurine of his wife, resting atop his map table. "I never wanted to be a general, I just wanted to make you proud of me." His lips contort into a snarl. "I should never have listened to that bastard Scipio."

That night, a somber Sempronius meets with his surviving officers. He sits at his map table, unshaven and unkempt.

"We count eleven thousand of their men dead," Atinius crows. "Their dead outnumbered ours more than two to one!"[xxi] He slaps his fist into his palm. "Tomorrow we can finish them off."

The consul stares at him with empty eyes. "Caduceus is dead. We lost five thousand men—*I* lost five thousand men, when I let them run wild. I'm not going to lose any more."

"Their army is in a shambles!" Britannicus declares. "If we destroy this group of Boii and Insubres, the northern border will be secure for years!"

The grizzled legate pounds his fist on the map table, sending its figurines flying. "Let's not retreat like Flaccus did, when he had a chance to destroy them!"

Seleucus looks at the Roman figurines sprawled across the table. He thinks of Caduceus, and of the four thousand bodies sprawled on the plain, waiting to be burned.

"We march southeast to the Placentia garrison.[xxii] We will wait for Scipio to arrive. Those are my final words!" He rises stiffly from the table and gazes at the tent exit, his face a stone. The officers eye one another. Without a word, they stalk from the consul's tent.

Once outside, Britannicus waves over two of his senior tribunes. "Come to my tent, friends. I need some wine to swallow this decision. Hades take me, I need an entire jug!"

"He is as bad as that Carthaginian Hannibal was at Cannae, when he was reluctant to march on Rome,"[xxiii] one tribune growls. "He doesn't know how to finish an enemy."

"I hear that Scipio will be here soon," the other tribune declares. "He'll not be running from a bunch of piggish Gauls."

Britannicus laughs grimly. "He had best not tarry, or Boiorix will soon be stalking the Forum!"

***Scipio Africanus***

# III. THE GRAY FOX HUNTS

ROME, 194 BCE. Philo stands outside Scipio's residence, grasping his horse's reins. The messenger is a man equally skilled with horse and sail, despite the fact that his right arm ends in an iron hand,[xxiv] artfully carved to grasp a horse's bridle or a sailboat's rope. For ten years, the war veteran has relayed Scipio's messages across continents and seas, earning his status as Scipio's most trusted emissary.

Philo strokes the muzzle of his slim gray mare. "Gods help us, Epona. The consul wants me in Numidia within three days, and I should have left hours ago. But here I stand, waiting for him to finish his stupid letter."

His gaze returns to the dark red doors of the Scipio manse, making sure he is not overheard. "Why Scipio would write to Masinissa is beyond my ken. Everyone knows what Scipio did to him—can't say that I blame him for hating Scipio."

Philo frowns at the descending afternoon sun. "We'll have to be faster than Apollo to get to the Ostia port before sunset." He stares into his horse's liquid brown eyes, gently shaking her head. "All this racing about with his big secret messages: he'd better give me enough coin for a good skin of Falernian—and a big bag of oats for you!"

Hoofbeats clatter upon the cobbled street, growing louder. The messenger spins around, his hand on his belt dagger. A lean young messenger draws in and eases off his mount. He slaps his heart in welcome. "Salus, good Philo! I wish you well."

"Salve, Glaucus. Where are you going?"

"Northern Greece. To find General Flamininus. The consul has a bee in his ass about sending him a message."

Philo chuckles. "I'd say he has two bees! I'm off to the court of Numidia, to see Masinissa."

"To the Numidians? Be careful, those horse-eaters may throw you into the pot with one of their broken-down stallions!"

"Ah, that is a child's tale. They are not cannibals—I hope."

Inside Scipio House, Scipio bends over his marble-top writing table in the manse's tablinum. He dips his wooden stylus into a bowl of octopus ink and scratches out a message in his bold, florid hand.

*Prince Masinissa,* Scipio starts. He stares at the papyrus for a moment, then crumples it up. Unrolling another scroll, he begins again.

*Masinissa, Rightful King of Numidia:*

*I write to an ally and friend of Rome, a man who fought beside me when we achieved glorious victories over Hannibal and Syphax, our mutual enemies.*

*As consul of Rome, I request that five hundred of your finest riders be sent to me before the next full moon. They will join me in my campaign against the Northern Gauls.*

*Rome has agreed to help you protect your borders. Now we—I—ask you for help in protecting ours. In return, I promise you that Rome will lend support to your effort to recover your ancestral lands from Carthage. You know me as a man of my word.*

*Consul Publius Cornelius Scipio*

Scipio rereads his message. He chuckles mirthlessly. *He'll probably set fire to it as soon as he reads it.*

Scipio dangles the papyrus in front of him, blowing upon it to dry the ink. He rolls it up, ties it, and dribbles hot red wax on its edge. He presses his owl's-head imprint into the wax and blows upon it.

"Rufus!" he barks. The old slave hobbles in, his grandson trailing behind him. Scipio hands Rufus the message and a bulging mouse skin purse. "Take this to Philo." As Rufus leaves, Scipio pulls another papyrus from his wicker basket.

General Titus Quinctius Flamininus

I would like one of your tribunes to accompany me in my campaign against the Boii and Insubres. You know him well. His name is Marcus Aemilius. His mountaineering skills will be a great help to my campaign against Boiorix and his Boii.

Scipio finishes the message and hands it to Rufus. *I hate to take Flamininus' best soldier, but he won't need him. He's so damn determined to withdraw from Greece, even though Antiochus is at their doorstep! It's like the sheep dog leaving the lambs, while the wolf is on the hill.*

Scipio peers into the family lararium, where his father's death mask hangs. He recalls his promise to defend Rome against all its enemies. *This trip to save Sempronius is bullshit! I have to get over to Greece, before Antiochus destroys it.*

Scipio pads into to his sunny atrium. Amelia sits on a couch by the fishpond, playing sticks and balls with young Cornelia. Scipio's son Publius grapples with Laelius, who is teaching him some new wrestling holds. Laelius whirls behind Publius and lifts the slim boy off his feet.

"Show me your forefinger," Laelius says, telling Publius to give him the sign of surrender.

"Never!" The boy squeals, kicking frantically with his feet. When Scipio enters, Laelius drops Publius to the ground and shoves him away. "Just like your father, too stubborn to know when you're beaten. Begone now, before I break your neck!"

Publius rises and smoothes his tunic. "Don't forget, you promised to take me sailing." He strides from the room, his posture as erect as a king's.

Laelius grins at Scipio. "Look at him. He thinks *he's* the consul in the family! So, did you finish your love letters?"

Scipio rubs the back of his neck. "I would not use the word 'love' in connection with a message to Masinissa. You know how he feels about me, after Sophonisba died."

"We were just doing our duty. We had to bring King Syphax and his wife back to Rome. They were our prisoners! Rome didn't care about Masnissa's little love affair with her."

"Do not make too light of his feelings. He saw her as the love of his life, his future wife and queen. And we caused her to kill herself."

Laelius snorts. "She took it upon herself, and now we suffer for it. But he will always be a part of my heart, regardless of his enmity." He slaps Scipio on the shoulder. "Be not so morose, friend. I have good news—I am going to run for consul next year!"

"And I'm going to help him," Amelia declares. "Prima will join me."

Scipio purses his lips. "Really? Don't you think it a bit early? You haven't been a praetor yet. You should complete the cursus honorum that leads to a consulship."

"A curse on the cursus!" Laelius barks. "The cursus is not mandatory, and you know it. Look, when you were dictator you made me an admiral, then a cavalry commander—and then I became a war hero![xxv] Our victory over Hannibal still lingers on the people's minds. I think I am ready."

"Based on my fading popularity, I would say our victory does not linger much," Scipio replies. "You will need a fresh reputation—and fresh campaign funds. Why don't you join me as cavalry commander in Gaul? Next year, you can run as a fresh war hero."

"Excellent," Laelius replies. "I'll help you pull Sempronius out of that Placentia garrison he's hiding in, and run those Gauls out of Italia! When do we leave?"

"On the full moon. Or as soon as a I get a response from Masinissa," Scipio replies. "If he will give me one."

ATLAS MOUNTAINS, NORTH AFRICA. It is a pleasant time in the village. The Carthaginians are busy skinning two aurochs for the night's celebratory feast, chatting and laughing as they chop up their food.

A hundred lean, dusky-skinned riders appear, their agile ponies clopping in between the thatched huts that encircle the dusty town square.

A tall man slides from his night-black mount, a man so sinewy that he appears to be carved of oak, every vein etched above his long, ropy muscles. Beneath his lion's head cap, his obsidian eyes burn with anger.

The man points his spear at a knot of men who stare defiantly at him, gripping the handles of their bush machetes. "Who is the chief here?" he barks.

A barrel-chested man steps out from a large hut, hastily tying on his loincloth. "I am Hiro. What are you doing on Carthaginian land?"

"This is not Carthaginian land. It belonged to my father Gaia. It was taken from him years ago. I have come to get it back."

Hiro sniffs. "That was then. This is now. I was born in this village, and my father before me. It is part of the Carthaginian Empire."

Masinissa laughs. "You say 'empire?' What empire? Scipio has taken your empire from you! But I will not let you take mine from me. You have one day to get off this land."

"You're a fucking idiot." The chieftain replies. Hiro stalks back into his hut. He emerges with a curved Carthaginian sword in his hand.

"This served me well when I was killing Romans," he says to Masinissa. "It will serve me well on Numidians."

He walks toward Masinissa, his busy brows knitted over his angry brown eyes. Masinissa's men crowd closer to him, holding their lances at the ready. The village men draw their machetes and step in behind their chief.

Hiro stops at arm's length from Masinissa. He throws his sword at Masinissa's feet. "You and me, we decide this."

A handsome young Numidian rides up behind Masinissa, adorned with the same pointed black beard. He leans to his father's ear. "You're a king now, you can't risk leaving our new kingdom leaderless. Let me take care of him."

"And how long would I remain a king if I retreated from a challenge, Sophon? How long before the word spreads that I let someone else fight my battles?" Masinissa reaches into his saddle sheath and extracts a short, double-edged sword. He hands his lion cap and horse's reins to his son. "Get back with the men."

The Numidians and villagers encircle the two warriors, each group poised to charge if the other interferes.

Hiro and Masinissa face each other. They heft their naked blades in their right hands, their left arms extended for balance. Hiro's teeth bare into a snaggle-toothed grin. "I've killed six Romans with this sword. You'll be my first Numidian."

A smile plays across Masinissa's lips as he stalks toward Hiro. The Numidian fixes his eyes on the Carthaginian's stomach, knowing it will tell him which way Hiro moves.

Hiro lunges at Masinissa's chest. Masinissa turns sideways and quickly steps past him, slicing the Carthaginian's shoulder. Hiro spins about and lunges again, ready for Masinissa to edge sideways. Instead, Masinissa steps in and blocks the Carthaginian's sword thrust. His knobby fist bashes Hiro in the jaw, stunning him. Hiro whirls his sword in front of him, trying to fend off Masinissa while he recovers his senses. But Masinissa does not grant him the time.

The king crouches so low his chest touches his bended knees. He ducks under Hiro's swipes and delves his sword into the side of his opponent's lower stomach. With a quick twist of his razored blade, Masinissa spills Hiro's intestines onto the sand. The Carthaginian wails in agony and horror. He drops to his knees, vainly trying to stuff his vitals into his gaping stomach.

Masinissa walks toward the villagers, ignoring his moaning opponent.

He wills himself not to grasp his throbbing knuckles. "Are there any others who dispute my orders?" He stands, sword in hand, rigid as a statue.

Long seconds pass. Hiro thumps down behind him, his legs scrabbling at the sandy earth. "I thought not. My men will be back here at sunset. I do not have to tell you what they will do to any who remain." The Numidian king springs onto his horse and gallops out of the camp, followed by his raiders.

The stunned villagers slouch about the square, muttering and arguing. An older woman emerges from her hut, towing a leashed goat and cart full of grain sacks and cooking pots.

"I go to Carthage," she says. "You can stay here and argue until he returns." The villagers watch her trundle down the pathway to the city. They shuffle into their huts and begin to pack their belongings.

Three days later Masinissa and his men arrive at Cirta, the easternmost stronghold of his vast northern kingdom. Riding into his mountain redoubt, he sees a gray mare tethered in front of his palace steps. The horse sports a red saddle blanket emblazoned with the spread eagle symbol of Rome. *Now what do they want*? he fumes.

Masinissa dismounts and stalks into the palace, his mood growing fouler by the minute. Philo the messenger stands in the vestibule, a papyrus roll wedged into his iron hand. He bows and extends the message.

"A message from Rome, honored king. I am to wait for a response."

Masinissa eyes the artificial limb. "A clever piece of work. Could one be fashioned to hold a lance?" Philo shrugs. "The Greek who made this is a wonder. He has made bronze legs and glass eyes. I wager he could make one that moves, if you gave him the time."

Masinissa takes the message from Philo. He marches across the stone slab floor of his oak-paneled meeting room, easing himself onto his gilt throne. Philo slowly follows, eyeing the six-and-a-half-foot guards who stand by the doors. Sophon walks in behind him, watching Glaucus' every move.

The king jams his finger under the edge of the papyrus, preparing to break its seal. He freezes when he sees Scipio's owl's head impression.

Willing himself to be calm, Masinissa takes a deep breath and unwraps the scroll. He reads it. He reads it again.

*He wants men from me. After what he did*. For the thousandth time, he envisions his beloved Sophonisba strapped to her throne, her dead face grinning at the Romans who came to take her. The fatal chalice lies at her feet, dribbling the remnants of its Sardonicus poison.[xxvi]

Masinissa crumples the papyrus and flings it into a corner. Sophon retrieves the message and reads it. He looks expectantly at his father.

Masinissa glares at Philo. "You need a reply, eh? Tell Consul Scipio he can go—"

"Father!" Sophon interjects. "I will go. Let me take my men there!"

"No. I'm not helping him," the king growls.

His son strides over to his father. "Can we talk privately?" he says softly, his voice tense with muted anger.

"Wait in the vestibule," Masinissa tells Philo.

Glaucus strides stiffly from the room. Sophon places his hand on Masinissa's forearm. "Give Scipio the men. You won't be helping him, you'll be helping yourself. Carthage will complain to Rome about your incursions into their territory. It will help if we have a powerful friend in the Senate."

"Do not use the word 'friend' with him," Masinissa replies peevishly.

"Do you want to fight Carthage *and* Rome, Father? After all the years you spent fighting to regain our Massylii kingdom from the Masaesyli, would you give it all away just to spite Scipio?"

Masinissa drums his fingers on the oak arms of his throne, his eyes staring straight ahead.

"Let me take them to Rome. Your refusal to marry has made me a bastard. The people do not see me as your legitimate heir. I need to make my reputation if I am to succeed you. Yet I have no foes to fight, now that the Massylii have fled from us. Fighting the Gauls would prove that I am a deserving heir to your throne, even if I am illegitimate."

Masinissa's hand flashes out, gripping Sophon's arm. "After Sophonisba, I could not marry anyone—I just could not do it. Even your mother, who was more woman than I deserved. I know I have made your way difficult. Go to Rome, and make your reputation."

Sophon's lean face splits into a smile. "Excellent! By your leave, I'll take our veterans from the war with Syphax. We'll sail for Rome in two days!"

"Take what you need," Masinissa mutters, dismissively waving his hand. Sophon strides for the throne room doors.

"Wait. There is one more thing." Sophon turns.

"For my parting words, I am telling you what the Spartan women told their sons when they went off to battle."

Sophon arches an eyebrow. "Which is?"

"Come back with your shield, or upon it."[xxvii]

ELATIA MOUNTAINS, NORTHERN GREECE. Marcus Aemilius lays the tip of his bare foot into the spot of bare earth between the dry leaves. He finds another spot in front of him and takes another step, soundlessly creeping toward the bear. His spear is poised above his shoulder, ready for the telling throw.

The bear raises its nose into the air, turning its head about. *Good thing I am upwind, or she'd be on me in a minute*. He holds his breath and takes another step. He draws back his arm.

A hoarse bawling erupts behind the bear. A cub pops its head up from the berry bushes, crying loudly for its mother. The she-bear rears up to her full seven feet, looking for her cub. She drops to all fours and barges through the bushes, faster than a horse can run. Her cub follows her, crashing through the brush.

Marcus remains motionless, watching the beasts disappear into the pines and alders. He smiles. *Go ahead, Mother. I don't like bear meat that much, anyway. You'd probably tear me to pieces before you died—mothers are like that.* He lowers his spear and begins his twenty-mile trudge to the Elatia fort.

As the tribune hikes down the switchback, he pauses beside a massive fallen cedar, thick as a child is tall. Marcus grabs a small boulder. Squatting low, with the rock cradled in his arms, he springs onto the top of the trunk.

Poised atop the tree, Marcus swings the boulder about him like a hammer thrower, grunting with effort. He springs down and repeats the maneuver a dozen more times. Panting from his efforts, he drops the stone and wipes the thin sheen of sweat that covers his body. *Father Marcus lifted boulders for years, but I bet he never thought of that routine! Good for fighting balance. I'll have to show it to the men.*

The stocky little soldier descends into the flatlands, following the crystal mountain stream that wends toward Flamininus' garrison. As he enters the flatlands a peasant gallops toward him, his tattered brown cloak flapping behind him. Marcus' hand strays to his hunting knife.

"Marcus, it's me!" shouts the rider.

Marcus withdraws his hand, saluting as the rider pulls up next to him. "Trobus! I did not recognize you. You really look like a local!" He sniffs. "You even smell like one. Is that pig shit?"

"The better to blend in," the speculatore replies merrily. "If you're going to be a spy, you have to be authentic."

"So you are here to spy on me?" Marcus says, chuckling. "That will be boring."

"I'm on my way to the Macedonia border. I have to make sure the Macedonians are adhering to the treaty, and not amassing troops in secret. You know King Philip, he is a wily one. But I have something for you."

Trobus hands Marcus a scroll. "From General Flamininus himself."

Marcus unrolls the papyrus and quickly scans it. "I'm to go back to Italia, and join Scipio Africanus' army?" He gapes at Trobus. "At the consul's personal request!"

"Fortuna smiles on you," Trobus says. "You get to serve under the great Scipio! Nothing is happening here, anyway. I heard we are all going home."

"I am honored to fight with the man my father so admired, but I hope you are wrong about us leaving. The Syrians are taking over Thrace and the eastern Greek colonies. I don't think they'll be satisfied with stopping there."

"Well, it is not your problem now, Tribune," Trobus replies airily.

Marcus snorts. "You think not? Thrace, Macedonia, then Greece. How long before Antiochus is in Italia? Then it is a problem for all of us."

LYSIMACHIA, THRACE. King Antiochus trots through the city gates, his face flush with excitement. He tows a rangy brown mule behind him, a lion carcass draped over its back. The king's guards follow him, scanning the populace for threats. One guard tows a horse with a ravaged corpse hanging across its saddle—the lion exacted a price for his death.

The king spies Hannibal standing atop the palace steps, watching his arrival. The Carthaginian is garbed in full battle regalia, his polished linen cuirass shining like a waxed egg. Hannibal spreads his arms wide in welcome.

"What did I tell you?" Hannibal crows. "The Roman Senate has forced Scipio to go to Gaul. He poses no threat to you!"

The king slides off his mount and gives its bridle to one of his Egyptian slaves. "Cure the hide and give it to the tailor," he tells him. "I want a new robe done in a fortnight."

Antiochus nods at Hannibal. "That is good news indeed. You were right, their Senate is very focused upon Gaul."

"And the Latins are very focused on Scipio," Hannibal says. "On minimizing his chances for glory!"

Antiochus the Younger strides out from the palace entry, his face set with purpose. "I take it you have heard the news from Hannibal?" Seeing his father nod, he continues. "Now is the time to strike, Father. We can be in Macedonia within a week. Then on to Aetolia!"

The king sees Hannibal pinch his eyes shut, as if willing himself to be patient. "It is too early. Flamininus' legions are still in northern Greece."

"Who cares?" The king's son declares. "We can mount a hundred thousand men against his twenty."

Hannibal sniffs. "Yes. A hundred thousand men from your so-called Army of a Hundred Nations, half of them wild and untrained. I, of all men, know the managerial nightmare that poses. We must bide our time. Flamininus will withdraw. In the meantime, we can get the men trained and ready."

"Then we will strike when the Romans depart." King Antiochus declares.

"The Lion of Syria should not hide from the Romans!" his son sneers. "I swear, Father, you have become timid in your old age."

"You dare talk to me like that?" Antiochus splutters. "My kingdom stretches across the earth!"

"Your father is a lion, young man," Hannibal says. "The lion is quick and strong, but it is his patience that makes him the victor. He bides his time before he strikes, watching his prey, conserving himself until he is sure of his kill. That is something you should learn."

The son shoulders his way between the two leaders. He glowers at Hannibal. "You don't even know if the Romans will leave!"

"Flamininus will withdraw. My spies tell me he loves the idea of being known as the liberator of Greece. He will take his army home to prove that he does not intend to occupy their country."

"And if he does not, and you cost us a valuable opportunity?" Antiochus the Younger snaps.

Hannibal nods toward King Antiochus. "You have six crosses outside your walls. If I am wrong, put me on one of them."

The king's eyes widen. "You are an audacious man! Very well, I will follow your words—and take you up on your wager."

He faces his son. "I do plan to take action. I will take my men to our coastal fortress at Ephesus. From there we can cross the Aegean and be in Greece within a day."

"Then let me lead our troops into Macedonia while you are waiting," says the younger Antiochus. "King Philip has been broken by the Romans. He will be easy prey."

"You march on Philip and you will give Rome a powerful ally," says Hannibal. "And give Flamininus a reason to stay where he is."

Antiochus frowns at his rebellious son. "Forget Greece. I have another mission for you. You will take an army and patrol Syria's northern and eastern borders, to prevent any disturbances after my men move to Ephesus."[xxviii]

Antiochus the Younger's face reddens. "You are exiling me to the desert? You two are wasting your chance to conquer the world. Shame, shame on the both of you!"

The burly young prince stalks into the palace, shoving the doorway guards aside.

"You must forgive him," Antiochus says. "He is bold, but a touch impatient."

*This boy will be the end of his father—and my chance to bring down Rome*. "I understand," Hannibal says. "I must say, your son Seleucus has the cooler head that a king requires." His voice lowers. "I do fear for you safety, King. Young Antiochus may not wait for your passing."

The king is quiet for several long moments. "Well, he *is* very popular with the people.[xxix] And he voices his dissatisfaction with me to them."

"All I am saying, is that he bears watching. Especially now, when you are on the cusp of great victory. You have the world within your grasp. It would be a tragedy if it were taken from you. Flamininus and Scipio may be the least of your problems."

"Ah, the dread Scipio," Antiochus chuckles. "I am taking steps to ensure that Scipio will never oppose me," Antiochus says.

"He is totally committed to the safety of Rome, King. He cannot be bribed."

"He cannot be bribed, but he can be bought," Antiochus replies, rubbing his hands together. "Bought with the life of the one he most loves."

PORT OF OSTIA. "Publius! Pull the damn sail in!" Laelius shouts from the shore. "You're fighting the wind too much."

Scipio's son grasps the catboat's sail rope. He hauls the sail closer to the boat, and jerks the rudder sideways. The little sailboat does a perfect about-face into the wind. When the boat completely turns around, he releases the sail. The linen square billows out, stiffening with the force of the wind behind it. The sailboat jounces across the waves, heading farther out to sea.

"Good work," Laelius bellows. "We'll make an admiral of you yet!" He plunks himself down upon the front of the dock, his legs dangling from the edge. Laelius watches the town fishermen coast out into the open waters. *Nice day for fishing, even if it's a bit choppy. I should have brought my bireme and joined Publius.*

He notices a weathered fishing boat edging sideways toward Publius' vessel, beating its sails against the wind.

*Why aren't they going out to sea? Those pot-lickers don't watch where they're going, they'll run into Publius!* He notices the fishing boat has no nets or floats in it, just two men sitting back by the rudder, their faces fixed upon the boy's bobbing boat.

Laelius jumps up and runs to the front of the dock. He dashes over to a fisherman who is pushing the nose of his craft into the breezy waters.

Laelius shoves the man aside. "Apologies!" he blurts. He scrabbles into his belt pouch and pushes a handful of denarii into the man's chest, the coins cascading onto the beach.

"I'll bring it back," Laelius tells him. He slides the small boat into the shallows and springs into it. Grasping the sail ropes, he loosens the sails and tacks out toward Publius' boat, angling back and forth to take advantage of the shifting winds.

A hundred yards from Publius' catboat, Jammal and Sami trim their sailboat's jib and mainsail, laboring to close on the young boy's craft.

"Can't you go any faster,? Jammal growls. "I thought you were this big expert sailor. If we don't get that boy this time, Antiochus will roast the both of us."

"I said I knew how to sail," Sami retorts. "But I haven't had to deal with these crazy Italian winds. Pull that rope tighter!"

"Should we ram him?" Jammal asks. "Knock him out of the boat and pull him up?"

"We can't risk it. The king wants him alive," Sami answers. "Just get me close enough to grab him." He snaps his fingers. "I have it! Let's see if we can get him to come closer to us!"

Publius spies the larger boat closing in on him, its occupants waving for him to come closer. *What do they want? Do they need help?* He turns his tiny catboat toward the approaching vessel.

Racing toward Publius, Laelius watches the boy sail toward the fishing boat. *Oh no, don't do that!* He pitches the fisherman's belongings off the boat and leans his upper body over the side, angling the boat out of the water. *Neptune, lend me wings!* The boat surges ahead.

"The boy's coming!" declares Sami. "Soon as he gets near enough, I'll jump in and get him."

"I'm not worried about him, I'm worried about that boat over there!" Jammal shouts, pointing his finger at Laelius' craft. "He's heading right for us."

"Get out of the way, you ass!" Sami yells, frantically waving his arms.

"He's not getting out of the way," Jammal replies. "I think he's aiming at us. Get us out of here!" The Syrians' fishing boat pivots sideways, steering away from Publius.

Laelius turns to starboard and pursues them. He shoots by Publius' catboat. "Get back to shore!" Laelius yells across waves. "Those men are pirates!" He closes upon the Syrians' craft.

"We can't outrun him," Sami growls. "When he gets close I'll jump in and kill him. Then we'll go get the boy." Jammal and Sami grab their daggers from the bottom of the boat and place them near their feet. They stand up and face the onrushing Laelius.

"What do you want, sir?" asks Sami. "Why are you chasing us?"

"I just want to ask you about the fishing here," Laelius says. He tenses his legs and prepares to spring.

Laelius pulls parallel to the side of the boat. At the last instant, he jerks the sail to the other side of the boat and yanks the tiller sideways. The speeding boat wheels around and crashes into the side of the Jammal and Sami's craft, splintering its side.

Jammal stumbles backwards and pitches into the sea. Sami falls to the bottom of the boat. Laelius leaps into the sinking boat, his dagger in his hand.

Sami scrambles to his feet, clutching his curved dagger. The muscular Syrian stabs at Laelius' neck. Laelius catches his hand by the wrist and thrusts his blade at the Syrian's face. Sami grabs his forearm. The two grapple inside the lurching boat, their feet sloshing in the bottom's deepening waters.

Straining against the Syrian's sword arm, Laelius sees the second assassin clambering up the rear of the boat. *You don't have much time*, he realizes.

The former wrestler surges forward and wraps his right leg about Sami's calf. Pivoting forward with all this strength, he flops the Syrian backward, striking his head on the thick seat board.

The stunned Syrian rolls onto his stomach. In a flash of motion, Laelius grabs the Syrian's hair, yanks his head back and slices open his throat. He watches the blood gush from his gaping artery, a dark cloud reddening the boat bottom's rising waters.

Laelius turns to face the other Syrian—just as Jammal rams his head into Laelius' chest, knocking him into the bottom of the boat. Coughing and choking, Laelius grabs for the railing, trying to push himself upright. Jammal grabs Laelius' hand and twists away his dagger. He pitches it over the side.

"Now it's your turn," Jammal spits. He leans his considerable bulk onto Laelius' back and wraps his forearm around his windpipe.

Laelius turns sideways and shoves himself away. He stoops down and yanks up the Syrian's leg, tumbling onto his stomach. Laelius scrabbles onto the Syrian's back and bends the man's knife arm behind his back. Jammal screams, and drops his dagger.

Laelius grips a sail rope and loops it about the assassin's neck. Bracing his knee on Jammal's back, he pulls with all his strength, shoving the Syrian's head into the boat bottom's waters.

The Syrian kicks and twists like a man possessed. Laelius wraps his legs around Jammal's submerged torso and jerks the rope tighter. A cloud of pink bubbles froths to the surface, then fewer, then none. The boat's edges sink underwater, but Laelius still clings to the rope. When the ship finally disappears into the sea, he releases his grip.

Laelius swims over to Publius' boat. The boy leans over the edge, watching him with eyes wide as saucers.

Laelius clambers aboard the tiny boat and collapses inside it, breathing heavily. He smiles groggily at Publius.

"If it's not too much to ask, could you give me ride back to the docks? I seem to have lost my transportation."

"Why did you do that to them? They were but two fishermen!"

"Those 'two fishermen' were out to sell you into slavery, or ransom you, or worse. I swear, ten years ago nothing like this would have happened here in Ostia. This place is going to the dogs."

Laelius and Publius guide the overloaded catboat into the Ostia docks. The two retrieve their horses from the nearby stables and begin their twenty-mile journey back to Rome.

Two hours later, Laelius is inside the Scipio atrium, relating the day's details to Amelia and Prima. They listen with a horror that soon turns to anger.

"You think they were going to kidnap him?" Amelia asks, looking toward the garden, where Publius plays with his sister.

"I would think so. Why would they kill him? He's worth more alive, unless you're trying to take revenge on Scipio—or you. But Jupiter's cock, even the Latins wouldn't do that. Well, maybe Flaccus would—but he's away down in Capua."

"Plots can be hatched from a distance," says Prima. "We should kill him on general moral principles, whether he did it or not." She smiles sweetly. "I'd be happy to do it!"

"Ah, I don't know," Laelius says. "They might have been just a couple of sea thugs. If so, there won't be any more problems. But we should put a guard on Publius, just to be safe."

"I'll watch him," Prima replies. "I can get our nurse to attend to the baby." She sees Laelius starting to speak, and raises her hand. "It is decided!"

Amelia smiles at the gladiatrix. "Gratitude, Sister. You are worth a dozen guards."

That evening, Scipio returns from his preparations for his departure to Gaul. He hears the news about Publius' assault. His face flushes with fatherly rage.

"I swear, if Flaccus is behind this, I will kill him myself!" he declares.

"It could have been pirates, or kidnappers," Laelius says. "I will ask around at Ostia. I still have some connections from my time there as a street boy." He frowns at Scipio. "Don't do anything to Flaccus, First man of Rome. You have too much to lose. Let me handle this."

Scipio's mouth tightens. "Fine, but I am doubling the patrols around the bay. Anyone who attempts a kidnapping will be flogged and crucified. Tell that to your Ostia friends."

An hour later, after Scipio has calmed, the four friends repair to the atrium for dinner. They recline on the manse's low-slung dining couches. The serving slaves circulate quietly with platters of food.

Scipio plucks a roasted pigeon from a silver tray. He crunches into the sesame-encrusted bird. "The Numidians have arrived in Rome, and so has Marcus Aemilius. We are ready to march to Placentia and succor that whining Sempronius."

He bobs his half-eaten bird at Laelius. "I leave it to you. Do you want to stay here and campaign for your consulship, or campaign with me against the Gauls?" He winks at Prima. "Perhaps you are more comfortable making speeches than fighting?"

Laelius flings a slice of quince at Scipio. "You know I'm not much for talking. I'd rather fight naked against a Gaul than stand on that speaker's platform in the Forum." He looks at Prima. "But I do not want to abandon my family."

Prima springs from her couch and strides over to her husband. The gladiatrix laces her long sinewy fingers into his dark curls, a gesture both tender and firm. "Go with him. You have a year before we get serious about running for consul. Until then, Amelia and I will direct your campaign. We have owners who will let us paint slogans on their houses, and speakers who will tout your glories in the Forum plaza. You can best serve our cause by giving us something to tout!"

Laelius clasps his hand over hers. "I hear and obey," he says, chuckling.

"Then it is decided," Scipio says. "You and I will fight together. With every city we take, every garrison, every cursed little town, we will send a messenger to Rome about our victories. Let the news of our successes be fodder for your campaign speeches."

Scipio breaks open a round loaf of emmer bread, gnawing on its leathery crust. "I would rather go to Greece, but Gaul is not a pointless mission. I am tired of the Boii's pestiferous invasions. We will run them from Italia, and be back home before the new year. Then we both can attend to this business about the election."

"I thought your business was rescuing Sempronius," Laelius says.

"He does not need rescuing as much as his men need leadership," Scipio replies. "My real business is that I have to figure out a way to get an army over to Greece before Flamininus takes his men back to Italia, and Antiochus fills his place."

Amelia pours some water into her wine, her face thoughtful. "I doubt the Senate will change their mind, Husband. The Latins treat you like you were our worst enemy, not Antiochus."

Scipio shrugs. "I see their point, because it is mine. We are both fighting for the future of Rome, not just its territories. They see conquests, I see alliances." He pops a grape into his mouth. "Perhaps they are right to fear me the more."

SABINA HILLS, OUTSKIRTS OF ROME. "You wanted to see me?" says Titus Paullus, carefully picking his way through the clods of fertilizer.

Cato rises from the furrow he has been tending and lays down his hoe. He wipes his hands on his sweaty gray tunic. "You are to be the quaestor for Scipio's army, correct?"

The stringy little man raises his chin, obviously proud of his appointment. "Yes. I am to be the army accountant, tracking all of its expenses."

"And the army's revenue as well? Its gains from ransom and plunder?"

Titus frowns. "You know that. You were the quaestor for Scipio's African campaign,[xxx] were you not?"

"I was, and I know how he operates." Cato replies, his eyebrows flaring. "He sent me home from Africa, that he might add to his personal coffers."

"I know nothing about that." Titus coolly replies.

"I know you are a member of that mystic Pythagorean sect that worships knowledge above all else.[xxxi] I ask you to gain some important knowledge for me."

The quaestor's lips furrow into a line. "Which is?" he mutters.

Cato takes a deep breath. "I think Scipio Africanus has violated the theft laws of our Twelve Tables.[xxxii] I need to you find out if he sequesters any war profits for his own purposes."

Titus stares, open-mouthed. "You want me to spy on Scipio Africanus?"

Cato pauses, feeling a rare moment of discomfort. "It is worth a purse of gold to me." He says, looking out toward his fields. "Even more if you find evidence."

Titus' back stiffens. "I am a quaestor. It is my sworn duty to ensure Rome receives her due." He stares haughtily into Cato's gray eyes. "I do not require bribes to do my duty."

The little man spins on his heel and marches toward his horse. He whirls upon Cato, his small fists clenched. "From everything I'd heard, I had thought you incapable of this." Titus clambers onto his worn brown mare and trots down the wide dirt pathway to Rome.

Cato watches him leave, his hands limp at his sides. *What did I just do?* "Continue your work," he tells his field slaves. He marches up the hillside to the back of his austere little villa.

"Aelius!" he shouts, looking for his senior house slave. "Come out to the garden." A middle-aged Gaul appears in the garden entrance, his thick arms luminescent with the blue tattoos of his clan.

Cato reaches into a wicker garden basket. He extracts a long, thick, willow branch, denuded of all but its knobby branch stubs. Cato shoves the branch in Aelius' hands. The Gaul nods, knowing its purpose.

Cato sheds his sweaty work tunic, then his loincloth. Naked, he kneels on the cobbled walkway, his broad back turned to Aelius. "Do it until I say stop. This time it will be a while."

"Master, are you sure—?"

"Commence!" Cato barks.

The powerful slave reaches back and whips his right arm forward. The willow rod slaps into Cato's back, laying a thread of welts across his back. "Again!" Cato says, his voice quavering. "Give me a dozen! And a dozen more! If you relent, I will know it!"

The Gaul sets to his task, laying stripes across his master's quivering back.

Cato grits his teeth, his head bowed. *Ancestors, help me. Let this pain purge me of my dishonor. Please, please, do not let me lose myself.*

Another blow strikes. Cato's cheeks quiver. Sweat trickles down his face. *Gods, what if Scipio was right, and Syria takes Greece when Flamininus withdraws. I will deserve more than this rod.*

CORINTH, GREECE, 194 BCE. Fifty faces stare at him, each one topped with a crown or circlet. The fifty rulers have come from all parts of Greece, here to absorb the words of General Titus Quinctius Flaminius, the conqueror of Macedonia.

The slender, dark-haired general stands at a marble podium in the midst of Corinth's gigantic Temple of Apollo. He is clad in a snow-white toga that flows to his silver sandaled feet, garb that conveys his peaceful intentions.

The young conqueror faces a three-row semicircle of Greece's most powerful leaders. He nervously scans the crowd, looking for friendly faces. Most eye him impassively, reserving judgment. One beak-nosed giant glares at him, his blue eyes burning from the thicket of his night black beard.

*That's Thoas, the magistrate of Aetolia. Look at him, the asshole still thinks I didn't give him enough credit for defeating Philip.*[xxxiii] *As if his men didn't prove to be more obstacle than aid. Ah well, best get on with this. They should be glad to hear what I say.*

Flaminius clears his throat. "As you know, there have been a number of rumors about Rome's intention to stay here. Chief among those rumor mongers were the Aetolians, my former allies in the war against Philip."

All eyes turn toward Thoas. He sits with his arms crossed over his broad chest, staring at the opposite wall. His face shows no more emotion than a statue, but his leathery neck has reddened.

"What do these rumors say? They say that Rome intends to remain here, that we intend to take over Greece. They say that Greece has no freedom, that you have exchanged a Macedonian master for a Roman one."[xxxiv]

Flaminius steps from the podium and walks around the semicircle of rulers, looking into each one's eyes. "Rome is ambitious, I do not deny it. Under Scipio Africanus we have taken Sicily and Iberia. And Carthage itself. Does Rome now set her eyes upon Greece? Thoas says so, but I say no."

The general spreads out his hands. "But how are you to tell who is lying, and who is telling the truth? Let me give you an answer to that question."

The dignitaries stir uneasily, unsure of what comes next.

"Starting tomorrow, I will begin to evacuate my troops from Greece," Flaminius declares. "In ten days I will withdraw my troops from our garrisons in Demetrias and Chalcis. Then I will remove all our men from Thessaly."

The chamber is quiet as a tomb. The flabbergasted rulers stare at one another. "Where will you take them?" the Athenian delegate ventures.

"To the port of Oricum, on the western coast." Flamininus pauses to let the implications of his words sink in. "My transports will sail out from Oricum, heading for Brundisium, our port garrison in Italia. I am taking my army home."

He sees the amazed looks on many of the delegates' faces, men not believing their ears. "Let me put it more simply. Rome is leaving Greece. You are free of our presence. You…are…free."

Scores of delegates unabashedly weep, tears of joy trickling into their manicured beards. Dozens hug each other, realizing their nations are finally free of Macedonia's domination, and the worry of Roman control. Flamininus raises his hands, a wry smile on his face.

The Roman general fixes Thoas with an insolent grin. "Now you can judge if Rome was lying, or if that is the specialty of the Aetolians."[xxxv]

Thoas springs from his seat, spreading his arms entreatingly to his fellows. "Do not be deceived, his words are empty! He speaks only of intentions, not actions. When will you accomplish this evacuation, Roman? That is the meat of the issue."

"Sixty days," Flamininus snaps. "We will be gone within sixty days."

"Hmph!" Thoas growls. "I will have my eye on you, to see that you do!"

Flamininus closes his eyes. *Patience. He is a pig, but a powerful one.*

The delegates turn to the details of the Roman withdrawal, arguing about the amount and location of Roman security troops that should be left behind. The meeting concludes two hours later. Thoas hastens down the steps of the marble columned temple, followed by his guards and attendants. He crosses the town square and enters the merchant's manse that is his temporary residence.

"You all wait outside," he tells his men. "Gravlix, you come with me." His scribe follows Thoas into his spacious receiving room. The Aetolian magistrate points to the oak slab that serves as a writing table.

"Compose a message to King Antiochus," Thoas says. "Tell him our rumors have succeeded. Flamininus is leaving Greece within sixty days." The king plops onto a pile of skins and stretches out, rubbing the soles of his feet.

*Fucking Romans. That pussy Flamininus couldn't have beaten Philip without us, but he takes all the glory—and then calls us liars! We'll see how proud they are when they face us across the battle lines, with the Syrians and Macedonians at our side. Maybe I can capture that young priss myself. Be fun to listen to him roasting inside the bull!"* [xxxvi]

He grins. "Gravlix, remind me to check on our bronze bull when I get back. We might have a new guest for it."

PLACENTIA GARRISON, 194 BCE. The gatekeeper's eyes bulge at what he sees below him. "Pluto take me, it's him! Open the gates, boys. open them!"

The recruits leap onto the tall pedestals on each side of the gates. Grasping the gate timbers by the six-inch handles nailed into them, they shove the thick timbers sideways. They jump from the pedestals and heave at the gates, pushing with all their might. The portals creak open, and widen. The recruits stand breathlessly at attention.

Scipio Africanus enters the Placentia garrison, his face as stern as a wrathful god's. He scans the garrison square, taking in the scores of soldiers who loll about the market stalls and walkways. Many of them wear only gray army tunics, neglecting their weapons and armor. The men gape at the legend who ride past them. Dozens hasten back to their quarters, seeking to properly outfit themselves.

Laelius and Lucius ride in behind Scipio, halting their horses next to his. "Well. this is a sturdy little city," Laelius remarks. "I could see why Sempronius would want to hide in here."

"He said he was waiting for us to join him,'" Lucius remarks.

"Yes, waiting for mother to come and save him from the big bad Boii," Laelius says, eyeing the unkempt side streets.

A tribune walks out from a stone block armory opposite the town square, hastily strapping on his cuirass. He snaps out his right arm in a crisp salute.

"Apologies, Imperator! Consul Sempronius did not know you were coming so soon."

Scipio looks at the officer's unpolished armor. "Obviously."

The tribune blanches. "Forgiveness! I did not you were…anyway, I will fetch him immediately. He is visiting with the citizenry."

"Visiting with the citizenry, eh?" snipes Laelius. "What whorehouse is he in?" He sees Scipio frowning at him. "What? That's what he's known for, isn't it? I heard he had three Nubians in bed, and he—"

Scipio raises his right arm. "You and Lucius stay here." He turns to the tribune. "Tell Sempronius I will meet him in his quarters in half an hour." Scipio trots his horse through the main street, his elite guard following. His eyes roam over its buildings and populace, taking in the garrison's organization and readiness.

A half hour later, Scipio strides into the limestone blockhouse that serves as Sempronius' command center. The consul reclines on a couch in front of a low slung table of hammered silver, its top laden with meats and pitchers.

"Scipio, you old tyrant!" He springs up and energetically clasps his mentor's forearm. "What a pleasure to see you!"

Scipio grasps Sempronius' lower bicep and quickly releases it. "I am glad you are safe," he replies, with a hint of sarcasm. His eyes flick over Sempronius' ample frame. *He has gotten heavier since he left Rome. A soldier isn't supposed to gain weight in the middle of a war.*

Sempronius furrows his brows. "Where is your army? My scouts did not report them coming."

"They are two day's march from here," Scipio replies. "I rode ahead, so I could talk to you about our campaign into the lands of the Boii and Insubres."

The young consul nods. "I am grateful you have come. I lost too many men in that battle with Boiorix."

"Too many because they were out of control," Scipio declares. Sempronius lowers his eyes.

*Don't break his spirit.* Scipio chides himself. *He'll have to lead his army into battle.* He squeezes Sempronius' shoulder. "Forgive my rudeness. Fortuna did not smile on you that day, but there will be more opportunities. We will march north and settle our score with this Boiorix. You will emerge victorious."

"He has assembled over sixty thousand men, according to my exploratores."

Scipio grins. "That just means their army is too large to hide from us!

We won't have to roam all over Gaul trying to find them."

A week later, thirty thousand legionnaires and allies venture into the Po Valley, destined for Milano. They pass through the site of Sempronius' last battle and continue north, following the trail of charred fields that marks the Gallic army's progress.

The Romans locate Boiorix's army northwest of Milano, camped behind a crude octagon of logs interlaced into eight-foot walls. Scipio and Sempronius ride out onto the plain, studying the sprawling emplacement.

"It's very large, but it's not a real fort," Sempronius declares. "It looks more like some gigantic child was playing with sticks."

Scipio chuckles. "And why should they worry about that? Who would dare attack that mob? Those logs are thick and heavy; it would be very difficult to knock them down. They've probably got a walkway around the inside perimeter, which makes it even easier to defend. Do you know what's inside?"

"I didn't think they'd build something like that. I didn't send any spies to get in there."

"You know nothing, then. And them with four gates wide open, with scads of locals coming and going! No matter. I have brought two of my own speculatores. They're very good spies. They'll tell us how we can defeat them."

"You know that the Gauls outnumber us two to one," says Sempronius, staring sideways at Scipio.

Scipio winces. "A good legionnaire is worth four of those unruly giants. I'd say we have *them* outnumbered."

"But we can't break through those tree walls!"

"Why should we?" Scipio retorts. "Those walls are going to be our greatest asset! Come on, let's get back to our men. I have a few tricks of my own for this tricky Boiorix."

The two generals return to the budding Roman encampment. They ride through hundreds of men digging an outside trench and piling the dirt into a rampart. Hundreds more shove stakes into the mounded dirt, finishing off the camp palisade. Scipio waves over the centurion of his guards.

"Bring Ros and Branus to my tent," Scipio tells him. "Tell them I have a mission for them."

An hour later, the centurion leads in two slightly built men with ragged tunics, their greasy brown hair roped into ponytails. The two men slink toward the generals, warily eyeing the stern centurion. They fall upon their knees and clasp their hands. "Mercy, Master! We have done nothing wrong!"

One prostrates himself, clawing the earth. He stares beseechingly at Sempronius. "Please Dominus, do not beat us."

Sempronius wrinkles his nose. "They smell like horseshit," he murmurs to Scipio.

"That's because they have horseshit on their tunics," Scipio says. "These two stinking slaves are Branus and Ros, my prize speculatores." He waves them upright. "You can quit the performance now."

The two men spring up and stand straight as an arrow, their white teeth grinning from their grimed faces. "Thought we'd show you we're not out of practice," one replies, laughing.

"You never seem to be," Scipio retorts. "If I didn't know it was part of your disguise, I'd flog you Gauls for being so repulsive."

Sempronius stares at Scipio. "Gauls? You trust a Gaul to spy on a Gaul?" The two spies grin at his discomfiture.

"I trust a Gaul who gets a purse of silver for the right information, and a lash for his back if he lies," Scipio declares. "These are two of the best spies in Rome. They are Montani, the mortal enemies of the Boii."

Branus grins. "You can trust us to deliver. I need some women money. When do we start?"

"As soon as you can," Scipio says. "I need to know how many men they have, and the locations of their huts and barracks."

"We'll join the next bunch of peasants heading into camp," says Ros. "We'll strap a pile of wheat sheaves on our back and join the parade."

"Return by nightfall, if you can." Scipio says. "There will be some wine money as a bonus." The two men trot from the tent.

"You wouldn't know it to look at them, but they are wealthier than many of Rome's merchants," Scipio says.

Sempronius looks confused, prompting a grin from Scipio. "The senators hire them to spy on their wives and enemies!"

The next morning, the two spies totter into Scipio's tent, interrupting his breakfast with Laelius, Lucius, and Sempronius. Branus snaps out his right arm in a salute. "It was a fruitful mission. We have learned much that is valuable."

Scipio eyes the two. "Why are you bent over?"

Ros grimaces. "One of the Insubres caught us poking around the stables. He laid a branch to our backs." His eyes flare. "I would welcome a chance to join your assault and repay him."

"You will not. I need you alive, and I pay you well for such indignities. Now what did you discover?"

"They have a wide pathway around the inside of the wall, allowing for troop and livestock movements. The barracks are stuck by the east gate, on the other side of that pathway. There are hundreds of huts outside the rear gate. Looks like most of them are filled with camp followers and families. The stables are at the rear of the west gate. Nothing by the front gate, except a clearing."

Scipio nods. "Those outside walls would be difficult to ignite, but if they did catch, they would be very difficult to extinguish. Those barracks, and the huts, they are quite another matter. They will burn readily."

Laelius crooks an eye at him. "What are you thinking?"

"Remember what we did in Africa, when Syphax and Hasdrubal had their camps near us?[xxxvii] We can use that strategy."

"But the Gauls have only one camp, not two," Lucius notes.

Scipio waves his hand, dismissing the remark. "I'm thinking of how we handled the overwhelming numbers we faced there, and what we did by their gates."

"I see. We use the forests as cover. What forests the Gauls have left here are near the mountains by the east and west gates."

"Mars' cock, what are you talking about?" Sempronius blurts.

"We are talking about some very un-Roman tactics we've used before," Laelius replies. "Night raids. Black raiders. Gauntlets."

Sempronius shakes his head. "I still don't understand."

"You will," Scipio says. "As soon as we talk with Prince Sophon and Tribune Marcus Aemilius."

The consul stares at him. "The Numidian prince? Who is this Marcus Aemilius?"

"He was the tribune who led a mountain ambush upon Philip's troops at the Aos River.[xxxviii] He's quite adept at surreptitious assaults."

"You're going to have him spy on them?"

"Gods, no," Scipio replies, enjoying his game. "I'm going to have an entire legion spy on them!"

Two nights later, the Roman horns call for the troops to retire to bed. Torches and campfires blink out, one by one. A blanket of darkness drops over the camp.

Sophon leads his horse out from the main gate, pulling it along by its rope bridle. The Numidian prince is covered with gray-black wood ash, as is his horse. Five hundred ash-covered Africans pad out behind him, leading their rangy little ponies. The warriors fan out and flow toward the quiescent Gallic camp, gray silhouettes outlined against the moonless nighttime sky. Each horse carries a sling of pitch-covered torches. Each man lugs a knapsack full of fist-sized, stoppered jugs.

General Sempronius trots his horse out from the gates, leading the fourth legion's cohorts. Five thousand Romans creep toward the front of the enemy camp, their shields covered with black cloth. The legion's ten cohorts divide into two groups. One group heads to the left of the front wall, the other to the right.

When the cohorts are halfway across the plain. they slow to a halt. The legionnaires drop to one knee and watch the flickering torches of the Gallic camp.

"What are we waiting for?" asks one of third cohort's legionnaires.

"We're waiting for the Africans to do their job," his centurion whispers.

"Where are they?"

"They're there, you just can't see them. Just get ready to march, triple time, when the signal comes."

"You mean when I hear the cornicen?"

"I mean when you see the flames."

While the Romans look on, Sophon and his riders creep toward the camp. Soon, Sophon hears the jangling of mail-covered horses, backdropped by the muted conversations of their riders. He crouches, pressing his hand upon his horse's neck. The pony silently kneels with him. All across the plain, the Africans settle to the earth, turning into indistinguishable black mounds.

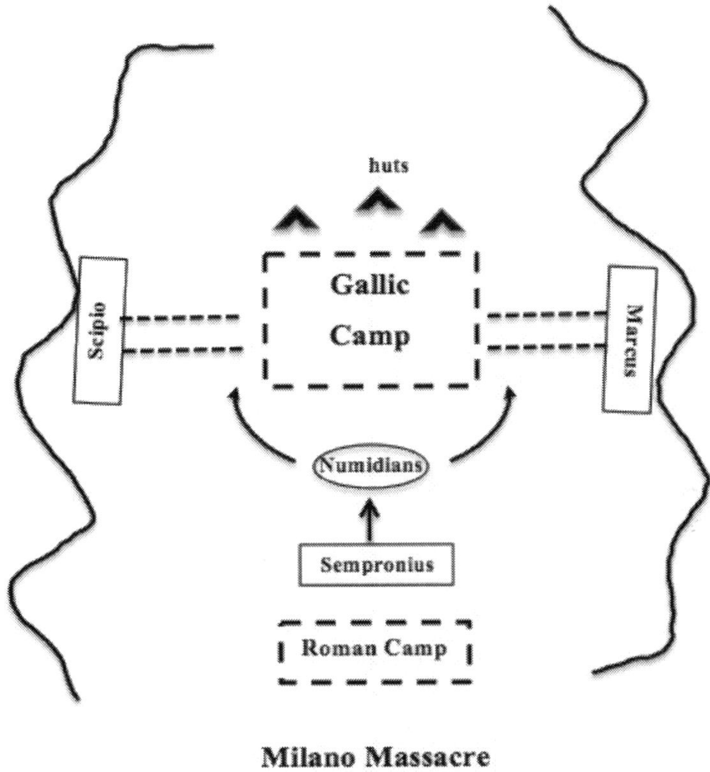


**Milano Massacre**
**194 BCE**

The Gallic patrol trots toward the Roman castra, heedless of the dark mounds about them. As they pass, a dozen Africans rise up behind them, scurrying forward with daggers drawn. Grunts and cries erupt—quickly stifled—followed by the thud of falling bodies. Two Africans lead the riderless Gallic horses toward the Roman camp, as their fellows creep closer to Boiorix's emplacement.

Sophon draws within three spear casts of the enemy. He whistles softly, imitating the trilling call of a night bird. He hears his signal repeated on both sides of him, an affirmation that all is well. Sophon peers into the foothills his left, his eyes straining into the darkness, looking for his signal.

Off to Sophon's left, Scipio leads a legion of his men through the lower foothills, down a winding game trail to the bottom of the forest. He treads out onto the darkened plain, his men lining up behind him. Scipio examines the side gate, estimating its width and thickness. He waves over Laelius.

"Get your cohorts ready to go to the left side of the gate. My cohorts will take the right. The triarii go in front, just like we planned it." He looks to the mountains on the other side of the camp. *Marcus, I hope you have done your job.*

"Silvus!" Scipio hisses. The archer appears next to Scipio.

"This is it. Give the signal." Scipio orders.

Silvus pulls two arrows from his sling and clasps them between his knees. Striking flint and steel, he ignites the arrows. He shoots one high overhead, then follows it with another.

On the other side of the Gallic camp, tribune Marcus Aemilius stands in front of the other legion. The night before, his legionnaires ventured deep into the mountains, drawing nearer to the Gallic camp by the next day's sunset.

Marcus has led the legion down the mountain pass toward the enemy emplacement, wandering ahead to dispatch the few guards that were placed along the trail. Now, he and Lucius wait on the wide plain facing the east gate, their cohorts arrayed behind them. They stare into the dark sky.

"Come on, brother, give us the sign." Lucius mutters.

Marcus glances over at him. "Be patient. Men will die soon enough." The words no sooner escape his mouth than a flaming arrow rockets high into the sky, followed by another one.

Lucius swallows. "This is it. Get the men ready for the charge."

Out on the plains, Sophon sees the arrows arc up into the sky. He rises from his concealment, puts his fingers to his lips, and blows one shrill note. He hears the rustling of his five hundred men as they climb upon their horses.

Sophon vaults onto his mount, his youthful heart hammering with excitement. He dives his long-fingered hand into his saddle sling and yanks out a pitch-covered arrow. The Numidian ignites the arrowhead and waves it slowly over his head. A constellation of tiny fires winks to life across the plain.

With an ear-piercing scream, Sophon digs his heels into his horse. He hurtles toward the Gallic fort. His men thunder in after him, abandoning all pretense at concealment. The riders stream forward like a horde of maddened fireflies.

The Numidians close in upon the front wall. Guiding their horses with their knees, they pull their bows off their backs and nock their flaming arrows. When they draw within a spear's cast of the front gateway the riders split to the left and right, each heading for his assigned target.

The riders on the left gallop past the front wall and head to the side gate. They shoot their flaming brands high over the walls. dropping them into the stables and hay bales. Flames leap up, followed by the whinnying screams of the stabled horses. The terrified beasts pound through their fences and stampede into the camp, crashing through the Gauls' tents and huts.

The west side riders loop around the west wall and unleash a storm of arrows into the thatched huts outside the rear gate, begetting another conflagration. Men, women and children dash madly across the plain, desperate to escape the leaping flames.

The Numidians wheel about and race back along the walls, dodging the spears hurled from above. They reach into their knapsacks and fling their pottery jars into the wall timbers, coating the walls with thick black pitch. Aided by the firelight of the burning camp, they shoot their flaming arrows into the pitch smears, setting them afire. The west wall becomes a sheet of fire.

The east side riders repeat the same maneuvers. They rocket arrows into the barracks clustered about the east gate, then set fire to the outside huts and east wall.

In the distance, Lucius and Marcus watch the African riders rush past them and set the rear huts aflame. Minutes later they see them return, setting fire to the camp walls.

"That's it," Lucius says excitedly, "Time to get out there and form our lines!"

"Sound the call," Marcus yells to the cornicen.

The horns blow. Thousands of legionnaires trot toward the east gates, encouraged by screams erupting from the flame lit camp. The Romans array themselves in a wide, three-deep gauntlet in front of the gates, their swords and spears at the ready.

Six hundred triarii form the front lines of the quarter-mile gauntlet. The elder legionnaires kneel and plant their curved shields into the ground, their seven-foot spears sticking out in front of them. A second line moves in behind the first, repeating the formation. The triarii form a double wall of bristling spears, backed by rows of hastati and principes. Hundreds of velites stand behind them, with dozens of pila at their feet.

While the east legion finishes forming its gauntlet formation, the east gates fly open. Thousands of Gauls dash from the burning camp, seeking the safety of the cool night air. Unarmed and unarmored, they run through the night-shadowed gauntlet, heedless of the death that awaits them on either side.

"Loose!" screams Marcus Aemilius. He draws his sword and steps into the front line of triarii.

The velites unleash their javelins, aiming them low to avoid hitting their compatriots on the other side. The pila skewer hundreds of unprotected Gauls. The night air fills with the screams of dead and dying. Wave after wave of spears fly from the velites. Soon, thousands of corpses lie silent in front of the flaming gates.

Mad with fear, the Gauls dash from the center of the path, only to run into the spear walls of the stone-hearted triarii. The triarii lance their spears into their vulnerable foes, lining the ground with their Gallic victims.

"Line change!" Marcus yells to the nearby cornicen. The hornsman blows the signal, which is echoed from the other side. On each side of the gauntlet, the triarii turn their shields sideways, readying for the legion's final assault.

The hastati and principes edge in between the triarii, their iron blades flickering in the firelight. They walk over the corpses strewn in front of them and close upon the compacted Gauls, stabbing down all within reach. The Gauls try to retreat from the walls of swords, but their comrades fleeing from the camp push them into the threshing Roman blades. Hundreds more fall. An hour later, all that remains is a thick band of Boii and Insubres pressed into the center. Hundreds of Gauls fall to their knees, begging for mercy.

The Gauls are struck down where they kneel. Many others attack with bare fists and javelin shafts, desperately beating upon the Roman shield wall. With the quick thrust of a blade or spearpoint, each of these attackers fall.

On the west side gate, Scipio's and Laelius' men are engaged in similar butchery, with an unanticipated obstacle. Scores of horses have burst out from the west side gateway, trampling through the Roman lines. Hundreds of barbarians sprint through the openings created by their mounts, frantic to escape the abattoir behind them. Dozens leap onto the backs of the panicky horses, careening toward the protective foothills.

Scipio and Laelius are on their horses, directing men to the gaps in their murderous shield wall. "A bunch of those bastards are getting away!" Laelius shouts to Scipio.

"They won't get far," Scipio replies. "Sophon has his orders." He points to the end of the gauntlet, near the foothills. "See?"

Sophon's Numidians gallop past the Roman lines, hurtling toward the escaping Gauls. As Laelius watches, they close upon the runners, striking them down with their short curved swords. The Africans amuse themselves by shooting the remainder of their flaming arrows into the Gauls' backs. They watch the flaming riders bob away into the night, soon to fall sideways to the earth.

Back at the front of the Gallic camp, Consul Sempronius has followed Sophon's men toward the front gates. He draws his legions into a wide semicircle about the main portal, knowing that the body of the Gallic army has yet to emerge—that there will be too many to contain within the gauntlet. He does not have long to wait.

The barbarians pull open the front gates and run madly out onto the plain, only to find themselves facing an enormous curved wall of ten thousand enemy shields. Avoiding the thick wall of legionnaires to their sides, the Boii and Insubres escape into the dimly lit darkness in front of them. They meet death in that darkness, cut down by men they can barely see.

Hearing the screams of their fallen colleagues, hundreds dash back into the main gates, running to their smoldering barracks and armories. They grab shields, swords, axes—whatever weapons they can find. The barbarians run back through the gates, determined to die as warriors.

Fighting with the desperate ferocity of doomed men, the Boii and Insubres batter openings into their enemies' lines. Scores of Gauls stream through the gaps and dash into the night. Mad with terror, they slash at any silhouette that appears nearby, heedless of whether they are friend or foe.

"Close ranks," Sempronius yells, riding along behind his lines. "Get the cavalry after those bastards!" He hears a rumbling coming from the camp, as if a herd of giant beasts were stampeding toward him. The consul squints into the cavernous gate opening.

With the sound and suddenness of a thunder strike, dozens of wagons burst forth from the front portal, drawn by horses desperate to escape the burning bales in the backs of their wagons. The maddened beasts careen into the Roman encirclement. The wagons pitch over, tumbling the flaming bales onto scores of helpless legionnaires. Their tunics and cloaks burning, the unfortunate soldiers scatter among the ranks, screaming in anguish and supplication. The hastati and principes rush to pitch earth onto them.

Squadrons of Gallic riders gallop out from behind the wagons. Boiorix rides in the lead, his helmet glinting redly in the flickering firelight. His brother Sudarix rides next to him, his head pressed tight against the neck of his fleeing mount. The squadron gallops past the sides of a large burning wagon and flees into the night, heading for the western foothills.

While the wagons are bursting from camp, Scipio is overseeing the slaughter in the west wall gauntlet. His eyes are captured by the fiery wagons careening out into the front of the burning camp. He watches a knot of Gauls gallop past a tumbled wagon, heading for the hills. *Clever ruse. Someone had the wits to devise that in the midst of all this insanity.*

He sees the glint of golden horns, and his mouth drops. *It's Boiorix! He'll get out and start this all over again!*"

"Laelius! Laelius! Damn it, where are you?"

"Quit yelling!" Laelius barks, trotting in next to Scipio. "Nothing to worry about, we've got them cornered like pigs in a pen."

"Boiorix! He's heading toward the foothills!" Scipio wheels his mount about and gallops off.

"Gods be cursed, I thought we had finished him!" Laelius slaps the neck of his horse and chases after Scipio. "Wait, damn it. Wait for the guards!"

Scipio angles to his right, intent on cutting off Boiorix before he enters the sheltering forest. He watches Sempronius' allied cavalry hurtle out from camp walls, aiming at the fleeing horsemen. *They won't get to him in time.* Scipio hammers his heels into his prize stallion. He races through the field of fleeing Gauls, his gaze fixed on Boiorix's horned helmet.

Boiorix sees two Roman horsemen racing across the plains toward him, one with a purple cape flapping from his shoulders. *That must be Scipio!*

"Come about, Sudarix," Boiorix yells. "Scipio's behind us!" The two brothers wheel about and race headlong toward Scipio, with six of their men following.

Scipio sees the two chieftains racing at him, followed by their guards. *Here they come! Now what are you going to do?* He draws his sword and leans into his horse's neck. *I've got to get Boiorix before his brother catches up to me. And the others.*

An arrow whistles out from behind him, then another. Scipio looks over his shoulder and sees Laelius guiding his horse with his knees, shooting arrows as he rides. *Good! Got to trust he'll get some of them.* He gallops straight for Boiorix.

As Scipio closes in, he straightens up. He holds his small round shield in front of him, his sword arm cocked for a skull-splitting blow. Boiorix charges in from Scipio's left, holding his hand axe over his head.

The two riders dash past each other, a hand's breadth apart. Boiorix chops his axe at Scipio's head. Scipio grasps his horse's mane and leans sideways toward Boiorix, just as the axe swooshes over him. He jabs out with his short sword, gouging his blade across the Gaul's exposed thigh.

Boiorix screams. He tumbles from his horse and crashes onto the ground. The chieftain totters to his feet, grasping his gushing thigh. Scipio veers about and closes upon Boiorix. The chieftain grabs his oblong shield and crouches behind it, axe in hand.

"Hold on, brother!" Sudarix cries. He charges in from behind Scipio, both hands grasping his long sword.

There is a flash of wood and feather. Sudarix jerks back in his saddle, staring at the arrowhead that juts from his breastplate. Another blooms next to it. Sudarix drops his sword. He fingers the twin arrow points, gaping at the bloodstreams that flow beneath them. The chieftain slides sideways and crashes onto the trampled earth.

Boiorix gapes at his brother's fate. An arrow thunks into the side of his neck. He grapples at his gushing windpipe, his eyes wide with horror.

Scipio hurtles into his enemy, leaning sideways from his mount. His sword arcs down. The Gaul's head tumbles from his body. His headless corpse joins his brother's body.

Laelius pulls up beside Scipio, gripping his horn bow in his right hand. "I got a couple of them, but I wasted some arrows trying to hit them. I need more practice!"

Scipio grins with relief. "That saggitarius training has proven to be beneficial."

"Maybe so, but here come the rest. Let's get out of here!"

Six Gauls close in upon the two men, fury upon their faces. Scipio and Laelius race for their lines, pounding their heels into the sides of their mounts. Six more enemy riders angle in from the foothills, their eyes fixed on Scipio and Laelius.

Scipio hears the thudding hooves growing louder. "We're not going to make it," he yells to Laelius.

"We don't have to," retorts Laelius, pointing off to their left.

Prince Sophon races across the plains, flanked by scores of his Numidian tribesmen. Facing certain death, the Gauls wheel about and race for safety.

Whooping and shouting, the Numidians thunder past Scipio and Laelius. They close quickly upon the Gauls' heavy horses. Minutes later, the enemy riders lie upon the ground, their bodies stitched with spear cuts. The Numidians weave across the plains, hunting down the last of the fleeing Boii and Insubres.

Laelius whooshes a sigh of relief. He grabs Scipio by the shoulder and shakes him. “Are you fucking crazy? Why’d you run after him?”

Scipio shrugs. “He’s the mastermind. He would have raised another army.”

Laelius shoves him backward. “So we lose *our* mastermind because he wants to kill some half-wit barbarian. That was more stupid than brave!”

Prince Sophon trots back to the Scipio and Laelius, his face as calm as if he were riding along the seashore. “It was fortunate you were wearing that purple cape,” he tells Scipio. “Else we would have left you to your own fortunes.”

“Gratitude,” Scipio replies. The trio trot back toward the burning camp, back to the screams of their slaughtered enemies. “Call the men back,” Scipio tells his lead tribune. “The Gauls are broken. More killing serves no purpose.”

The next day’s dawn breaks upon a battlefield strewn with thirty thousand Boii and Insubres, a sea of bodies interspersed with five hundred Romans. Though the dead lie silent, the field is a hive of activity. Hundreds of Romans and Umbrians pick their way through the fallen enemies, bared swords in hand.

Wounded comrades are pulled from the mounds of bodies, and wounded enemies are quickly dispatched. Few words are spoken by the Romans, so intent are they upon their hunt. The Romans’ vengeful blades strike home. The quiet field is punctuated with the enemies’ agonized cries.

Hundreds of villagers congregate at the edges of the charnel landscape, which was once the site of their tall, waving grainfields. They wait for the invaders to finish their killings and plunders, anxious to pick through the remains. After decades of battles, the locals are quite expert and finding treasures that the victors overlook.

The Roman armies tread back to camp, so weary from stabbing and throwing that they can barely raise their arms. Still, many of them manage an anticipatory smile. Tonight, they know, there will be much feasting, drinking, fighting, and singing—all celebrated with the giddy desperation that only men who have escaped death can feel.

That night, as thousands of drunken soldiers careen through the camp, Scipio, Sempronius, Sophon, Laelius, and Lucius sit at the map table in Scipio's command tent. Goblets of wine replace yesterday's battle figurines.

Marcus Aemilius stands to the rear of the tent, standing at attention behind the senior officers. He forsakes any drink, contenting himself with tidbits of the roast mice that the camp cooks have prepared for them.

Sempronius raises his bronze goblet. "Let us toast our victory. We estimate thirty thousand enemy slain, and at least another five thousand captured," he crows. "It is a great victory, Rome will give us a triumph when we return!"

Scipio plunks his goblet upon the table. "Perhaps, but we are not going home."

Sempronius gapes at him. "What? We've killed their chiefs and broken their army. Our mission is fulfilled."

Scipio slowly shakes his head. "There are a dozen Gallic garrisons between here and the northern highlands. The Gallic threat remains."

"Pish!" Sempronius snaps. "The remainders can be attended to by next year's consuls. We have done more than Flaccus did last year. Let's go home and receive our honors."

"You think you will be honored?" Scipio says. "Rome still remembers that you lost a legion's worth of men in Milano. It will take more than one victory to erase your foolish mistakes."

"You cannot address me in such a manner!" Sempronius huffs, his face reddening. "I am a consul!"

"And I am the man who got you elected, or did you forget that? Your losses are the Hellenic party's losses. If I don't help you out of this mess, we will never win another election!"

"This matter does not concern me," Sophon says, rising to leave. "I'd rather brush my horse than listen to you two argue." He opens the tent flaps and strides into the tumultuous night.

Scipio's voice softens. "It's not just for politics, Sempronius. I'd like to go back, too, because Antiochus is the real danger. But we have to eliminate the Gallic presence. If we don't the Senate may send another two armies up here, and neglect the Syrian threat. Can you see that?"

"When we get back, I will speak on behalf of committing troops to Syria," Sempronius says. "Wouldn't that suffice?"

"No. We are going to take all of the Po Valley. You will return with such a load of plunder that the Senate will have to give you a triumph." He crooks an eye at Sempronius. "Of course, you will receive a sizable portion of that plunder."

*I could buy a larger farm. Get out of Rome forever*. Sempronius sips his wine. "Well, I suppose we should make our borderlands safe for Italia."

"That is a noble sentiment," Laelius says, his voice dripping with sarcasm.

Scipio slaps Sempronius on the back. "So it will be, Consul. We will march out after the men have rested. The Gauls have a fort near Comum, that will be our next objective."

"I am going to check on my men," Sempronius says, stalking out from the tent.

"That's is a good idea," Marcus says. "I don't want my men too hung over." The stocky young tribune follows Sempronius.

As soon as they leave, Laelius plops onto Scipio's sleeping furs, his hands behind his head. "I am yours to command, pumpkin-head. I just hope we are back in Rome at year's end, so I can begin my campaign for consul."

"Agreed," Scipio says. "I think you would be best served by accruing more victories here, anyway. We will report each one to Rome. Your reputation will grow."

"What about me?" Lucius interjects, his face anxious. "Do I have to go with you?"

Scipio flicks his eyes at Laelius, who gives the barest of head shakes. "After that incident with the pirates, I am worried about Amelia and the children. I would feel much better if you were there to guard them."

Lucius laughs, relieved. "Of course! Anything to help my brother! I just hope you can get along without me."

"We will manage," says Scipio. Laelius and Scipio fall silent, looking at the floor.

"I think I'll go out and join the festivities," Lucius says stiffly. "Who knows when I'll have another victory to celebrate." He pushes through the tent flaps and merges into the night.

"Who knows when, indeed," Laelius says.

"He tries his best, Laelius. He just has more to overcome than some of us." He frowns. "I recognize the burden he carries as my brother."

"You know he will not rest until he becomes a consul, like you,"

"There have been worse than he would be."

"If you say so. But then he won't be yours to command, like he is now. He may have to lead an army into battle. Against the Gauls—or the Syrians!"

Scipio purses his lips. "I made a promise to my mother. I intend to keep it,"

Laelius swirls the wine in his goblet. "You promised your father you'd protect Rome, and you promised your mother you'd help Lucius make his way. The day may come when you can't do both."

"Gods, I pray that day never comes," Scipio mutters. He springs up. "Come on, why speculate about gloomy possibilities? Amusement awaits us, just outside my tent!"

Laelius laughs. "I do not believe it! Somber Scipio telling Laelius he should lighten his spirit! Yes, let us cut loose from dreary speculations, and celebrate with our men."

The two step out of the tent—and quickly jump back in. Eight naked legionnaires barge past them, clanging pewter spoons upon the tops of their plundered Gallic helmets.

"Those men know how to celebrate," Scipio declares.

"I like getting naked and screaming, but I prefer it with a single partner," Laelius replies. He tugs at Scipio's tunic sleeve. "I have the urge to deprive some men of their wages. I'm going to pitch some knucklebones. Come with me."

"I'll come, but only to watch. It's unseemly for a consul to participate. If I lose, it lessens the men's confidence that I am favored by the gods. If I win, they resent a wealthy patrician taking their hard-earned money!" He spreads his hands. "I cannot win, even if I win!"

"Huh, Then maybe I shouldn't be a consul, I enjoy my recreations too much." Laelius grins. "What would the men think if Consul Laelius stripped naked and challenged them to wrestle?"

"You would give them confidence," Scipio replies. "One look at your tiny thing and they would feel much better about themselves!"

Laelius punches Scipio in the shoulder. "You are just jealous! Come on, you can at least watch—and drink!"

Arm in arm, the two childhood friends walk into the heart of the raucous camp, heading to the dice games at the back of the stables.

Four days later Scipio rides out from camp, weaving through the carpenters who are disassembling the front gates and towers. Sophon and his Numidians follow behind him. The wary Africans scan the flatlands and foothills, still searching for attackers.

The party halts near the head-high ash piles of the army's funeral pyres. Scipio grasps Sophon's forearm. "We part here. A turma of my cavalry will accompany you to Rome as an honor guard. I give you thanks for all your help."

Sophon bows his head. "It was an honor to work with you. I have learned much." He jerks his fist into the air, signaling his men to follow him.

"Sophon!" Scipio yells. The Numidian prince looks over his shoulder. "Send my regards to your father, Masinissa."

Sophon smiles tightly. "I will tell him, though I doubt they will be well received." The Numidians gallop across the plain.

Scipio nods, his mouth pinched into a line of regret.

For the next three months, Scipio and Sempronius' armies storm across North Italia. The Gauls' Comum fortress falls to them, its walls scaled by hundreds of escaladers. That victory is followed by successful sieges of the Clastidium and Ticinum garrisons. After each conquest, Scipio sends messengers back to Rome, alerting the people of their victories. Their conquests become the talk of Rome—and the envy of the Latin senators.

Scipio and Sempronius ride together in the vanguard, but they speak little to each other. Chastened and resentful, Sempronius acquiesces to Scipio's directives, knowing they give him the best chance for victory—and a safe return home. The young general's mind often wanders to the Sabina Hills of Rome, to the farm and family he envisions for himself.

After months of campaigning, the legions return to Placentia, laden with wagonloads of money and valuables. The Romans pitch camp around the city. Scipio personally directs the storage of the plunder into the city's storehouses.

"We can leave for Rome with the week," Scipio tells Sempronius. "With all these riches for the treasury, the Senate should readily approve your triumph. The quaestor can tally all of it in a few days, after we have sorted it all out."

The young consul smiles. "Then let us depart as soon as possible. I ache to be done with the military life."

The next night, three wagons trundle from the rear portal of the sleeping town, their oaken axles groaning under the weight of their load. Scipio stands next to the wagons, his hooded face in shadow.

Two sentries approach the portal. They spy the wagons departing and run toward them, their hands gripping their sword hilts. "Here now, where are you going?" one of them shouts to a driver.

"Let them go," says a commanding voice behind them.

The two legionnaires march toward the hooded figure. "And who might you be?" one of them blusters. Scipio throws back his hood.

"Ap…apologies, General," the lead guard stammers. "We did not know…at this hour we see wagons leaving, how could we—"

"We are sending some captured armament to Tibur,"[xxxix] Scipio replies. "They need weapons to protect themselves against the Sabines."

The guards nod. They continue their rounds.

One sentry pauses. He looks back at Scipio. "I am one of the survivors of Sempronius' second legion. I have to tell you, were you in charge at Milano, we would not have lost all those men." He turns about and marches into the night.

*I wish I were, too,* Scipio thinks. *And I would not carry the guilt of getting that puff elected.* Scipio ambles toward Placentia's main street, intent on offering a sacrifice at the temple of Clementia, the goddess of forgiveness.

Scipio rounds the street corner. Titus Paullus walks out from the horse stable's shadows, pulling his dark gray hood from his head. The camp accountant takes out a wooden stylus and carves some numbers and dates into a wax tablet.

*Well, Cato, it seems as if you had cause for concern.*

TEMPLE OF BELLONA, 194 BCE. "You are denying us a triumph?" Scipio blurts incredulously. "We have secured all of northern Italia, and brought enough plunder to buy the city! We have eighteen tons of silver, and two tons of gold! Does any of that mean anything to you?"

Following custom, Sempronius and Scipio are meeting with the Senate outside of Rome, so that the army may be disarmed before it returns. Sitting on the semicircular steps of the beautiful little temple, the senators stolidly endure Scipio's outrage.

Senator Laxtus rises from the temple steps. The senior senator smiles ingratiatingly at Scipio. He spreads his arms in a placating gesture. "It's not that you two have not achieved great victories, honored general. But we lost a legion's worth of men at Milano, a very severe loss. That has palled the shine of your conquests." The senator glances at Flaccus, who makes a circle with his thumb and forefinger.

*And you wouldn't want to honor two Hellenic consuls right before the elections, would you, Senator?* Scipio glares at a smirking Flaccus. *This smells of your doing, prick.*

Scipio sees Sempronius' head droop in defeat. *Poor bastard, you are the one who needed this.* "I am not going to beg for honors," Scipio declares. "That is an act dishonorable in itself. I would only ask that we be allowed to parade through the gates, that our men may receive their due respect."

Flaccus stands up, his eyes alight victory. "Of course, Consul." He spreads his hands. "We are not unreasonable men! You and Sempronius can have your parade. There will be no gold wreaths for you, but we will provide a welcoming speech at the Forum Square." He grins. "Why, I will give it myself!"

Scipio winces. *The Latins will throw a bone to us so the people aren't angry with them. At least Laelius and Sempronius will get some recognition.*

Scipio turns his back on the senators. He walks to Sempronius, and grasps his shoulder. "Come on, General. There is nothing left to do here. Let us take our men home. We will leave our weapons at the gates."

Sempronius shrugs off Scipio's hand. "This is your fault. If they didn't hate you so much, they would have given it to me."

Sempronius treads over and faces the senators. He unclasps his purple cloak and lets it fall to his feet. "I am done with your political bullshit!" he declares. "And done with fucking Rome!"

Laxtus rises. "Please, Consul, do not take this as—" But Sempronius is already marching away, head held high. He climbs onto his white stallion and gallops down the pathway that follows the Tiber River, heading for his farm in the Sabina Hills.

Scipio watches Sempronius disappear down the cobbled roadway. He turns back to the senators, nightfall on his face. "For any one of you who denied us because we are Hellenics, I will tell you this. You have soiled your robe of office."

Scipio whirls about and marches back to his horse. Laelius stands there, holding the bridles their mounts. The two mount their horses and trot toward Rome.

"Well, you said they might not give it to us," Laelius says, shaking his head. "So much for my consular campaign."

"They did not, but we will give it to them—up the ass. We are going to get you elected. We will host something memorable. Something the Latins cannot diminish."

"What? A three-day public orgy?"

Scipio smiles grimly. "Nothing with that much group participation.

We'll organize our own gladiatorial games, in honor of our legions' glorious victories. That will remind the people who won this war. You think Prima would be willing to participate?"

Laelius rolls his eyes. "Willing? I can only hope she doesn't get the baby to fight!"

***Thracian Warrior***

# IV. WARS OF DIPLOMACY

LEPCIS, CARTHAGE, 193 BCE. Masinissa and Sophon ride down the roadway between this port city's fields of barley and millet. The rising sun sets the Mediterranean aglow before them, its light dancing atop the choppy turquoise waves. In spite of the beauty about them, the Numidians' faces are grim. They know their mission may end in their immediate death.

"You think this will work?" Sophon asks.

"Why not? We are not their enemies, though we are not their friends," the king replies. "I can't see why they'd kill us outright." He snorts. "Then again, Carthaginians are very unpredictable."

Father and son enter the clearing that encircles the block-walled fortress. They halt in front Lepcis' twenty-foot doors. Masinissa draws a long silver spear from his saddle sling. He wheels his horse sideways and pitches his spear into the earth. He and Sophon withdraw several paces, watching the spear's white pennant flap in the gusty sea breeze. An hour passes. Neither man moves.

The heavy doors slowly creak open. A squadron of Carthaginian cavalry file out in wedge formation, their linen cuirasses gleaming in the high desert sun. The squadron halts near Masinissa and Sophon. A brown-bearded rider trots out from the group. He removes his purple-plumed helmet. His green eyes stare insolently beneath his coal-black brows.

"What are you two doing out here?" he demands.

"Reclaiming our lands," Masinissa replies. "The Numidians owned this land until Hamilcar took it from my grandfather. I, King Masinissa, am here to reclaim the property. Its tenants will now pay taxes to me."[xl]

"Psh!" the officer replies. "These lands are always being taken over by someone or another. And now it's part of Carthage. Get on your way, before I make a rug of your skin."

Masinissa smirks. "It is you who will 'get on your way,' as you say. I am giving you a chance to go back to Carthage—alive."

The Carthaginian flushes with anger. "I'm not wasting words on a fool." He beckons his dozen riders. "Take them in."

"You were a fool to leave your walls," Masinissa replies. He flicks up his right hand.

Five hundred cavalry rise up from the tall fields behind the Numidians. They leap onto their horses. Riding fast as a desert wind, the Numidians whirl across the clearing and encircle the stunned Carthaginians.

Two thousand Numidian mountain men lope in behind them, lugging the spears and shields that Masinissa recently gave them. The recruits race across the plains, eager for their first taste of battle and plunder.

Forty Numidian foot soldiers trot past the cavalry, lugging the trimmed pine trees that serve as their ladders. They line themselves along the front wall of the city.

Shouts of alarm erupt from the walls. Scores of Carthaginian militia level their spears over the ramparts.

"As you can see, we are ready to defend ourselves," the squadron leader says.

Masinissa watches the Numidians line up along the walls. "Now!" he says to his son.

Sophon whistles two short, high-pitched notes. Another five hundred cavalry rise from the fields and mount their horses. They gallop in and line up behind their infantry. The wall defenders peer anxiously at their bewildered captain.

"You have maybe three hundred men in the town?" Masinissa says to the Carthaginian. "Do you think you have a chance for more than token resistance? I don't want to kill your men, but I will. Your choice."

"Are you mad? Carthage will destroy you when it hears of this!" the leader blusters.

"Then go tell them!" Masinissa replies irritably. "Or stay here and die. What will it be?"

The captain is silent, studying the Numidian forces arrayed about his city. Sophon draws his curved sword and pulls his horse next to the captain's mount. He points it between the captain's eyes.

"Make a decision. Or I will make it for you."

The captain stares at the gleaming blade. He swallows. "I will come back and rectify this outrage."

The prince withdraws his blade. "Of course you will. But for now, you will wait here with me. Tell your officers to bring out the rest of your men. I swear on my mother's spirit, no one will be harmed."

An hour later, two hundred unarmed Carthaginian cavalry stand in the Lepcis square, surrounded by a matching number of foot soldiers. The captain leads his men down the northern road to Carthage.

"Aren't you worried about a counterattack?" Sophon asks his father.

"No. Rome's treaty has cut Carthage's balls off. They don't have the men to handle border incursions. They'll just complain to Rome." He shrugs. "Let them."

"That does not worry you?" Sophon asks.

"No. These lands are rightfully ours, and you have recently done a great service to Rome. That is why I sent you to help them."

The king's eyes grow cold. "And Scipio is the most powerful man in Rome. He owes me a debt he can never repay. But he will try."

LYSIMACHIA, THRACE. *They're almost there. Come on, you dogs,*

*Just a little farther. There.*

Thrax is satisfied. The Syrians are right where the Thracian chief wants them, heading for the narrowest passage in the Chersonese Mountains. He leans over his skeletal brown horse, beckoning to the five hundred Thracians strung along the chasm trail, hundreds of feet above their enemies. *Get ready*, he signals.

For three days, Thrax and his raiders have followed the Syrian war party. Scrambling over brush and boulders, the rebels have stalked them through Thrace's rugged peninsular mountains. Thrax himself has followed every move of the four Syrian scouts that rode in advance of the party, learning their signals and motions. Now he's ready to spring his trap.

*They're heading north to take Pontike town, I'd bet my children on it. The townspeople won't surrender. The Syrians will murder them all. We have to take them here, before they get out onto the plains.*

The rangy old warrior examines the tops of the jagged peaks that surround him, recalling every trail and passage of his childhood hunting grounds. *The upper routes are too narrow for their horses and wagons. They'll have to take the Ludi gorge. That's our best chance.*

Thrax sends a hundred men ahead of him. The Thracians march along the trail, each lugging a stout pole upon his shoulder.

Thrax watches them disappear around a bend in the trail. *Now to prepare a welcome for those scouts*. He dissolves soundlessly into the trailside scrub.

The next morning, the Syrian war party enters the mouth of the Ludi Gorge, the cavalry splashing through the rocky stream that carved this precipitous passage. The Syrian scouts ride along the mountains ahead of the army, traversing the high mountain passages. Seeing no sign of enemies, they wobble their polished bronze shields, flashing the signal that all is clear.

The scouts do not see Thrax and three of his men lurking along the deer trail above them, slowly edging downward.

The Syrian cavalry enter the mountains' narrowest defile. Thrax crouches down, his hunting knife clenched in his teeth. He motions for his men to do the same. The scouts trot by below them. Thrax chops down his hand.

The Thracians leap upon the startled scouts, tackling them off their mounts. Minutes later, the scouts lay dead and naked. Garbed in Syrian armor, Thrax's men ride along the trail, continuing the scouts' route. Thrax flashes his Syrian shield at men below, assuring them that all is well.

Five hundred infantry and two hundred cavalry turn into a rocky passage. Thrax watches the Syrian columns fill the gorge below him. When the last column of Syrians marches into the gorge, Thrax grabs his ram's horn and blows three short blasts.

The mountainsides swarm to life with warriors. Hundreds of Thracians spring up from the scrub trees and boulders above the Syrians, seemingly rising from the earth. The warriors jam their poles into crevices beneath mountainside boulders. Grunting and straining, they pry huge rocks from the mountainside.

Rolling, bouncing, and crashing, the heavy stones plummet into the surprised Syrians, bashing into their heads and bodies. The passage echoes with the screams of men trapped under the avalanche. Scores of Syrians crawl along the ground, stunned by blows to their heads and back. The cavalry mill about their fallen comrades, uncertain about what to do.

The Thracians scramble down the mountainsides, shields and swords strapped upon their backs. As they near the bottom of the gorge, the warriors leap upon the milling cavalrymen, knocking them onto the earth. The Syrian riders die where they land, too dazed to block their enemies' killing blades.

Thrax stabs a rider off his mount and vaults upon it. He arcs his dripping sword above his head. "All die!" Thrax screams.

The Thracians charge into the surviving infantrymen. Hundreds of individual duels erupt inside the narrow, rock-filled passage. The lightly armored Thracians dodge the strikes of their heavily armored opponents, swarming around them until they can administer a fatal thrust. After several hours, no infantrymen remain to oppose them. The vengeful Thracians crawl from boulder to boulder, executing the wounded that lie beneath them.

"Back to the city!" yells the cavalry captain. The Syrian cavalry stampede from the slaughter, racing back for Lysimachia. Thrax grimaces. *Shit! We should have set up a boulder field to block them. Now they'll return with an army.*

"Come on, we've got lots of work to do before we get back to our retreat," Thrax says. "Get the poles. Grab the bodies. You know what to do."

Hours later, as the sun creeps behind the westernmost pinnacles, the Thracians finish their grisly task. The horns sound, and the Thracians hike up the threadlike trail that leads to their hidden camp.

The evening moon finds Thrax's men ensconced in a high valley, feasting on venison and wine. Thrax sits by a campfire in front of his cave, sharing battle stories with his men. His tattooed face beams with mirth.

"It was a good fight today," declares Zalmoxis, Thrax's one-eyed cavalry leader.

The smile disappears from Thrax's face. "Is this what we are reduced to? Nibbling at the edges of Antiochus' armies while they destroy our towns?" He pounds his fist on his thigh. "There just aren't enough of us! The Greeks need to come after him. Or the Romans. Then we can join them. Vulcan's balls, even Philip of Macedonia would be better than these Asian butchers!"

"Aye," Zalmoxis growls. "That silver-faced bastard is the worst of them!"

Thrax recalls the Battle of Lysimachia two years ago, when the Syrian hordes slaughtered thousands of his men. Nicator the Assassin was there, slashing down Thrax's men. He remembers Nicator's scarred and pustulent face when Thrax yanked off his mask. He shudders.

Thrax pokes at the campfire's orange-red embers, watching them flare back to life. *You killed many of my men, soup-face. We have a score to settle.* He grins to himself. *I left you a memento in the gorge.*

Two days later, the Syrian army marches into the Chersonese Gorge, seeking their comrades' bodies. They do not have far to look.

From that day on, the Syrians will refer to the gorge as the Passage of Fifty Crucifixes. It is so named to commemorate the fifty comrades hung along the high mountain trail above the gorge, each cross angled southeast toward Syria. Each corpse's right arm sags limply next to its side, but the left arm points toward Antiochus' homeland, sending their comrades a message from the grave. *Go home.*

The Syrian raiding party stares mutely at their comrades' bodies. "Leave them," the commander orders. "Nicator will want to see this."

Days later, an army of riders gallops out from Lysimachia. A thousand of Antiochus' elite cataphractii rumble out in the vanguard. Horse and rider are armored head to foot, impervious to the blows of sword or spear. Five hundred Parthian horse archers follow, men experienced in mountain warfare. The army enters the Chersonese Gorge, preceded by twenty advance scouts.

Soon, the lead explorer returns. He pulls up to his silver-masked commander and points to an outcropping a thousand feet above them. "Up there, Captain. Look at what those fucking Thracians did!"

Nicator tilts his face upward. He sees a limp body hanging from a cross, its left arm nailed to the crossbeam. He nods appreciatively.

*Using corpses to tell us to leave. Very clever, Thrax.* He smiles inside his mask. *I am going to burn a village for every one of those men you've put up there. Maybe rage will bring you down to confront me, you pig.*

"Leave them to the vultures. We don't have time to bury them," he commands. The Syrian squadrons gallop through the mountain passage, their eyes fixed on the trail of crucifixes.

Thrax watches them leave. When the last rider has filed past him, he rises from his rocky niche at the top of the mountain. He waves his hand. Hundreds of Thracians rise from the pinnacles, their bodies wrapped in leafy branches. Their eyes follow the departing Syrians.

Thrax eases his sword into its scabbard. “Come on, get the horses. We’re going to hound those bastards until they sail back where they came from.” He gazes westward, toward Greece and Italia. “Or until someone comes to help us destroy them.”

SENATE CHAMBERS, ROME. Menippus bellows with laughter. “You want us to withdraw from Lysimachia?” the Syrian commander blurts. “And give up Pergamum, too? You want us to just walk away from the lands of Antiochus’ ancestors?” He throws up his hands. “Zeus take me! Who says Romans have no sense of humor?”

A young senator rises from his seat in the back row. He glares at the Syrian general. “You have no right to those lands anymore! The Greeks claimed them years ago.“

“We preceded them. They do not have the right to claim anything! I will speak no more about such silliness!” The rotund Syrian hoists his black robe above his ankles and lumbers to his seat next to the Cyprian the Senate Leader, his back stiff with resentment.

The Leader’s wattled neck reddens, but his voice remains unruffled. “Three days ago we received ten commissioners from Greece, Menippus. They were very concerned about your incursions into the Lysimachia region. They insist that you return to your Syrian homeland. We are in sympathy with their desires.”

The second Syrian delegate rises, his fists clenched. “I assure you, we resent even listening to this proposal that we vacate Thrace and its environs.[xli] Antiochus’ great grandfather Seleucus won these places. The people who live there are the better for him ruling them. He has restored Lysimachia to its former glory. Come visit it, and see!”

General Flamininus rises from his bench in the second row. "If you want to be friends with the people of Rome, you must promise that you will keep your hands off the cities of Greece! If you move any farther into Greece, Rome has the right to protect her existing friendships over there."[xlii] The senators roar their approval of the young general's words.

Scipio sits in the front row, resting his elbows on the marble bench behind him. Listening to Flamininus' shout out his warning, Scipio cannot help but smile. He turns to the two Hellenic senators sitting behind him. "Flamininus was so damn eager to withdraw our troops and become Greece's 'liberator.' Now he threatens to declare war against Syria, when his hasty withdrawal only encouraged their advance!" He rolls his eyes. "Does he not see the irony?"

Menippus shakes his fist at the red-faced Flamininus. "You threaten those who would be your friends? You made the Greek city-states into your amici, into friends of Rome. We only ask that you do the same for us. Yet you treat us as if we were conquered enemies, dictating terms of conquest to us!"[xliii]

Flamininus springs to his feet. "That is because you act like an enemy, when you transport your armies across the Aegean!" Several senators shout their agreement.

Scipio rubs his eyes. *Gods help us, this is getting out of control!* He pushes himself up and walks to the center of the Senate floor, facing Cyprian and the two Syrian envoys.

"This discussion seems to be generating more heat than light, so let me propose an alternative. We will send envoys to negotiate with King Antiochus, the same ones who met him at Lysimachia.[xliv] Let us see if we can come to some agreement about Greece and Syria's borders, before war breaks out between us. I would be happy to lead the delegation."

Scipio smiles impishly. "I hear my old friend Hannibal is acting as Antiochus' advisor. Perhaps my presence there will make him sympathetic to our cause—if he doesn't slit my throat first!" The senators chuckle, aware of the admiration and enmity shared between the two former foes.

"We will vote on Scipio's proposal," the Cyprian declares. He turns to the Syrian delegates. "Please wait outside the chambers."

The elder watches them go, then turns to the Senate. "Before we take a voice vote upon Scipio's suggestion, I propose an amendment to it."

He faces Scipio. "I have learned that Carthage will be sending envoys to us. They will lodge a complaint about King Masinissa's incursions into Lepcis and its surroundings. We should send a delegation to settle this dispute. Scipio, you are respected by both the Carthaginians and Numidians. I suggest you lead that delegation."[xlv]

"Respect from the Numidians?" Scipio says. "You had better ask Masinissa about that! Besides, I believe the greater issue is Antiochus. I would be of greater service leading a delegation to him."

The aged Leader rubs his chin. "Well, if you say so…"

Flaccus realizes that the Leader preparing to accede to Scipio's words. The storklike senator levers himself from his front row seat.

"With pardon, honorable Scipio," Flaccus says unctuously. "I think the African issue is the greater problem. The envoys from Carthage have told us that Hannibal is pressing Carthage to ally themselves with Antiochus.[xlvi] If we do not settle this dispute with Masinissa, they may take it as a sign that we favor the Numidians. That may be just the push they need to join the Syrians."

He turns to his fellow senators. "Think of it! The Carthaginians allied with the Army of a Hundred Nations! Greece would not be their only conquest—we would be their next victim!"

Dozens of Latin senators nod their agreement. Flaccus eyes Cato, a demand in his eyes. Cato grimaces. *Why are you looking at me? Scipio has the right of it, We disarmed Carthage, and it is no threat.*

Flaccus continues to stare at Cato, his eyes urging him to reply.

*You need Flaccus,* Cato reminds himself. *He will help you gain the power to save Rome from degeneration.* With a heavy sigh, he rises slowly from his seat.

"You all know I think Carthage is too dangerous to exist, that we must destroy it.[xlvii] So, we must certainly prevent them from allying with the dread Antiochus. That is the greatest threat to Rome."

Cato plops onto his seat, his face sour. *I have earned myself another flogging. Politics are truly the bane of virtue.* He looks at his fellow senators, recalling the ones that have accepted Flaccus' bribes and favors. *Gods help me from becoming like them.*

Scipio rises. "I am puzzled by Cato's words about a 'Carthaginian threat.' He knows we have a peace treaty with Carthage. He knows that the Carthaginian Senate opposes Hannibal, to the degree that they were going to capture him and send him to Rome for imprisonment. Cato knows this, yet he portrays them as Antiochus' potential allies. This is, at best, an inconsistency on his part."

He eyes Cato. "At worst, it is a lie."

Cato stares at his feet. *Flaccus can go to Hades, I need to speak the truth of this.*

Before Cato can speak, Cyprian pounds his oak staff. "It does not have to be one or the other," he says. "Senator Scipio, if you settle the issue in Africa, you can then venture to Antiochus' court. If Fortuna smiles upon you in Africa, there will be ample time for you to do both. What say you to that?"

Scipio closes his eyes. "If the Senate agrees with your amendment, I will follow it. I will set off for Africa as soon as possible."

"I call a voice vote," Cyprian quickly interjects. "All in favor of my proposal?" The chamber rings with hundreds of 'ayes'. The Leader's milky eyes gleam with pride. "Good. It is settled. Now, to our next order of business, a proposal for a new slave tax..."

Hours later, the meeting adjourns. Scipio walks out into the afternoon sun, following a handful of his friends down the steps. He spies Cato at a vegetable vendor's stand, haggling over a large basket of turnips at his feet. Scipio excuses himself and approaches Cato.

"I would speak with you," Scipio declares, standing right behind him.

Cato ignores him. He leans into the vendor's face. "Ten sestertii or nothing!" The intimidated vendor nods.

Cato hefts the wicker basket under his left arm, his rounded bicep bulging. "Now, what do you want of me?"

"I know we have had some strong disagreements, but I always believed it was because you were as concerned for Rome's welfare as I was. But this argument that toothless Carthage is a danger? I do not criticize your reasons for sending me to Carthage, I only seek to understand. Why?"

"You know the Carthaginian and Numidian rulers, and they respect you. We already have plenty of negotiators for Antiochus."

Scipio snorts. "Who? Flamininus? He has already generated irreparable enmity there. Senator Tiberius? He hates everyone who is not a Roman? You? Are you thinking you will go? You hate the Greeks!"[xlviii]

Cato sets his chin. "We have others who could serve there."

"I am best suited to bring Philip of Macedonia to our side, and you know it!" He eyes Cato speculatively. "They say if you lie with dogs, you will soon get fleas. I suspect you have been too long in the Latin kennel."

Cato flushes. "And you have had your hands too long in the Roman till! Oh yes, I know what you're doing. You think that *I* have strayed from my concern for Rome's welfare? What about someone who steals from Rome, Scipio? Theft is theft, no matter how lofty the reason!" Cato stalks off to a cobbled side street, a turnip tumbling from his basket.

"And lying is lying, no matter the reason!" Scipio yells.

He rubs the back of his neck. *Gods, I am sick of arguing with people! I need a friendly face*. He weaves through a web of side streets, drifting toward a streetside popina he visited five years ago.[xlix]

Scipio arrives at a house-sized corner cafe. He slides between the worn stone stools that encircle the popina's soup and stew urns, heading for a small wooden table in a darkened corner. A duck-bodied matron trundles out to meet him, her careworn face beatific with joy.

"Fortuna be thanked, you've come back to see me! This is truly an honor!"

Scipio smiles, "Hello Livia. How fares your husband Sertor?"

"He is alive, what else can I say? You'd think an old cripple couldn't cause as much trouble as he does, with all his dicing and wining!" She smiles. "You know, he still talks about fighting for you at Zama."

Livia lays her calloused fingers on Scipio's forearm, her eyes twinkling. "He'll fall dead when I tell him you came here—so you have done me a great favor! Now, what can I bring the Savior of Rome?"

"A cup of mulsum." Scipio mutters. The owner quickly returns with a brimming silver chalice of honeyed wine. She lays down a small covered platter. "Here's a breast of roast goose. Killed it myself this morning!"

Scipio reaches for his belt purse. Livia shakes her head so vigorously, her turtle shell comb flies from her graying brunette bun. "No, no, no. Do not deny me the honor!"

Scipio pulls her hamlike hand to his mouth and kisses its reddened knuckles. "Gratitude, Citizen."

Livia flushes. "Ah, you! I…" She turns and bustles away, shouting imprecations at the two boy slaves ladling soup to her customers.

*You still have your seductive powers*, Scipio thinks, chuckling to himself. He sips the sweet red wine, inhaling the mulsum's aroma of cloves, cinnamon, and nutmeg. Mulling over the day's affairs, his mind turns back to Africa.

*What will Masinissa say when he sees me?* He recalls when the African king ordered him from his palace, bared sword in hand. *Worse, what will he do?*

Scipio pops a chunk of the sesame-encrusted goose into his mouth. *He'll probably cut my head off, and I'll never get to talk Antiochus out of invading Greece.* He upends his chalice, drinking deeply. *If Antiochus gets Macedonia to join him, we'll all be fucked!*

Scipio twirls his empty goblet, studying its stamped impressions of centaurs and satyrs. *Good a reason as any for another drink.*

An hour later, Scipio totters from the popina. He ambles to the Scipio town house. As he approaches the door, Amelia flings it open.

"Where have you been?" she snaps. "Laelius and Prima were waiting here for an hour! They wanted to talk about our candidates for the city aediles."

Scipio waves his hand in front of his face. "I had to get away from politics for a while. See what it feels like to be a normal person." He burps loudly. "Should have told my father to go to Hades, and become a teacher."

Amelia glowers at him, hands on her hips. "I can see you are in no state for rational discussion. At least get some food in you."

"Already dined," he replies. "Had some goose and bread. And a bit of love." He stretches out his arms, yawning. I am for a quick nap. Got to go out later, check on our resources for the coming elections."

Night falls on the city. Scipio eases from the front door, clad in an indigo hooded cloak. Rufus hands him the bridle to a swaybacked brown mare. Scipio clops down a side street, bound for the rough-and-tumble Aventine Hill district. When Scipio's horse turns into a side street, a small, tousle-haired figure sidles from a darkened doorway opposite the Scipio manse.

Runner peers down both sides of the cobbled street, making sure no one is watching him. For weeks the boy has sat in the darkened doorway, waiting for Scipio to ride out. Tonight, finally, he sees his opportunity.

The street urchin takes a deep breath and dashes after Scipio, monitoring the sound of his horse's hooves. The boy lopes between the narrow passageways that Scipio negotiates, his bare feet slapping softly over the inlaid river stones.

A mile becomes two. Runner's breath quickens, but he does not relent. His mind is fixed on his reward. The gray man has promised him a wonderful toy horse if he succeeds in his mission—and a beating if he does not.

Scipio enters the stone block buildings that fill the industrial section near the Porta Collina. He halts before the windowless stone granary that he has rented there for years—under a different name.

He halts his horse in front of the arched entry. He pauses, motionless, listening for voices, for any sound of movement. Satisfied, Scipio slides off his horse walks to the granary's oak door. He takes out a finger-length key and unlocks it, exposing the iron door hidden behind it. Scipio unlocks the second door and pushes it open.

He pushes into the inky darkness, his right hand searching for the wall torch he knows will be there. He strikes iron to flint, and kindles the brand. After closing the doors, Scipio holds up the torch and surveys the room's contents.

Hundreds of gold neck torques are piled into a back corner, resting next to tall mounds of Roman and Gallic coins. They lie near piles of Carthaginian gems and stacks of Iberian silver bars, the remnants of plunder from his previous campaigns. Scipio nods with satisfaction. *Good. There's enough here for a dozen local elections, if I spend it wisely. Maybe enough for several consular campaigns. What should I sell for Laelius' election?*

A half hour later Scipio extinguishes the torch and exits into the darkened street, his hand at his dagger belt. He mounts his horse and quickly trots away, weaving between the silent warehouses and granaries.

Runner steps out from the shadows and dashes in the opposite direction, eager to get to the gray man's house.

Several miles later, the street boy enters a mud brick apartment house and trots up its rickety stairs. He knocks on a door near the third floor landing, gasping to regain his breath. The door creaks open. A gaunt hand motions him inside.

Titus Paullus resumes his seat in his wicker chair, pushing aside the backgammon game he had played earlier with a tenant. The gray-bearded man wears a hooded gray tunic.

"Did you learn anything. boy?" he demands.

Runner bobs his head, his dark eyes shining with pride. "I followed him all the way to the old warehouses. He was on a horse, but he couldn't shake me!"

"Charon take you, what did you find out?" Titus raises his hand. "Speak, or I'll slap the spit from your mouth!"

The boy cowers. "Not again, please! General Scipio went into a granary building there. I could not see inside, but I know where it's at."

"That is enough. I think I know what is inside." He leans over the boy, his eyes demanding truth. "Can you take me to it tomorrow? To the exact place?" The boy nods meekly.

Scipio's old army accountant rises. "Good. You have earned your reward." He reaches into a wicker basket and pulls out a carved wooden horse, its feet equipped with shining ivory wheels. He hands the toy to Runner.

The boy's eyes widen. He runs the horse back and forth over his forearm, watching its wheels turn. He clutches it to his breast, eyeing

Titus suspiciously. "It's mine?"

"Go on, get out." Titus says. "Come back tomorrow at the second hour. There's a silver coin in it for you."

The boy dashes out the door. Titus listens to Runner's feet clacking down the pine slat stairway. He hears the lower door rattle shut. The old quaestor lays back in his chair, eyeing his backgammon board.

*Best get my horse and go see Cato. Then it will be your move, Senator.*

PELLA, MACEDONIA, 193 BCE. Philip steeples his spiderlike fingers and gazes over them, a wry smile tugging at his long, thin lips. "Let me see if I understand you, Nicander. King Antiochus proposes that I ally myself with him and Hannibal. And together we will to do what? Conquer the world?"

Antiochus' emissary shifts his bony, sandaled feet over the throne room's marble tiles. "That is the heart of it. Hannibal has sent men to Carthage's court. The Carthaginians will soon come along with us. Together, we will take all of Greece. And then we sail to Italia."

"You mean first you take Thrace, don't you?" Philip snaps. "Your men have already invaded it, the land that was ruled by my ancestors—and by me—until the Romans took it."

Nicander flaps his hands. "No, no, those are baseless rumors! Antiochus is merely advancing through it, my King. His mind is set upon Greece—and Rome. Antiochus says that Thrace will be yours to rule."

*He says that, does he? How condescending.* "I have a treaty with Rome," Philip says. "One worked out with Scipio Africanus himself, and that pup Flamininus. Scipio's vengeance would be terrible if things went awry for us."

Nicander waves away Philip's objection. "We do not ask that you declare war on Rome now, only that you join us after we cross into Greece.[1] Our invasion would violate Rome's agreement to protect you, and you could honorably declare war on them."

Philip snorts. "You want me to declare war on the greatest military power in the world? Led by Scipio Africanus? That might be honorable, but it's also stupid."

"Why? You almost defeated the Romans by yourself. If you joined Antiochus, who also has the warlike Aetolians waiting to join him, how could the Romans withstand such a force?"[li]

The king's eyes narrow. *You mean the capricious, addle-brained Aetolians, who serve only their own interests. And you have said nothing about your overtures to my enemy Nabis, dictator of Sparta.*[lii]

Philip gazes at the battered Roman shields that hang from his palace walls, souvenirs of his earlier victories. *The Romans are too crude to be devious. At least I know where I stand with them.*

"This is a momentous decision, Nicander. Let me give it due consideration," Philip replies.

"I shall await your decision in my chambers," says Nicander, turning toward the entryway.

"You will await it at home, because I will not be hastened to judgment," Philip says. "My men will see you safely to the city gates."

"Time is of the essence," Nicander declares. "You must—"

Philip rises from his seat, his face contorted with anger.

"I must? You seek to make demands on me?" His eyes burn into Nicander's. "Hear me now, Minister. You are one step from being flayed to death. So tell me again. What *must* I do?"

Nicander prostrates himself, his arms splayed toward the angry king. "Nothing, you have to do nothing! Forgive my temerity." He crawls backwards through the open palace doors.

When the gold-paneled doors boom shut, Philip collapses into the purple silk pads of his ten-foot throne. *Ares save me, what a choice!*

*Take a chance on conquering the world, but risk Roman annihilation!*

Philip rubs his eyes. "Phoebe! A goblet of Aglianika," he says to the empty chamber. A comely Cretan girl appears from the rear curtains, bearing a tray with Philip's favorite wine vessel, a clear glass goblet. She gives the precious glass to Philip and pours Aglianika into it.

Philip squeezes her gowned buttock. "Come to my chambers tonight," he says. "And bring Iselda."

The king lifts the wine to the torchlight, admiring its deep purple color of a quarter-moon sky. *As beautiful as my jewels. And much more useful.* He sips meditatively. A thought comes to him. He grins.

Philip stretches back into his pillowed throne, tapping his fingers on its arm. *Nothing, I'll do nothing! Let the Romans and the Syrians play out the first act of this play. I need not intervene. Best I learn which way the die rolls before I make my bet.*

He drains his cup in a single gulp. *Antiochus and Hannibal can get fucked. Come to think of it…* "Phoebe, get me a pitcher of wine. Bring it to my chambers with Iselda." He grins wolfishly. "I feel the need to retire early tonight."

LYSIMACHIA, THRACE, 193 BCE. "Give me ten thousand infantry, a thousand riders, and a hundred ships. Give me that and we'll win the war," Hannibal declares.

Antiochus looks up from his map table. "Oh really? Will you march on Rome? Perhaps you will take on Scipio himself?"

"Victory is not assured through numbers, it is assured through strategy," Hannibal says. "Diversions are as valuable as invasions." He sticks his forefinger on a map of Northern Africa. "If I land in Carthage with that army, they will be persuaded to join me."[liii]

"And if they do not join you, you are stuck in an African prison while I fight alone in Greece," Antiochus muses.

"If Carthage does not capitulate, I will land in Italia, and you move into Greece, near the ports.[liv] Rome will have to divide their forces, or one of us can attack unencumbered. Believe what I say. I conquered Italia before, I can do it again."

Antiochus shifts uneasily in his seat. "Let me take the matter up with my son Antiochus. And with Nicator."

Hannibal stifles a grimace. "Very well. Where is Nicator? He is usually with us."

"It's a full moon. He is out hunting."

"Out hunting bears? Or is he after deer?"

"He's hunting for men. Hunting for Thrax and his Thracians."

While Hannibal and Antiochus mull attack strategies, Nicator stalks through the upper Chersonese Mountains, following a moonlit animal trail. His silver mask is stuffed inside his goatskin pouch, ready to wear when daylight arrives. When humans can see his face.

The assassin loves hunting alone at night. In darkness, he can expose his ravaged face to the cool caress of the mile-high mountain breezes. There are no slow-moving colleagues to impede him, no awkward attempts at conversation. There is only him, the trail, and the prey.

Nicator turns east at a crossroads, following a path of broken scrub branches. *You're back in the caves, aren't you? You think I don't know where you hide? Do you think your missing men were deserters?*

Nicator spies a light on the opposite mountainside, a faint flickering among its thick-bodied pines. His heart quickens.

Nicator tramps down the saddle that joins the two mountains, his eyes fixed on the twinkling fire. He halts when he is within a spear's throw of the flames, holding his breath. The Syrian listens to the low mutter of campfire conversation, straining to identify each voice.

He unlaces his calf-high sandals. He places them behind a trailside scrub oak, along with his mask, sword belt, and back pack. Wearing only a hooded dark green tunic, he trots silently toward the Thracians, dangling his curved swords next to brown thighs bulging with muscle.

Nicator halts near the edge of the firelight. He peers into the campfire clearing between the pines, counting the illuminated faces. *Four. All young. Not too bad.*

The Syrian crouches. He pulls his purpled lips back into the rictus of a grin, and springs into the firelight.

The Thracians look up and see a vision from hell. A demon strides toward them, its snaggled teeth bared from stringy, leprous lips. The demon's ice-gray eyes stare from a face purpled with pockmarks and pustulent sores, eyes shining with murderous anticipation.

"It's a monster!" screams one. The four warriors leap up, yanking out their blades. Nicator rushes in.

The Syrian's left sword flashes up, blocking the skull-splitting blow of the Thracian in front of him. He plunges his right blade into the stomach of the warrior next to his fellow. A deft twist of Nicator's blade and the Thracian falls by the edge of the fire, hugging his spilled intestines. Nicator leaps back, just as a Thracian sword slices through the space where his head had been. He twists his body sideways and lunges, skewering its owner in the heart.

The two surviving Thracians spring away from him. They glance at one another. "Left and right, together," says the oldest warrior. The two step warily toward the Syrian. Nicator stands with his arms outspread, blood dripping from his twin blades. His snaggled grin widens.

"Come on, my beauties, come strike down the ugly man." The Thracians stalk forward, eyeing each other. The elder soldier nods to his compatriot. "Now!"

The two jab their swords at Nicator's unprotected chest. The Syrian blocks each blade with one of his own, and quickly steps closer. He hooks his left foot about the older Thracian's foot and scoops it sideways, tumbling him to the ground.

In a single flash of motion, Nicator's ducks low and lunges to his right, thrusting his right sword upward. His blade plunges into the underside of the younger Thracian's jaw, delving deep into his skull. The youth's eyes bulge. He falls face first onto the bloodied earth, his eyes glassy with impending death.

Nicator whirls upon the remaining soldier, just as the Thracian shoves his blade at the Syrian. The long sword gashes across Nicator's thigh. A thick ribbon of blood pours from it.

The assassin frowns at the flowing wound. "You will pay dearly for that!" he murmurs.

Nicator springs upon the kneeling Thracian, his blades whirling like the wheels of a scythed chariot. A slash to the left, and the Thracian's ear plops to the ground. A side cut to the right, and the tip of his nose hangs from his face. The Thracian battles his way to his feet, ignoring the blood that streams from his head wounds.

"You are a tough one, eh?" Nicator says, thoroughly enjoying himself. "Try this." He blocks the Thracian's stab at his gut and flashes his left blade down in a wide arc. The Thracian's head tumbles to the ground, rolling to Nicator's feet.

"That wound hard to ignore, eh?" says Nicator to the head.

He pulls the other three corpses near him, and busily sets to work. Soon, four heads stare glassily into the dwindling embers, jammed onto their sword hilts. Each face bears its own demonic visage, noseless and eyeless, its features sliced into bloodied strips.

Nicator smiles to himself as he wipes off his blades. "You say hello to Thrax when he comes," Nicator tells the heads. He retrieves his clothing and begins his long hike down to Lysimachia.

When the morning sun rises, Nicator sees the city's rounded towers shining before him. He straps on his mask and trots toward the city, eager to recount his mission. *I'll get me some boar's head and cheese first, report the kills later. They are dead—no rush.*

Later that morning, Nicator presents himself at Antiochus' throne room. He wears a hooded black robe, his waxed mask gleaming from its shadows. Antiochus and Hannibal are seated at a side table finishing breakfast.

Antiochus studies Nicator's freshly polished face mask. "I take it your hunt went well?" he says, popping a date into his mouth.

"Four dead, I take their head, spread Thracian dread!" He says in a singsong voice.

Antiochus rolls his eyes. *Now he thinks he's a poet*! "That is good, I suppose. Maybe they'll be more reluctant to ambush us." He raises a palm toward Nicator. "You have done well, Commander." The Syrian bows, and glides from the room.

When the doors close behind Nicator, Hannibal leans toward Antiochus. "You know what Thracians are like, King," he says. "They will be more careful about attacking us, but not more reluctant. You need more patrols out there."

"We'll wipe them out eventually, but they are not our immediate concern," Antiochus replies. "We will journey to Ephesus next month. The Romans and Greeks are sending envoys there." He snorts. "They think they'll talk us out of invading Greece!"

Hannibal grins. "Keep them talking. It keeps them from acting."

"I suppose I should call Antiochus the Younger to join us," the king muses.

Hannibal's mouth tightens. "As you say. But he does have a certain, uh, impatience about taking the throne—I'd say he wants it right now."

Antiochus is silent for a moment. "You have concluded such?"

"Just speculation on my part. But you should bring him along, anyway. If he comes with us, he will gain experience in negotiating with those hard-headed Romans." He glances sideways at Antiochus. "So he will be better prepared to replace you!"

"He *is* busy with the Galatian invaders," Antiochus remarks absently. "But going to Ephesus would do him good. Scipio himself may be there."

"I would love to meet Scipio again," Hannibal says, spooning yogurt onto his soft-boiled egg. "He was ruthless in war, but merciful in victory. I have such mixed feelings about him."

Antiochus sips his black tea. "Just don't kill him. That would give the Romans an excuse to declare war on us. We must delay *that* until we are well inside Greece."

"I may not have the chance to kill him," Hannibal says, smiling. "Scipio has gone to see Masinissa. The Numidian may do the job for me!"

CIRTA, NUMIDIA. It is midnight. The city gates crack open. A solitary figure eases his horse from the opening, trotting down the fortress' precipitous trail. The tall, sinewy figure rides with his head down. He is oblivious to the million-star canopy that soars above him, pulsing with the paths of a dozen falling stars. His mind is fixed on obtaining counsel—from the dead.

A cheetah scampers across the rocky trail in front of his mount, but the night-black war horse does not shy. The beast has fought in a score of cacophonous battles, with a dozen men crushed beneath his heavy trampling hooves. A mere cheetah does not alarm him.

Horse and rider are soon at the bottom of the winding incline. They trot over to a threadlike stream and enter a grove of stately palms. The rider ties his beast to one of the trees and walks onto the arid plain in front of the grove. He pauses before the twenty-foot stone pyramid that squats there, facing the dancing elephant that is carved into the center of it.

King Masinissa prostates himself in front of the tomb, his regal face buried in the sand. *My Queen, I come to you with heavy heart. Your killer comes here again, in spite of my warning that he stay away.*

He listens for an answer. All he hears is the dry rustling of palm fronds, stirred by a susurrating breeze. *I want to slash his throat, see him bleed out before me. He says he was following his laws when he sent men to capture you, but...*

*Listen!* comes a whisper inside his head.

Masinissa strains his ears. He hears his horse pawing the ground. It neighs nervously. Masinissa holds his breath, his heart pounding in his ears. Then he hears it.

A footfall, soft as a cheetah's step. Two more, coming from the grove near his horse. Masinissa remains prostrate. "Sophonisba, please forgive me that I have not joined you," he says aloud. "I want nothing more than to be by your side." As he talks, his right arm edges toward his belt. The footfalls grow louder.

There is a quick flurry of footsteps across the sand. Masinissa rolls sideways, flashing out his wave-bladed dagger. A black spear crunches into the spot where his head just lay, shoved there by a wiry little man in black pants and tunic, his face wrapped in midnight cloth.

Quick as a striking cat, the king springs upon the assassin. He shoves his blade into the man's eye socket, burying it to the hilt. The man screeches, once. He collapses onto his face, his body quaking in its final death convulsions.

Masinissa straddles the corpse. He bends down and yanks out his blade. Pulling back the assassin's facecloth, he wipes his dagger across his victim's cheeks. *Wear your blood, son of a dog!*

The king pulls up the man's right sleeve and searches his arm. He gapes at the blue leopard tattoo halfway up the underside of his attacker's forearm. *A Masaesyli assassin. Vermina*[lv] *must still be out there, trying to regain control of Numidia.*

"Thank you, Sophonisba," he says to the dancing elephant. "I did not know my enemies were so near."

*You are surrounded by enemies,* comes the voice. *Rome is all that stands between you and the loss of your kingdom.* Masinissa nods to himself. "I see your truth, and I know what I must do." He mounts his horse and trots back to his palace, lost in thought.

Two days later, Scipio Africanus strides through Cirta's palace doors, garbed in his purple-bordered toga. He is flanked by senators Gaius Cornelius and Marcus Minucius, his fellow delegates.[lvi] Masinissa descends from his ivory throne. He grasps forearms with the three men, but his eyes avoid Scipio's entreating gaze. He waves the delegates to a silk covered settee, and resumes his seat.

"You know why we are here," Scipio says. "Carthage has told us that you have penetrated the Emporia region and seized Lepcis."

"That much is true," Masinissa says. "What import is it to you?"

"When I defeated Carthage and brokered a treaty with them, Rome became obligated to defend Carthage. It was part of our agreement that they would reduce their forces. Now you have occupied their lands, and forced us to respond."

"*Their* lands?" Masinissa says, his hands gripping his throne. "The Carthaginians came here as immigrants. We, the people of North Africa, granted them a parcel so they could build a city.[lvii] And what have they done to repay us? They take over our ancestral lands."

"Perhaps so, but Emporia was in their control when we made the treaty," says Senator Minucius.

Masinissa snorts. "Emporia has changed hands many times, ruled by the country with the greatest military strength. That is how we determine who has the right to it.[lviii] Leave us to settle this in our own manner."

"Carthage is under our protection!" blusters portly Cornelius. "That is in the terms of our treaty!"

"He speaks the truth," Minucius adds. "If you do not leave Emporia, Rome will have to intervene—with our legions."

Scipio frowns at the two senators' words. "May I speak with him privately?" He says to his colleagues.

"If you must," Minucius snipes. The two envoys exit the chambers. When the doors close behind them, Scipio approaches Masinissa, pausing at the foot of his throne. Masinissa glares down at him, his stern visage masking the anxiety that pulses inside him.

"I cannot grant you rightful ownership of those lands," Scipio declares, "but I can grant your wish that you settle it based on rule of might. I can do that by leaving the entire matter unsettled—for now."

"That is desirable," Masinissa says, his face as flat as a stone.

Scipio stands silently. "There is one condition," he says.

"Which is?"

"If I should engage in battle with Syria, you will send your cavalry to our side. We both know they are the finest in the world."

A long minute passes. Masinissa nods. "It will be done."

"And you will lead them," Scipio adds.

Masinissa springs from his throne. He steps down and pushes his face into Scipio's. "Fight with you? After what you did? I would sooner give my kingdom to the Masaesyli!"

"And that is just what you will be doing!" Scipio says. "Rome will send its legions against you, and Carthage will willingly join us. Your Massylii tribe will be back to hiding in the hills while Vermina's Masaesyli hunt you like dogs! Is that what you want? Is that what Sophonisba would want?

"Masinissa's grabs the hilt of his dagger. "Do not speak her name, murderer!"

"I did not kill her," Scipio blazes, "*she* killed her! She poisoned herself. I only intended to take her back to Rome with her husband Syphax—you know he was Rome's mortal enemy! I swear by all my gods, Masinissa, I never thought she would do anything like that."

"Sophonisba was proud, and strong of will. You must have known she would never tolerate such a disgrace."

Scipio spreads his hands. His voice grows husky "I had to take her back, it was dictated by Roman law. You think I wanted that? Gods above, do you know how many nights I've spent regretting that decision?"

Masinissa gazes at the lionskin hanging to his right. "All my triumphs, everything I have gained—it is as nothing without her."

Scipio glares at him. "All I know is that you risk losing everything for nothing, because we cannot change what happened!"

The palace falls silent. The two commanders stare at each other, their faces flush with emotion. The doorway guards stir uneasily. Masinissa steps back from Scipio and resumes his seat on his throne.

"I will fight with you," the king says coldly, "if you will abandon this matter about Lepcis—and Emporia."

"It will be done," Scipio states. "The dispute will remain unresolved.[lix] I will tell Carthage you and I are still finalizing your plans for withdrawal." He strolls toward the chamber doors.

"I believe you," Masinissa blurts. Scipio halts. He turns to Masinissa, looking expectantly at him.

The king takes a deep breath. "About what you said, not wanting to hurt Sophonisba." A long, silent, moment passes. "I believe you."

"Gratitude, " Scipio replies huskily.

He studies Masinissa's stony visage. His mouth tightens into a bitter grin. "But it changes nothing between us, does it?" Hearing nothing, he strides for the door.

"I am off to see Hannibal," Scipio tosses over his shoulder. "It is an unfortunate day when the man whose army I slaughtered bears me greater friendship than the one whose nation I saved!"

Scipio shoulders his way between the guards. He jerks open the foot-thick doors. They boom shut behind him. There is the sound of a muffled argument, cut short by Scipio's stern voice. Hob-nailed sandals clack across marble tiles, fading into the distance.

"Get out," he says to the guards. The doors ease shut behind them.

Masinissa lays his face in his man-killing hands. He quietly sobs.

SABINA HILLS. "You say you know where Scipio keeps his hoard?" Cato gapes at Titus Paullus, not believing his ears. Cato reclines on a couch outside the entry to his humble farm house, studying the little man who stands before him.

"I have been to the place where I think he keeps it," Titus replies. "But I have yet to catch him there."

Cato grimaces. "Then you know nothing. Why have you come to me here at night, with nothing of worth?"

"What I will find will be priceless to you. But it may take weeks of following Scipio before I can catch him there," Titus rubs his fingers together. "I need an incentive for such an arduous task."

"Money. You want money to catch this thief, to do your duty as a Roman? When you were Scipio's quaestor, you told me that it was enough for you to do your duty, that you could not be bribed."

"And that was true, when I served as his accountant. Now my term is over, and I have other obligations." He leers at Cato. "Come on, how much is it worth to the irreproachable Cato the Elder, to see his nemesis lowered into the prison pits of the Mammertine?"

Cato flushes with anger. His stony hands curls into fists. "Get off my land."

Titus shrugs. "As you say. But this may be your only chance to catch him." He strolls down the steps that lead to Cato's humble wheat fields, his back stiff as a board.

Cato's eyes follow Titus. They turn to gaze across the roadway, to the lush, sprawling fields of Flaccus' estate. "A hundred denarii," Cato blurts, surprising himself. Titus continues his walk.

"Two hundred denarii!" The wiry little man skips down the rough stone steps, disappearing into the night.

"Five hundred!" Cato yells into the dark, his face flush with embarrassment. Titus ascends the steps and pauses in front of Cato. His beady eyes shine with victory.

"I want the time and place he enters, and two credible witnesses," Cato mutters, avoiding the quaestor's eyes.

"Whatever you say, *Senator*," replies Titus. He trots back down the steps.

Cato sits on his patio, head in hand, listening to the deafening buzz of the nighttime cicadas. He stares in the direction of the legendary Manius Dentatus' hut, recalling the times he stood there and prayed to lead as honorable a life as he.

*I am paying a man to spy on a Roman consul, and a war hero*. He rubs his eyes. *But Scipio must have stolen plunder in Carthage—he just sent me away before I could catch him.*[lx]

The thought comes to him, unbidden. *Who are you most like now, boy? Flaccus, or Dentatus? Or Scipio, who believes his noble end justifies its means?*

Cato peels off his tunic. He kneels on the roughshod patio stones, feeling its edges bite into his knees. *It hurts. Good.*

"Aelius! Bring the rod." The burly Gaul ambles in, clutching the willow whip.

"Give me six," he tells him. Aelius whaps the rod into Cato's bare back.

Cato jerks with each blow, remonstrating himself. *I must cease the act, instead of punishing myself for it.*

He jerks at the rod slaps wetly into his bleeding back. *Or is it the nobler task, to sacrifice my honor for a higher purpose?*

He looks over his shoulder. "Six more."

TADMAR, NORTHWEST SYRIA, 193 BCE. Antiochus the Younger flips the goatskin scroll from his bed couch, smiling to himself.

*Father has summoned me to council with him. At last, I can escape this camel pen and help him take over Greece. We must attack immediately, before they can mount an army against us.*

The prince studies the wall tapestry of his Assyrian ancestors riding war chariots over their supine Egyptian enemies. He slaps the goatskin palm in his hand. *I have to pry Father from that meddling Hannibal's clutches.*

Antiochus' chief attendant shuffles past the prince, his puffy eyes fixed on the floor. The prince grins. *I'll bring Fish with me. He is good with all kinds of potions.*

Antiochus the Younger beckons the fleshy older eunuch. Fish slowly approaches, kneading the folds of his black silk robe. *Gods, what did I do now? Not another ear twist!*

"We are going home, Fish! Bring us some wine!"

Fish's clasps his hands together and smiles broadly. "Of course, Master! I have some waiting for you." The eunuch lumbers through the chamber doors. He returns with a brimming stone pitcher of deep red Bargylus wine.[lxi]

"Try this, my prince. An excellent vintage from the coastal mountains. I picked it out myself, just for you!"

Antiochus the Younger grins. "You are an obsequious dog, but you are my dog nonetheless. Pour us both a drink!" The eunuch fills two goblets with the heady wine. He proffers one to his owner.

"Ah-ah," Antiochus says, waggling his finger. He nods at the burly

Parthian standing guard at his chamber door. “Him first.”

The eunuch lays his goblet upon the chamber’s red wool carpet and carries the other goblet to the guard. He pours a small portion into the guard’s pottery cup. The Parthian sniffs it, then sips. He waits. Antiochus watches. The guard downs the rest and smacks his lips.

“Very good,” he says to Fish, after resuming his post. Fish brings the cup to the Syrian prince. He raises the cup toward his eunuch.

“To reunions. And to my father’s glory.” He downs his wine in one long gulp. Fish does the same, carefully watching his master.

“Thank you,” Fish says. “That was delicious. Shall I prepare for our departure?”

“I’m not staying here any longer than I have to,” the prince replies, “but it can wait until tomorrow.” He stretches out upon his bed furs. “Leave me. Tomorrow we set out for the port of Tripoli!”

Fish bows. “I will be outside your chamber door, should you want anything.” The eunuch closes the door behind him and stands in the hallway, hands folded in front of him. He studies the patterns in the intricately woven hallway carpet, humming an ancient Syrian lyre song.[lxii]

Fish hears a soft thump on the other side of the door, followed by faint choking noises. Hands scrabble at the bottom of the chamber doors. The door handle twitches. It turns.

Fish leans his considerable bulk against the door. He feels the door shove against his buttocks. The door opens a crack. Gurgling noises creep from the opening. Fish braces his legs and shoves with all his might. The door slams shut, followed by frantic scratching noises. The scratches lessen, then cease.

Fish leans against the door, his heart hammering. An eternity later, he opens the door and peeks inside.

Antiochus the Younger lies sprawled against the bottom of the door, his glassy eyes bulging from his purpled face.[lxiii] *Very fitting,* Fish thinks, *Carthaginian purple.*

He grimaces at the guard's motionless body. "Sorry, friend. He didn't pay to have you killed, but it was necessary."

The eunuch eases the door shut and locks it with his key. He pads quickly down the hallway, his baggy cheeks quivering with excitement. Fish turns into his small chamber at the end of the hall and grabs the bulging camelskin bag sitting on top of his skeletal sleeping pallet. The bag jingles with the weight of its coins. *Merciful Mother, it's heavy! I should have asked for payment in saffron—it's a damned sight lighter.*

Walking quickly, Fish exits from the palace's side door and clambers on top of a waiting mare. He pulls a hooded robe over his head and trots away, heading to a side gate that he knows will be open and waiting. He looks back, once, over his shoulder.

The eunuch trots down a sand-strewn side street, his head bowed over the neck of his horse. He dreams of date palms swaying in the breeze along the Euphrates River, trees that will be part of his new estate. Part of his life as a free man, once again.

EPHESUS, SYRIA, 193 BCE. The Syrian guard peers down from the watchtower ramparts. He sneers at the two middle-aged men perched on horses below him. The men wear hooded cloaks with a spread eagle imprinted on the chests. A squadron of equites rides behind them, staring insolently at the guard.

*Just what I need, a bunch of fucking Romans at the gates.* "What is your business here?"

"General Publius Cornelius Scipio, here to see King Antiochus," Scipio shouts. "I am here with Senator Villius. We came to speak on Rome's behalf."

"Forgiveness, Envoys," the guard stammers, "I did not know you were arriving so early!" The man's head disappears from the ramparts. Minutes later, the iron-clad gates creak open. A Syrian officer rides into the opening, his black-feathered helmet tucked under his arm.

"I am to escort you to your chambers," the captain declares. He leads the Romans to a three-story palace fronted with rose marble columns.

A tall, regal figure stands at the top of the steps, wearing an indigo linen robe. He grins at Scipio.

"Well, well. Charon has not taken you to Hades yet! I am pleased to see you."

"And I am pleased to see you in some place other than a battlefield. I have wearied of plotting your destruction!"

Hannibal laughs heartily. "Ah, those days at Zama are far behind us now, aren't they?" A mischievous twinkle lights his eyes. "But who knows? Perhaps new adventures lie ahead!"

"Gods, I hope not. I'm getting too old for this!" Scipio gestures at the stern, muscular man next to him. "This is Senator Villius."

Hannibal waves them up. "Come on, let us celebrate your safe arrival. You can get as drunk as you like tonight. Antiochus is returning from his son's funeral, so we will not meet for two days."

"I heard about Antiochus' the Younger's death," Scipio says, eyeing Hannibal. "Most unfortunate."

"Yes, a tragedy," Hannibal declares, his voice flat. "But then, perhaps fate favored the king. He was worried that his brash son would move to replace him.[lxiv] No matter, he's gone now. Let us celebrate the peace between Rome and Carthage."

*A peace you would sooner upset,* Scipio thinks. "Tonight we will have many stories to tell, about times when there was no between us."

"Those were eventful times," Hannibal declares. *And they may not be gone yet, friend Scipio.*

At sunset, Villius and Scipio don purple-bordered white tunics. They stroll into one of the palace's dinner chambers, a house-sized space filled with statues and murals from across the world. Hannibal sits on the edge of a low feasting couch, his bare legs dangling from his black silk tunic. His black silk eye patch sports a purple phoenix sewn into it, evidencing his continued loyalty to Carthage, the nation that exiled him.

"Come and join me. I'm starving and there is a feast for the ages here! The delegates from Greece will arrive soon, they are meeting among themselves right now." He grins. "No doubt they are organizing all their whining complaints about Antiochus!"

For the next hour, the three men savor boar, peacock, pomegranates, and other treasures from Antiochus' kitchens. As the wine flows, the conversation turns to reminiscences of the Punic war, and of generals past and present.

"You are acknowledged as a great commander," Scipio says, sipping at his watered wine. "I have even heard our officers call you Hannibal the Great, in grudging admiration to your conquests. So I ask you, Hannibal the Great. Who is the greatest general of all time?"

Hannibal rubs his curled, graying beard. "Hmm. Alexander of Macedonia, because he conquered so much and so many, with such a small force."[lxv] He smiles into his goblet. "As did I!"

"And who would be second?" asks Villius, eyeing Scipio.

Hannibal notices Villius' look. "Why, Pyrrhus of Epirus, for his skill in choosing the best fighting ground, and in arraying his limited forces." He grins. "And then I would place myself third!"

Scipio laughs, slapping his knee. "Such modesty! So where you would you place yourself if you had defeated me?"

Hannibal grows somber. He fixes his green eye upon Scipio, and raises his cup. "Why, then I would be the greatest of them all!"[lxvi]

Two days later, the peace negotiations commence in Antiochus' meeting hall, though the king has not yet arrived. The delegates from Greece's city states fill the thirty-foot meeting table, joining Villius and Scipio.

As with their meeting in Rome, the Greek representatives air their grievances to Scipio and Villius, complaining about Antiochus' incursions into Corinth, Thrace, and the Greek colonies near Syria.

Minnio, Antiochus' senior delegate, listens without comment. When it is his turn to speak, the tall old commander rises from his place next to Scipio.

"You Romans complain that we are exacting tribute from the Greek colonies on our lands, that we have no right to them. Yet how are they different than the Greek colonies you control in Italia? I speak of Naples, Rhegium, Tarentum, and a dozen others.[lxvii] If you abandon your claim to them, we will abandon ours—but not until you do!"

The Romans and Greeks rise in protest. The meeting quickly degenerates into isolated shouting matches.

"Silence!" Scipio shouts. "This is unseemly for men of your station!" His entreaties fall on deaf ears.

After a half hour of unruly debate, Villius and Scipio stomp out from the proceedings. Hannibal rushes after them, vainly entreating them to stay. Minutes later, the Greek delegates walk from the table, save for the Aetolians. Minnio smiles. *I have played my part. We can say they rejected our peace efforts.*

Two days later, Antiochus returns to his palace. He enters his chambers and sheds his indigo robes of mourning. "Get Minnio in here," he says to his guard. Minnio appears, a smile tugging at the corners of his mouth.

"So, everything went as planned?" Antiochus says, noticing Minnio's expression.

"I got nothing, but I gave up nothing," Minnio replies.

"That is all you needed to do," the king replies. "We will take the lands we want, they don't have to give us anything. Send the Greeks and Romans home. We'll call a war council when they leave."

"It will be done," Minnio replies. He stares at the floor, fidgeting with his dagger belt.

"There is something else?" Antiochus says.

"I must tell you, I saw Hannibal consorting with Scipio and Villius, the Roman delegates. He seemed very friendly with them."

"Really?" Antiochus says, steepling his fingers. "He met with Scipio?"

"They broke bread and wined together. The three left the meeting together, as if he were one of the Roman delegates!" Minnio smirks. "You know these Carthaginians. They shake your forearm with one hand while they knife you in the back with the other."

The king slides a knee-length brown tunic over his head, smoothing down its gold-embroidered sides. "This is very unexpected, I have always trusted his loyalty."

*Now's my chance to replace that one-eyed prick.* "You might consider convening our war council without Hannibal. We can inform him of our decisions afterwards, and choose what we want to tell him."

The king nods, his expression uncertain. "Very well. We can try it."

Days later, Antiochus' commanders gather around the meeting table, with King Alexander of Acarnania attending. The ruler of that western Greek region has decided that Syria is unstoppable, and he chooses alliance over conquest.

Thoas of Aetolia sits next to him. The Aetolian king is committed to defeating his former Roman allies. A dozen minor rulers join the two rulers, all ready to join the Army of a Hundred Nations.

Nicator sits in a chair behind Antiochus, there to fulfill his role as army commander. One by one, his masked face fixes upon each ruler at the table, making them squirm.

"Let us start with the most important question," Antiochus says. "Are we strong enough to contest with Rome?" He turns to Nicator. "What say you?"

"We have at least twice their manpower," Nicator says, his voice tinny. "But many of them are recruits who have yet to taste blood or battle."

"But our ships outnumber theirs, and we are superior sailors," adds Prostus, the Syrian navy commander. "We can control the seas. That would keep them from sending troop transports."

"I am a great friend to Philip of Macedonia," replies Alexander. "I tell you now, he will spring to arms the moment he hears your trumpet call to battle."[lxviii]

Seleucus rises from his place at the table. Antiochus' son slowly shakes his head. "It is too risky. The Romans are a rising power. They have conquered half the world. Would you risk adding our homeland to their dominion?"

The meeting room echoes with the sound of a fist pounding upon the door.

"See who it is," Antiochus says, dreading it is whom he expects. The Syrian guards pull out their swords and open the doors. Hannibal stands in the opening, glowering at those within the room.

Antiochus grimaces. "Let him in."

The Carthaginian general marches past the guards. He stops in front of Antiochus, his hands balled into fists. "Why was I not invited to this council?"

"Well, these are but preliminary meetings," Alexander says. "It was not necessary that—"

"Shut up," Hannibal barks at him, his eye never leaving Antiochus.

"I will not lie to you," Antiochus says. "You have been consorting with the Roman delegate Villius. And Scipio himself.[lxix] These men are our enemies."

Hannibal laughs. "That is ridiculous. Villius is an insect. It was a mere cordiality that he remain while Scipio and I talked. As for Scipio, I count him as both foe and friend. Friend because he is a fellow soldier, foe because he is a Roman general. I would divulge nothing to him."

"He is the most powerful man in Rome. It would not be unreasonable for you would ally yourself with him," Antiochus replies coolly.

Hannibal fixes his green eye on the king. "When I was a mere child, my father Hamilcar bound me to an oath never to be a friend to Rome. Under this compulsion, I have fought Rome for thirty-six years. Thirty-six years! Accordingly, whenever you are thinking of war against Rome, count Hannibal among your first friends!"[lxx]

The room is silent, as the rulers take in Hannibal's words. The king rises from his chair and puts his hand on Hannibal's shoulder.

"I have done you a grievous wrong. I swear I will never mistrust you again." The king pulls a chair next to him. "Take a seat. We are airing our opinions of Rome's proposal that I withdraw from Greece and its protectorates."

Hannibal sits down, his face grim. He looks at the rulers gathered at the table, searching their faces. *Someone put him up to this.*

Spurred by Hannibal's commitment to defeating Rome, the commanders propose strategies for combatting a Roman intrusion. After an hour of heated discussion, Antiochus makes a proposal—a show of hands is unanimous in support of it.

"It is settled," Antiochus declares. "Syria will advance into Greece, and declare war upon Rome.[lxxi] Hannibal will be one of our lead commanders." He turns to Hannibal. "Will you accept the charge?"

Hannibal raises his right hand. He gazes into each ruler's face before he speaks. "By sea or by land, I will battle Carthage's conquerors, until one of us has died."

Eight days later, Minnio is found stabbed to death in his bedroom chamber. His tongue lies on the floor next to his head, the sign that he has suffered an informant's fate.

SABINA HILLS, OUTSKIRTS OF ROME, 193 BCE. "So, Scipio's friend Laelius is running for consul this year," Cato says. "I think it a bit premature for him to run, but he has proven to be a man for the common people. Rome could do worse."

"You and your 'common people,'" Flaccus retorts. "It's the patricians who run this city, and you're one of us now. Get used to it."

*That is what I most fear*, Cato thinks. *That I am becoming one of you.* "I am a farmer, now and forever."

"Well, farmer, you had best help the party get a Latin into office, or you will see all our tax monies going to museums and libraries! The Hellenics will turn Rome into another decadent Athens!"

"I would be more worried if Scipio's cousin Nasica gets elected," Cato says. "He is running for consul, too."

"The right candidates for patrician and plebian consuls can defeat the both of them." Flaccus says.

"You have someone in mind, don't you?" Cato says.

"Of course," Flaccus purrs. "Am I not the leader of our party?"

"But you have been strangely quiet about elections over these last two years," Cato notes.

*That's because I was threatened with death if I interfered,*[lxxii] Flaccus thinks. *But best you didn't know that, farm boy.* "We will back Lucius Quinctius Flamininus."

"Titus Flamininus' brother?[lxxiii] Titus was one of Scipio's favorites. Is his brother any better?"

Flaccus smiles. "Lucius Quinctius opposes the Hellenics' proposals for the slave tax and salt tax. Those proposals would directly affect his land holdings and businesses." He gazes at Cato. "He also supports Gnaeus Domitius, our plebian candidate for consul. You know him, Cato. He has spoken of reducing the taxes on small farms."

Cato eyes Flaccus. "But why do you support Domitius? You don't care about farmers."

Flaccus summons a wounded look. "Oh, but I do! Just because I have a large estate doesn't mean I'm not sympathetic to their welfare! Don't I pay a dozen of them to work my land?"

"At a slave's rate," Cato growls. "So they can ill afford to buy plots of their own."

"The point is, Quinctius and Domitius are viable opponents to Laelius, and to Scipio's cousin. We will throw our support behind them."

"Agreed. We can speak in their favor at the Senate, and in the Forum."

"Why don't you do the speeches," says Flaccus, recalling the death threat he received. "You are a much better speaker. I will deploy my talents and money elsewhere."

"Doing what?"

"I will act as the minister of propaganda for our party," Flaccus replies. "Believe me, I know how to send a powerful message."

"You plan to tout Quinctius and Domitius through banners and murals?" Cato says.

Flaccus chuckles. "Oh my, no. It is your job to elevate our candidates. It is my job to diminish their opponents!"

ROME, 193 BCE. Laelius and Publius ride in from their trip to Ostia, filled with bittersweet melancholy. It is the end of the year, and winter has come upon the land. The two have spent the morning dragging their sailboats onto land and covering them with worn linen sailcloths.

Young Publius has been especially unhappy; he aches to do more sailing. When he celebrates his fourteenth birthday next year, he plans to seek duties with the Roman navy. His mind is set on following the path of his mentor Laelius.

Though his father Scipio has urged him to become a scholar, the youth dreams of leading ships into battle. He wants to protect Rome from its enemies, as his father has done.

As they trot through Rome's Porta Carmentalis, Laelius reaches over and taps Publius' shoulder.

"Look, I know it has been a long day for you, but I have to do a little politicking. Now that I am a declared candidate for consul, I have to be seen in public. Let's ride through the streets and say hello to the people."

Laelius passes through the stalls that line Market Street, stopping to grasp forearms with dozens of commoners. He notices that many passersby gaze at him with sly smiles, whispering among themselves. A pair of comely maidens titter as they look at him, glancing back into a side street.

"Just a minute," he says to Publius. The two trot their horses into the alleyway. Laelius halts in front of a crudely painted drawing of two men in anal congress, the receiving one grinning fatuously.

*Laelius takes it in the ass from Scipio!* The graffiti declaims.

Laelius flushes with anger. His eyes dart about, vainly seeking a perpetrator.

"Why do they say such mean things?" Publius says.

Laelius tousles boy's hair. "Because a lie repeated enough soon becomes a truth—at least to some idiots. Let's get back to the house."

As they enter Market Street, Laelius notes the bright blue banners that float from the windows of several upper story insulae. *I ask that you elect Laelius for consul,* some declare. Others say *The late drinkers ask you to elect Laelius,* and *The worshippers of Jupiter call for Laelius.* [lxxiv]

"Your mother has done her work well," he says to Publius. "Probably with Prima's assistance, though she prefers to threaten rather than encourage."

As they near their turn to the Scipio manse, a second-story drawing catches his eye, this one of a man on all fours being led on a rope. *Laelius is Scipio's mule*, it reads.

"I've got to find who is spreading these lies," he growls to the confused Publius.

The two turn into a broad avenue near the Scipio manse. Laelius yanks his horse to a halt. He stares at the ten-foot letters painted upon the walls of a two-story apartment house. *Laelius will raise your taxes!*

"I have never seen such slander! I swear, I will kill whoever is doing this." He forces a smile to his face. "No matter, let's go home. I've got to get up early and start campaigning again." *And hunt down the bastards that are doing this.*

"You think this silliness will hurt you?" Publius asks.

Laelius musters his best grin. "I trust the people. They know me better than that!" *I hope.*

SCIPIO MANSE, TWO MONTHS LATER. Laelius slumps on the edge of the couch, his hands folded between his knees. Prima sits at his side, her arm around his shoulders.

"How could this happen?" he laments, his teary eyes staring up at Scipio. "I lost! I thought I was the people's favorite!"

"But not the patricians' favorite," Scipio murmurs. "Too many wagging tongues were slandering you."

"If they gave you a triumph after for defeating the Boii, that would have sealed it." Prima declares. "They deny it to you, yet they give one to that limp-dicked Flamininus, when he parades in from Greece!"[lxxv]

"Which he should never have left," Amelia adds.

"This slanderous propaganda has Flaccus' mark," Scipio says. "And Cato's as well. They are both former consuls, their words weighed heavy against us."

"Do you think Flaccus is the one that spread the rumors about…about you and I," Laelius says to Scipio. "If he did, I'd—"

"We know nothing for certain, but I will make inquiries," Scipio replies. "Now we must plan for the future, and guarantee your election next time."

"How do we do that?" Laelius says bitterly. "Make more bribes than the Latins?"

Scipio shakes his head. "Our party needs a military victory. An momentous victory. And there will only be one man who can give it to us." He sits next to Laelius and grasps his forearm.

"We are going to defeat Antiochus. Because as sure as Jupiter rules the heavens, if we don't, he will be coming for us."

*Antiochus III*

# V. THE TINY ARMY

ROME, 192 BCE. “I do swear to uphold Roman law, to defend its interests, and to govern with honesty and wisdom.”

Their oaths completed, Lucius Quintus Flamininus and Gnaeus Domitius Ahenobarbus move to the Senate chamber’s altar of Minerva. Tiberius Gracchus, the high priest of Rome, stands next to the warrior-goddess’ statue, cradling a large wicker cage in his muscular arms. Two clucking roosters stick their heads out, blinking at the solemn senators who encircle them.

“Please accept our humble sacrifice of these proud birds,” Tiberius intones. He extracts the wood pin fastener that holds the cage door. “Go ahead,” he says softly to the two men.

Each consul removes a rooster from the wicker cage. Quintus steps forward. He positions the rooster over the wide marble bowl on a pedestal in front of the goddess. He stares upward at Minerva’s helmeted visage.

The high priest spreads his arms and looks skyward. “Gods and goddesses, look with favor upon these men. Let them serve Rome with honor and courage.” Tiberius nods at Quintus.

An attendant places an ivory-handled knife in Quintus’ hands. The new consul pulls the rooster up by its neck. The bird squawks loudly, flapping its wings. The chamber echoes with its protests. With one swipe, Quintus severs the bird’s head, grasping its twitching body.

The new consul pours the rooster’s blood into the marble bowl. He dips his fingers into the bowl and marks red stripes upon his forehead and cheeks. “All glory to Minerva,” he declares. Quintus steps back from the statue of the goddess. The priest’s attendants replace the brimming bowl with an empty one, and Domitius repeats the ceremony.

Laelius sits in the back row, slumped over his clasped hands. When the new consuls take their oaths, he stares at the ceiling's frescoes of battle scenes. *I can't believe I lost to those overprivileged morons! Did they kiss more rich asses than I did? They must have called in every favor they were owed.*[lxxvi]

With the ceremony concluded, the consuls assume the two rectangular wooden seats that face the senators, flanking the Senate Leader's padded one. Cyprian pounds his staff upon the floor, calling the meeting to order.

"Now to the first order of business, called by Scipio Africanus. It deals with the protection of Greece."

Scipio rises from his front row bench. "Syria has taken the Thracian city of Lysimachia," he declares, facing his fellow senators. "There are rumors that they are taking over the entire region, and will soon be marching on Macedonia. One of our new consuls must take their consular army to oppose them."

The two patrician consuls exchange alarmed looks. "But we are not at war with Syria!" Consul Quintus declares.

"Based on their actions, they are at war with us," Scipio counters. "They are venturing into the lands of our amici, our allies. That is reason enough to go."

Quintus envisions the Syrian hordes, their brutal scythed chariots descending upon him. "There are more pressing matters here."

"Then give me your army and I'll take care of him!" Scipio blazes. He glares at the Latin senators clustered in the third row. "This matter transcends politics, do you hear me? Every day, Antiochus gathers more men. And Hannibal is with him. You know he seeks Rome's destruction. Those two will take Greece, and move on to Italia!"

"Calm yourself, Imperator," says the Senate Leader. "We all have the best interests of Rome at heart."

"Do we?" Scipio says. He cuts his eyes toward Flaccus. "Or do some of us place the importance of our party first? Why are we even debating this issue? Antiochus has already moved on Thrace!"

Flaccus grimaces with disgust. *They're going to give him an army for Greece!* He rises up from his front row seat and faces the two new consuls—the men he helped elect.

"Antiochus has caused mischief in Thrace, that it true. But he has not moved into Greece proper, into the Achean or Aetolian regions. Macedonia still stands in his way, and King Philip will not allow him to pass. We need to send our forces to Iberia, where there is an active rebellion against us. And to North Italia, where the Ligurians are massing again. Those are the most immediate threats, my fellows."

Flaccus winks at Quintus, who responds with the faintest of nods. The consul rises from his seat. "I have discussed this matter with Gnaeus Domitius. We agree that Iberia and Liguria are active threats."

"Pah!" replies Scipio. "The Iberians are not an issue There are a just few Celtiberian tribes stirring up trouble. The Ligurians, they are no more than a band of raiders who have taken advantage of our lax security. The praetor at Placentia could run them back to their forests in a fortnight!"

Flaccus spreads his arms entreatingly. "Do you hear him? Scipio is obsessed with taking an army against Syria. Scipio, who favors diplomacy over force! He would precipitate a war against the vast Syrian empire, before we have fully explored our diplomatic options!"

"I have explored our diplomatic options," Scipio growls. "I was at Antiochus' court last year, talking to Hannibal and Antiochus." He fixes his eyes on the Latin senators. "Hannibal has the king set on invading Rome. Greece is just a byway in his road to conquest!"

The new consuls receive Scipio's words with equanimity. Quintus leans in behind Cyprian, craning his neck toward Gnaeus Domitius. "Tell them about the delegation." He tells his fellow consul. Domitius stands.

"I am with Flaccus. We have not negotiated enough to abandon peace as an alternative. I propose we send a delegation to Greece, to talk with the Syrians. We will see if we can settle this peaceably."

"I move we vote on that proposal," Flaccus quickly interjects.

"We will take a voice vote," Cyprian declares.

The peace proposal wins by two votes. Four envoys are delegated to sail to Greece and reassure Rome's allies of Rome's intention to protect them, and then seek an audience with King Antiochus.[lxxvii] The meeting concludes, and the senators file from the chambers.

Scipio stalks down the Senate steps, stunned with disbelief. *There was a time my recommendations were taken as commands. Curse it, sending envoys will just give Hannibal more time to plot against us.*

Laelius draws up next to Scipio. "That was an unfortunate session, my friend. I thought that Tiberius and Gregorius would vote with the rest of the Hellenics." His mouth tightens. "I'd bet my firstborn that Flaccus had a hand in that. Or the consuls."

"The consuls are but Latin Party dogs," Scipio mutters. "They do their master's bidding. We have to get our own men in office, whatever the price."

"Fear not. I'm going to run again as the plebian candidate," Laelius says. "This time I'll campaign here instead of marching off to war." He sniffs. "You'd think the people would have been more grateful to me, after I helped defeat the Boii."

"They are grateful, but they are also poor—and hungry." Scipio says. "A small bribe to a hungry man is enough to turn his vote—especially if he believes the elections are fixed."

"You are saying I have to stoop to bribery?" Laelius says. "I'm not sure I have the will to do that."

"You have a conscience. That's why you would be a good consul," Scipio says. "But you must wait a few years before you run. Your loss is fresh on the people's minds." He shakes his head. "I will help you, but it is obvious that I no longer wield the influence I once did.[lxxviii] I must build up my political capital."

"Scipio!" comes a voice behind him. Tiberius Gracchus hurries down the stone steps, his sandals clopping.

"Oh gods, here comes the pontiff," Laelius remarks. "I have to go. Priests give me diarrhea." He trots to his right and joins two young senators, draping his arms about them.

"Honorable Scipio, I want to talk to you about marrying your daughter," Gracchus says.

"Again? She is but a child," Scipio replies irritably.

"It does not matter. The auguries have foretold it. I had a vision that Cornelia and I would be joined. We should make arrangements."

*He is one of the most revered and powerful men in Rome*, Scipio reminds himself. "Well, I could use your support in my affairs this year. That would favor my decision on making you a member of my family."

"She would become a Gracchus, a member of *my* revered family," the priest calmly replies. "The gods will not be denied in this, but your support will ease the path. I will support any of your actions, provided they promote Rome's welfare."

"I swore to my father that I would do the same, so we should not be in conflict," Scipio replies.

"I would hope not. But this war with Syria issue, I am not so sure about that. I am glad we are giving peace a chance, first." He grins. "Who knows? Perhaps King Thoas of Aetolia can sway Antiochus. I have heard he is close to him."

"Too close to him, and too far from us," Scipio replies, shaking his head. "You are a good man, Tiberius, and that is the problem. Good men do not grasp how evil men can be, when lusting for power or revenge. Thoas lusts for both. I fear our 'ally' will soon send his armies to join Antiochus—while we do nothing but talk. That could make the Syrian unstoppable."

EPHESUS, SYRIA, 192 BCE. Antiochus leans back in his gold-gilt throne. He eyes Thoas skeptically. "You are sure of this? The Aetolian League is coming over to our side?"

"The magistrates from its tribes and cities will join us in just a matter of weeks. Central Greece will welcome you with open arms." King Thoas says. "Why, even Sparta is coming up from the south."

"That is surprising." Antiochus says. "Nabis of Sparta rejected my overtures to join forces with me."

Thoas bows his head. "Nabis has met with an unfortunate hunting accident. When I sent a delegation to the funeral, they found that the Spartans are ready to fight. And so is the rest of the Aetolian League."

Hannibal listens to Thoas with half-lidded eyes. A slight smile plays about his lips. *'Unfortunate accident?' My spies say your men slew the Spartan king and took over his city. No matter, your lies have the desired effect. Sparta will go to Antiochus.*

"There are so many differing factions in the League," Hannibal says to Thoas. "How can you be sure they will all come over?"

Thoas pounds his chest. "I will deliver them! In a few weeks, I will have them all together at Thermos, when we meet with the envoys from Rome. I will secure a binding agreement from each of them."

Antiochus rises from his seat. "You are giving the Romans a hearing?" he says, his brow furrowed. Hannibal nods approvingly, anticipating what Thoas will say.

"The Roman delegates requested an audience with the Aetolian League. That meeting will bring magistrates from all over my country. That gives me the opportunity to unite them to your cause."

*Your own cause,* Hannibal thinks. "May fortune smile on your enterprise," he says.

"Go then, and bring me more men," Antiochus says, waving Thoas toward the doors.

"I will see to it immediately." Thoas marches from the meeting room.

Hannibal turns to Antiochus. "This Thoas could be a powerful ally, but he is as sly as a fox. He bears watching."

Antiochus snorts. "Right now, I am more worried about the Roman bear than an Aetolian fox."

THERMOS, AETOLIA, NORTHERN GREECE. "That stupid slave of mine wrapped my underwear too tight, I can hardly breathe," Titus fumes. "He does this again, I'll sell him to the Sicilians!"

Senator Titus Julius wriggles his ample bottom back and forth across his saddle blanket. *I itch worse than a Libyan dog! When we get to Thermos I'm going to buy me a clean subligaculum.*

Rome's lead envoy glances at his three fellows. *Look at them, slumped in their saddles. Old Benedictus, he's about ready to fall off his horse! Well, they'd better get ready for an argument. The Aetolians are not going to welcome us with kisses.*

Titus Julius summons a cheery tone to his voice. "This is it, my friends. We've done Athens, Chalcis, and Thessaly. This is the last stop before we talk to Antiochus."

"I don't know why we are bothering with him," Senator Gaius snipes. "You heard Scipio. The bastard's going to storm across Greece, soon as we go home!"

Julius rolls his eyes. "You Hellenics! You act like Scipio is the oracle of Delphi! We do it because the Senate commissioned us to talk to him, in hopes we can strike a treaty, a cessation of hostilities."

"A cessation of hostilities?" blurts Benedictus. "The Syrian has already invaded Thrace. And what do we do about it? We send troops way down to Sicily, on the rumor that he's going to invade it.[lxxix] That's Hannibal spreading those rumors, as sure as my cock rises in the morning!"

"He must be talking about his rooster," snipes senator Gaius, prompting weary laughter.

Benedictus waggles a bony finger at his fellows. "You can laugh, but all we're doing is giving the Syrian more time to gather allies. If Philip of Macedonia joins him, we might as well fortify the Italian coastline, because they're coming across the sea for us!"

"I think Antiochus has already got to the Aetolians," interjects young Battista, "King Thoas has been visiting him."

"And we are visiting him, too," retorts Gaius. "So who's to say who the enemy is?"

The party trots on. An hour later, Julius points to his right. "Look over there, on the other side of that hillock. You can see the top of Thermos' white walls. We're almost there!"

"Thank the gods," Gaius mutters. "I haven't had a bath in three days."

"We are well aware of that," Benedictus replies.

Late that afternoon, the refreshed envoys negotiate the fifty steps to the landing of Thermos' magnificent Temple of Apollo. They are accompanied by a score of personal guards, retired veterans of Scipio's sixth legion. The Roman delegates pause under the thirty foot-statue of Apollo, waiting for the guards to lead them in.

The guards pull open the towering brass doors, and the four envoys enter the temple's central hall. Twenty Aetolian League magistrates stand along the marble-columned walls inside the chambers, rulers who have come from the regions of Thessaly, Dolopia, and Acarnania. The magistrates stand motionless as statues, their faces grim.

Julius glances at the blood-stained marble altar at the far side of the temple. *We're in the sacrificial chambers. Very appropriate.*

Thoas, the chief magistrate of Aetolia, stands in the center of the house-sized chamber, resplendent in a black toga bordered with silver lacework. He spreads his angular, bony arms, his gold teeth gleaming from his bristly brown beard.

"Welcome, Senators," Thoas declares tonelessly. "We are pleased that you have come to see us."

"We came to talk about a treaty between us, preparatory to us making one with Antiochus," declares Gaius.

Thoas spreads his hands. "I fear that discussion is a bit premature, Senator. We have a number of grievances to air, matters that you must first resolve."

Julius blinks in surprise. "If you have a grievance against Rome, it were better you came to Rome and complained to the Senate, instead of promoting war between us and Antiochus."[lxxx]

"Do you hear this?" Thoas tells the attendees. "He's ordering us to go to Rome! He wants us to beg for scraps from the senators' table!"

A half dozen rulers shout out their protests, men Thoas has prompted beforehand. Thoas walks across the line of magistrates, nodding his head.

"I hear you, my fellow rulers. Such a proposal is demeaning. You have heard what Cato and his Latin Party think of us: they say we Greeks are weak." Several rulers hiss their agreement.

Thoas' eyes shine, knowing he has the crowd in his hand. "The Latin Party swears they will keep Rome from becoming like Greece! Do you think those men will be sympathetic to our plight?"

Julius shakes his head. "You know that Scipio Africanus has always been a friend to Rome. And General Flamininus liberated Greece just a year ago. As our amici and allies, you should go talk with them. We can renew our loyalties to each other."

"Listen to him, telling us what we should do!" Thoas says. His eyes grow fierce. "I have heard enough! Let me issue a decree that we want

King Antiochus to come to Greece, and settle this dispute. He will set us free from the dictates of Rome!"[lxxxi] The Aetolians roar out their agreement, thrusting their fists over their heads.

Julius stands silently, eyes closed, listening to defeat wash over him. When the tumult has quieted, he looks to several magistrates that he has known for years. They avoid his eyes.

*This matter was decided before we came here.* Julius decides. *This Thoas will not rest until he's marching into Rome.*

"I would like a copy of this decree about Antiochus. I will take it back to the Senate," Julius says. "Perhaps we can still find a way out of war."

Thoas glances over at Democritus, his chief magistrate. Democritus leaps to his feet." I am the one who will formulate the decree, Senator."

The senator nods in his direction. "Might I have it before we leave tomorrow?"

Democritus rolls his eyes skyward. "I am very busy right now, so I cannot give you the decree before you leave. But I promise I will deliver it to you personally—when our army is camped on the banks of the Tiber, right outside your gates!"[lxxxii]

The magistrates laugh uproariously, snapping their fingers and flapping their togas. Titus Julius bows his head. *There's no reasoning with them now.* He huddles with his three fellow delegates, talking softly so as not to be overheard.

"We might as well abandon the visit to Antiochus," he murmurs to his companions. "War is coming. We have to prepare our ships and legions."

Julius breaks from the group and walks back to face the magistrates. He smoothes his toga and raises his chin, staring imperiously at them.

"We are done," he declares. "We leave you to the fate you have chosen before we came here."

The Roman delegation shuffles from the chamber, ignoring the hoots and whistles that follow them. Thoas watches them go, his eyes aglow with delight.

Democritus sidles up to Thoas. “That’s it. They’re going back to Rome. Their Senate will be furious at our insolence. What do we do next?”

“We wait. Antiochus is coming. And when he does, we will start this war in earnest.”

SCIPIO MANSE, ROME, 192 BCE. Scipio unrolls the butter-soft goatskin scroll. He rubs his hand across it, flattening it across the bronze table in his sunny atrium. He runs his finger along a black ink drawing of a large, columned, rectangular building.

“What do you think of it, Glabrio?” Scipio says. “It would be the size of two large mansions. The walls would be lined with nooks holding scrolls of the world’s finest writers, people such as Aristotle, Plato, Euripides, and Sappho. There’d be a big table in the middle of the floor, where people could request a scroll from one of our tutors. The patron could make his mark and take the scroll to a reading table.” He grins. “Of course, we’d have tutors to help people read them.”

The severe-looking young man scratches his blond curls. “And you call this a what?

“I call it a ‘library,’ Glabrio.” Scipio says. “Athens has one, and there is a magnificent one in Alexandria. Why, even the cursed Syrians have several of them! It’s time Rome grew up and built one of their own.” Scipio rolls up the drawing. “And it’s time Rome had you as consul.”

Glabrio’s brown eyes start from his face. “Me?”

“It’s your time,” says Scipio. “But you have to decide now. The delegates to Greece have failed, and the Senate has finally woke up to Antiochus’ threat—to what I’ve been telling them for a year! We are having the elections early this year, to send out an army as soon as possible.”

The blond-haired young man blinks nervously. "Are you sure the patricians will allow a novus homo to be elected consul, even if I run as the people's choice?

Scipio pats him on the back, chuckling. "My fellow patricians do not readily embrace someone who is the first in his family to become a senator, but they will if I back you. I have that much influence left!"

"Why me? There are older senators who have not had the chance. There's Caeso, Augustus, Vitus, a dozen others."

"You are educated, ethical, decisive, and popular," Scipio says. "We need your kind of man to lead us against the Syrians."

"I'd take an army against the Army of a Hundred Nations?"

"Yes, If you draw the lot for Greece." He puts his arm around Glabrio's broad shoulder. "You are ready. Remember when you served under me as my tribune? I recall how you led your men on that flanking attack at Zama. You did not waver, even while Hannibal's elephants rampaged around you."

"Even if I am elected, I may not draw the lot for Greece."

Scipio nods. "True enough. My cousin Nasica is running for the patrician consul.[lxxxiii] He has distinguished himself almost as much as you have. Either way we will be in good hands for this war. As long as a Latin isn't elected."

"I know we need to repel the Syrian threat, but I may better serve Rome if I fought as a legate, directing one of its legions."

Scipio's voice grows stern. "Now look. I have brought you along for years, educating you in Hellenic philosophy. As my protégé,[lxxxiv] you will now become the people's candidate for Rome. The matter is settled."

"But I'd have to sponsor games and feasts, and pay some bribes," Glabrio mutters. "My family is newly rich. We do not have that kind of money yet."

"Do not worry about the money, I will provide you with a thousand denarii," Scipio replies. He picks at a fingernail. "But there is one condition."

Glabrio's mouth tightens. "Which is?"

"You appoint my brother Lucius as a legate in of one of your legions."

Glabrio's eyes dart about. He takes on the look of a trapped man. "I could not put him in charge of my men," he says, his jaw set. "I owe that much to them."

Scipio sighs. *And I don't blame you.* He begins to nod his assent, then he pauses. *You promised Mother you'd help him. He needs this post if he is to be consul some day*. Scipio's minds races for a solution.

"What if I give you Marcus Aemilius as your legion's First Tribune? He fought over there for a year, and knows the terrain better than anybody."

Glabrio shrugs noncommittally. "I know of him. He led his men through the mountains on a sneak attack upon Philip."

"That was him. He won the battle of the Aos River for Flamininus! He will direct Lucius' legion. My brother will be commander in name only."

"Lucius might interfere." His eyes stare challengingly into Scipio's. "Or run."

Scipio flushes. *Be calm. Lucius needs this.* "I will talk with him. I promise he will not interfere with you—or with Marcus." He raises two fingers. "And I will give you two thousand denarii for your campaign. Amelia and Prima will provide you with the necessary propaganda. You will win."

Glabrio sighs, shaking his head. "I don't know. It's just that he hasn't done anything without you, Scipio.[lxxxv] We all know that."

Scipio steps closer to Glabrio's face. "I have made you, Marcus

Acilius Glabrio. I can just as easily break you."

Glabrio turns his head from Scipio's gaze. He stands silent. "When can I have the money?" He finally asks.

"Within five days. You will have to start campaigning immediately. Amelia has already made the banners."

"You must have been very sure I would accept." Glabrio says bitterly.

Scipio shrugs. "You are a novus homo. As a new man, you have fought your way from humble upbringings to the top rungs of power. Why would you jump off now?"

He slaps Glabrio on the back. "Be not so morose, future consul. You have learned a valuable lesson about negotiations: dangle a carrot, but carry a stick! Come on, let me show you the banners."

The two walk past the atrium's fishpond, heading toward the manse's tablinum. Amelia and Prima stand in the office room doorway, their arms laden with paint pots and bright blue banners.

A thought flashes into Scipio's head. *You promised your father that you'd protect Rome. What would he say about placing Lucius as a legate?*

"Shut up," Scipio says aloud. He smiles, embarrassed. "Talking to myself."

Glabrio gapes at him. *Charon take me, I am taking orders from a moon-head.*

The veteran warrior's eyes grow steely. *You think you can push me around? If I get the Greece campaign, I will have a big surprise for you, First Man of Rome.*

LAMIA, WESTERN GREECE,[lxxxvi] 192 BCE. "This kykeon needs more goat cheese," Thelonika declares.

Nestor, his fellow sentry, shakes his pewter spoon at Thelonika. "I'd add more honey, to it, too. But we have to take whatever the cooks give us for breakfast. You ask for something extra, they'll spit in it!"

The two watchmen lean out over the stone-walled parapet, moodily swallowing their barley porridge. Bored to distraction, they fling rocks off the tower, watching them splash into the glistening blue Aegean.

The two spy a group of frolicking dolphins. "I bet you ten sestertii I can get closer than you can!" says Nestor.

Nestor and Thelonika spend a half hour pitching stones at the bounding animals, arguing over who has gotten the closest. The dolphins cavort farther out to sea. The sentries resume staring into a featureless expanse.

Thelonika's head jerks up. "Look, there's a herd of sperm whales out there! See the dark bumps on the horizon? Gods take me, they're as large as a quinquereme!"

"I care not," Nestor replies. "I haven't hunted whales years. Their meat is good, but it's just too dangerous!"

"Does everything have to be about killing and food with you?" says Thelonika.

"Of course not. Sexual congress is most important—after I've killed something to eat! Now, you see that group of whales out there, I'd...Wait, those aren't whales. See the masts? Those are ships!"

Thelonika, leans out from the parapet, staring until his eyes water. "Zeus' cock, there's a bunch of them! They're all across the sea!"

"Sound the alarm!" cries Nestor. "We're being invaded!" He grabs the curved bronze horn and blows a deep, lingering note. The warning is repeated below them, resounding through the Greek fortress. The sea wall is soon lined with soldiers and citizens, watching the flotilla approach.

"There's at least forty big warships out there, and twice as many smaller ones!" Thelonika blurts. "And hundreds of transports. It's an army!"

"Ah gods, I bet it's the Achean League, come to destroy us for siding with Syria." He slaps a hands to his cheek. "Why am I standing here? I've got to get my family out of town!"

A gruff voice erupts behind them. "Stay where you are and be quiet!" A barrel-bodied dwarf barges between Thelonika and Nestor. "Let me take a look out there."

"Apologies, noble Phaeneas," Nestor says, drawing back two steps. A guard places a short ladder against the wall. The regional magistrate clambers up the ladder and peers out. A grin splits his face. "It's not an invasion, you mule-heads. That's Antiochus' fleet out there!"

The Aetolian glowers at Nestor and Thelonika. "Look at the insignia on the sail, dog-wits! Does that look like a Greek centaur to you? That's an anchor, the symbol of Syria.[lxxxvii] They are coming to free us from Rome. Just as King Thoas said they would."

*I didn't know we were prisoners*, Thelonika thinks. "As you say, Magistrate."

Phaeneas jumps off the ladder and hurries toward the steps. "We've got to prepare a reception for our liberators! We'll need dozens of squids and goats. I want to give them a feast for the ages!"

Two days later, Antiochus stands before a bevy of Aetolian officers and politicians, gathered at a dozen banquet tables in the city's dining hall. He stands at the head of an oak table fashioned like whale's head, resplendent in his gold-bordered black robe.

"I thank you for your enthusiastic welcome," the king says, beaming at his audience. "As you have heard from the reports, I have come with ten thousand infantry, five hundred cavalry, and six of my finest elephants.[lxxxviii] My army is small, but this is just an advance force, to establish a beachhead in Greece. I promise you, as soon as the winter weather subsides, I will fill the whole of Greece with men and armaments, and line the coast with my ships!"[lxxxix]

"That is just what I am worried about," a Thessalian general says to his lieutenant. He frowns at his ecstatic colleagues. "Am I the only one who is suspicious of a Syrian conqueror coming to 'liberate' us? Am I insane, or them?"

"I think not, Procyrus," his lieutenant says, nodding toward the back of the room. Procyrus notices that three of his infantry commanders remain stone-faced amidst the thunderous roars of approval. One looks at him and shakes his head.

Antiochus jabs his finger at the commanders. "Some of you may be apprehensive about another war, since Rome so recently settled one with nearby Macedonia. But it will come to an all-out conflict with them. We merely have to demonstrate that we will not back down from their threats. Rome will withdraw from any further interference."

"Rome won that war with Macedonia," shouts a man in the crowd. "It defeated King Philip!"

"Rome did not fear Philip, but Rome fears me!" Antiochus shouts back. "Look at the facts. They keep sending delegates to make peace with me. And General Flamininus withdrew his legions as soon as he knew I was coming! Are those the acts of a nation that wants to fight? They have neither the stomach or monies for another war. Together, you and I, we will conquer the Achean league and take southern Greece. Greece will be united once more!"

Antiochus raises his head high, savoring the cheers that wash over him. As he exits the chamber, he hears the crowd chanting his name. His aide Demoncritus draws up beside him.

"Do you hear them?" Antiochus crows. "We hold them in our hand!"

"Not all of them," Democritus replies. "The Thessalians refrained from honoring you. I am afraid you do not have Thessaly's full support yet. Some are still loyal to Rome."

Antiochus' eyes flare. "Thessaly serves whoever poses the greatest threat to them. We will ask King Amynander of Thessaly to meet with us at his fortress in Pherae. Tell Thoas I want him to assemble his troops and meet me there. Once Amynander sees our armies, he will come to our side. And the rest of Thessaly will follow."

A month later, Antiochus draws his army of ten thousand near the ancient city of Pherae, accompanied by a half-dozen rulers of the local tribes. He enters a plain surrounded by low-slung hills. The plain is lined with a grisly crop of gray-white bones.

"Why are all those bones out there?" he asks the tribal chiefs.

Philip of Megalopolis draws his horse next to Antiochus' mount. "Those are the skeletons of the Macedonians slain in the battle of Cynoscephalae," the fox-faced old chieftain replies. "King Philip retreated from the Romans so fast, he never paused to bury them."

"Warriors should be given a decent burial," Antiochus mutters.

"You are right, I should have taken care of it myself. I would be happy to put my men at your disposal, and do the task for you." *And shame King Philip in the process*, the Megalopolis chieftain thinks, his mind set on ruling Macedonia.[xc]

"That is a noble gesture, Philip," replies Antiochus. "Please take care of it."[xci]

"It will be my pleasure," Philip of Megalopolis replies.

ROME. Amelia rolls off Scipio's naked body, stretching out next to him. "Well, that was momentous!" she remarks.

"There is still some trot in this old horse," Scipio says, grinning. "And the horse is grateful you took time to ride him!" He glances out the doorway, squinting at the six-foot water clock in the atrium.

"The float is almost at the ninth mark," he says. "I had better wash up."

"Bring me a basin!" Amelia orders, snapping her fingers at the bedroom portal.

An Iberian slave girl steps into the bedroom, carrying a wide bronze dish and a bundle of linen squares. Scipio rises from his sleeping pallet and spreads his arms. The slave girl dips a square into the basin and laves his naked body.

"Where are you going at this hour?" Amelia asks, as the girl swabs Scipio's thighs. "Laelius hasn't talked you into another dice game, has he?"

Scipio takes a deep breath. *Here we go again.* "I have to visit the granary," he tells Amelia. "I promised Glabrio some money if he'd run for consul."

Amelia props herself on an elbow, her breasts swaying. "We talked about this before! You've got to quit going there. What if someone catches you with all that plunder?"

"Puf. I can kill any thieves that would come after me."

"Thieves? Who is talking about thieves! What if someone saw you, and knew who you were? That's all Flaccus and Cato need, an excuse to bring you to trial!"

"I need the money, Carissima. I had to offer Glabrio two thousand denarii to get him to run for consul. I know it's a lot, but he's won battles in Iberia, and he comes from an illustrious family—he's bound to win! He can clean up the mess left by those milk-spined Latins consuls."

Amelia purses her lips. "You know I love campaigning for our candidates, but perhaps we should put this one aside. You have served Rome for decades. Isn't being a senator enough for now?"

"I promised Father I would protect Rome. We need Hellenics in office to do that. The Latins are as great a threat as Antiochus."

"You promised your *father*? What about your promises to us? We have children to care for—living children, not some dead parent! What happens if you are arrested? They could take everything from us! What future would our children have then?"

"What future would they have in a city where women are kept as chattels, denied the right to dress themselves as they see fit?[xcii] A city where freemen lie idle, while the slaves of wealthy landowners take all their work? Is that what we want to leave them? Let Flaccus' minions control us, and you'll see what we get!"

Amelia's green eyes flash. "You are as stubborn as that old mule you ride! At least wait until Laelius gets back from Ostia, so someone can guard your back."

"Laelius will run for consul someday, I don't want him involved. Besides, I must go tonight. I want to put the money in Glabrio's hand before he changes his mind."

Amelia pitches herself from the bed. She slides her gown over her shoulders, and straps on her ankle-length sandals. "Go on, then. Keep your precious promise. But what will you say to your ancestors' death masks, when the censors come to pry them from the wall?"

She throws up her hands and storms from the bedroom. "I have things to do!" she barks, her sandals clacking across the atrium tiles.

Scipio stares into the empty doorway. "I have to!" he shouts. *Who would I be if I didn't?*

Rome's First Citizen pulls on a stained grey tunic and belts it with a greasy rope. He tucks his oiled gray curls inside a tattered indigo cap. After throwing a burlap sack over his shoulder, he considers himself in his polished tin mirror. *Not bad, but I should dirty my face more.*

After streaking his face with ashes, he pads into the empty atrium. "Amelia? I'm off. Amelia?" He shrugs. *Probably went to Prima's, to get some gladiator sweat for her complexion.*[xciii]

"Rufus!" Scipio shouts. The aged house attendant shuffles in from the walled courtyard, gumming a slice of citron. "Fetch the old mule," Scipio says.

"Another late trip?" Rufus asks. "Be careful, Imperator. The night has a thousand eyes. Rome needs you!"

"I'm sick of being needed," Scipio snaps. "Now go get the mule."

Soon, Scipio is riding his nondescript mount toward the gritty

Aventine Hill neighborhood.

When Scipio turns left into a side street, Runner emerges from an alleyway opposite the Scipio manse. He trots after Scipio, his small calloused feet flying over the thick black paving stones.

Runner hurries to the end of the street and turns right onto the spacious Via Lata. He dashes for Titus Paullus' house, anxious to lead him to Scipio.

After Runner disappears around the corner, a rider clops past the Scipio manse. Cloaked in black with a stallion to match, the figure blends seamlessly into the moonless cloudy night.

Scipio wends his way through narrow side streets and alleyways, being careful to take a new route to his destination. He arrives at his storehouse two hours later. After tying up his horse, he slides between the storehouse's two layers of doors.

The inner door rasps shut. Titus Paullus and Runner emerge from an alleyway down the block. Titus pulls a wax tablet from his cloak. He marks the street intersections by the storehouse.

"It is as you said." He hands Runner a silver sestertii. "Off with you."

Runner turns, ready to dash back down the alley. He freezes, staring at the hooded figure who appears there, silhouetted by the torchlight. Runner tugs at the quaestor's cloak.

"I told you to get out of here!" Titus growls.

"A man is coming!" Runner whispers.

Titus spies the approaching figure. "It's one of those Aventine thugs," he mutters to Runner. "I'll take care of him."

The former legionnaire draws his army short sword. He crouches down, arms spread for balance, his blade pointed at the intruder. "Stay right there, or you will regret it."

There is a flash of silver, followed by another. Titus Paullus crumples to the earth, a knife hilt jutting from his forehead. Runner rolls moaning upon the ground, clutching at the knife in his bowels. He jerks himself upright and stumbles toward the street, his heart thundering in his ears.

A third blade arrows through the night. Runner falls. He grapples for the knife hilt protruding from his spine. "Please," he mews. "Don't—" The boy's body convulses. He says no more.

The assassin hurries over and pulls out the three blades, pausing to slice open Runner's jugular. The bodies are dragged into the shadows, and the alley is quiet once again.

A half hour later, Scipio eases out of the darkened granary doorway. He carries a bulging burlap sack in one hand, and grips his bared sword in the other. Scipio peers into the darkened streets and alleyways. Satisfied that no one is about, he climbs onto his mule and canters toward the northern side of the Aventine slums.

Scipio pulls up in front of a mud brick apartment and dismounts. He knocks on the wide green door that fronts the street. Two large Gauls appear in the doorway. Each grips a double-bladed hand axe.

"Welcome, General," a guard says. The two step aside. Scipio enters a room packed with coins and treasures, its air clouded with a sickly-sweet fog of kannabis smoke.

Celsus the Syrian reclines on an indigo pillow bed, his thin blue lips pursed about his long-stemmed clay pipe. He grins dreamily at Scipio. "Ah, my favorite consul! I am honored—and I hope enriched—by your presence."

Scipio pitches his burlap sack at Celsus' skeletal feet. "Here. I want two thousand denarii for these Gallic gold coins. They are worth at least twice that much."

The Sicilian flutters his spiderlike fingers. "Oh, I am certain they are, but I have to sell those to other buyers, who also want their profit, and then there's transport—"

"You will give me two thousand denarii."

The two Gauls edge closer to Scipio. He feels their breath wafting his neck hairs.

"Do you know what would happen to you if you were even suspected of killing me?" Scipio says. "Romans can be quite inventive when it comes to torture."

Celsus fingers the stem of his pipe. A long, silent, minute drifts through the clouded air. "Two thousand, then," he replies. "But not a sestertius more than that."

Scipio snorts derisively. "Whatever you say."

"Let us seal the arrangement with a celebration," Celsus says. He proffers a clean pipe tamped full with gray-green buds. "Smoke?"

"Wine." Scipio replies. "I have had enough smoke just standing here."

After half an hour, a woozy Scipio eases through the door with small linen sack, its contents wrapped to prevent them from clinking. He slides onto his mule and clops down the cobbled street. A block away, a cloaked figure watches him depart, then walks down the alleyway and remounts, galloping toward the Capitoline Hill neighborhood.

Scipio decides to take a safer but slower return route to his domus. He rides through the capacious avenues of Merchant Street, nodding at the torch lighters and night women that populate the hour. As dawn cracks the horizon, he arrives home and ties his mule to the doorstep's three-foot statue of Minerva, goddess of wisdom. He strolls into the atrium, gripping his sack of denarii.

Amelia slumps on the edge of the fish pond, her black-gowned back to him. She hugs Cornelia against her, her arm tightly encircling her sleeping daughter.

"You are up late. Are you still mad at me?"

Her shoulders shrug. She shakes her head.

"I got the money. Old Celsus tried to haggle me down, but I wouldn't do it! Glabrio should have enough to win the election."

Another shrug.

Scipio places the bag on the floor and sits down next to Amelia. She continues to stare into the pool, watching the carp mill about. Scipio bends over and peers into her face. He leans back, startled by her haunted look.

"Are you all right? Did something happen at Prima's?"

"Prima is out of town. I had to take care of it myself," she says in a monotone.

"Take care of what?"

Her eyes wander across the frescoes that border the ceiling. "Nothing. Just taking care of the family."

Scipio rubs her slumped shoulders. "Well, I hope your chores were not too unpleasant. At least you were not skulking in the night like a common thief, as I was!"

Amelia laughs hoarsely. "I daresay we are all doing things we never expected to do." She glances at Cornelia with distant, teary, eyes. "Things we never, ever, wanted."

DEMETRIAS, AETOLIA. Hannibal paces back and forth in front of Antiochus' throne, his lips twisted in rage. "I'm being ignored again. There's something going on," He says, staring straight at the king. "Something you haven't told me about."

"What can you mean?" Antiochus replies irritably. "You have been with me for almost a year now, as an honored member of my court."

"Honored? You exclude me from your military meetings. You have ignored my counsel,[xciv] much to your detriment!"

Antiochus cocks his head. "To my detriment?"

"Thoas has misled you about the value of your Greek alliances,"

Hannibal says.

Antiochus blinks. “Really? How so?”

“He’s convinced you to waste your time wooing all these petty little kingdoms. You only need one ally, and that is Macedonia. Bring Philip into alliance with us, by any possible means. Thessaly, Boetia, and the other provinces of northern Greece—they are all weak. Macedonia is the only one that has defeated the Romans. With the Aetolians and the Macedonians on our side, we can take all of Greece.” His eyes light with excitement. “And then all of Italia.”

“Italia is a formidable undertaking,” Antiochus says uneasily.

“Formidable, but obtainable. Summon all your land and sea forces. Sail them across the Adriatic and land at Brundisium. Use the west coast as a base to march on Rome, The Romans have few outposts over there. They would pose no problem to such a mighty force.”

“Still, Rome could put four legions against us in the blink of an eye,” Antiochus counters. “They recruit quickly. Could we overcome such a force, fighting in their homeland?”

Hannibal smirks. “I may not be the most experienced of men in every kind of war, but I have at least learned how to fight the Romans and win.[xcv] Who else can say that.?”

“You certainly have done that, more than any man,” says Antiochus. “I promise you, my council will consider your proposal.”

“May the gods approve whatever proposal you select,” Hannibal replies, realizing he will not be invited to the meeting. “But I tell you now, you need more men over here. Do you know what the Achean League Greeks call your force? The ‘Tiny Army!’[xcvi] That should tell you all you need to know about how much they fear you. Bring all your forces here immediately. Such a display will help bring Macedonia to your side.” Hannibal stalks from the room.

Shaken by Hannibal’s words, Antiochus calls a midnight meeting of his Syrian commanders. He relates the details of his conversation to the half-dozen officers who are gathered there.

"Hannibal's words make sense to me. I have eighty thousand men scattered across Syria. They could cross the Aegean and join me," he says.

Menippus shakes his head. "It could take months for them to assemble. I think it more important that you move on Thessaly now, and western Greece. We can take those territories while before Rome lands on the eastern shore."

"What about King Philip?" Antiochus says. "We will be invading Thessalian lands that he considers his."

"Do you not remember what Thoas said?" Menippus replies. "Philip is waiting to be our ally. He will welcome our appearance at his borders."

PELLA, MACEDONIA, 191 BCE. "Antiochus did what?" Philip bellows. He flings his golden goblet across the room. The cup clangs off a statue of Ares, barely missing the head of Philocles, his stocky infantry commander. "That Syrian dog has the temerity to bury the bones of my men? Then he tells my subjects that it needed to be done?"

He clenches his jeweled hands, throttling an imaginary throat. "Fuck the Romans, I'll destroy him myself!"

"I'm sure Philip of Megalopolis put him up to it," says Philocles. "He has been seeking your crown for years."

"I know that, but Antiochus didn't have to listen him," Philip replies. "That stupid Syrian has undermined my authority within my own kingdom! As if things weren't bad enough after our defeat by Rome."

"Our scouts say Antiochus is moving west, my King. The Syrians and Aetolians have taken Crannum, Cierum, and Metropolis.[xcvii] Antiochus will be coming into Macedonia, and the Romans will come to fight him there. We have to make a decision. Do we side with Rome or Syria?"

The king rubs his chin. "I hate Rome, but our treaty is clear about the lands and forces that Macedonia may keep. This Antiochus, with treacherous Thoas at his side, who knows what he would do?" He glares at Philocles. "And that bastard humiliated me!"

Philocles watches Philip expectantly. "Do we ally ourselves with Rome, then? They still have your son as hostage."[xcviii]

"I know, I know," Philip says, waving his hand as if swatting a fly. "But the future of Macedonia is paramount."

Philip rises from his throne and paces about the room, clasping his hands behind his back. "If we ally ourselves with the Romans, I risk losing my kingdom if Antiochus defeats them. If we ally ourselves with the Syrians, I risk losing my kingdom if the Romans win—but I also risk it if this sneak Antiochus wins. That alternative is twice as risky."

He rubs his eyes and grimaces. "Send a message to Praetor Marcus Baebius. Ask him to meet with me, that we may decide what to do next—as allies."[xcix]

"Immediately," replies Philocles. He hurries from the room.

Philip slouches in his gold-gilt throne, his eyes staring angrily at an unseen enemy. "Bury my men's bones, will he? I'll bury *his* bones!"

A week later, King Philip rides out from his capitol, riding west toward the Pindus Mountains. His entourage pulls into a tiny village at the base of the mountains, stopping next to a house-sized tent that bears a spread-eagle blazon upon its roof.

A lean, gray-haired man emerges from the tent, clad in a gray tunic with SQPR branded upon it. A half-dozen armored tribunes surround him, intently watching Philip's armed guards. Philip slides off his horse and strides over to the man, his arm extended.

"You are Governor Marcus Baebius?" Philip says.

"No other, King," the praetor replies, clasping forearms. "Come inside, I need to learn more about the Syrians' advance toward your homeland."

The two venture into the praetor's tent, followed by his praetorian guard. After the two renew their countries' pledges of support, Philip details Antiochus' recent conquests.

"Charon take me," Baebius exclaims. "I did not even know he had landed in Greece, and now you tell me he is marching across it!"

"He has already taken parts of Thrace and Thessaly," Philip replies. "And now he is besieging Larisa, a city that is loyal to Rome."

"I don't have enough men to take on an army," Baebius replies. "Even one as small as his. But I can send out a cohort of men with Tribune Appius Claudius. He will slow their advance."

"There are a lot of mountains in that area. You had best have someone who knows how to fight in them," Philip advises.

"Appius has been in the service for a dozen years," Baebius says. "He fought with General Flamininus and knows the terrain."[c]

Philip grimaces. "Flamininus should never have taken his army away from Greece. The fool only encouraged Antiochus to come over here as soon as he could! If the Syrian moves his entire army over here, he can take northern Greece before he goes to winter quarters."

"There is still hope," Baebius replies. "Tribune Claudius is quite crafty—he might figure out a way to slow him down. General Glabrio, our new consul. He is supposed to be here before the new year begins. Then we'll see how Antiochus' tiny army fares against Glabrio's twenty thousand men!"

"He had best fare well," Philip growls. "Or I will have lost a kingdom."

ROME, 191 BCE. Scipio flings his accounting tablet against his office wall. It explodes into shards of wax and pottery.

"Why did that stupid bastard do that?" he fumes, stalking around his writing table. "He picked Cato and Flaccus to go with him to Greece!"

"You said Glabrio is a proud man," Amelia says. "Perhaps he resented your forcing Lucius on him."

"I had to get Lucius this opportunity. He may not have another chance," He grimaces at his wife. "Gods above, Glabrio could have taken anyone but those two!"

"I would think the Latins had a hand in Cato and Flaccus' selection," Amelia says. "You said they readily agreed to his demands for extra troops and resources."

"A bit too readily," Scipio replies. "Now I wish my cousin Nasica had drawn the lot for Greece."

Amelia shakes her head. "No you don't. He would never have taken Lucius—you know what he thinks of him."

"Ah well, that horse has left the stable. All we can hope is that Flaccus does not make a mess of whatever he does over there. And Cato does not find some reason to bring Glabrio up on charges!"

LARISA, 191 BCE. "Winter is coming," Antiochus says to Hannibal and his generals. "We will retire to our fortress at Chalcis, and gather all our forces. "When spring returns in a few months, we will storm across Greece."

The officers look at one another, sharing an unspoken thought. Menippus raises his hand. "My King, we still have time to drive out the last of the Romans in Greece. Appius Baebius only has a few thousand men here. We can start with that outpost to the west of us—it only has a few hundred men. We can take it within a week, and move on the remains of Baebius' men. Two victories before we go to winter quarters, and we remove any Roman threat."

"That can wait until spring," Antiochus says. "Philip of Macedonia has not yet agreed to join us."

Hannibal shakes his head. "In spring you will have to fight an entire Roman army. If you took out the last of the Romans here, the rest of Greece might flock to us. We wouldn't need Philip yet."

He sees Antiochus is wavering. "You would still have time to bring over the bulk of your army, and prepare them for battle against Glabrio."

*A victory over the Romans might bring Philip to my side.* "Very well. Menippus. Prepare to march west. We will take all ten thousand men. I will summon another fifty thousand to come over from Syria, with more after spring."

Hannibal's heart leaps at Antiochus' words. *Finally, he's acting like a conqueror!* "An excellent plan, King. Nothing can stop you now."

CHALCIS, WESTERN GREECE. "Father, I'm off to visit the Courtyard of the Gods."

The raven-haired young woman shouts into the arched passages of the family mansion, hearing her voice boom off its block limestone walls. A voice echoes back from its recesses.

"I want you home before I meet with the council," Cleoptolemus shouts. "Be back before dark!"

Clea rolls her eyes. "Gods, Father. I am almost sixteen years old. I know how to take care of myself!" She bends over and picks up a small cage. A white hen clucks inside it.

"You be back before dark or you can't go to the play tonight, you hear me?"

Clea sticks out her tongue at the darkened hallway. She hurries through the door and strolls down the wide dirt street that is Chalcis' main thoroughfare, walking with the sinuous grace of a practiced dancer. The men stare at her as she passes, watching her hips sway beneath her thin green gown. Clea ignores them—she knows her father would reject any man who does not ride in a carriage with a retinue about him.

The young Grecian enters the town square and walks into the low-walled Courtyard of Erotes situated next to it. The courtyard is lined with small altars, each topped with a marble statue of one of the many

Erotes, the Greek gods of love and sex.[ci]

Clea strolls past the statues of Impetuous Passion, Desire, and Requited Love. She pauses near Pothos, the god of Longing for One Who Is Absent. A disheveled young woman kneels in front of the statue, her hands clutching a bouquet of orange-red poppies. A small child kneels at her side, his pudgy fist gripping a broken-stemmed flower. Clea bends to the woman's ear.

"Still no word about Egan?" she says softly. The woman turns her tear-stained face to the girl. She shakes her head, her unkempt brown hair dangling across her face.

"He went off to join Antiochus' troops. There was a battle to take over Pherae. I haven't heard from him since."

Clea squeezes her shoulder. "I am sure he will be fine, Sister. This Antiochus is supposed to be an invincible conqueror. He might have taken Pherae with no resistance at all!"

The woman nods mechanically. She turns back to face the statue, her back convulsing with sobs.

Clea tiptoes away. She halts before an altar with man-sized statue of a winged youth balanced on one foot, aiming his bent bow into the sky. Clea bows low before the figure.

"Eros, please accept this sacrifice, that you may soon bring love to me. Bring me a husband my headstrong father will finally find worthy." Clea pulls out the squawking hen. In one practiced move, she slits the hen's neck and empties its blood into the marble bowl beneath the statue's pedestal.

"Another sacrifice, Clea?" says a throaty voice behind her. Clea turns. She smiles at the tall, white-gowned woman who stands near her. "The gods do not hear me, Priestess. They have not yet cracked my father's stone heart."

"Be not so hard on Cleoptolemus, he is wise to be so selective. You are the most beautiful woman in Chalcis—no, do not deny it—and you will have many suitors. He only wants the best for you." She winks. "And for him!"

"His 'best' is a man of power and station," Clea says. "Mine is a man who will love and respect me. A man who pines for a family, not a throne."

"He is simply concerned about your welfare. The priest at the temple of Apollo conducted an augury for your father, to see about your prospects. The scapegoat's entrails foretold that you will soon marry someone with wealth and power."

"What about happiness? Did it foretell anything about happiness?" Cleo asks.

The priestess stares past Cleo's pleading face, watching the supplicants at the statues. "Well, the entrails do not tell *everything* that will happen. Some of it is left to you. Perhaps if you sacrifice a sheep, the gods will help you obtain your wish. But expecting to have both power and happiness—that may require an ox!"

"I don't want power," Clea blurts angrily. "I don't want anything like that at all!"

The priestess raises her eyes to the skies. "We can only take what the gods give us. I think they have something momentous in store for you."

"That is what I fear most of all," the girl replies, looking down at the twitching hen.

TEMPE PASS, THESSALY PROVINCE, NORTHERN GREECE, 191 BCE. The tribune peers out over the rocky ledge. He studies the Syrian encampment six miles away, encircling the front of Larisa. "Look at them, Glaucus," Tribune Appius Claudius says. "How many do you think there are?"

The veteran centurion squints down onto the plain. "The camp's big enough for eight, ten thousand of them. But that's just a guess. Hard to tell how many of them are holed up inside the city."

As the two legionnaires look on, four riders in conical helmets race in from the mountains to the fort's entryway. The sentries yank open the camp's timbered gates. The riders hurtle inside.

Appius grimaces. "Ah, shit! Their scouts probably ventured out near Gonni, and found our camp. They'll be coming after us."

"We only have four hundred men. Not enough to withstand all those camel-fuckers," Glaucus murmurs. "Best we retreat."

The tribune shakes his head. "It's too late for that, we'd never make it back to our main garrison. And even if we did, Baebius would have our hides nailed to the wall for retreating." He grimaces. "We've got to face them."

"So we stay out here and die? Is that your solution?"

"Not necessarily. I remember a tactic General Scipio used in Iberia. He said he learned it from Hannibal. Let's just hope the Carthaginian isn't there with him. He'd remember it."

"We're going to ambush them?"

"No, we're going to fool them. We have to move our camp near the Tempe Pass, so we'll have the rocks at our back. Go to Gonni and get us a hundred torches. And send a rider to the Macedonian outpost."

"The Macedonians won't have any men to lend us. It's too small."

"We don't need their men. We need their uniforms."

Two mornings later, General Menippus leads four thousand of Antiochus' infantry from his fortress at Larisa, accompanied by two hundred of his cavalry. His orders from Antiochus are simple: destroy the scouting party near Gonni, so that the king may achieve a token victory over the Romans.

That evening, as the phalanxes approach the Roman camp, the Syrian scouts gallop in to report to Menippus.

"What is the problem?" Menippus says, noticing their troubled faces.

The lead scout nods toward the faint outline of a jagged mountain defile. "The Romans have moved from Gonni. They are camped at the base of Tempe Pass."

Menippus frowns. "That means they have the mountains protecting their flanks. How many are there?"

"More than we anticipated, but it is difficult to tell. Best you see for yourself, Commander."

Darkness creeps upon the land. Menippus ventures out with his royal guard, heading toward the pass. An hour later, he halts on a hillock facing Tempe.

The Roman camp sprawls out before him, a palisaded emplacement large enough to encompass two legions. Hundreds of smoke clouds waft into the fading light, drifting from the camp's scattered campfires. Scores of soldiers line the walls of the front wall. Many of them wear the sunburst standard of Macedonia.

"Zeus be fucked, they've got an army out there!" Menippus says.

"And the Macedonians are with them," adds the lead scout.[cii]

Menippus stands transfixed. Minutes pass. "Curse it!" he exclaims.

The commander wheels his horse about and waves over his lead scout. "Report what we've seen to Antiochus. Tell him I'll be back in Larisa by tomorrow afternoon." The party trots back to camp, led by a fuming Menippus.

Tribune Appius Claudius stands in a sentry tower above the Roman camp gates. He watches the Syrians retreat from the ridge. "Send out some scouts to follow them," he orders. "I want to know if they're really leaving." The scouts return two hours later, bearing the news he has prayed for.

"The phalanxes are marching east," a scout says.

Claudius turns to his centurion, beaming from ear to ear. "They're returning to Larisa! Fortuna has smiled upon us, Glaucus. Tell the men to take their rest. They can sleep as late as they want."

Glaucus nods. "Good. They have worked night and day, building this big camp and tending to all those fires." He glances at the front rampart. "What should I do with the Macedonian standards?"

"Oh, leave them up. The Syrians may be spying on us. And leave some of our men in the borrowed armor, just in case the spies get close enough for a look."

"What a narrow escape!" Claudius declares. He stretches languidly. "I'm going ride over to Gonni and get myself a bath and a massage." He winks. "And maybe a little something else. Would you join me?"

"The men would notice if we were both gone," says Glaucus. A wry smile crosses his face. "But then, if we went one at a time…"

That evening, a Syrian scout gallops through the gates of Larisa. He heads straight for Antiochus' temporary palace. When the scout relays Menippus' message, the Syrian king slumps down in his throne, kneading his gold-wreathed brow. Hannibal sits at a map table below the king, mulling over the scout's news.

"The Romans must have taken an army in under our noses, and brought Philip with them!" Antiochus says. "We don't have the men to risk a battle. We'll have to get out of here before they surround us!"

"Perhaps, perhaps not," Hannibal says. "You know, I used to set up false campfires as night, and sneak out under cover of darkness. They might be trying the same tactic, to make it look like an army's there."

Antiochus snorts. "Your ingenuity is legend, Hannibal. But Romans have not the imagination for such trickery. They would think it cowardly."

"Not all of them are so dull. Scipio was quite inventive. If he was there, or one of his lieutenants, he would pull such a trick."

Antiochus pounds his fist on the throne table. "I'm not going to risk losing the war before I even begin it! I'm taking my men to Chalcis, its walls are unassailable. It won't be a retreat, I'll tell the men we're going there for winter camp."[ciii] When the rest of my men to come over, there will be too many of them to stop, no matter what tricks the Romans play!"

Hannibal frowns. "Why don't we investigate their camp? We could send some scouts to into the heights above it, the could see if—"

Antiochus jerks up his hand. "We go to Chalcis."

Hannibal bites his lip. *Trick or not, if he'd brought more men with him, we could have taken the fort!* He looks at the brooding king. *What manner of man have I allied myself with?*

Hannibal recalls his midnight flight from Carthage, running from the Romans who came to capture him, betrayed by his fellow senators.[civ] *But then, what other choice did I have?*

**Thermopylae Pass**

# VI. THERMOPYLAE

CHALCIS. The two commanders pause on a hillock overlooking the Chalcis fortress. Behind them, the Syrian horns call the army to a halt.

"Well, they certainly built the walls high enough," Hannibal remarks, eyeing the fortress' towering limestone ramparts.

"Look at the ditch around it, it's deep as a chasm!" remarks Antiochus. "The Romans could never get in there. That's why I chose it."

The Carthaginian general glances sideways at the king. "I think you are making overmuch of the Roman threat. That was likely a ruse they set up at Tempe Pass. Why, they might only have had a few hundred men in their camp! Instead of worrying about them invading us, you should get some spies over there, and find out their numbers."

"Look, I'm not hiding inside Chalcis," Antiochus replies irritably. "I'll get several thousand of Thoas' Aetolians to join me here. Then we can march east and destroy the Romans."

"You have a hundred thousand men in Syria, King. Bring them across before the winter seas become too violent. Then no one can stop you. You can take northern Greece. In spring, you move on Italia."

The king shakes his head. "For now, let us settle in here."

*You will 'settle in' instead of setting out,* Hannibal thinks. *If only you hated the Romans more and feared them less.*

Antiochus snaps the reins of his horse and walks it down the hill, surrounded by his royal guard. Hannibal follows, studying the hundreds of men who are massed in front of the open gates.

A rotund little man trots his white horse toward the king's party, a man richly dressed in green silk pantaloons and tunic. A conical silver helmet rests atop his head, its sides inscribed with dancing centaurs.

*Who is this dandy?* Hannibal wonders. *He's dressed like a Cretan juggler.*

The man draws near Antiochus. He removes his helmet and bows his head.

"Good morning, mighty Antiochus. I am Cleoptolemus, magistrate of Chalcis. Your messengers alerted me of your coming. I have prepared a fine reception for you!"

"Who are those men behind you?" Hannibal asks, eyeing them warily.

The magistrate gapes at Hannibal. "My gods, you must be the legendary Hannibal! It is truly an honor to meet you!" He jerks his head back toward his guards. "They are just city militia. Did you notice that they bear neither shield nor sword? I wanted to show you that we welcome you unconditionally."

*A wise move when you have ten thousand soldiers at your door*, Antiochus thinks. "I am touched by your generosity, Magistrate. I would love to see your city."

"And I would be honored to show it to you!" Cleoptolemus exclaims. He eyes the phalanxes lined up on the hillock, a forest of tall spears pointed to the sky. "And what of all your men up there?"

"I would hope we could camp near your gates," Antiochus says, his tone brokering no disagreement.

"Oh, of course, of course. The barley harvest was good this year, we have plenty of grain for them."

"And?" Antiochus says, glowering at him.

"And cheese! Plenty of cheese!" Cleoptolemus adds.

"I would pay, of course," Antiochus says. He eyes Cleoptolemus. "If it is a reasonable amount."

"I am sure that whatever you pay will be enough," the magistrate stammers. "Please, come inside and refresh yourself."

The magistrate leads Antiochus' party into Chalcis. They ride through the city's well-tended streets and buildings, halting before a three-story manse with silver-studded bronze doors.

"This was the residence of Konstantin, a wealthy wheat merchant. He met with an unfortunate end recently, and his house is at your disposal. It still has all his slaves!

"An unfortunate accident?" Antiochus says.

"Robbers! His caravan was waylaid. They took all his money and killed him and his family!" Cleoptolemus vigorously shakes his head. "Terrible, just terrible!"

Hannibal eyes him. "He was a friend of yours?"

"Konstantin was my competitor." The magistrate's eyes narrow. "Oh, people say we fought bitterly over politics and business. But the truth is, I respected him."

"That is laudable of you," Hannibal says, his tone tinged with sarcasm. "I am sure you gave him his due."

Cleoptolemus dismounts and bangs on the entrance. "Open now, open for the king!" Two bear-bodied Egyptian slaves emerge and hold open the doors.

"Please come in," Cleoptolemus urges. "You can rest and refresh yourself. Tonight we will have a feast at my house. In your honor, of course. Chalcis' finest will all be there."

"It will be an honor," Antiochus replies, rubbing his eyes. "Now, if you can show us to some sleeping pallets, I would be most grateful."

That evening, Antiochus and Hannibal enter a temple-sized mansion in the heart of the city, accompanied by a half-dozen of the king's elite guards. The Syrian king wears a flowing black toga bordered with gold threading, a slim gold wreath upon his brow. Hannibal is clad in a knee-length tunic of Phoenician purple, eschewing his senatorial finery for the simpler garb of a Carthaginian officer.

Cleoptolemus meets them at the door, his white-robed chest draped with gold chains. "Come in, come in! The people of Chalcis are anxious to meet you!"

Hannibal's eye roves over the scores of elegantly dressed men. *I doubt if there are any 'people' of Chalcis here. Only the ones that prey off of them.* He musters a smile and proceeds inside.

The evening drifts by with continuous feasting and drinking, backdropped by the music of lyre-players and pipers. Antiochus moves from one group of politicos and merchants to another, outlining his plans to unite all of Greece.

For all his humble dress, Hannibal becomes the center of attention. He regales the Chalcis nobility with tales of his Roman conquests, answering their many questions about his duels with Scipio. They listen raptly as he describes his defeat at Zama.

"So Scipio is the only man who defeated you?" murmurs a slave merchant, his voice blurred with drink.

Hannibal winces. "Yes, I lost a battle to him and his numerically superior forces. But the tally is not yet complete. I have a feeling we are not yet done with each other."

Antiochus takes small sips of his chilled white wine, careful to maintain his composure. *Remember your story*, he reminds himself. *You are here to free them from Roman domination.* The king pulls the goblet from his lips and frowns. *Blah! It's grown tepid.*

Cleoptolemus is instantly at his side, his face contorted with concern. "The Byblos does not please you? May I get you something else? A red? Some opium?"

"It's quite tasty, magistrate," Antiochus replies. "It had grown a bit warm, is all."

"Then let me chill it up for you!" Cleoptolemus peers into a darkened doorway. "Clea, bring snow for our king!"

Clea strolls in from the doorway, her gold-sandaled toes peeping out from her diaphanous white robe. Her carmine fingernails cup a large golden goblet heaped with snow.[cv]

Antiochus is struck dumb. *Gods above, who is this? She is Aphrodite come to earth!* He watches the girl's hips undulate beneath her gauzy dress, at the swaying globed shadows of her fulsome breasts. The king glances at the men around her, and notices that even the oldest are staring at her. The tall young woman pauses in front Antiochus, her eyes downcast.

"This is my youngest daughter, Clea," the magistrate says. "Go on, girl, fill his cup."

Clea spoons two mounds of snow into the king's goblet. He stares at her tapered ivory fingers as if she were spooning gold into his hands. "Gratitude," he mumbles.

Clea raises her dark blue eyes to meet his, quickly averting them from the intensity of his gaze. "Is that enough, my King?" she says.

"Uh, more…two more," he stammers.

The girl glances up at him. Her full lips arc into the hint of a deprecating smile. "I fear your cup will run over."

The conqueror of nations laughs giddily. "Oh, of course! Just one, then." His eyes rove over her body. *I want her!* is all he can think.

An iron hand clasps Antiochus' forearm. "There are some merchants over here who are very anxious to meet you," Hannibal says. "Can you come with me for a minute?" He interposes himself between Antiochus and Clea.

"You will excuse us," Hannibal says to Cleoptolemus, making it more an order than a request. The rotund magistrate jumps back from him as if he has seen a snake. Antiochus and Hannibal head toward a group of togaed men stretched out on thickly padded dining couches.

Antiochus turns back toward the magistrate. "I want to talk to you tomorrow! About your daughter."

Cleoptolemus bows low, sweeping out his arms. "It would be an honor!"

As the two men walk toward the couches, Hannibal leans into Antiochus' ear. "What are you doing, making pigeon eyes at that girl? You risk loss of dignity."

"You think I care what these pot-carriers think? I can destroy them all. I want that woman to be my wife."

"You have a wife," Hannibal retorts.

"Not here. This one will be my Grecian wife."

Hannibal grits his teeth. *We're on the cusp of conquering a nation, and he has to stop and chase pussy. If I ever get my own army again, I'll run his ass into the sea.*

The next morning, Antiochus and Cleoptolemus ride out the city gates, pausing by the hundreds of tents that sprawl among the denuded barley fields. The Syrian king sweeps his arm across his encampment. "Magistrate, I have over ten thousand men here, and ten times that many coming over. I will soon liberate Greece from any trace of Roman influence. And then, who knows? The rest of the world beckons."

"I have heard about your Army of a Hundred Nations. I am sure no one can withstand them."

Antiochus takes a deep breath. "I would like you to join me. As one of my regional advisors."

Cleoptolemus sweeps off his particolored turban. "It would be the honor of my life."

"And I would like your daughter by my side, as my queen."

Cleoptolemus' heart leaps. *Steady, boy. Strike a good bargain.* "Forgive me for what I must ask you, but as a father I must protect my daughter. What about your other wife? Will there be difficulties?"

*I should kill you for your insolence*, Antiochus thinks. He envisions Clea's nude body. "That one stays in Syria. I will rule my new empire from here, with Clea." His eyes bore into the magistrate's. "And you."

"And the wedding dowry?"[cvi] Cleoptolemus murmurs expectantly.

"More than the wealth of kings."

The magistrate's grin splits his face. He extends his forearm. "Welcome to the family."

Two weeks later, all of Chalcis fill the flower-strewn streets, celebrating Antiochus' and Clea's three-day wedding feast. Thousands of Syrian soldiers wander through the city, laughing and drinking with its people. The soldiers are careful to keep hands off the local women. They know that Antiochus crucifies rapists—after slowly castrating them.

On the third wedding day, bride and groom celebrate inside the city's main banquet hall, surrounded by Chalcis' rich and powerful. Clad in a flowing white gown, Clea stands next to her fifty-year old husband. She bears the look of a captured slave.

Clea glances sideways at the king, who is preoccupied welcoming the wedding guests. *He's got scars all over his face. Not much fat, though. Hera help me, I should have run away with Nikos. Well, at least this old man will be gone on campaign.* She brightens. *Maybe he'll get killed!*

Hannibal lurks in a corner of the hall, his mood as bitter as the fish sauce he pours on his flatbread. *The Romans are sailing into Greece, and we're standing around getting drunk. I've got to get him to bring his entire army over here, before the Romans are battering at Chalcis' gates.*

Lost in love, Antiochus spends the rest of winter immersed in sex and celebration. His mind wanders far from the liberation of Greece and his war with Rome.[cvii]

While Antiochus languishes, Hannibal stalks the streets of Chalcis. He fumes at the idleness of his Syrian ally, knowing the Romans draw ever closer to them.

EPIRUS, GREECE, 191 BCE. "I can see it. We're almost there!"

Glabrio leans over the bow of his quinquereme, watching the Neptune-faced prow head slash through the churning Adriatic. Flaccus and Cato stand by his side, shifting about to dodge the cold February spray. The three men watch the shadow of the northern Greece coastline grow ever larger.

"So, Consul, are there any changes to our plan?" Flaccus asks.

"Our path is clear," Glabrio replies. "We march to Thessaly and join forces with Philip. Together we take back Thrace and Thessaly."

Cato barks a laugh. "So you and Philip are going to take back the land from which we expelled him just six years ago?"[cviii]

Glabrio's severe countenance breaks into a smile. "Politics are all about reversals. An enemy becomes an ally, when a greater enemy looms for the both of you."

"Scipio is the greater enemy," Flaccus interjects. "I would like to think that you are now aware of that."

"I am aware that he is the one who warned us to keep Flamininus' troops in Greece," Glabrio says. "Had we listened to him, Antiochus would not be there right now."

"And you two Latins would still be back in Rome, figuring out ways to undermine Scipio," replies a voice. "So perhaps it is not so bad we are taking you over here."

Lucius Scipio walks in to join the three men, glowering at Cato and Flaccus. "I'm surprised you two even left Rome. Gods know what

Scipio will accomplish without you dogging his every step. Will your thugs and rumor-mongers assume your duties while you are absent?"

"I level no falsities against any man," snaps Cato.

Glabrio grimaces. "Best we focus our attentions on debarking quickly. We have to move across Greece as quickly we can, to keep Antiochus from gathering strength."

"A good plan," Lucius replies. "I heard that the Aetolians are bringing ten thousand men to join him."

"Then Antiochus' Tiny Army will double in size, to become a Small Army," Flaccus says. "But they will still be no match for us."

"Unless he puts them in the mountains," remarks Tribune Marcus Aemilius, as he strolls in to join them. "There are places where a handful of men could hold an army at bay."

"You mean Thermopylae," Glabrio says. "Where the three hundred Spartans held off Xerses' Persian hordes."[cix]

"Just so," replies the tribune. "I have been through that pass. It is narrow and steep, just as the legends describe it."

"Psh," says Flaccus. "Antiochus is from Asia. What would he know about ancient Greek history?"

"He may not," Lucius says, his voice grim. "But Hannibal is with him. He knows all manner of military history, just as my brother does."

"Yes, too bad Big Brother Scipio is not here to save us from him," snipes Flaccus.

"Too bad, indeed," Marcus Aemilius declares, his eyes fixed on Flaccus. "Our greatest commander is at home."

*Scipio again!* Glabrio fumes. "The task is mine to accomplish, all else is speculation," he huffs. "Scipio has given us his guidance and his veterans, but it's up to us to wrest Greece from Antiochus before he amasses more troops."

"I trust your strategy, and your leadership," Marcus replies. "Nevertheless, keep your messengers at the ready. We may yet have need of Scipio's counsel."

ROME. "Today, I have fourteen years. I begin my passage to adulthood," Publius Scipio intones. He lifts off the gold chain necklace that he has worn all his life, his face as solemn as a priest's. He lays the necklace upon the family altar, carefully placing the owl-faced amulet in front of the family gods. [cx]"

"Ancestors, I give you my bulla, this symbol of my childhood, that you may recognize that I am an adult. Today, I am a man."

Scipio's son unwinds his toga praetexta, the red-bordered garment he has worn since he was four. His father hands him a plain white toga virilis, a man's toga, and watches him wrap the wool garment about his spindly torso. A minute later, Publius clasps the toga's end piece onto his chest. He gazes up at his parents, his eyes glowing with pride.

Scipio bends over and kisses his son on both cheeks. "I am proud of you," he declares.

Publius beams at him, his eyes moist with tears. "I am honored, Father. I pray I will grow to be like you."

Scipio places a plate of honey cakes in front of the small bronze statues of the family's five household protectors. "Accept our offerings, ancestors, and bless us with your continued protection this year."

Unable to restrain herself any longer, Amelia grabs Publius and presses his head to her green-gowned bosom.

Publius squirms away from her, tugging down his toga. "Please, Mother. I am no longer a boy!"

She kisses the top of his tousled brown hair. "You may be a man, but you will always be my baby!"

Publius rolls his eyes.

Scipio hands Publius a supple leather belt rimmed with silver. "A present from us, for your new career as a marine. A belt fit for an admiral!"

"I am but a junior officer, but I shall wear it proudly," Publius says.

"Well, we all start somewhere, and work our way up. Now go get a bath," Scipio says. Publius' lips curl into a pout. "I mean, Laelius and Prima are coming over to celebrate. You might want to prepare."

Publius grins. "Old habits die a slow death, don't they, Father?" He walks toward his room near the open air kitchen, fingering the rough-cut wool of his new toga virilis.

Scipio and Amelia stroll into the manse's enclosed gardens, savoring the perfume of the freshly bloomed roses. Scipio slides out his belt dagger and severs a carmine-colored rosebud. With a bow, he hands it to Amelia.

"For you, Mother. You have raised him well."

Tears streams from her eyes, furrowing her chalk-powdered cheeks. "Oh god, he's going off to be a soldier. I feel so old."

Scipio wraps an arm about her, running his hands along her back and buttocks. "You are as enticing as ever you were. He pinches the knife hidden inside the sleeve of her gown. "And just as dangerous."

"But I won't be able to protect him out there," Amelia says. "All those raiders and pirates!"

"He is merely going on patrols as a junior administrative officer, a beneficiarius," Scipio says. "He'll be back in a few months, safe and sound."

"I do hope you are right," Amelia says. "He is so strong and bright. What a fine consul he will make some day!"

Scipio's face darkens. "He'd make a better consul than Glabrio. I cannot swallow the way the fool has treated me."

"You still harbor ill will toward him?" Amelia asks, wandering over to the opposite side of the garden. "He is a Hellenic Party man."

"The whelp betrayed me!" Scipio growls, pacing about the cobbled walkway. "He took Flaccus and Cato with him, just to spite me!"

"You spent a lot of money for his campaign." Amelia says. "We will have to pick this year's candidates more carefully."

Scipio pauses near a large rosemary bush. He pinches its spiky needles and inhales the piney fragrance. "Well, at least Flaccus and Cato served as consuls several years ago. They can't run again for a while."

"No, but they can use their influence to elect those who will—just like we do. Suppose they back Tiberius Glaucus, or Junius Paullus? You've heard them at the feasts we go to. They want to conquer the world!"

Scipio nods. "They would turn Rome into a military society, a second Sparta." He sits down on one of the garden's marble benches, his hands clasped between his legs. "They think the most powerful nation is the greatest one. Same old mistake."

"Just like Flaccus thinks the richest would be the greatest," adds Amelia. "At cost to our arts and culture."

Scipio's fist slaps his palm. "We can't have another candidate who turns to the Latins. It will take us on a pathway we cannot escape! I have to know our candidates will be loyal to us, and to the party." He looks expectantly at Amelia. "Lucius would do that. He'll do whatever I tell him."

Amelia sits next to him. She drapes her arm about his shoulders. "Really? Lucius?"

Scipio shrugs. "It is not so far-fetched. If Glabrio repels Antiochus, Lucius would return as a war hero. It may be his best and only time to become consul. And I promised—"

"Yes I know, you promised your mother you would protect him,"

Amelia interjects. "I swear to Juno, sometimes I wish you were less allied to your promises!"

"My mother knew he would need help to make his way in life, and I am here now to help him." He squeezes her hand. "My war wounds still tax me, now more than ever. Who knows where I will be ten years from now?"

Amelia leans over and firmly kisses his cheek. She draws back and smiles. "You'll probably be in India then, winning another momentous battle to save Rome!"

He chuckles. "I hope you are right about me being here. But India? It is too cursed hot!" Scipio raises his head, his chin set. "Support my folly, Beloved. Together we can get Lucius elected."

Amelia says nothing. She rises abruptly and grasps her bronze garden shears, nipping off a crocus' deep purple blooms. "Who will run as the plebian candidate?" she says, turning the bloom in her hands.

"Laelius."

Amelia points the shears at his head. "Laelius? Again? It's only been two years."

"He is honest, intelligent, and immensely popular with the people. He just lacks the, uh, determination that's needed to win."

Amelia inhales the crocus' peppery scent. She smirks. "You mean the determination to do what must be done, regardless of honor. You sound like Flaccus."

Scipio smirks. "I have learned much from coping with Flaccus' political depredations. Someone must do the dishonorable to get an honorable man elected. And that will be my task."

Amelia hands him the crocus. "Have caution that you do not endanger those who love you, Publius Cornelius Scipio. That would be the greatest dishonor of all."

CHALCIS. "You are sure of this?" Hannibal asks, his voice heavy with dismay.

Nicator nods slowly, his silver mask flashing in the angular throne room sunlight. "Two of my spies confirmed it," he says in a muffled voice. "Neither knew the other was there at Linnaeum, and they came back with the same story."

"So Glabrio is leading a consular army toward Chalcis," Hannibal says. "That means he has at least twenty thousand foot soldiers, and most of them are probably veterans. And cavalry."

"That snake Philip will likely join him," mutters Nicator.

"If only we had that snake on our side," Hannibal says. "We'd better notify Antiochus. We have to get out of here before they lay siege to us."

"We could march to Thrace, and hole up in the Lysimachia garrison," Nicator says, his mind on finding Thrax. "Its walls are thick and high."

Hannibal shakes his head. "It would not protect us if Philip is with them. He is a master at undermining walls."

"So what can we do? Run home to Syria and stick our heads in the sand? Give up all that we have gained?"

Hannibal stands silent, thinking. He points a finger into the air. "Not necessarily," he says. "There is one place. A place where a handful can hold off an army. Come on, we had best rouse Antiochus."

The two commanders tramp up the winding staircase centered in the palace's throne room. They march down the rug-lined hallway and halt at the doors to the king's bedchamber, guarded by two enormous Syrians.

"We need to see the king," Hannibal declares.

The lead sentry raises himself to his full six-and-a-half-foot height. "He is not to be disturbed under any circumstances," he declares. His bass voice booms through the hallway.

"This is an affront!" Hannibal barks. "Do you know who we are?"

The sentry stares into space, his face blank.

Nicator grasps Hannibal's forearm and pulls him back. "They know very well who we are," he says. "And they know who I am. Let me take care of this."

He pulls out his curved sword and fronts the scowling guards. "Must I force my way in there?" he says, his bloodshot eyes glaring out from his mask. "I will take you both down before you can raise your swords."

The two guards glance at once another. An unspoken agreement passes between them. They step to the side.

"You are wise men," Nicator says. The Syrian captain pushes open the doors and steps inside.

Antiochus' snores emerge from an oak canopied bed the size of small room, its green sheets pooled at his feet. His bride Clea lies naked beside him, her limp arm curved across his wine-spattered chest. The smell of opium hangs heavy in the air.

Nicator steps to the bed, his eyes riveted upon Clea's globed buttocks. "My King," he says.

Antiochus raises his head. He blinks blearily at the intruders. "What are you doing here? I gave orders not to be disturbed."

*You have not been disturbed for over two months*, Hannibal fumes, *doing naught but feasting and fucking.*[cxi] "The Romans are coming. Twenty thousand men are heading toward you."

"What?" The king scrambles from the bed, his eyes alert with panic. He pitches the silk sheet over his bride and stands naked in front of Hannibal and Nicator, his limp manhood dangling beneath his gray-streaked stomach. "This can't be happening! We have only eight thousand men here. The rest are in the garrisons up north!"

Antiochus pulls his black tunic off the floor and slips it over his head. “Nicator, send messengers to those five Aetolian chiefs that promised us troops. Tell them to meet me in Lamia day after tomorrow. We have to prepare for battle.”

“As you command,” Nicator replies. He stalks from the room. Clea sits up, rubbing the sleep from her eyes. “What is happening, Husband?” she murmurs. Hannibal averts his eye from her nude torso—but not before he feels a stirring inside himself. *Baal take me, no wonder he has dallied in bed all these months!*

“Rest yourself, Wife. We men have plans to make.” Antiochus beckons to Hannibal. “Come on, let’s find out where they are.”

The chamber door closes behind Antiochus. Clea leaps from the stained and rumpled covers. She walks to the arched opening that leads to the attendants’ chambers.

“Gwenn, do you hear me? Prepare the bathing tub! I have to go into town and see some friends.” *Young, handsome friends.*

Hannibal and Antiochus stride to the back of the palace anteroom and enter the king’s war room. The chamber’s twelve-foot table is covered with an elaborately drawn terrain map of northern Greece and Macedonia. The two lean over the map, studying the terrain around Chalcis.

“How many men will the Aetolians provide?” Hannibal asks.

“Thoas said the chiefs could recruit twenty thousand men to my cause.” That would give us enough to stop the Romans.”

“Are you certain? General Glabrio will likely have Philip with him. He may bring ten thousand Macedonians to the fray. And forgive me for what I say, King, but your men have grown soft these recent months. They do not don armor when on duty, and show up late for their watches.[cxii] They are not ready to face the Romans.”

Antiochus’ face flushes with embarrassed anger. “I don’t know whether to thank you for your honesty or kill you for your impertinence," he says.

"I only speak the truth, as one general to another." Hannibal calmly replies. "Deal with it as you see fit."

The king sighs. "If I don't have enough men to fight them, what other recourse do I have?"

"What about bringing in your armies from Syria?"

Antiochus shakes his head. "Menippus sent me a message. The main body of troops were sent to Tadmar, to quell a native rebellion." He shakes his head. "The fool should have asked me before he did that. I would have held some back for situations such as this."

A short, sun-browned man enters the chamber, clad in worn wool pants and tunic. "You summoned me, King?"

"Come in, Abraxis. You reported that the Roman army is heading this way? How far away are they?"

The scout begins to count on his fingers. "Well, they were at Antigonia a few days ago. I'd say they are five, six days' march from here."

"Were the Macedonians with them?"

Abraxis looks at the floor. "Philip was with Baebius' cohort. Those two have taken a dozen of your Thessaly garrisons."[cxiii]

"The gods shit on me again!" mutters Antiochus. He points toward the door. "Go on, get back out there. I want a daily report on Glabrio and Philip." Abraxis trots from the war room.

The Syrian king slumps in his chair. He glances sideways at Hannibal, who silently watches him. "I know, I know. I brought this upon myself. I just didn't think they would come over when winter was still upon the land."

"Spring comes early to warriors who want to fight," Hannibal says. "We had best hope that Thoas is true to his word, and his chieftains have a host of soldiers for us."

Two days later, Antiochus and Hannibal sit in the weapons blockhouse of the Lamia garrison, facing five Aetolian chieftains.

"Where is Thoas? He should be at this meeting," Antiochus says to Bemus, the senior chieftain.

The red-bearded old warrior averts his eyes. "He had to deal with an assault from Corinth and Aegium," he replies. "Apparently the Achean League has cast their dice with Rome."

Hannibal studies the chieftain's stiff posture and averted gaze. *He's lying about Thoas. But to what end?*

"That is most disappointing," Antiochus says. "But we will succeed without him. How many men did you all bring with you?"

The chieftains study their hands. A stocky, bearded man nudges Bemus with his elbow. Bemus takes a deep breath. "We came here alone, King Antiochus. We do not have any soldiers for you."[cxiv]

"What?!" Antiochus flies from his seat, his eyes boring into the chieftains. "You don't have *any* troops out there? The Romans are coming!"

Hannibal smiles bitterly. *I told you the Aetolians cannot be trusted. But you had to listen to Thoas' rosy promises.*

"We have to protect our own cities," Bemus says. "The Macedonians are besieging Elyrissa, and we could be next. We simply cannot spare any men."

Antiochus gapes at the Aetolians. "You brought no one?" he splutters, still not believing what he hears. "Not even one cursed phalanx?" The room is silent.

"Get out, all of you!" Antiochus splutters. "I will deal with you later. When I do, you will wish it were the Macedonians who were at your gates! Get out!" The Aetolians rise from their seats and slowly file out.

None glance back at the angry king.

When the door closes behind the last of the Aetolians, Hannibal turns to Antiochus. "They are lying. They have the men, but they fear the Romans more than they fear you," Hannibal says. "They think your Tiny Army cannot possibly defeat Glabrio's and Philip's men.

The king raises his eyes to the heavens. "I feel like the world has abandoned me. [cxv] Thoas lured me to Greece with promises of countless allies, and he doesn't even show up." He nods toward Hannibal. "You were right about not trusting them. We should have pursued the Macedonians more strongly. You have been like a prophet to me, yet I shunted you from my counsel."

Antiochus grasps Hannibal's shoulder. "I will regret that for the rest of my life. But regret does not solve our problem. How can we defend ourselves against the Romans?"

"Once you recall your garrison troops, we will have ten thousand men. They will have twenty or thirty thousand. We have to use the terrain as our ally. Fight in a place that restricts their numbers.

"Is there such a place near us? We only have a few days."

"It is three day's march south of Chalcis, a narrow passage buttressed by the mountains and the sea. A place where three hundred held off a hundred thousand. That is where we make our stand."

Recognition dawns in Antiochus' eyes. "You speak of the legend of the Three Hundred Spartans?"

"Yes, the Pass of Thermopylae. We can use that spot to repel the Roman forces. We cannot defeat them, but we can prevent them from defeating us." Hannibal rises and extends his hand to Antiochus.

"Come, King, we have no time to lose. We march to Thermopylae, to make the legend anew."

PELLA, MACEDONIA. "Who's side are we on?" asks Boban, King Philip's portly minister of war. "Are we on Rome's or Syria's?"

"My alliance with Rome's provincial governor has been very productive," Philip says. "Marcus Baebius and I have taken back a dozen of Antiochus' cities and towns.[cxvi] And Baebius has returned them to me, as per our agreement. It would be foolish to break off now."

"Hmph! They have given back only part of what they took from you five years ago."

Philip grimaces. "You think I am not aware of that? But I do not have the forces to overthrow them." He rubs his chin. "Now, if I did join forces with Antiochus, we'd have well over a hundred thousand men."

"Not really. He has what they call a 'Tiny Army' over here. Barely ten thousand men."

Philip grimaces. "Still, he does have Hannibal with him. That man could win a battle with a herd of sheep." He rubs his eyes and gapes at the ceiling. "Aaagh! Sometimes I just hate being a ruler!"

The minister stands silent, accustomed to Philip's outbursts. *He is like water—he will find the path of least resistance.*

Philip peeks out between his fingers. He pulls his hands down and smiles. "Why do we have to decide about it right now? We can wait to see how their fight plays out at Thermopylae. Then we ally ourselves with the winner!"

"But you have an agreement to fight with consul Glabrio. You made it with that praetor Baebius, did you not?"

Philip waves his hand. "Psh, Baebius and I have done most of the hard work for Glabrio. He has a clear path to Thermopylae.[cxvii] Why waste any more of my men on fighting the Romans' battles? It won't get me any more of my original possessions."

"But your agreement with Baebius," says the minister. "He will expect—"

Philip bends over, grasping his stomach. "Oooh, I don't feel so good!"

He glances mischievously at his minister. "I may have a touch of cholera.[cxviii] I don't think I can lead my men to Thermopylae!"

*With you, gonorrhea is more likely*, Boban thinks. "Illness! A brilliant way out! I will prepare a letter of apology and send it to Glabrio."

"Do that immediately." Philip lays back in his throne, smiling to himself. "And bring me a pitcher of red wine for my…malady."

"I hasten to fulfill your desires," the minister replies, with the barest hint of sarcasm. "I will send several scouts to observe the battle at Thermopylae. Perhaps their information will help you decide who we should join."

"Excellent idea, but I already know one thing for sure. Hannibal is very clever. He will have a surprise or two for the Romans." He grins. "That is, if Antiochus does not get in his way."

THERMOPYLAE PASS, 191 BCE. "Move our six elephants over to the right, by the swamplands," Antiochus tells Menippus. "Line them up facing the mouth of the pass, so they can charge the Romans at a moment's notice."

"That is a worthy idea," Hannibal says. "Though Glabrio has fifteen of Scipio's African elephants, their horses may not be used to the size and smell of your Indian beasts."

Antiochus nods. "I had not thought of that. All the more reason to keep them near the front lines." He points to the mouth of the pass. "See where my men are digging a trench? I'm going to put in an eight-foot palisade behind it, with staked ends. We'll pile the trench earth inside the wall for our phalangites to stand upon. That will be our first line of defense."

"Put in a second barricade behind that one, where the pass begins to narrow," Hannibal says. "That will slow any Romans who manage to get that far."

"I already have it planned," Antiochus replies. *You are not the only military genius, Carthaginian.* "I'll have the men put a rock wall on the left side of the ramparts, near the side of the hill. That will keep the Romans from sneaking around our flanks."

"Best we put a rock wall behind the barricade," Hannibal tells Antiochus. "If the Romans get past the elephants, like they did at Zama, your right flank will be unprotected. This way you can send your light infantry to man that back wall, and mount an adequate defense." He turns his horse toward the inside of the pass. "Come with me, I'll show you where we can build it."

Hannibal, Antiochus, and Menippus walk their horses a hundred yards farther into the narrowing pass. Hannibal stops his mount at a pathway section flanked by pinnacles on one side and swamp on the other.

"The trail is only sixty paces wide here. Put up a thick, waist-high wall here and station the rest of our troops behind it. They can be the last line of defense. The Romans cannot get over this wall without breaking up their precious formations."

"You keep talking as if we were going to be beaten back, and have to retreat." Antiochus mutters.

"With Scipio's veterans here, that is a distinct possibility. Besides, I think it is wise to prepare for every eventuality. We can use this treacherous terrain as our ally. Just like Leonidas the Spartan did, two hundred years ago."

Antiochus pinches his nose, pondering Hannibal's strategy. He turns to Menippus. "See it done."

"We will finish it by tomorrow morning." Menippus says. The Syrian commander trots toward the hundreds of light infantrymen lolling along the brush-lined beach. Hannibal and Antiochus hear him shouting commands. The young soldiers march gloomily into the passage. They grab the jagged rocks that sprinkle the landscape and begin piling them into a wide, shallow wall.

Antiochus and Hannibal return to the front of the Thermopylae pass. The Syrian phalangites are hard at work with mattocks and shovels, digging out a two-hundred-foot-wide trench.

Nicator is there, fully armored. He sits upon a flat boulder embedded into the side of the hill. Nicator watches the men work, their white loincloths splotched with dust-grimed sweat. Those digging the trench have only to glance at Nicator, inscrutable in his silver mask, to find the motivation to dig harder.

Seeing his king approach, Nicator springs off his rocky perch. "How goes the work, Commander?" Antiochus asks. Nicator glances at his men. "They will have it done by dusk, or I'll cut one of their ears off. I have told them that."

"Good. We'll put up a palisade right behind it. The Dahae infantry are coming over to build it."

"Dahae!" Nicator snorts derisively. "They are dog eaters!" His red-rimmed eyes fix on Antiochus. "When is the battle? I want to see how good these vaunted Romans fight."

"You will soon have your chance," Hannibal replies. "The scouts say Glabrio's army will arrive by afternoon tomorrow. They will likely come at us a few days after that, after they have established their camp."

"Now we will settle this thing, and prove who's best." Nicator points his forefinger at Antiochus. "I make you this promise. They come and fight us, I will bring you a commander's head. You can make a drinking bowl from the skull."

Antiochus chuckles uneasily. "Well, I suppose that would be a very unique goblet. Why, two of those skulls would be even better. In case I have a drinking companion!"

Syria's deadliest warrior genuflects. "It will be done, or I will not be upon this earth." He stalks back toward his boulder.

Hannibal chuckles. "You know, I believe he'd come back with the consul's head, if you just asked him to do it."

"His skills are only matched by his devotion," the king replies. "I'm glad he is fixed on a goal. It will get his mind off that Thracian he has sworn to kill."

Hannibal cranes his neck, studying the castle-shaped peak above him. "You know, if I were Glabrio, I'd lead a war party down from those mountains. That's what their general Flamininus did when he defeated Philip at the Aous Gorge."[cxix]

"We can prevent that. There are thousands of Aetolians inside nearby Heraclea, they fled there when the Romans approached. I will tell them that they must send half their men to guard the mountaintop passes, or I will take their city myself."

Hannibal snorts derisively. "Yes, I think threatening Aetolians works better than requesting." He points to a peak towering in the distance. "Make sure they put the main force around the goat path on top of Mount Callidromum. That's the trail the Persians used to get at the Spartans."

"The Aetolians will be up there by tomorrow night, or I'll declare war on them!" Antiochus declares. "I'd rather have them as a certain enemy than a dubious ally. That way I know whom I'm fighting!"

* * * * * *

Two days later, the Roman army camps out a mile from the mouth of Thermopylae Pass.

Consul Glabrio holds a final war meeting in his consular tent. The young commander stands over the oak slab that serves as his map table. Baebius, Lucius, Cato, Flaccus, and Marcus Aemilius circle the table, studying the scouts' recently-drawn map of Thermopylae. All are clad in the simple gray tunics that soldiers wear, the Roman eagle blazoned across the chests of their garments.

Glabrio runs his finger along the thick black line that depicts the Thermopylae Pass. "Antiochus has blocked the pass with staked palisades and stone walls. We will need more than a frontal assault to take them."

"We can't get through the swamplands. That leaves the mountains on the other side," Baebius says. "If we can make our way to the top of the pinnacles, we can descend upon their flanks."

"We can ambush them," Flaccus says. "Excellent!"

Cato shakes his head. "I doubt we will surprise them. Hannibal is in his camp. The Carthaginian is an expert on military history. He will know that Leonidas was surprised by the Persians there."

"He's right," Lucius adds. "The Syrians will have scouts patrolling that goat path the Persians used. They might have troops stationed up there, too."

Glabrio purses his lips. "So, we have no choice but to storm the pass? We will lose many men."

Cato snorts. "Just because they know we're coming doesn't mean we can't kick their asses! Give me a cohort, and I'll cut through whoever is up there." He nods at Flaccus. "My fellow consul can join me."

Flaccus gapes at him. "Uh, I am more successful at fighting on the plains. Perhaps someone else?"

The room is quiet for a moment. "I will be that 'someone else'," says Tribune Marcus Aemilius. "When I served under General Flamininus, I led a cohort up into the Aous Mountains, and we managed to sneak down upon Philip's flank.[cxx] Give me a day and a night to explore the animal trails. I will find a way for us to ascend undetected."

Glabrio nods, relieved. "I have heard about your mountaineering skills, Tribune. Consider it done."

"Good," Cato says. "But we still need you, Flaccus. We will have to split our forces to cover all that terrain. You can take one half of them."

Flaccus starts to protest. Glabrio raises his palm. "Cato, you will take two thousand men up near Mount Callidromum,[cxxi] above the front of their ramparts. Flaccus, you take two thousand more to Rhodontia and Tichius, the two lower mountains by their rear.[cxxii] Marcus, explore the routes that lead up to there, and come back with a plan."

The tribune snaps out a salute. “I will leave after this meeting.”

“Very good,” Glabrio replies. “That leaves us to finalize the frontal attack. Praetor Baebius, you will lead the eighth legion into the mouth of the pass. I expect you will encounter a phalanx formation. But Hannibal is with him, so be prepared for anything.” He shakes his head. “We don’t know what they’re going to do with their elephants.”

“I’ll keep my cavalry ready on the flanks,” Baebius says. “They can move swiftly to counter whatever occurs.” He grins tightly “Whatever it is, we will handle it.”

“I trust you to hold the point of attack,” Glabrio says. “Your heart would not quicken if Jupiter himself appeared before you.”

The consul glances sideways at Lucius. “Lucius, I need you to lead the sixth legion, and take charge of our elephants. Your men will back up the eighth.” *In this narrow a passage, I doubt if we’ll need him.*

“As you command, Consul,” mutters Lucius.

“What about that trench they’re digging?” says Baebius. “If my men have to crawl in and out of it, they’ll be easy prey for the phalangites on the other side.”

“We’ll give you a hundred escaladers to solve that,” Glabrio replies.

“Ladder men? That trench isn’t deep enough to need ladders.” Baebius says.

Cato shakes his head. “They will go across the trench, not in it. Remember what our ancestors did at the Battle of Comitium?”

Baebius grins. “Of course! I’ll get the carpenters working on the ladder modifications.”

“Any other details?” Glabrio asks. The officers stare at the map, then at each other. No one speaks.

The young consul takes a deep breath. “That’s it, then. We march into the pass the day after tomorrow. Cato and Flaccus, you will lead their advance troops out tomorrow, after Marcus returns with a route."

Cato nods his assent. "I suggest we ascend the mountains at night, to gain the cover of darkness. We can sneak up on any who wait up there."

"I did not think you one to stoop to a sneak attack, Cato," snipes Flaccus, still irritated at him. "You always choose the direct approach."

"I know, but I have learned a few things from you," Cato replies.

Glabrio rolls up the goatskin map. "Enough talk. Prepare the men for battle. Two days hence, we'll test the mettle of these Syrians."

Cato spreads his arms above his head, taking in his fellow officers. "May Victoria favor you, and Mars be at your side." The Roman commanders hasten off to prepare their men—and themselves—for the conflict.

The ten flap closes behind the last to depart. Glabrio holds his right hand in front of his eyes, watching it quiver. *Gods, I'm shaking like a dog shitting olive pits! Did they notice?*

He pours himself a goblet of watered wine, and flops onto his sleeping pallet, staring up at the gray tent roof. *Get some sleep, boy. You have lots of planning to do tomorrow.*

He suddenly leaps up and marches over to the corner of his tent, rummaging through his armor. Reaching into his belt purse, he pulls out a ivory figurine of a fox-faced woman in a flowing gown, her hair piled high on her head. He takes it back to his sleeping pallet and lies on his back, sipping wine as he holds it in his palm. *I promise you, Livia, next year this will all be over, and I will return to you. We get us our villa, and Rome can go to Hades.*

* * * * *

Two days later, Marcus, Cato, and Flaccus lead their mountain assault troops out into the predawn morning, riding in front of four thousand legionnaires.

The soldiers carry only a sword, helmet, and two javelins. Following Marcus' directive, they have forsaken their armor so they can travel quickly up the mountains. The hastati and principes have exchanged their cumbersome rectangular scuta for the lightweight circular parma used by the velites, a shield small enough to maneuver through the dense mountaintop foliage.

Marching double time, the assault party quickly crosses the mile-wide plain that fronts the rocky foothills of the Thermopylae Mountains. Marcus leads them to low rise between two hillocks, where they pause to take in water.

"We have to leave the horses here," he says to Cato. "They won't make it along the upper trail." The three officers dismount. Marcus walks over to a pine tree marked with two slashes. He waves over Cato and Flaccus.

"This is our trail to the three mountains. I marked it last night."

Flaccus peers into the dense stand of scrub oak and pines. "What trail?"

"Here," Marcus replies. He bends over and points to a foot-wide thread of trampled vegetation. "This is an animal trail, used by the generations of elk and deer. It will take us to the saddle between Callidromum and Rhodontia. From there we split into two groups and take separate paths. We can attack the Aetolian camps that are stationed at each peak.

"How many are up there?" Cato asks.

"There must be, oh, two thousand or so, from what I could see." He nods at Cato. Most of them are on Callidromum, overlooking the front of their battle lines." He chuckles. "Aetolians are so cocky! They only have a dozen sentries guarding the Callidromum camp, and most of them seem half asleep."

"All the better," Cato replies. "I'm not looking for a noble battle with our former allies. I'd rather murder them in their sleep."

The Romans tread silently up a steep forested switchback, with Marcus Aemilius leading the way. Hours later, they come to a high country meadow ringed with jagged pinnacles. Marcus signals for a halt. He walks to the edge of the meadow and whistles shrilly. An answering shrill comes from the opposite side. A young man pops up in the midst of the meadow grasses, clad in green tunic and leggings. He smiles and waves.

"That's my local man. He says all is safe," Marcus tells Cato and Flaccus. "Come on. We can take refreshment while we wait for the night."

The Romans sprawl out among the tall, golden grasses, chewing on the dried fruit and cheese that are their only rations. Marcus leads the brown-skinned youth over to Flaccus and Cato. "This is Castos, one of the local hunters." Marcus says. Castos greets the commanders with a gap-toothed grin.

"Castos will lead Flaccus' men up a hidden trail up to Rhodontia and Tichius." He points to a large boulder on the right side of the meadow. "Cato and I go to the left of the boulder. You and Castos take the right."

"Why do I get him? Why not you?" Flaccus snaps.

"I want to be where the fighting is the worst, Flaccus. The greater danger is at Callidromum. Many more men are there." He grins at the youth. "Besides. Castos has hunted here for years, he knows the woods better than I do." He eyes Flaccus. "You'll be much safer with him. Isn't that what you want?"

Before Flaccus can reply, Marcus stretches out and puts his hands behind his head. "We have to wait for dark. Best you take some rest while you still have the time."

As the sun creeps behind the mountaintops, the assault parties set out on their missions. Marcus leads Cato and his men on a winding trail around the midpoint of the mountain, hiking toward the side that overlooks Thermopylae Pass. Finally, near midnight, he calls a halt.

"We're close," he says to Cato. "Follow me, and walk quietly. Tell the men to sheathe their swords, their blades could shine off of the camp firelight." The tribune disappears into the murky forest.

Cato follows Marcus' shadowy outline, his feet crunching softly upon the path's dried pine needles. After an hour of weaving through scrub and pine, Cato sees scores of flickering lights ahead of them. A spear's cast farther, and the lights become campfires.

"That's them," Marcus whispers. "There are twelve, maybe fourteen hundred infantry. Most of their guards are facing the other side of the mountain, near that trail Leonidas used. That's where they think we'd come, if we came at all."

"We can take them at dawn, when Glabrio's men attack the pass below us," Cato says.

Marcus nods. "Soon as there's light enough to tell who we're killing."

For the next two hours, the Romans slowly through the trees along the camp perimeter, stringing out into a semicircle. Cato murmurs a command to his cohort's tribune, who relays it to the centurions. The command is whispered from one soldier to another: wait for the battle horn, then rush in like madmen.

The first stripe of dawn glows above the eastern ridges. Marcus tiptoes barefoot toward a sentry dozing upright against a pine. In one swift motion, Marcus jerks the man's head back and slices his throat, then pulls the gurgling corpse into the bushes. Behind him, hundreds of legionnaires step closer to the camp. Marcus repeats the maneuver two more times, quietly removing the bodies. He sees that only one guard remains.

Marcus nears the fourth guard, his dagger gripped in his bloodied hand. A twig snaps beneath his feet. *Shit!*

The sentry jolts upright and peers behind him. He sees Marcus rushing toward him. "Romans!" the Aetolian yells. "Alarm! Alarm!"

Marcus lunges forward. He tackles the guard and wrestles him onto his stomach, slipping his forearm under his neck. He jerks his arm back, snapping the guard's neck. Rising from the spasming corpse, Marcus draws his sword and rushes into the heart of the camp.

Cato elbows the cornicen standing next to him. "Blow, curse you, blow!" The hornsman trumpets a long, lingering blast. Screaming like a mob of berserking Gauls, the Romans flood into the camp. The legionnaires plunge their spears into sides of the Aetolians' tents, jabbing until the screams inside turn silent.

Hundreds of Aetolians scramble from their tents, grasping whatever weapons they can find. The campsite soon becomes a swirling, dawnlit melee. The Aetolians and Romans dash in every direction, fighting whatever foe they stumble upon.

Ducking and stabbing, Marcus Aemilius fights his way into the center of the camp, heading for a cluster of large black tents. *That must be the officer's quarters.*

He sees a silver-armored Aetolian standing in front of them, a tall man flanked by two armored soldiers. Crouching low, the blocky little tribune weaves his way between the surrounding tents.

A rangy young Aetolian leaps out from behind a tent. Screaming like a madman, the Aetolian swings his axe toward the top of Marcus' helmet, seeking to split his skull. Marcus' shield arm flashes out and rams against the underside of the Aetolian's forearm, knocking the blow aside. The tribune lunges forward and chops the man's arm off at the elbow, leaving him with a spurting stump.

The Aetolian youth falls to his knees, screaming in pain and despair. Without a backward glance, Marcus rushes toward the captain.

The Aetolian's screams alert the two guards. They march toward Marcus, their swords raised to strike.

Running at full speed, Marcus bends over and snatches a tent from its tethers. He flings the eight-foot sheet into the faces of the oncoming Aetolians, draping it over their heads. Sliding to the earth at their feet, he plunges his blade into the arch of the first Aetolian's foot, cutting through bone and tendon. The groaning soldier hops sideways, grabbing at his foot, He loses balance and crashes to the earth.

Marcus blocks a downward sword thrust from the other guard and jabs his blade into a bare spot above the man's greaves, delving into his kneecap. The Aetolian bellows in pain. He chops his blade at Marcus' head. The blow rings off the side of the tribune's helmet, stunning him. Marcus falls to one elbow, his shield raised over his face. The relentless Aetolian limps forward. He kicks Marcus' shield aside and leans over him, his sword raised for the killing blow.

The Aetolian's head jerks back, his face contorted into a rictus of agony. A swordpoint juts through the chest of his cuirass, thrust by an arm powerful enough to cut through solid bronze. The Aetolian falls on top of Marcus, feebly clawing at the tribune's face.

Marcus rolls sideways and flings him off, pausing to crunch his gladius into the Aetolian's forehead. The tribune totters to his feet, shaking his head to clear it.

Cato stands before him, wiping his blade on the edge of his tunic. He frowns disapprovingly. "Will you come on? Their commander's getting away!"

Cato wheels about and runs toward the Aetolian commander, who is vainly shouting for help. Marcus dashes after him, his blade dripping a trail of blood.

The Aetolian captain sees the two Romans rushing toward him, their faces fixed with murderous intent. He looks about for his guards and sees none, only the press of enemies drawing ever closer. He drops his sword and raises his arms.

Cato and Marcus slow to a walk, scanning the surroundings for attackers. Cato halts in front of the captain. He presses his swordtip against the commander's throat.

The captain leans his head back as far as it will go. "I surrender!" he blurts. "Thoas talked us into fighting for Antiochus. Fuck them both, they're not worth dying for."

"Will you tell your men to surrender?" Marcus asks.

The commander smiles bitterly. "From the looks of it, there aren't many left to tell."

Cato grabs the Aetolian by his shoulder straps and pulls him forward. "Come on, you have men's lives to save." He drags the commander into the center of camp.

"Go on, tell them!" Cato barks.

"Drop your weapons!" The Aetolian shouts, time and again. Soon, several hundred unarmed Aetolians are gathered about their crestfallen commander, listening to the cries of triumph and pain from those still fighting.

As the sun peeks over the eastern mountains, the last of the Aetolians are rounded up and tied together. Marcus and Cato stand in the midst of the ravished camp, watching their men drag the Aetolian wounded from their collapsed tents.

"We have to hurry. General Glabrio will soon begin his assault," Cato says. "We've got to get our men to the edge of the descent, so they're ready to come down upon the Syrians."

"That's fine," Marcus says. He points to the east end of the camp. "There's a narrow trail where we can march down undetected, at least until we get to the rocky sections just below the floor."

Cato shakes his head. "No more sneak attacks. We want them to see us coming. And I want us to come down on that goat trail, the same one that the Aetolians used to get up here. The one that the Persians took to foil the Greeks."

"You want us to be seen?" the young tribune says, bewildered.

Cato's lips draw into a tight smile. "Exactly. The Greeks are decadent weaklings, but that philosopher Aristotle made sense on one point. Men are creatures of impulse, and they are controlled by them."[cxxiii]

Cato chuckles dryly. "We are going to give those Syrians a mighty strong impulse."

*THERMOPYLAE PASS. Calm, be calm. The men are watching you.*

Consul Glabrio rides out in the vanguard of his army, watching the pinnacles of Thermopylae Pass grow ever larger. Ahead, thousands of Syrian light infantry straddle the pass, unarmored young soldiers grasping a brace of javelins and a sling.

The Syrian phalangites stand behind them, bunched in a narrow phalanx that is sixteen men wide and sixteen men deep, squares bristling with the eighteen-foot spears Antiochus has commissioned for defense of the pass.

Glabrio sees a wide trench lying before his men, backed by a staked palisade. He swallows. *That looks impassable! Gods, I hope Cato and Flaccus have done their job.*

The army halts within several hundred yards of the Syrians. The consul waves over Baebius, his legion commander. The two study the compact Syrian phalanxes.

Glabrio frowns. "Once we get through the light infantry inside the pass, we'll have to break through those phalanxes, somehow."

"The ground is uneven behind them," Baebius notes. "It's lined with rocks and furrows. That could work to our advantage."

Glabrio nods. "I remember Scipio saying that was how he defeated the Macedonian phalanxes who fought for Hannibal. He got them on uneven ground, where they couldn't hold formation."

"If we use a maniple formation, our men would be more mobile than if they were in cohorts," Baebius notes. "We could get inside any gaps that appear." He grins. "Those phalangites have got to use both hands to hold those oversized lances. If we get inside them, our short swords could cut them to pieces."

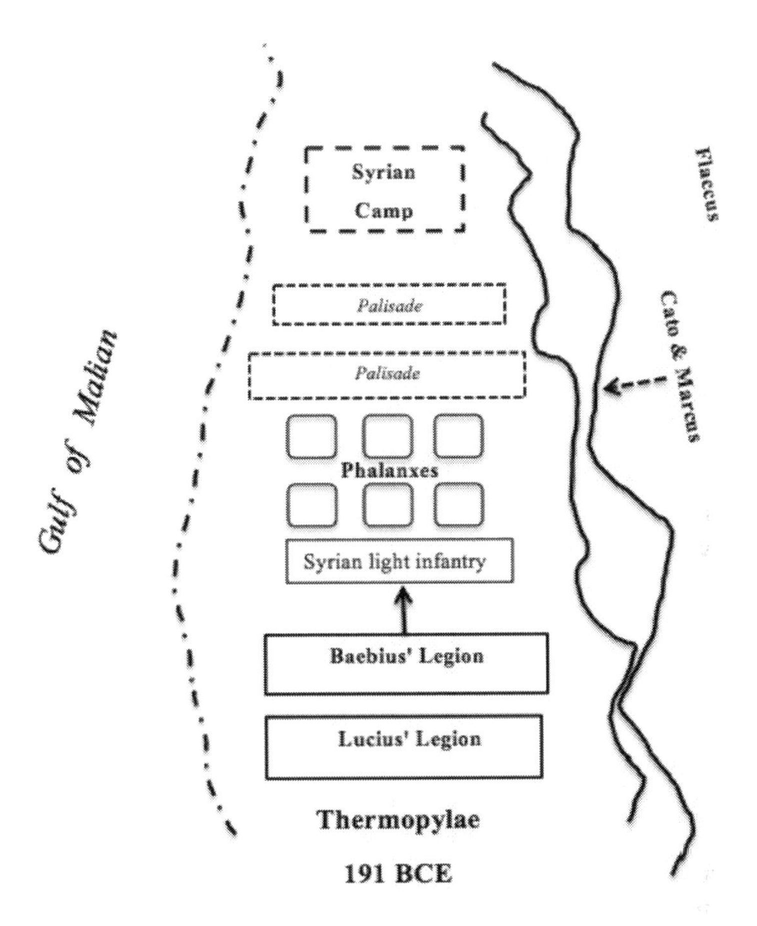


"Relay the message to your tribunes. Maniple formation on the front lines. Use the principes instead of the hastati on the front—we need our best men first."

Baebius' legion quickly divides into maniples of one hundred twenty men. The veteran principes form into an attack column four maniples wide. Glabrio watches his soldiers fall into formation and stand at the ready, waiting for the order to attack.

He feels his stomach flutter. *Gods curse it, I should have ate a pancake or something this morning. Ah, I'd probably throw it up if I did.* He looks to the front of Baebius' maniples and sees the praetor expectantly watching him.

*Come on, no turning back now,* Glabrio leans sideways on his horse, inclining his head toward his hornsman.

"Sound the charge!"

The cornicen raises his e-shaped horn and blows a deep, lingering note. A score of his fellows echo the order, the signal resounding through twenty thousand men. His heart pounding in his ears, Glabrio snaps the reins of his horse and moves forward. The maniples tramp in behind him.

King Antiochus hears the Romans' brassy call to battle. He watches Glabrio's maniples marching toward him, their brightly colored standards bobbing above the rows of glistening helmets.

He glances at Hannibal. "This had better work. We have nowhere to go."

Hannibal scans the pinnacles above his head. "Thermopylae Pass is a legendary redoubt. As long as your Aetolians can hold the mountains, we can hold the bottom." *Just be glad your men aren't fighting them on the plains,* he thinks. *The Romans would cut through your men like a honed scythe through grass.*

Nicator kneels on a rock outcropping twenty feet above the Syrian light infantry and phalangites, his eyes fixed on the Romans' maniples. The Syrian warrior hears the Roman attack signal. He rocks back and forth, stirring with excitement. *Now I kill Romans. Bring my king some skulls.*

He bends over the edge of the ridge. "Put up the planks!" he yells. A score of rear-line infantry scurry over to a pile of planks near the swamplands. Working in groups of four, they lug the twenty-foot boards to the trench and lay them across it, creating a temporary roadway toward the barricades.

Nicator waits until the last board is laid into place. He peers down at his men and raises his curved sword. "Get ready!" The phalangites raise their spears. The velites load their slings and grasp their javelins.

"Charge on my command!" Nicator shouts to the light infantry. He looks up to a rock shelf directly above him, where forty archers and slingers stand. He raises his fist toward them. "At my signal!"

When the maniples arrive at the mouth of the pass, Consul Glabrio draws his horse to one side. "They are yours to command, Praetor."

Baebius dismounts and marches to the front of his principes. "On to victory!" he shouts, waving his gladius over his head. Baebius leads his men toward the waiting Syrians. The maniples draw within two spear casts of the Syrian infantry.

"Charge!" Nicator screams. The Syrian light infantry dash forward, screaming their battle cries.

"Loose!" bellows Nicator. The Syrians stop, plant their feet, and fling their javelins into the oncoming legionnaires.

"Testudo!" yells Baebius, raising his shield.

The maniples lift their scuta above their heads, creating a turtle shell of interleaved shields. Hundreds of spears thunk harmlessly into the sturdy shell. Scores find an opening, however, felling dozens of Romans. As the velites drag back the wounded, the principes yank the spears from their shields and fling them down. They march farther into the narrowing pass, crunching the spears beneath their hob-nailed sandals.

The Syrians unleash a second volley. When the rain of spears diminishes. Baebius trots to the right flank and vigorously waves his arm. "Come on! Get at them!"

The velites dash in from the flanks and unleash a torrent of javelins. With only a helmet and plate-sized shield to defend themselves, hundreds of Syrian light infantry are struck down by the Roman missiles. The survivors grab their wounded and drag them into the pass, slinging rocks as they retreat. The velites jog back to regroup behind the heavy infantry. And the maniples march on.

"Get ready!" Nicator shouts to the phalanx captain.

"Lower your spears!" the captain barks. The first four rows of phalangites level their sarissas, creating a thickly layered spear wall. The Romans approach, every step in unison, every face set with purpose. The principes lower their shields and place them in front of their chests, ready to barge into the sarissas.

Nicator raises his fist, his eyes on the ridge above him. He jerks it down. "Loose!" he shouts.

The archers and slingers rain missiles upon the advancing legionnaires, downing scores of them.

"Testudo!" Baebius shouts, holding his shield over his head. The Romans reform their shield shell and step forward, leaving a trail of wounded behind them. The Syrians rain down more arrows and stones.

Baebius grits his teeth. *We've got to kill those pricks up there!* He beckons the velites forward, jerking his index finger at the rock shelf in front of him. "Strike them down!" he commands.

The Roman light infantry rush past the legion's right flank, their small shields raised to block the Syrians' fire.

"Loose!" the velites' tribune yells. The young warriors fling out a hailstorm of javelins. A handful of Syrians plunge from their rocky perch, crashing down onto the phalangites.

"At will!" the tribune shouts. Loading and firing as fast as they can, the velites release a steady stream of missiles. A score of slingers and archers fall. The others cower beneath the relentless onslaught.

Nicator waves for his men to retreat. The relieved Syrians hurry down a steep trail that leads behind the ramparts, seeking succor within the main body of troops.

Marching in unison, the Roman maniples collide with the Syrian spear wall. The Roman shields grate and clatter against the thick, immobile lances. The Romans batter their swords against the jabbing Syrian sarissas, but the wall does not move.

"Back!" Baebius shouts. The Romans back up twenty paces, leaving a line of principes' corpses in front of the staggered spear wall. The Syrians hoot and jeer, flinging stones and food scraps.

*We'll kill ourselves trying to break through that mass.* Baebius decides. He calls over the velites' tribune.

"Help us out, Justus. Those first four lines don't have any spears held above them. Can you concentrate your fire on them? Just give us a few openings, and we'll take care of the rest."

The lanky old warrior slaps his palm to his breast. "It will be done, Commander. Get your men ready to charge." The tribune strides back to his velites, barking orders at them.

Baebius call a hasty conference with the centurions leading the front line maniples. He grabs a stick and scratches a new attack plan in the dirt. "Get back there and get ready. We will only have a few moments for this to work. Do not waste it!"

Minutes later, the Roman horns sound a call to retreat. The legionnaires step back a spear's cast from the phalanx. The Syrians cheer again.

Baebius smiles. *Good. There's nothing like dashed hopes to demoralize a man.* He snaps down his arm.

The velites trot into the space separating the Syrians and Romans. They hurl their javelins on a low trajectory, arrowing them into the faces of the phalangites along the front rows.

Though many javelins clack off the Syrians' spear shafts, scores plunge through to their mark. The phalangites grab their faces and shoulders, screaming in testament that the javelins have found their mark. The ground becomes mounded with fallen, squirming, phalangites. Scores of Syrians stagger about, clutching at their bleeding heads and torsos. Man-wide gaps appear in the spear wall.

"Replacements to the front!" Nicator shouts down to the phalanxes. He scurries from the ridge, intent on rallying his men.

"Double time! Charge!" screams Baebius, frantic to seize the opportunity. The Romans trot forward, their eyes fixed on the gaps in the phalanx. Ducking low and turning sideways, dozens of legionnaires manage to edge their way into the second and third lines of the phalanx, slithering through the forbidding spears.

Striking to the right and left, the penetrators cut down scores of the unprotected phalangites, creating more openings in the wall. Many Syrians drop their spears and grab their dagger-swords, intent on protecting themselves. The front wall disintegrates, and the Romans rush in.

Nicator barges into the back lines of the phalanx. Screaming and cursing, he shoves men into the breaches, only to see more fall to the methodical Roman assault. His eyes grow black with fury. "Get up there, or I'll kill you myself!" he yells, to no avail.

The Roman attackers cut into the rear lines, scattering the Syrians. The terrified phalangites rush toward their fortifications.[cxxiv] They clatter across the trench planks and file into the sides of the timbered ramparts. The last men to cross remove the bridges.

The phalangites regroup behind the barricade, their lines spanning its perimeter. The Syrian light infantry hasten to the sides of the barrier. They pile rocks into a thick five-foot high wall, blocking any flanking incursion.

"To the wall, spears first!" Nicator shouts. The phalangites march up onto the packed earth walkway that lines the inside of the ramparts. They level their long spears over the wall, forming a dense row of deadly spearpoints.

Praetor Baebius watches the Syrians form a new spear line. He waves over his senior tribune. "Jupiter curse them, I thought we had them whipped. Send out the escaladers!"

The Roman laddermen rush forward, lugging two ladders lashed together and covered with wood planks. The Syrians rain arrows and stones upon them, felling dozens in mid-stride. Still the laddermen run on. They throw their narrow bridges across the trench, stacking them side by side until they span the opening.

"Come on across!" Baebius orders, beckoning his legionnaires with his blade. He marches over the rude bridge, stones bouncing off his chest-high shield. The maniples rush past him, intent on breaking through the staked ramparts.

"Stop! Get organized!" Baebius screams. His shouts are drowned by the din of battle. Scores of legionnaires rush headlong into the spear wall.

Nicator has been waiting for just such a moment. "Stab them!" he shouts.

The phalangites retract their eighteen-foot spears and thrust them forward. Hundreds of lances plunge into the Romans from every angle, cutting into heads and bodies. Dozens of Romans die upright, futilely squirming upon the spears that impale them.

Behind his silver mask, Nicator grins wolfishly. "Look at you, stuck like pigs on a spit. Come on, charge us again!"

Baebius runs to the rear of the attacking principes and beats them on the back. "Get back to your lines! Gods curse you, get back!" The wayward attackers retreat to their maniples They resume their places along the front lines, wrapping their wounds with bandages from their belt pouches.

Baebius surveys the rows of phalangite spears. He notes the enormous elephants poised near the swamp border, their mahouts standing ready with their goading lances. *Trying to take that barricade will cost us hundreds of men. Maybe a flanking maneuver into the swamp? No, we'd just get bogged down, they could pick us off at will. We could use our elephants, but they could cause more havoc than good.*

General Glabrio rides in to join Baebius, his face lined with concern. "What is happening? Why are we stalled?"

"I'm trying to figure out how to get through the ramparts," Baebius snaps. "It's not so fucking easy to do, Consul."

Glabrio's face flushes. "We have to get through it," he replies. "I leave it to you, but you have to do it." He wheels his horse about and walks it toward the mouth of the pass.

Baebius feels his stomach turn. *Gods save me, we're going to have to charge right into them.* He calls over his tribunes. "Prepare for a full attack. There will be no retreat."

"You know what that means," says a grim-faced tribune.

"I do, and it will be on my head."

The officers solemnly return to their men. Baebius waves over his cornicen. "When I jerk down my hand, sound the charge." The praetor raises a trembling fist.

A hand grips his shoulder.

"Hold, Legate," says Glabrio. "I have a plan. We will attack the ramparts, not the Syrians."

Baebius blinks at him. "What?"

"The triarii," Glabrio replies, looking expectantly at Baebius. "They can use their barbed spears."

Recognition dawns in Baebius eyes. "That may work!"

The young consul looks over his shoulder. He smiles wryly. "It is good you agreed, because I have already summoned them. They are yours to command." Glabrio rides back to his place between the two legions, halting his mount next to Lucius.

Baebius smirks. *The pup is smarter than I thought.*

The elder triarii edge into the front, sliding sideways between the rows of principes. Their lead tribune marches over to Baebius and salutes. "We are ready," the middle-aged legionnaire says, gesturing toward the three hundred soldiers who stand behind him, each man gripping a barbed twelve-foot spear.

"Let me talk to them, Caldus." Baebius steps past the tribune and faces the battle-hardened triarii, the middle-aged soldiers who act as the legion's last line of defense.

"That barricade needs to come down, or all is lost. You have one task before you—one great, glorious task. Pull it down!"

A voice rings out from the ranks. "Don't you worry about that, Praetor. We'll pull down their little stick fence, though Pluto himself rise to stop us!"

Amid scattered nervous laughter, the legate grins. "I do believe you would, Legionnaire. And I'll be up there watching you do it."

Caldus turns toward the Syrians, and raises his sword. "Together now!"

Baebius raises two fingers toward the cornicen. The hornsman blows the attack signal. Caldus and Baebius tramp forward, the leather-tough triarii following in two ten-wide columns.

Perched on top of the barricade, Nicator watches the spearmen march toward him. *What are they up to?* He runs to the rear lines, where the slingers and archers stand at the ready.

"When I raise my fist, you unleash everything you have," he tells the light infantry captain. "Just over the top of the barricade." Nicator returns to his place along the rampart, watching the Roman advance.

The triarii cross the improvised bridge. The Syrian captain rises his right fist and jerks it down. The Syrian missiles fly out over the phalangites' heads, swooping down upon the oncoming Romans. Four of them fall, then four more. The triarii raise their shields and march on, unperturbed.

"Just a few more steps," Baebius yells to the spearmen, holding his scutum over his head. "Then we'll be too close for them to fire on us!"

The Romans stride toward the rows of spears jutting down from the top of the barricade.

The triarii arrive at the barricade. They quickly kneel down, raising their shields up to block off the spears that are jabbing at them. They jam their spears between the stakes and turn them sideways, hooking the barbed end into the wood. Grunting and cursing, the triarii yank backward with all the strength in their iron-muscled bodies, dropping their shields to pull with both hands.

With a grinding crash, a stake topples out in front of them. Four more follow, then a dozen. Pulling, pushing, and prying, the Romans wedge the ramparts apart. Two man-sized openings appear, then four. The barricade's packed earth walkway collapses in front of the legionnaires, tumbling out the phalangites who stood upon it. They are cut down before they can rise.

"Into the breaches!" Baebius shouts. He runs at the wall, screaming like a madman. The triarii plunge into the openings, holding their long spears in front of them. The principes follow them and spread out to the sides, slashing into the unprotected phalangites. Within minutes, hundreds of Romans are inside the wall.

The rampart battle becomes a freewheeling swirl of phalangites and legionnaires. Scores of Syrian spearmen fall during the first few minutes, their unwieldy weapons providing little defense. The Romans wedge their shields between the spears and jab into the men holding them, methodically stabbing down the first rows of defenders. The Syrians retreat, slamming into each other in their haste to escape.

"Come on, boys, we have them!" Baebius shouts. "Follow me in!"

A silver masked warrior appears before him, shoving his way through the fleeing Syrians. Baebius watches him slide between the press of fighters. Baebius stalks toward Nicator, his sword arm cocked.

Nicator watches Baebius approach. His eyes rove over Baebius' stance, studying the way he angles his body. He sees the Roman is readying himself for a quick, short strike. *You want to stab me? Good,*

*I'll let you!*

Nicator spreads his shield a little farther from his body, presenting the Roman with a larger target area. He raises his sword arm high, knowing it will be easy for Baebius to block at his chest.

Baebius lunges forward, his scutum raised to block an overhead cut. He jabs his sword at Nicator's unguarded chest. With the speed of a striking snake, Nicator spins sideways and lunges past the stabbing sword blade. He whirls down his arm, changing his overhead sword cut into an uppercut.

The Syrian's curved blade crunches through the side of Baebius' jaw. The legate's eyes start from his head. His lips flap spasmodically as they spew out streams his life's blood. Baebius swings feebly at the Syrian. Nicator swats away the blows.

The Syrian yanks out his sword and steps back, watching the Roman crumple to the ground. "You think to kill me?" he barks at the spasming corpse. Nicator spreads his arms apart and bellows out his victory.

Caldus glances toward the screams. He stares at the sight of Baebius lying on the ground, his scarlet cape spread under him like a blood-flower.

"Baebius has fallen! Get that bastard in the mask!" A quartet of principes dash toward Nicator, with Caldus and two triarii following them.

Nicator stoops over and saws off Baebius' head, throwing the helmet to the side. He holds the head aloft by its hair, laughing as he brandishes it at the Romans.

The assassin spins around and dashes into the thick of his phalangites, intent on giving his prize to his king. *I'll come back and get that tribune. And the consul. That will break them.*

Caldus straddles his commander's headless body, ready to kill any enemy who dare approach it. "Avenge him!" he screams. "Avenge

Baebius! Kill them! Gods damn them, kill them all!"

The Romans attack the packed Syrians with renewed vigor, slashing and stabbing like demons gone mad. The Syrians retreat, step by step. They battle back with spears and swords, but the enraged legionnaires refuse to relent. Soon, the narrow pass becomes an open graveyard. Piles of Syrian bodies lie heaped upon one another, scattered boulders serving as their unmarked tombstones.

* * * * *

Hannibal and Antiochus observe the Roman advance from a high point farther up the pass, surrounded by their reserve troops.

Antiochus rubs the back of his head, frowning at what he sees. "They made it through our first wall, but our second rampart will be more difficult for them. We have a thousand men behind it, ready to refresh the men along the front of it. I've already ordered replacement stakes if they try to yank them out again."

"They'll have to charge through it, there's no other way." Hannibal observes. "Then they'll have to get past the other rock wall. They'll lose thousands. It may cost them the battle."

Nicator trots up to Antiochus, carrying Baebius' dripping head by its hair. He lays the head at the feet of Antiochus' mount. "This is the skull of their legion's commander," he says proudly. "I'll bring you his tribune's in a moment." The Syrian trots back toward the battle.

"Charming little fellow," Hannibal remarks dryly. An uncomfortable thought occurs to him. "There's only one way the Romans can get to us. Are you sure the pass is guarded up there?"

"Did I not tell you before?" Antiochus snaps. "I put two thousand Aetolians up there. Look, you can see them moving around on the Callidromum. See the shine of their helmets? They'd let us know if anything is amiss."

MOUNT CALLIDROMUM, THERMOPYLAE. Poised on the edge of the five-thousand-foot peak, Cato studies the battle below him, its insect-like figures swarming around the floor of the pass. He grimaces at sight of the Romans battling their way toward the second Syrian rampart. *They'll lose a lot of men fighting their way through a second spear wall, and that rock pile behind it. The Syrians will be ready for them this time.*

He turns to Marcus Aemilius. "We have to get down there. Is the way clear?"

"There were three sentries," Marcus says. "They never saw me coming." He gazes across the valley, peering at Mounts Rhodontia and Tichius. "Where do you suppose Flaccus is doing?"

Cato snorts. "He's probably lost. Conveniently lost, if I know him.[cxxv] No matter. We cannot worry about where he's at, we can only control our own fate."

Marcus looks inquisitively at Cato. "I have to remind you. We don't have to take that trail the Persians took. We can sneak down upon them on a narrow side trail. It'll take a little longer, but they won't see us. We'd have the element of surprise."

"That is not my way," Cato growls, thinking of Flaccus' jibe about him being sneaky. "Would Dentatus or Cincinnatus sneak in like some cowardly Carthaginian? No, we raise our standards high, and let our trumpets blow. Let them see the mighty Romans descending upon them. March down in a narrow column, so it looks like we have an endless line of soldiers."

Marcus grins. "That will not be a problem, the trail's barely wide enough for several goats!" He turns to the tribune behind him. "Take the men down behind us, Cassius."

Cato and Marcus begin to tramp down the winding goat herder's path, marching in full view of the Syrians. The Roman battle horns sound the call to attack, their brassy notes echoing through the canyon.

The Syrians see the glint of armored soldiers descending upon them. Their hearts soar with the notion that reinforcements are coming to aid them.[cxxvi] Then the Roman horns sound out above them, blaring the notes of their enemies.

"Romans!" A Syrian captain calls out. "The Romans are upon us!" The warning spreads like wildfire through the ranks. Terror grips the massed Syrians. Hundreds throw down their arms and run,[cxxvii] swarming past the second rampart.

Glabrio hears the echo of the Roman cornu. He peers at the mountain, searching for signs of Roman standards. He sees a bright red pennant fluttering atop a tall pole with a brass serpent coiled atop it. His heart soars. *It's Cato's men!*

The consul pushes his horse to the second barricade, shouting as he wedges his way through them. "We have the pass! Look, we're coming down upon them! Victory is ours!"

The Romans swarm over their demoralized enemy. They stab into the backs of their fleeing Syrians, flinging victims aside to get at the men behind them.

The velites run to the rampart on the left side of the pass and fling javelins into the elephants stationed there. Maddened by the stinging spears, the elephants rampage up through the pass, trampling over friend and foe alike. The beasts mill about the narrow passage, slowing the Roman pursuit.[cxxviii]

"Get at the drivers!" Glabrio screams.

The velites spear down the mahouts driving the elephants. They jab at the beast's haunches, herding them into the Syrians' front lines. The maddened beasts crash down the rampart and rock wall.

While the Syrian elephants wreak destruction on the left. Cato and Marcus lead their men down into the right flank of the Syrians, slashing through the terrorized phalangites and light infantry. Dozens of legionnaires remain on the hillside, flinging boulders into the compressed masses. Terrified by the attack from above, hundreds of Syrians run toward the pinnacles bordering the pass, seeking shelter among its trees.

Hannibal watches the rout unfold below him. His feelings shift from disappointment to dread. "We have to get you out of here, Antiochus."

The king stares glassily at the massacre, his mouth agape. "The pass is supposed to be impregnable!" he stammers.

Hannibal suppresses a sneer. "It is, when you hold the high ground. Come on, we can go to the Elatia garrison and gather your men before we go to Chalcis. You have a hundred thousand men in Syria. This war is not yet lost."

"As you say," Antiochus replies numbly. Hannibal grasps his shoulder and gently shakes it. "Get your guards."

The king calls his elite guard to his side. "Follow me to Elatia," he says. "We will regroup there." The riders gallop through the narrowing pass. Turning left, they start up a switchback pathway to the mountain valley town of Elatia.

While his king rides from the scene of the battle, Nicator wades into the maelstrom of men and beasts. The Roman equites have charged over the crumbled second rampart, only to find that their horses are terrified by the foreign smell of Antiochus' rampaging elephants.[cxxix] The horses stampede across the battleground, trampling Roman and Syrian alike.

A wide-eyed stallion thunders toward Nicator, its equite futilely yanking at its mane. Nicator pirouettes to the side of the rampaging beast. He slashes upward with his sword, skillfully severing the equite's artery. The young patrician careens away, grasping at his gushing groin. "Ride away, boy," Nicator shouts. "Go ride to your death."

Scanning the battlefield, Nicator spies the black-plumed helmet of a tribune nodding above a mound of fallen phalangites. *There's the head I want.*

The Syrian crouches down and weaves his way toward the Roman officer, pausing only to pierce the heart of an attacking principe. He springs over two Roman corpses and stalks toward the tribune.

Caldus stands in a small clearing, shouting orders to his men. A glint of silver catches his eye, and he looks to his left. He sees a masked Syrian stalking toward him, poised to attack. The old tribune looks about and sees his triarii are occupied with pursuit. He shrugs. *No way out, it's him or me*. Caldus pulls his shield close to his chest and strides toward Nicator. The two draw within arm's reach of each other.

Caldus thrusts his blade at Nicator's stomach, aiming for the spot where his silver cuirass ends. The Syrian dances to the side of the tribune. He suddenly lunges in and batters his sword against Caldus' shield, driving him backwards. Caldus retreats three steps, then counters with a slash at the Syrian's sword arm.

Nicator skips sideways and repeats the attack, driving Caldus back another two steps. He notices that the tribune is standing directly in front of a Syrian corpse.

Nicator leaps upon the tribune bashing his shield against his scutum. Caldus staggers back. He trips over the corpse and crashes to the earth. The Syrian is instantly upon him. His blade plunges toward Caldus' throat.

A large rock clangs off the side of Nicator's helmet, hammering him sideways. He tumbles to the ground, rolls over, and instantly springs up, his sword poised to kill.

A short, stocky, tribune faces the assassin, his sword arm cradling two jagged rocks. "Come on, pot-face," says Marcus Aemilius. "I'll give you a fight." Marcus surges toward him, flinging one rock after another. Nicator takes the blows on his shield. By the time he lowers it, Marcus Aemilius is upon him.

Marcus sweeps his foot under the Syrian's ankle, tumbling him to the earth. He lunges in, stabbing at the side of Nicator's head. The Syrian jerks his head sideways. Marcus' blade rasps into the gravelly earth.

The assassin springs up and jumps forward, his sword darting for the tribune's unprotected shoulder. Marcus turns sideways, catching the blade on the edge of his shield. He spins completely around, swinging his razored blade in a backhand cut. The blade slices across Nicator's triceps.

Nicator yelps with pain and drops his sword. He quickly lunges down to retrieve it. Marcus kicks him backward and pinions Nicator's blade under his hob-nailed sandal. The tribune points his sword at Nicator's face. "Surrender, or I'll cut your throat."

Inside his mask, Nicator's lips twist into a snarl. *I'll have to beat this little bastard to death.* The Syrian grabs the edges of his shield with both hands and slams it into the tribune's chest. Marcus staggers backward. He plants his foot and batters back with his scutum, readying his blade for a cut to the Syrian's throat.

Nicator slides his left hand into his shield. His right hand grabs the dagger from his belt. *Come on, a little closer.*

"Let me have him," cries Caldus, rushing toward the dueling warriors. "I'll cut his fucking balls off!"

Nicator grabs his dagger and trots back several paces. The two legionnaires stalk toward him, their eyes fixed on the Syrian's blade. Nicator shifts his weight to his rear foot, preparing to leap at Marcus.

"Hold on, Caldus! We'll get him!" comes a cry.

The Syrian glances to his right and sees four triarii marching toward him, aiming their twelve-foot spears at him.

Nicator spins about and runs into the press of Syrians retreating into the rear end of the pass. "I'll get the bastard," Caldus tells Marcus, his face flush with excitement.

Marcus yanks at his forearm. "Let him go, Tribune, you won't catch him in that mess. We have to organize the pursuit, before our men get too scattered."

"We should send the cavalry after him," Cyprian replies. "He is a very dangerous man."

"I'd rather they went after Hannibal," Marcus says. "He is the mind behind the throne."

Nicator pushes his way to the base of the foothills. He clambers onto a boulder embedded in the hillside, intent on rallying his men. "Halt!" he screams, blood streaming from his arm cut. "Reform ranks! Halt! Do you hear me?"

The Syrians rush on, trampling each other in their haste to escape. *Cowards!* He shakes his head in frustration. *This battle is lost, I've got to find the king.*

Four Roman cavalryman ride by beneath him, slashing at the fleeing phalangites. Nicator throws down his shield. He springs onto the back of the last horse, grasping its rider about the middle. With a quick swipe of his jagged dagger, he saws through the Roman's jugular and pitches him off the horse. Nicator steers the horse through the fleeing Syrians, screaming for them to get out of his way.

The Syrian captain comes to the spot where Antiochus and Hannibal last stood. He scans the Syrians fleeing past him, noticing that none of Antiochus' royal guard are among them. *He's run for Elatia, or Chalcis.*

Nicator spots Baebius' dust-grimed head lying on the ground near him. He slides off his horse and picks the head up by bloodied hair, ready to stuff it into his saddle sack. He pauses. *Best to leave them a reminder.*

Nicator grabs a fallen javelin and shoves its butt end into the ground. He grasps the legate's head by the ears. With an audible crunch, the Syrian jams the head onto the spearhead. He puts heels to his horse and gallops into the side of the foothills, heading toward Elatia.

A half hour later, General Glabrio trots up to the spot Nicator vacated. A centurion stands next to the spear holding Baebius' head.

"I thought you should see this before we took him down," says the middle-aged soldier, his voice breaking. "You go tell the Senate, tell them what they did to him. Don't let them get away with this."

The young consul eases off his horse. He walks to the centurion and lays his hand onto the back of his neck. "This is just our first encounter. We will have our chance to revenge him."

Glabrio's cavalry commander pulls up next to him. "The elephants have jammed up the other end of the pass, but we'll get them out soon. When we do, should we go after the remains of his army?"

Glabrio looks to his left. He sees scores of Syrians swimming into the Gulf of Malian, their armor scattered across the shore. To his right, hordes of weaponless Syrians swarm into the pass' foothills, scattered in every direction.

"They are broken," he answers. "We only have a few more hours of daylight. We'll resume the hunt tomorrow."

Glabrio glances at Baebius' skull. His eyes take on a vengeful light. "Take a week's supplies with you tomorrow. Get as many of them as you can."

"It will be my pleasure." The cavalry leader turns his horse about and rides into the pass.

Cato marches up to Glabrio, his armor spattered with blood. He nods toward the corpse-strewn passage leading down to the Roman camp. "There's five, maybe six thousand Syrians dead there, to go with all the Aetolians we wiped out on the mountain. His army's gone. What next?"

Glabrio stretches out his arms, easing the tensions of battle from his shoulders. A great weariness comes upon him. "We celebrate tonight, then we rest. At week's end we start reclaiming the towns that went over to Antiochus. Most will capitulate without a fight."

"If they don't we'll burn them down," Cato says. "You do that once or twice, and you won't have any trouble with the rest!" He gazes up into the mountains above the Syrian camp. "Antiochus is still out there, with that cursed Hannibal."

"He'll have to return to Chalcis—it's his base of operations. We'll head there, but we have dozens of territories to reclaim before we do." He grins wearily at Cato. "Perhaps Philip will be feeling better, so he can help us."

Cato snorts. "Philip! I wager his stomach problem was that he had no stomach for a fight! I trust a Macedonian as much as I trust an Aetolian."

The consul remounts his horse. "Come on, I've got to sound the recall. If we leave our men here, they'll spend all night pillaging." He rides down Thermopylae Pass, searching for his cornicen.

ROMAN CAMP, THERMOPYLAE PASS. It is midnight, but the camp still echoes with songs of drunken revelry. Lucius Scipio enters Glabrio's tent, summoned by the consul's messenger. Glabrio is sprawled upon his sleeping pallet, his eyes puffy from interrupted sleep. Lucius pulls up a stool, warily eyeing him.

Glabrio yawns. "Apologies. I have only had an hour's sleep. Wanted to finish my duties before the night is over." He sniffs, grabs a linen scrap, and blows his nose. "I hate all this dust! How can it be so dusty near a swamp? Anyway, I need you to go back to Rome and report our victory to the Senate."[cxxx]

"A victory in which I had little part," Lucius replies testily.

"You were in charge of our reserves, Lucius. It just happens that we did not need them."

He shakes Lucius' shoulder. "Come on, be a good soldier! I need someone with prestige to relay the details of our victory. The quaestor can give you an estimate of all the plunder we gathered. When you tell the Senate what we're bringing back for them, they will look upon you as a hero."

Lucius feels a surge of eagerness to go home, followed by the shame that he is so eager to do it. "Whatever you command, Consul." He stalks from the tent.

As the tent flaps close, Glabrio falls back upon his padded bed. *There!*

*He's been in a battle. I've kept my promise to Scipio.*

Glabrio drapes his arm across his eyes. He heaves a deep, satisfied, sigh. *Come to me, Hypnos*, he beseeches the god of sleep. *Take me to your kingdom.* Glabrio's prayers are soon answered. The tent echoes with his snores.

The next morning, Glabrio hosts a victory breakfast with Flaccus, Cato, and Marcus. As they dip their bread into the watered wine bowl, Flaccus leans toward Glabrio's ear. "Where is Lucius?" he asks. He chuckles. "Did he run away when the battle started?"

"Last night I asked him to go to Rome and report the news of our victory. He may have left already."

Glabrio's three officers look at each other. "He may not be the most reliable person to do that," Cato says. "Lucius may play up his own part to the disadvantage of others—including yourself."

"I heard he wants to run for consul this year," Flaccus adds. "And candidates do lean toward self-aggrandizement, consul."

Cato feels a stab of alarm. *Flaccus is going to volunteer to go back. He'd be just as bad*! "I can go to Rome. My work is done here."

Glabrio grins, relieved. "Agreed. Best the Senate hears it from a reliable authority.[cxxxi] They know your morals are irreproachable."

*Would that were true*, Cato thinks. "I will leave day after tomorrow. After I say farewell to my troops."

"Leave now, or Lucius Scipio will arrive in Rome before you," Flaccus says.

Cato shakes his head. "Lucius is not one to ride all day and into the night. I will be there before him, if I have to sprout wings!" His eyes flare. "Anything to prevent another Scipio from becoming consul."

ROME, 191 BCE. "At that point, after my men descended from the mountain, the Syrians fled their barricade. And Antiochus disappeared into the mountains."

Cato stands in the middle of the Senate floor, relating his account of the Battle of Thermopylae. The senators listen raptly, not believing their ears.

"And you say we only lost a few hundred men?" says Senator Tiberius Gracchus, high priest of Rome. "And they lost thousands?"

"Eight or nine thousand," Cato replies. "We were still counting bodies when I left."

Lucius Scipio stands to one side of Cato, listening to Cato's account. *How did he get here ahead of me?* he fumes. *I left days before he did.*[cxxxii] *Curse him to Hades, I could have been the center of attention.*

Cyprian, the Senate Elder, turns to Lucius. "Senator Lucius Scipio, you have heard Cato's words. Do they have the ring of truth?"

"He has captured the gist of it," Lucius mutters. "As he says, it was an overwhelming victory."

"Cato has related his role in the attack," Cyprian declares. "What was your role in the fight?"

"I directed the sixth legion," Lucius moodily replies. The room quiets, as the senators wait for Lucius to elaborate.

Scipio sits in the front row, smiling encouragingly at his brother. When he hears Lucius' terse reply, the First Man of Rome grows anxious. *They're going to ask him what he did with the sixth legion, and he'll have to admit he did nothing. He'll waste my efforts to get him over there.*

Scipio stands and sweeps out his arms. "Need we hear any more? It was a glorious victory! I would like to applaud our two Senators for their valuable service to Rome—and to our Greek amici!"

The senators clap the flats of their hands together. The stone chamber echoes with the sound of their approval. Cato stands stolidly, his face expressionless. Lucius raises his chin high, a beatific smile on his face.

Cyprian pounds his oak staff of office upon the floor. "We thank Lucius and Cato for their efforts. I motion that we have them give their account to the People's Assembly, followed by three days of public thanksgiving!"[cxxxiii] The Senate roars its approval, and the Leader closes the meeting.

As the elated patricians file out, Cato watches a handful of senators congratulating Lucius. Cato resists the urge to spit on the floor. *You did nothing to reap our victory, yet you stand there enjoying its fruits, grinning like a shit-eating monkey.* He watches Scipio lead more senators toward Lucius. *Your brother engineered all of this.*

Cato takes a deep breath and lets it out. *No matter. Now I can get back to my farm and get my hands into the earth. Away from the pandering and lies.*

Scipio and Lucius trip down the Senate steps, pausing to accept more congratulations. When they step onto the Forum's broad avenue, Scipio pulls Lucius aside.

"You have to run for consul now," he urges. "This is your best opportunity. Your name is linked with to the victory at Thermopylae. Laelius will run as the plebian candidate, and you as the patrician nominee."

"I'm not sure I'm ready," Lucius says. "That Glabrio, he does not like me. He gave Cato and Flaccus better assignments than me—Flaccus, of all people!"

"You led a legion into battle against Antiochus, that is all the people need to know. One of the new consuls will have to lead our legions against him. You will be an appealing candidate because you've fought him, don't you see?"

"But what about Glabrio?"

Scipio's eyes darken. "I will take care of him. You and Laelius just have to get ready. We are going to give Rome a campaign they will never forget!"

ROMAN CAMP, THERMOPYLAE, 191 BCE. "King Philip of Macedonia is here to see you," announces Glabrio's captain of the guard.

The consul looks up from his charts of the Malian Gulf territory. "King Philip, eh? Did he say what he wants?"

"Something about an apology. And a plan."

"Hmph. Let him in." Glabrio bends over his charts, his lips pursed with irritation.

Philip strides into the tent, brushing the dust off his black riding breeches. He wears neither crown nor jewels, appearing before Glabrio as a plainly dressed rider. A black silk knapsack dangles heavily from his back.

Philip bows with a flourish. "General Glabrio. I have come to congratulate you on your victory. And to apologize for my untimely illness."[cxxxiv]

"Yes, most unfortunate it happened right before our battle," Glabrio mutters, his eyes on a chart of the Aegean.

"This is a token of my heartfelt apologies." Philip slings the knapsack off his back and reaches into it. "This has been in my family since the time of Alexander the Great."

The young consul stares at the knapsack, attracted by the glint of gold from within it.

Philip extracts a foot-high gold crown, its points encrusted with rubies and emeralds. He holds it out to Glabrio. "Consider it a gift, a symbol of your victory over Antiochus." He smiles ingratiatingly. "I needed to get it off my head. The thing weighs as much as an ox!"

Glabrio takes the crown in his hands. He hefts it. Philip smiles encouragingly at him.

"I cannot accept bribes or remunerations," Glabrio mutters, fondling the base of the crown.

"This is a personal gift. A gift from your cherished ally, who deeply regrets his could not join you in battle." He arches an eyebrow. "I would be greatly offended if you rejected it."

"Hmm." Glabrio says.

The consul lays the crown upon his chair. He flips his cape over it. "Gratitude for your gift. Think no more of your absence. The pass was so narrow, I am not sure we would have found room to deploy your men, anyway."

"You are as gracious as you are wise, General," Philip says, staring through slitted eyes. "Still, my absence stings my heart. I am ready to help you take back the rest of the region. I offer a simple plan."

*Now he wants to fight, after all the fighting is settled.* "Which is what?"

"As you know, my treaty with Rome forbids me from having a large army. I have barely enough men to defend what's left of my kingdom! But you, you have a mighty force, one that emerged unscathed from Thermopylae. I propose that we divide our forces so that we can regain Thrace, Thessaly, and the rest of Northern Greece."

"And how to we do that?"

"Let me take on the small towns and garrisons, while Rome takes over the main ones, the fortresses that are too strong for me. I have enough men to garrison those small ones, but I wouldn't have enough for the major cities. I'd lose half my army if I tried!"

Glabrio's lips tighten. "Well, we were going to besiege the mountain fortress of Heraclea next. It's one of Aetolia's major fortresses." [cxxxv]

"That makes sense," Philip says. "I could move on Lamia.[cxxxvi] It's smaller, and on level ground. More suited to my tactic of digging under the walls. You Romans, you favor going over them. Your tactics suit Heraclea."

He edges closer to Glabrio. "You take the big ones, and I take the small ones—what could be simpler?" He leans closer. "You know you don't have the time to get to all of them."

Glabrio's glances back toward the shrouded crown. His face becomes stern. "It is decided. You start with Lamia, then take Demetrias and the ones around Dolopia. I will march on Heraclea and then Naupactus."

Philip's right fist taps his chest. "As you command, Consul. I will muster my forces immediately."

"Good," Glabrio says. He walks to his wicker wine basket and grabs a corked jug. "A glass of wine to seal our agreement."

"A drink to our mutually profitable arrangement," Philip says, grinning broadly.

The Macedonian exits the tent an hour later. His cavalry commander stands waiting for him, holding the braided leather bridle to Philip's black stallion. Philip springs onto his horse. "Let's get back to camp, Niklas. We have a campaign to organize."

The two men trout out from Glabrio's encampment. Forty hetairoi, Philip's elite cavalry, follow behind them. Niklas turns to Philip. "So, did he buy it?" he asks, grinning.

Philip nods. "Completely. I gave the boy that old crown we looted from Thebes, told him it was a family treasure. It was easy then. He was more than willing to take on Heraclea and Naupactus."

Niklas chuckles. "He'll spend a year trying to break into Heraclea."

"And while he does, we stock a dozen garrisons with our men. The towns surrounding them will capitulate, and we'll own all the territories."

Philip grins at his commander. "That's what I like about Romans. They are willing to tackle the most difficult obstacles!"

**Hannibal the Great**

# VII. THE SCIPIOS AT WAR

CHALCIS, 191 BCE. “Look at that, the gates are wide open,” Hannibal says to Antiochus.

“And why not?” the king morosely replies. “The Romans are far away, and my bedraggled force poses little threat to them.”

The king snaps the bridle on his exhausted mount, and trots slowly into the fortress. The remnants of Antiochus’ army file in behind him, five hundred survivors of Thermopylae.[cxxxvii]

“I will be with you in a bit,” Hannibal says. He gallops north of the city, riding to a hillock overlooking a narrow channel of water that leads to the Aegean. His emerald eye evaluates the calmness of the strait, the movement of the cottony clouds that drift across the azure autumn sky.

He inhales deeply and slowly lets it out, releasing a lingering sigh of resignation. *He lost, and he lost his army. We have to leave Greece before the winter storms come upon us—before Glabrio arrives.*

Hannibal looks back toward the city, watching the last of Antiochus’ phalangites tramp inside. His hand clenches into a fist. *I can’t let him lie around all day with that girl—he’ll get us both on crosses.* He turns his horse around and trots toward the city gates, his mind awhirl with his latest plan.

Two hours later, Antiochus sits in his throne room, draped in a gold-hemmed black toga. His bride Clea sits at his feet, slumped against his legs.

Cleoptolemus stands to the side of the king. The city magistrate anxiously shifts his weight from one foot to another, ready to react to Antiochus’ slightest whim.

Antiochus sits, chin in hand, pondering his next move. "I should have put my own men on that mountain," he says to no one in particular. "Fucking Aetolians."

"That breeze has blown," says Hannibal marching into the room. "The question is: what do we do now? Winter approaches, but not so soon that it will stop the Romans from coming after you. You have to get back to Syria."

"Soon enough, soon enough," the king says, waving his hand. He runs his jeweled fingers across Clea's veiled bosom. "I need a few days of relaxation."

*Which you will turn into weeks of sex and opium,* Hannibal thinks. As Antiochus caresses Clea's breasts, her lips wrinkle into faint lines of disgust. Hannibal smiles. *There's the lever to pry him from his bed.*

The next afternoon finds a cloaked Hannibal wandering through the slave market near Chalcis' busy port. He walks past several dingy wine bars, examining their roughshod patrons.

Hannibal stops at a mud brick house filled with men lolling about the weedy grounds in front of it. The men pass around a large jug of wine, guzzling its contents. Six young women sprawl across the wooden plank porch, each clad in stained, gauzy gowns.

A man rises from his spot and walks toward one of the women. The woman takes his hand and leads him inside.[cxxxviii] The drinkers hoot and laugh.

A stout, bald-headed man sits at a circular table on the lawn. He rolls dice from an empty drinking cup, cursing profusely after each throw. The men around the table lean toward him, attentive to his every move.

There is a scream. A woman rushes out from the house and leans into the bald man's ear, whispering urgently. The man shakes his egg-shaped head. He shoves her back toward the house, cursing at her as she scurries inside. He leans toward the men at the table and says something in a low voice. The men laugh loudly.

*That's the leader*, Hannibal decides. He watches the man until he catches the house leader's eye.

The leader notices the stranger's silk eye patch, manicured beard, and thick gold earring.

"Hera's cunt, it's him!" the bald man blurts. His associates stare dumbly at him. He rises from the table and lumbers over to Hannibal.

"This is indeed an honor," the man gushes. "Please come in and sample my wares. I promise you the finest woman in the city!"

"I have need of a service," Hannibal says. "Is there a place where we can talk?"

"Come," the man rasps. Hannibal follows him across the lawn and into the house. The two enter a corridor of curtained rooms that resound with moans and cries. The bearlike man opens a door and waves Hannibal inside.

"What can I provide you, General?" the brothel owner says.

Hannibal steps back a pace, withdrawing from the his fetid breath. "I have need of a man, a slippery man, a man who can scale walls and roofs. A man skilled in using the tube."

"That is quite a lot to ask." He raises his head and grins. "I can get such a man, if you have the money. He is not far from here."

"Bring him," Hannibal says. "I have need of his services immediately."

"He'll be here in a moment!" The man steps into the hallway, and looks back at Hannibal. "I hope this has something to do with getting rid of that fucking Antiochus," he growls. "All this fighting has been bad for business!"

Late that night, Clea rises from her place next to a snoring Antiochus. She grabs a linen towel and wipes the sweat from her naked body, grimacing at her husband's mole-spotted back.

A breeze blows in from the open window. Clea shivers, clutching herself for warmth. *What fool left that window open? Do they think it's summer?*

She stumbles to the wicker basket that holds her robe, and bends over to grab it. Clea hears a faint click above her head, followed by a click on the floor. She looks down and sees a small fly lying motionless at her feet. She notices the bug glistens in the torchlight.

Holding her robe in one hand, she picks it up and examines it. She sees it is not a fly, but a small, feathered dart.

"Ow!"

Clea jerks upright, feeling a sharp prick in her side. She pulls out a fly-shaped dart. A drop of her blood drips from its tip.

Clea crumples to her knees. She grasps the edge of a nearby stool, and topples sideways to the floor. As she lays there, gasping, she sees a spidery figure crawl in from the open window, almost invisible in dark grey pants and tunic. The figure clutches a skein of rope and a long, wooden dart tube.

The invader unfolds a dark blue bag and hurries toward her. Clea opens her mouth to cry out, but no words can escape her. She feels ropes tightening about her ankles. The bag is pulled over her head, and night descends upon her.

Clea wakes to the sound of roaring surf. She touches her chest and loins, feeling the rasp of a rough wool robe. *Who put this one me?*

The girl props herself up and rubs the bag's lint out of her eyes. She sees a wide strand of empty beach, its shore lined with rows of gently swaying sea oats. A single bireme bobs at anchor a few yards from shore. Three men stand on board, watching her.

"I was wondering when you would wake up. That poison is only supposed to last a few hours."

Clea turns. A slim woman sits on a moss-dappled boulder, clad in charcoal pants and tunic. She nods at Clea.

"Where am I?" Clea blurts. "Who are you?"

The woman grins. "I have no family name any more, but you can call me Nyx, after the goddess of the night." She flips her cascading raven hair over her shoulder, her bright teeth flashing in a gamin smile. "Where are you, you ask? Why, you are on your way out!"

"Out? Out to where?"

Nyx laughs. "Anywhere you want—as long as it's Athens!" She jerks up her hands. "Do you grasp what I'm saying? You are taking a trip!"

Nyx tosses a bulging goatskin purse at Clea feet. "That is enough to keep you entertained for several months, even at Athens' prices! Now come on, it's time to set sail. We want to get you out of here before your husband sends a search party."

Clea pushes herself upright, wobbling on her feet. "I'm not going anywhere," she sobs angrily. "This is my home!"

Nyx pulls out a long, slim dagger and waggles it at Clea. "Look here. You are lucky to be alive at all. The man who hired me cares enough to have you kidnapped instead of killed. He just wants you gone until your husband leaves for Syria."

Nyx rubs her cheek with the flat of her dagger blade, smiling seductively at Clea. "I hate to harm women, but I *will* kill you, unless you get on that boat!"

Clea remembers the touch of Antiochus' clammy, grasping, hands—of his rapacious lips upon her. She recalls the young men she played with just a few months ago, innocent boys with sparkling eyes and slim, firm bodies. Boys who delighted—as did she—in the simple pleasures of wine, bread, and sea. *This is your last chance*, she realizes. *If you don't, you'll end up with him forever.*

The girl fingers the hem of her simple robe. "I hear Athens is magnificent. As great as Rome."

Nyx sniffs disdainfully. "Rome? That pig farm? Athens is twice as beautiful, and ten times as cultured! Your beauty will take you far there. Men will crawl at your feet!" She nods toward the bireme. "Now get your ass on that boat!"

"How do I know you won't kill me and throw me overboard?"

Nyx chuckles. "The man who hired me was clear about what would happen to me and my crew if you didn't appear in Athens." She grins. "Believe me, girl. He is not a man I would want to betray."

Clea rises slowly. She raises her head, mustering the remains of her dignity, and strides toward the bireme. Nyx walks behind her, scanning the sea oats for hidden intruders. They climb into the boat. The three crewmen grab oars and push the bireme out into the emerald shallows, releasing its sails to the welcoming wind.

Clea watches the shore fade from sight. She opens the sack at their feet and tugs at the bulging purse inside it, hearing it jingle. Her eyes widen.

Nyx grins. "He has been most generous with you. Perhaps you remind him of someone he knew, in a place far away."

Clea nods. She looks back to the thread of shoreline. "Tell him I am grateful he has saved me from my golden cage. But I have a question?"

"Which is?" Nyx says.

"Do I have to come back?"

Nyx laughs.

The next day dawns bright and clear. Hannibal sits at a marble table near the palace kitchen, dining on figs and barley bread. He relives the times he would rise among his Carthaginian soldiers and break bread with them, chatting before he led them to another victory over the Romans.

For the twentieth time, he reflects on the strength of Antiochus' vast troops and resources, wondering if they can defeat the Romans. He scowls.

"Clea! Where is Clea!" Antiochus rushes down the palace steps, his silk gown billowing behind his naked body. A dozen guards hurry after him. They scatter through the hallway, searching every nook of the palace.

"My wife has disappeared!" Antiochus blurts. "I've looked all over for her!"

Hannibal dips his crusty bread into a bowl of watered wine. He bites into it, chewing slowly. "I am distressed to hear that, King. But girls are as capricious as the Aegean winds." He pops a fig into his mouth. "She may have run away."

Antiochus stares at him. He sweeps his arms about his palace. "Run away from all of this? Ungrateful bitch! I'll send out search parties. I'll comb every field until I find her. And when I do…"

Hannibal shrugs. "She likely ran to one of the cities taken by the Romans, so what good would it do to go looking for her? I am sorry for your loss, but our time would be better spent preparing to cross into Asia."

Antiochus is quiet. "I'll search the city. If she's not here, then we will go. There will be nothing to keep me here."

"Whatever you say," Hannibal says, flipping a fig into his mouth.

Three days later, Antiochus and Hannibal stand on the rainswept Chalcis docks, watching the army's supplies being loaded into transports. A rider gallops in from the roadway, clots of mud flying from his horse's hooves.

"This looks like trouble," Antiochus says. "Guards! Gather to me!" A score of Syrians encircle their king.

Hannibal detects a glint of metal from inside the rider's hood. "He's only trouble if you're a Roman," Hannibal says.

The hooded rider pulls up in front of the guards and leaps off his mount, clutching a muddy burlap bag. He pulls off his hood and genuflects in front of his king, raindrops pattering off his silver mask.

"Apologies for being late," Nicator says. "The Romans were out hunting our men, and I was out hunting them." He upends his soggy sack. Two heads tumble from it, their sightless eyes staring into the clouds.

"This one is a cavalry captain," Nicator says, pointing at a head ringed with auburn curls. He points to the balding head. "This one, he was a squadron commander. He was only a decurion, but he was an officer. Their skulls will make good drinking bowls!"

Antiochus swallows. "Gratitude. I will keep them for future use. The greater gift is that you have returned to me."

Nicator snorts. "Romans can't kill me. I wait in the trees, jump down on them. Kill ten, twelve, maybe more. Then I come here."

"And just in time," Hannibal says. "We are leaving for Ephesus day after tomorrow."

Nicator nods. "That is good. Romans and Macedonians, they take many towns around here. They will be here soon."

"I might as well leave," Antiochus says. "My wife is no longer with me."

"She die?" asks Nicator, trying not to sound hopeful.

"She ran away," Hannibal declares. He and Nicator exchange a look. Nicator gives him the barest of nods.

"Too bad. But good we go now."

"We'll go now, but we will be back," Antiochus says. "This time, I will bring the full fury of my army with me. We will cover Greece with our men and our ships. No more Thermopylaes. This time, we'll be the ones outnumbering them."

NAUPACTUS,[cxxxix] AETOLIA, 191 BCE. *Pushy bastard, making me travel halfway across Greece. I'm going to stick his head in a night pot!* The purple-cloaked rider presses on, his praetorian guard struggling to keep up with him.

General Titus Quinctius Flamininus gallops along the packed earth roadway that borders the indigo waters of the Gulf of Corinth, spurred on by his unrelenting irritation. The former consul is angry at Glabrio and angry at himself. Most of all, he is angry at Scipio, the man who wrote the letter that he carries in his purse.

The missive reached Flamininus in Athens five days ago, as he concluded a peacekeeping meeting with Rome's Greek allies in the Achean League. The words still burn in Flamininus' memory:

*General Titus Quinctius Flamininus:*

*I hesitate to remove you from your valuable work with our amici, but you must attend to a matter of the utmost importance.*

*For two months, Consul Glabrio has encamped his army about Naupactus, laying steady siege to it. In the meantime, Philip of Macedonia has taken a score of towns and garrisons, populating each with its own soldiers. While Glabrio's army lies idle at siege, the Philip has quietly regained much of western Greece. Glabrio must recall him before he gains any more power.*

*You may be reluctant to leave the friendly confines of Athens and make the three-day journey to Naupactus. Just remember, had you not been so eager to withdraw your troops from Greece—a measure that I strongly opposed—this problem would not exist, and you would not have to pursue this task. It is time for you to rectify your mistake.*

*Your friend and former mentor,*

*Publius Scipio Africanus.*

Flamininus spits off the side of his horse. *It's Glabrio's fault. I'm not the one that turned Philip loose to wander across Greece.*

He digs his heels into his horse, urging it faster. *If you think Philip is such a threat, Scipio, why didn't you come over here yourself? No, you're too busy turning the wheels of politics back at Rome.*

The general races into a rubbled chasm, searching its crags for lurking enemies. He soon emerges into the winter-browned plain surrounding the port city of Naupactus, and enters a scene of utter bedlam.

A thick ring of legionnaires encircles the fortress' landside walls, their catapults hurling rocks into its thick limestone walls. Scores of man-sized arrows fly out amidst the boulders, launched by Glabrio's twenty-foot scorpios.

The Aetolians return fire. Dozens of rocks and firepots shoot past the Roman missiles, catapulted from the Aetolians' ramparts. The firepots burst upon men and machine, spewing fingers of flaming oil. Four siege engines lie covered with flames. Screaming soldiers careen through the siege lines, their backs flaming like torches. Others roll madly about the ground, begging their colleagues to fling dirt upon them.

Flamininus slows his horse to a trot, studying the carnage. *He might have won Thermopylae, but he's making a mess of this siege.*

Flamininus dismounts in front of the consul's tent. "Where is General Glabrio?" he asks a sentry. The scar-faced veteran jerks his thumb toward Naupactus' towering walls.

"Over at the front, with the eighth legion," he says.

The general eyes him. "You are a veteran?"

"Twenty years," the guard replies. He raises his chin. "I fought with Scipio in Iberia and Africa. Now there was a general! Best we've ever had." He stares past Flaminius. "He would have taken all of Asia by now. We wouldn't be sitting around this dump-hole, pulling at our dicks."

Flamininus bows his head. "Gratitude, soldier. I wish you health."

The general trots out the camp gate, heading toward a boar's head standard that looms above the soldiers by Naupactus' left wall. He spots Glabrio's flowing purple cloak near the front maniples, and gallops over to him.

Glabrio stands in the midst of the muddy field, shouting orders to his assault team. "Up to the walls! First man on top gets a gold corona muralis!"

Eighty escaladers trot toward Naupactus, their grappling hooks slung over their shoulders. Glabrio stands by a half-built attack tower, conversing with two engineers.

Flamininus dismounts and approaches. "General Glabrio!" He shouts. The consul looks over his shoulder. His eyes widen. "Quinctius Flamininus! Juno's tits, this is a most pleasant surprise! Just a minute."

Glabrio walks over to his army engineers. A flaming pitch-pot crashes a spear's cast from them. Screams erupt from the unfortunates spattered with its burning resin. Unperturbed, Glabrio leans in toward the engineers, shouting over the din.

"I want a ballista mounted on the second and third levels of this thing. We're going roll these towers in and shoot stones right into their faces! And I want it finished day after tomorrow!" Glabrio spins on his heel and marches over to Flamininus. The two embrace heartily.

"You old war dog, it is good to see you! What brings you from central Greece?"

"I was sent here at the behest of Scipio," Flamininus replies. "When the First Man of Rome calls, you listen." He puts his arm on Glabrio's shoulder. "He is concerned about this siege—Rome is concerned about this siege."

"Why? I will be inside Naupactus within the week."

"It's taken you too long," Flamininus replies. "After defeating Antiochus, you have spent all your time attacking two cities, and now your year of command has almost expired. And Philip, who has not had a glimpse of an enemy's battle line, he has attached himself to many of the region's cities!"[cxl]

Glabrio shrugs. "So? He does not have the men to fully occupy them. He only staffs them with a skeleton force."

"And all the while Philip's men convert the city's militias to the Macedonian cause," Flamininus replies. "They become his soldiers, though they are not really a part of his army. So he does not violate his treaty with us." He shakes his head and grins. "A work of genius. Pure, devious, genius."

The young consul flushes. "It sounds to me like old Scipio is meddling where he should not. You are the one who defeated Philip and ended the war. You know the king better than Scipio does!"

"Scipio has the right of it, Glabrio. It is not so important for our cause that the Aetolians' power should be reduced as that Philip should not increase his beyond measure."[cxli]

Glabrio purses his lips. He looks out at the jagged openings in Naupactus' thick walls, openings it has taken him months to make, at the cost of scores of soldiers. "I can't abandon this, I am on the verge of taking it. Besides, what could I do about Philip?"

"Recall him," Flamininus says sternly. "You are the consul, he is yours to command. If he refuses—which he will not—he violates his treaty with us. Rome will order us to wrest him from his throne. He will know that."

"Well, I am not withdrawing from my siege to go chase Philip," Glabrio replies. "What would that look like to my men?"

*His pride clouds his judgment. I'll have to take care of this myself.* "I have a solution. The Aetolians may not love me, but we fought together. What if I got them to surrender to you, would you quit then? We could take the army north to deal with Philip, and take Antiochus' towns ourselves."

Glabrio stretches out his foot. His toe carves wavy lines in the mud. "That would be agreeable," he mutters. "Then I would have accomplished my objective."

*And you will have your little victory over Naupactus.* "Very good. Take your men back to camp. Leave the siege engines here, so that the Aetolians understand you are only giving them a respite. I will go out tomorrow and settle this thing."

The next day dawns on an empty battlefield, save for a single rider. Flamininus approaches the gates of Naupactus and dismounts. He cradles his helmet in his arm and strides along the base of the ravaged walls,[cxlii] weaving his way between the boulders and bodies. The Aetolians watch from the ramparts, captivated at the sight of a lone commander risking his life.

As he walks, Flamininus gazes up at the walls, his heart hammering with fear. *Come on, someone say something!* Long minutes roll by. Flamininus continues his march, sweat trickling down his forehead.

A voice rings out above him, saying the words he has been hoping for. "General Flamininus! Is that you? "

Flamininus squints into the sunlight above him. "It is I. Who addresses me?"

"Phaeneas, magistrate of Heracles. I fought with you at the Aous River."

The general grins up at him. "We tasted victory that day, didn't we?"

"Ran old Philip up into the mountains, we did!" comes the reply. "Your presence is a welcome sight!"

"General Flamininus is here!" shouts a soldier near Phaeneas. Flamininus hears the cry relayed across the wall.

Scores of townspeople appear along the top of the wall. Hundreds more soon join them. Women, children, and elders reach out from the ramparts. Their cries cascade upon him, scores of voices beseeching him to save them.[cxliii]

"Quiet!" Phaeneas bellows. His soldiers move through the crowd, shoving the townspeople to silence. A burly spearman leans over the walls. "You can see how it is. General. We know we cannot defeat you. But we're not going to allow ourselves to get killed like cattle."

"Come out and talk to me," Flamininus says. "Perhaps we can reach a settlement." He walks to the city gates and stands in front of them, arms crossed, eyeing the stern warriors that loom above him.

The foot-thick gates creak open. Phaeneas walks out, accompanied by six white-haired men. The elders prostrate themselves in front of Flamininus, their faces buried in the moist trampled earth.

*Leave them there for a minute*, Flamininus decides. *I want Glabrio to see this.* "I am furious that you Aetolians have turned against us. You, who fought and died next to me, and promised loyalty forever."

"Forgive us," Phaeneas says. "We are under King Thoas' command. Antiochus promised him all of northern Greece!"

"As if that excuses your treachery!" Flaminius snaps. He stands silent, forcing them to listen to his angry breathing. "Two years ago, when I took my armies home, I swore that I would liberate all of Greece. I would just as soon keep my promise and not see you sold into slavery. Will you strike a truce with Glabrio, so you can go plead your case to Rome? Rise and answer me."

The town officials stumble to their feet, brushing the clotted earth from their snow-white togas. They huddle together, muttering among themselves. Phaeneas steps out from the group. He nods solemnly.

Flamininus exhales. "Good. Come to the camp gates tomorrow morning. We will see if we can end this amicably." He walks to his horse and mounts it.

"My army is but two days march from here," he lies. "If you and Glabrio cannot come to a truce, my men will join him. Then I will keep my promise to keep Greece free, because there will be no one left alive here to sell into slavery!"

Six days later, Glabrio and Flamininus ride into Philip's Macedonian camp, a quarter mile from the Phalanna fortress in Thessaly. Two turma of cavalry follow them, their red banners flapping in the early winter winds.

The camp is an acres-wide sprawl of rectangular canvas tents, bordered with improvised stables. Philip's black linen tent dominates the camp center, a mansion among its hut-sized companions.

"Look at his tent—it's larger than my house," Glabrio says.

"Philip was never one to be inconspicuous," Flamininus replies. He grins. "Unless it were to escape Roman detection."

Niklas, Philip's commander, is there to receive the two generals. He leads them near the front of Phalanna's walls, halting near a gaping mineshaft. Philip stands next to a brace of elephants at the mouth of the shaft. Thick ropes dangle from the elephant's trunk-sized shoulders, trailing into the darkened hole behind them.

Philip gapes at the sight of the two Roman generals trotting slowly toward him. *Flamininus and Glabrio!* His body stiffens.

He forces a smile and spreads out his arms. "Welcome, honored consuls. You are just in time—time for the fall of wall!"

Flamininus eyes him coolly. "Phalanna would not surrender? There can't be more than a few Aetolians inside. Or some Syrians."

Philip flaps his bejeweled hands. "Stubborn little bastards wouldn't give up to anyone but Romans. I *told* them I was your designate, but they just wouldn't listen." He spreads his hands, his expression doleful. "So I had to take drastic action."

"We are here now," Glabrio declares. "Let me talk to them."

"Certainly," Philip says stiffly. "But why waste a good mine shaft? Here's something that should smooth your negotiations."

Before the generals can reply, Philip jerks down his hand. "Pull!" he shouts. The elephants' mahouts slap their guide poles into the sides of the two elephants. The beasts surge forward. The thick ropes tighten, stiff as iron. The mahouts jab the elephants' shoulders with their barbed poles. The beasts dig their table-sized feet into the earth, trumpeting with effort.

A loud creaking emanates from the tunnel, followed by splintering crashes. As Glabrio and Flamininus watch in amazement, a gaping hole appears beneath Phalanna's front wall. The base of the wall topples into the breach, its ramparts cascading into the plain. The wall defenders plummet into the wreckage, crushed by the falling rubble.

Philip claps his hands. "I love undermining an enemy's walls! You ruin their defenses without losing a man." He eyes the Romans, his eyes mischievous. "Better than the way *you* do it, scrambling about with your ladders and catapults."

Flamininus' mouth tightens. *Yes, you are quite good at undermining people.* "It is good you mentioned defense. That is why we're here." He nods at Glabrio, a command in his eyes.

Glabrio steps closer to Philip, his face flush with embarrassment. "Your mission is ended. My army will assume the defense of central and eastern Greece." He looks away from Philip. "I have orders from Rome. They request you return to your capital."

"I think you should reconsider, Consul Glabrio. You will be leaving soon. Who will assume the duties of protecting Greece?"

*I am more worried about protecting it from you,* Flamininus thinks. "The consular elections are coming early this year, King Philip. A new army will soon arrive." He stares at his former enemy. "I will maintain order until then. And our ships will patrol the coast."

"What if Antiochus should come back?" Philip retorts. "In two months he could be halfway across Greece!"

Flamininus smiles. "Antiochus is still at Ephesus. He will not be here for a while, if at all. And when he comes, our new consul will be ready for him." He grimaces. "Whomever it may be."

The two generals, ride back toward their men. Flamininus leans sideways toward Glabrio. "What will you do now?"

"I'll establish control of the operations here, leave a couple of cohorts with one of my legates. Then I will take the rest of my army to Rome."

His eyes light with excitement. "Flamininus, I am going to request a triumph for my men, for all they achieved. If Fortuna smiles upon me, they will get it."

Flamininus chuckles. "You had best hope Scipio smiles upon you. He is the god that rules over Rome."

TEMPLE OF JUPITER OPTIMUS MAXIMUS, ROME, 191 BCE. General Marcus Acilius Glabrio rubs tears from the corners of his eyes. *Gods, this dye is killing me. Did they really have to paint my face red?* He wears the gold-hemmed purple toga of a general celebrating his triumph, a laurel wreath set upon his painted brow.

Two white oxen lie on a burning pyre at the entrance to the temple of Jupiter, their throats slit by Tiberius Gracchus, the high priest. Hundreds of senators crowd the temple steps beneath the entryway, there to conclude Glabrio's three-day triumph. Many of them smile as they watch the dark smoke billow into the sky. The smoke flows straight up, a sign that the gods are pleased.

Scipio stands next to the consul. He holds a leather thong necklace with a gold figurine of Jupiter grasping three thunderbolts. He drapes the necklace over Glabrio's bowed head.

"Like Hercules, you have labored selflessly for the benefit of man," Scipio intones. "We declare you a friend to the gods." The senators applaud, energetically snapping their fingers. Dozens shout Glabrio's name. Scipio steps away from the entrance of the temple, letting Glabrio have his moment of glory.

When the applause dies, Scipio returns to the consul's side. "Do not forget, fellow senators. We conclude Glabrio's triumph tomorrow at the Circus Maximus games. I trust you all will attend."

Tiberius Gracchus offers a concluding prayer. The senators descend the lengthy steps, heading for one of the many private feasts being held in Glabrio's honor. The senators' guards barge through the thousands of plebians that jam the Forum, leading the patricians to their carriages.

Glabrio appears at the top of the steps, his arms spread toward the people. The citizens of Rome roar his name. They push against the guards blocking the lower temple steps, their arms outstretched toward their latest hero. The guards ram their shields into them, knocking scores of them sprawling. The angry plebians surge into the guards, pushing them backwards.

*Vulcan's balls, they're going to attack me!* Glabrio thinks. With a final wave, he hurries back into the temple and slams shut its doors.

Scipio stands beneath the thirty-foot statue of Jupiter, resting his hand on the thick marble slab that supports it. He catches the eye of Tiberius Gracchus, and gives him the barest of nods.

"Go with the gods," the priest says to Glabrio. He disappears behind the statue. A rear door booms shut.

Glabrio approaches Scipio, his face wary.

A wry smile twists Scipio's lips. "Honors to you, General. You are a god in the people's eyes."

The young consul takes a deep breath. "I must thank you for getting me elected. None of this would have happened without you."

"You should also thank me for getting Flamininus to drag you from that siege," Scipio snaps. "You would have driven off one enemy only to hand the region to another. Philip is not to be trusted."

"I would have taken Naupactus and Heraclea in another couple of days," Glabrio declares. "Anyway, I thank you for paying for the upcoming games. I do not yet have the coin for it, but I will repay you."

Scipio waves his hand. "It cost me dear, but it was worth it. And you will certainly repay me! I need you to publicly endorse our Hellenic candidates."

"Laelius? He is a warrior and leader. I will be glad to speak out for him at the games."

"And Lucius?" Scipio says.

The room becomes silent. "No." Glabrio blurts. "He cannot be trusted to lead an army. What if he drew the lot to go to Greece, and Antiochus came back? The Syrians would destroy him. No, not even if you put me on a cross."

"You owe this to the party that got you elected, General," Scipio growls. "You owe it to me."

"I have a greater debt to Rome," Glabrio replies. He glares disdainfully at Scipio. "I am now the First Man of Rome. The wealthy geese will now flock to me, seeking favors. I will repay you soon—with money."

Scipio bites his lip. *I hate having to do this, but this may be Lucius' last chance.*

"Do you know why I pushed you to run for consul?" Scipio says. "Part of it was that you are ambitious, clever, and headstrong. I knew you would make a good leader."

"Good enough to make up my own mind," Glabrio retorts.

Scipio stares into Glabrio's haughty face. "The other reason was that I knew I could control you."

Glabrio barks out a laugh. "You make overmuch of your influence, Senator Scipio. You might have forced me to abandon my siege, but that is the last time you will ever tell me what to do."

Scipio reaches into his belt pouch. He pulls out the Nike figurine his son Publius carved for his birthday. He rolls the goddess of victory in his fingers, avoiding Glabrio's eyes. "Before I spoke to you about becoming consul, I had several of my army's speculatores talk to a few of your friends. And bend the arms of a few others."

He jerks his head up, his eyes boring into Glabrio's. "Do you know what they found out? Your father's sudden death was not as mysterious as it seems. There were several herbalists you talked to the week before his death. Conversations about poisons that leave no trace."

Glabrio blinks at him. His mouth works, but no words come out.

Scipio chuckles mirthlessly. "Oh, I am not saying you were not justified. A father who abuses his son—in every way imaginable—is worthy of the worst. But you don't want Rome knowing about that, do you?"

"You can prove nothing," Glabrio splutters. His face darkens with rage—and fear.

Scipio shrugs. "I am still Scipio Africanus. The weight of my words still bear weight. And I have freeborn citizens to testify that what I will say is true."

Scipio's cocks his head, his eyes searching Glabrio's. "Do you know the punishment for patricide, young man? Do you really want to risk being sewn inside a bag of snakes and being thrown into the Tiber? Do you want your mother left impoverished? All I ask is a few choice words from you. If you endorse Lucius at the games, and all is repaid."

Tears of frustration roll down Glabrio's cheeks. "Gods curse you, you wheedling snake!"

Scipio stares at Glabrio, waiting.

Glabrio's shoulders quiver. His head falls to his chin, and his wreath tumbles onto the floor. "I'll fucking do it." He flutters his hand at Scipio. "Just leave me alone. Just go. You'll get what you want."

Scipio walks for the temple entrance. He halts, and looks over his shoulder. "You'd better wipe your face, Consul. You have streaked your face paint."

Scipio yanks open the stout temple doors. The crowd's roars wash into the vast chamber, echoing from the walls. Scipio closes them behind him. The room falls silent.

Glabrio rubs his face with the inside of his triumphal toga, staring at the dark red streaks across its lush purple wool. He stares at the closed temple doors, listening to the muffled roars of the crowd.

*I will repay you for this. Cato and I, we will figure out a way.*

LYSIMACHIA FOREST, THRACE. Lying under a pine-shrouded rock shelf, Thrax counts the Syrians marching out from the fortress. His brows furrow with concern. *Almost a hundred this time. Why so many? They must be expecting an attack from a larger force. Someone other than my men.*

For the last two months, Thrax has studied the patrols' comings and goings, trying to figure out their schedule. Now he knows the Syrians venture south along the sea cliffs every second week. Forty cavalry and a hundred infantrymen march through the Bakali Hills and head down the Aegean peninsula, reversing course when they near Gallipolis.

*I've seen enough.* Thrax crawls out from the overhang, plucking the glued leaves off his helmet. "Come on, let's go!" he says to the forest.

The surrounding scrub trees rise from the ground. They reveal themselves as Thracian warriors, their bodies covered with leafy branches.

"Back to camp," Thrax orders. "We've got an ambush to prepare."

Thrax and his men dissolve into the forest, hiking a mile to their tethered horses. They ride back to their mountain hideaway, following a faint animal trail. That night, Thrax convenes with his chieftains. He pulls out his dagger and etches a map into the campfire dirt.

"The Syrians will march through the passage between the Bakali Hills, and follow the Gallipolis road near the cliffs. That's our best chance." Thrax throws a handful of branches into the campfire, watching the flames crackle.

The chieftains shake their heads. "It won't work," replies a gray-haired warrior, waggling a forefinger stub. "Their scouts will be roaming all over those hills. We can't ambush them again."

Thrax nods. "No, we can't ambush them that way. But the Gallipolis road runs by the straits. That gives us another way."

“The sea?” mutters the chieftain. We don’t have any ships—they burned them all. And they’d spot our horses, if we ever got close enough for an attack.”

“We don’t need ships or horses. We need shovels. And a score of polearm fighters. I’ll show them a little trick the Iberians used on me, when I fought with the Romans.”

Two weeks later, the Syrian troops march out on the sea road toward Gallipolis. Captain Madsa eyes the looming hills, well aware that the Thracians always attack from there. He beckons his cavalry leader.

“Asor, I want a dozen scouts on each side of those hills. They should not take the same trails that they did two weeks ago. We can’t fall into a pattern.”

Asor shrugs. “As you say. But we never find anyone. Just a few shepherds.”

“More men die from rashness than caution,” Madsa snaps. “Next week we sail out to rejoin Antiochus at Ephesus. I intend to be alive to get there.”

The Syrian scouts venture out from the roadway, each carrying a warning horn. The riders comb through the low-slung hills, peering into the rangy pines and squat junipers. Madsa halts the infantry, waiting for the scouts’ signal to proceed.

A half hour later, a horn sounds three times. The call is echoes from a dozen horns. Madsa nods, satisfied. “Up and onward,” he says, trotting his horse toward the front of his train.

The Syrians negotiate the mile-long passage without incident. The patrol enters the spacious plain that borders the Hellespont, trekking along the wide dirt road that parallels the deep blue Sea of Helles.

The sun rises high. The day warms. The soldiers grow drowsy, lulled by the roadside’s gently waving stalks of green-gold sea oats.

One by one, the scouts descend from the hills and ride toward the front of the infantry, lining up behind their commander.

Madsa rubs the back of his neck, rolling his head back and forth. *Ishtar take me, I feel like I slept on a rock last night. Should have thrown that girl out of bed after I was done with her.* The scout leader approaches Madsa. He raises his right hand in salutation.

"What news, Babo? Any signs in the hills?" He grins. "Find any comely shepherdesses up there?"

Babo's mouth drops open, his eyes starting with alarm. He yanks out his sword and gallops straight toward Madsa.

"What are you doing?" Madsa bellows.

"Look out!" Babo screams, wheeling his horse to the left. Madsa gapes at the Syrian scout galloping madly toward him, clenching a javelin in a fist snaked with blue tattoos. *It's a Thracian!* Madsa realizes, just as the scout flings his lance.

Thrax's javelin buries itself in Madsa's eye socket, its shaft jutting out from his skull. The commander clutches at his face, his feet kicking madly into his horse. The beast rears. Madsa crashes to the ground, his mouth working soundlessly.

"Thracians!" Babo screams, waving over his cavalry. He hurtles toward Thrax.

Thrax races from the captain, his cheek resting against the neck of his mount. He pulls up at the edge of the seaside roadway and yanks off his helmet. "At them!" he screams into the empty strip of field.

A hundred Thracians rise from the ground, clumps of sea oats falling from the curved wicker shields that covered them. The rebels stampede toward the Syrians, screaming like madmen. A score of them wield the deadly Thracian rhomphaia, six-foot polearms that are half sword and half handle.

The Thracians fling themselves into the Syrian infantry. Ducking and leaping, the unarmored Thracians weave through their slower-moving opponents, jumping in for lightning-quick thrusts. Soon, scores of Syrians lie upon the blood-spattered ground, their torsos furrowed with blade cuts.

Babo waves over his riders. "Get behind them!" he orders. He gallops around the front edge of the fight, his men racing to catch up to him.

The Syrian cavalry loop in behind the Thracians and trample into the preoccupied foot soldiers, jabbing their spears into their backs. A dozen Thracians fall, then six more. The vengeful Syrian infantrymen swarm over their fallen enemies, hacking their blades into any who move.

Thrax gallops to the Thracians wielding the polearms. "Get at the cavalry. You know what to do!" The polearm warriors dash for the Syrian riders, swinging their rhomphaia like scythes.

Thrax weaves through his battling infantrymen, directing them toward the Syrian cavalry. "Onto their backs!" he shouts.

Dozens of Thracians drop their swords and shields. The soldiers leap upon the backs of riders occupied with the polearm fighters. They yank at the Syrians' spear arms, leaving them vulnerable to the polemens' thrusts. Within minutes, a dozen Syrian riders lie dead and wounded.

Thrax pulls on his Syrian helmet. He steers his mount through the milling soldiers and riders, his eyes fixed on Babo's crimson crest. He edges his horse toward the Syrian's back.

A rail-thin Thracian runs toward him, his polearm raised for a killing strike. "Zoltus, it's me!" Thrax hisses.

The young warrior halts. A bright smile gleams from his sand-grimed face. "Apologies. I just wanted me a Syrian head, is all."

Thrax points to his left. "Get at that fat rider over there. But wait for one of ours to jump on his back!"

"He'll be dead in a minute!" Zoltus declares. He stalks toward the Syrian, his rhomphaia cocked for a thrust.

Thrax eases his horse toward Babo. The Syrian leans over his horse and lances a Thracian poleman in the back.

Thrax grimaces. *Get him before he kills anyone else!*

The Thracian digs his heels into his horse. He draws his mount alongside Babo's horse, vaults sideways, and lands on Babo's back. The two crash to the earth. Thrax lands on top of Babo, slamming his face into the earth.

"Eat your blade," Thrax snarls. He twists Babo's sword arm and shoves his own blade into his throat. The Syrian jerks back his head. His mouth gapes in a silent cry. He grasps Thrax's iron forearms, feebly pushing at them.

*He's done*, Thrax decides. The chieftain walks over to the wounded poleman. The Thracian soldier sits on the ground, wrapping a tunic scrap around his chest.

"I need to borrow this, Oxus," Thrax says, grabbing the polearm.

Oxus coughs, spitting out a clot of blood. He grins, his eyes squinted with pain. "Go on, Chief. I won't be needing it for a while."

Thrax walks back to Babo. He hears a thump behind him, and peers over his shoulder. Oxus lies on his side, his eyes glassy. *Go with the gods, warrior.* His mouth sets with determination. *Now I will enjoy this*.

Thrax stoops over the gurgling Syrian. He arcs down the polearm's thick blade. There is a loud crunch. Babo's head rolls sideways, its brown eyes staring sightlessly.

He yanks off Babo's helmet and grasps the head by its dark oiled curls, shaking the gore from its neck stump. Thrax remounts his horse and rides through the fighters, holding his prize high above his head. The Syrians cry out in dismay. Thrax grins.

The dispirited cavalry wheel about and retreat toward Lysimachia, forsaking their infantry. The Thracians surround the remaining Syrians.

Step by step they close upon them, swords drawn.

A half hour later, the eighty-four surviving Thracians step slowly through the field of the dead, looting the Syrian corpses. Several Thracians amuse themselves by tumbling the enemy bodies over the sheer cliffside, watching them dance as they bounce down the rocks.

"Come on," Thrax says. "We have to get back to the hills before they send out more men. Strap the wounded onto the horses."

That night, the raiders busy themselves lugging in armfuls of coins, weapons and armor, piling their plunder in front of the campfire. As the wine flows, some Thracians take turns plucking a helmet from the pile, relating how they killed the man who wore it.

Others joke about a personal items they pull from the plunder: a lock of hair, a carved figurine of a child, a pouch with needle and thread. Several dig out rumpled letters and pretend to read them, much to their compatriots' amusement.

Thrax watches the proceedings from his log at the edge of the fire. The former legionnaire grimaces with distaste. *They are a bunch of heartless bastards. But they fight like demons. If I had ten thousand of them, we'd run Antiochus back to Syria.*

He pitches a dollop of dried horse dung into the fire, watching the sparks dance. *But you don't have ten thousand, so what's next?* He smiles bitterly. *You know what you have to do.*

The next morning, Thrax reveals his plan to his hung-over chieftains. "We are going to ally ourselves with Rome," he says. "They give us the best chance of ridding ourselves of the Syrians."

An auburn-bearded chieftain shoulders his way to the front of the crowd. His bloodshot eyes glare daggers at Thrax. "The Romans are our enemies. Our ancestors have fought them for centuries!"

"True, Abraxos. We have fought them, as we have fought the Athenians, the Scythians, the Macedonians, the Dacians, and the Persians.[cxliv] And anyone else who threatened our lands. But many of these enemies turned into allies, when a common threat emerged. These Syrians are too many for us. I have fought with the Romans, seen their discipline and will. They will not be defeated."

"Perhaps you are a bit too familiar with Rome," Abraxos mutters, looking back at his fellow chieftains. Several nod.

Thrax pulls back the sleeve of his wool undershirt. He points to the black words tattooed on the top of his forearm. *Gaius Acilius Marius.*

"I was a Roman slave, doomed to follow the whims of lesser men. I do not love Romans, but I hate Syrians even more. Rome will be coming here, as sure as I wear their brand. And when they do, we will join them against Antiochus."

ROME, 191 BCE. "Here now, let me show you. You take the tamper and stand directly over the stone. Hit it squarely on the head."

Laelius grasps the tamper's worn oak handle with both hands and braces himself. Shoving it vigorously downward, he pounds a wide, flat river stone into the roadway, snugging it against its fellows. A muscular Roman freeman stands to the side, glumly watching him.

Laelius wipes the dust off his new white tunic, grinning through the sweat that runs down his face. "I love manual labor," he says to the knot of senators watching him. "I'm not afraid to get my hands dirty—in work or politics!" The officials laugh, appreciating the joke's appropriateness from the commoners' candidate for consul.

"That stone is placed perfectly," says Procus, one of Rome's two Tribunes of the Plebs. "You act like you've done this before!" The gray-haired fisherman stands with the patrician senators, watching Laelius work.

Laelius drops another travertine stone onto the new roadway. "That's because I did," Laelius replies. "I worked on these when I was a dock orphan. Worked all day for a hunk of bread and chunk of cheese." He points at the road crews working in front of him. "Just like those poor bastards!"

Four work crews labor in front of Laelius. They work steadily, ignoring the politicians. The crews are on a deadline to complete the new public road to the Port of Ostia. The plebian aedile has promised them each a purse of denarii if they complete it before October's Festival of Wolves.

The first crew lays down the hand-sized boulders that form the road's bedrock, while the second crew fills in the gaps with shovelfuls of pebbles and rubble. The third crew pours in barrow loads of volcanic ash concrete, making for a smooth under layer. The fourth crew pounds in the tight-fitting finishing blocks.[cxlv]

"Your work looks good," Laelius says to the laborers. "Looks like it'll last for a thousand years!"

"Longer than Rome will," snaps one of the freemen, pounding in a rectangular block.

"You never know, Citizen," Laelius says. "Rome could rule the world for a thousand years!" He grins at the Roman officials. "With the right leadership, of course!"

"And you are the right leader!" shouts Scipio, who is standing in the back of the crowd. The senators snap their fingers, applauding Scipio's words.

"Gratitude to you all for coming out," Laelius says, stepping from the nascent roadway. "Just remember, when I am consul we will build these roads to Capua and Napoli. And way up north to Milano!"

"Without raising taxes, of course!" Scipio chimes in, provoking more laughter. Laelius smiles, "Of course. We just have to spend our denarii more wisely." He hands his tamper back to the Gallic slave. "That's enough for now, I'm getting my tunic dirty."

He spreads his arms toward the politicians. "Let us return for the afternoon games. My wife Prima is appearing in them."

"I thought she retired from the ring," Proxus says. "She must be a little rusty."

"You will not be disappointed, Proxus. She has maintained her skills. She fights with me every day, using words instead of swords!"

The city politicians hurry to their horses and carriages, ready to take the three-mile journey back to Rome. Scipio brings over Laelius' toga candida, the chalk-white toga of consular candidates.

"Here, this should warm you from the winter breeze."

Laelius glances at the workers. "I'm fine. The work has warmed me, as it has my fellows over there. They sweat in spite of the chill."

"You are the perfect people's candidate," Scipio says. "You truly believe you are one of them."

"And who else would I be?" Laelius says. "I'm not a patrician. No matter how rich I become, I'll never be one—and I don't want to! Rome needs rulers that are commoners. Men who appreciate the glory of good, honest work."

"Have a care," Scipio says, chuckling. "You are beginning to sound like Cato!"

"Well, Cato is not all wrong," Laelius replies. "He respects the working man. He hates to see Romans lying idle, their jobs replaced by slaves."

"As do I," Scipio says. "You don't have to be a pleb to know that we are becoming a nation of idlers."

"Thank Jupiter for wars," Laelius says. "It gives men something honorable to do."

Scipio grimaces. "If Antiochus invades Greece again, we will all have plenty to do. Now come on, we have to get ready for your appearance."

The two friends enter a waiting carriage. The carriage jounces along the newly paved road, heading back to Rome's Porta Collina entryway. As they ride, Scipio and Laelius share drafts from a skin of watered wine.

“Where’s Lucius, our patrician candidate?” asks Laelius. “He’s only got a few weeks before the election. He’s not hiding in your house again, is he?”

“He’s at the Avenue of Merchants, doing what he does best,” Scipio murmurs. “Shaking arms and making promises.” He nudges Laelius. “Just like you.”

“He’s not like me. *I* keep my promises,” Laelius snaps.

Scipio lowers his eyes.

“Apologies,” Laelius says. He grasps Scipio’s wrist. “I should not have said that. He is your brother.”

Scipio glances out the carriage window, watching the farmers gather their dried sheaves of wheat. “He is my brother, so I know who he is. And who he is not.” He turns to face Laelius. “And he—“

A coughing fit seizes Scipio, interrupting his words. He pulls out a linen scrap and slaps it against his mouth. Laelius pounds him on the back. “Brother, are you all right?”

Scipio’s convulsions subside. He pulls the linen away from his mouth, studying its red blotches. “Ah, you know. The winter brings visits from Febris, goddess of fevers and coughs. She has been particularly persistent this year.”

“And the dreams? She has gifted you with them, too?”

“Ah, such a gift! Night sweats and trembles. But yes, the visions come to me. Always the future, never the past.”

“What do you see?” Laelius asks.

Scipio recalls his dream of Laelius and Lucius fighting over command of an army, while the Syrians sweep down upon them. “Why, I see you both as consuls,” he replies. “With momentous decisions ahead of you.” *And one I will soon have to make.*

Laelius smirks. “Knowing you, you will likely be involved in any decisions we have to make."

Scipio chuckles wearily. "That would be my worst nightmare."

The carriage passes through the Porta Collina and trundles down the Avenue of Merchants. Minutes later, it halts at the Scipio domus. Rufus stands at the doorway, a broad smile splitting his workworn face. He opens of the manse's thick red doors.

"Salve, Laelius, future consul of Rome! I feel your victory in my bones!"

"That's what he said the first time I ran." Laelius whispers.

Scipio smiles. "This time he'll be right. Come on, we have to prepare for the games." Scipio and Laelius pass through the vestibule and enter the sun-washed atrium. Prima and Amelia stand at a table near the fish pond, dabbing chalk dust onto their faces.

"We'll be there is a minute," Amelia says. "We're just making up our faces."

"Making them up into what?" Laelius asks. Prima glares him into silence.

Amelia dips a small horsehair brush into a bowl of red wine finings and carefully brushes it onto her lips. After dabbing charcoal onto her eyebrows, she glances into a tin mirror held by her Indian slave girl.

She scowls at her image. "Well, that will just have to do." Amelia smoothes her emerald green gown over her hips and sticks a silver comb into the front of her auburn hair. She whirls about and faces her husband.

"What do you think?" she says, pulling out the sides of her gown.

Scipio feigns amazement. "You are Aphrodite come to earth!"

"Curse you," Laelius says. "I was going to say that."

"Then you had best think of something else for me—something

better," Prima growls.

"Words cannot describe your beauty," Laelius says, sweeping out his hands as he bows.

Prima sniffs. "That is the best you can do? I think I'll vote for one of the Latin candidates." She waves over the slave. "Come here and tie me up."

Prima's attendant pulls at the back straps of Prima's floor-length crimson dress, drawing them tight against her sinewy back. "Have a care," Prima says. "I want to breathe."

The gladiatrix yanks up the plunging neckline of her gown, waggling her breasts sideways. "That's better. All this fuss, and I'll have to take it off halfway through the games."

"You'd best wait to get naked until you are inside the gladiator cells," Scipio chirps. "We don't want you drawing attention from our candidates."

"I wouldn't mind a little less attention," remarks Lucius. Scipio's brother sits on a padded stool in the corner, his chin resting on his hand. Ursus, the family dog, rests his pot-sized head upon the hem of Lucius' bright white toga. Lucius pets him. "I'd rather stay here with Ursus. We'll keep an eye on the place."

*Juno give me patience!* Scipio thinks. "Come on, you need the exposure. Glabrio is going raise your hand."

"I know, Big Brother," Lucius replies. "I was just kidding."

An hour later, Scipio, Lucius, Laelius, Amelia, and Prima ride a gilded four-horse carriage to the arched entryway of the enormous Circus Maximus. A gold-tuniced piper helps them down from their ornately carved vehicle, one of the musicians Scipio hired to lead the entry procession. General Glabrio stands waiting for them, resplendent in a gold-hemmed purple toga. A large cadre of senators encircles him, eager to be seen with Rome's latest hero.

Scipio approaches Glabrio, smiling broadly. As the two shake forearms, Scipio leans in next to him.

"You know what to do, right?" Scipio says. "A word of endorsement, then you raise our candidates' arms."

Glabrio flushes. He sets his chin. "Look, I don't mind being seen with them, but I'm not going to—"

Scipio's grip tightens. "Must I remind you that former Senator Postus Novus is going to be a special participant in these games? Would you like to join him?"

Glabrio grimaces. He looks away from Scipio, gazing at the Circus' forty-foot walls. "It will be done," he mutters, "and then I am done with you." Glabrio stalks back to his admirers.

The trumpets sound the start of the game's entry procession. A dozen pipers prance through the Circus portal, welcomed by the cheers of fifty thousand Romans. They are followed by six of Scipio's African Campaign elephants, each caparisoned with a red blanket bearing a gold, spread-wing eagle. Ten chariots follow, the drivers waving enthusiastically at the crowd.

The gladiators march in, ten each from the schools of Murmus and Capitolus. At the sight of their favorites, the crowd's roars reach deafening heights. The warriors raise their swords and tridents, glorying in what may be their last hours on earth.

The Scipio entourage strolls through the entryway, led by Laelius and Lucius. The group moves up the stone steps to the dais set in the center of the oblong stadium. As sponsor of the games, Scipio assumes the high center chair, flanked by Glabrio and Amelia. Lucius and Laelius sit directly below Scipio, their chalk-white togas glowing in the bright winter sun.

Cato and Flaccus sit on benches three rows behind Scipio, occupying two of the purple-cushioned seats assigned to former consuls. Dozens of Latin senators encircle Cato and Flaccus, their faces sullen. The Latins know that their presence lends credence to Scipio's event, but they also know that the crowd must see them attending it.

Tiberius Gracchus steps to a small altar ten rows down from Scipio. The high priest of Rome spreads out his arms. "Gods and goddesses, we ask that you bless these games!" he shouts. The crowd hushes.

Two red-tuniced attendants raise a white sheep onto the altar, gently removing its two rose garlands. Gracchus raises his eight-inch sacrificial knife, clutching it with both hands. The knife flashes down. There is a single, mournful bleat.

Tiberius opens the sheep's vitals, carefully examining the globes of its liver. He lays down his dripping knife and raises his arms to Olympus, signaling that the gods have approved the games—as they always do.

The crowd cheers with relief. When the cheers have lowered to murmurs, the cornu sound the commencement of the games. Scipio rises.

"I declare these games in honor of General Glabrio's glorious victory at Thermopylae," he declares. Glabrio stands, head held high. Cheers wash over him as he waves his hands and smiles.

Scipio nudges Glabrio. "Go on."

Glabrio grits his teeth. He steps in front of Lucius and Laelius and raises their hands. The crowd cheers madly. The surrounding senators watch Glabrio carefully, waiting for him to speak the crucial words.

The consul takes a deep breath. "I, Marcus Acilius Glabrio, consul and general of Rome, hereby endorse Gaius Laelius and Lucius Cornelius Scipio to be the next consuls of Rome!"

Scores of Hellenic senators jump up and cheer, accompanied by the hisses of a dozen Latins. "You shame yourself, Glabrio," Cato barks. The consul's face reddens.

Scipio pats Glabrio's arm. "Ignore him. Their candidates would have us all barefoot again, living in farmer's huts. Who is the bigger fool?"

The cornu sound again. The two-man chariots line up in front of Scipio. A single horn blares. The chariots race off, circling the half-mile track for seven laps.

When the lead chariot finishes the sixth lap, its runner leaps from the wagon, racing to complete the final circuit. Three chariots immediately pull up behind the first one. Their runners dash out to catch the leader, legs and arms pumping furiously. The crowd screams for their favorites, laying bets on who will win.

The lead chariot runner crosses the finish line. Scipio descends to crown the driver and runner with a wreath of laurel leaves, kissing each upon both cheeks. When the brief ceremony is over, he hastens up the steps and plops down next to Amelia, breathing heavily.

"I'm getting too old for all these stairs. They're worse than fighting an Iberian!" He grins. "They ought to make stair-climbing an Olympic event!"

"This is so exciting! I wish Publius were here to see this," Amelia says.

Scipio chuckles. "He would only be interested if we were reenacting a naval battle! You know he is happiest where he is at, Mother. Sailing on a ship."

She shakes her head. "I just never thought of him as a marine. Perhaps a scholar, or a tutor. Not someone chasing pirates."

Scipio shrugs. "I encouraged him to be a teacher, to take the opportunity that I couldn't. But he feels the weight of the Scipio name, thinks he has to be some great military leader."

"As you did, after your father made you swear to become one," Amelia says.

"And yet Tiberius Gracchus augurs greatness for our daughter Cornelia—as his wife," Scipio says. "That is truly the greatest mystery of all."

The horns sound the next event. A quartet of armored dwarves tread into the arena. One bears the signifer of the Scipio family, another wears the eye patch and armament of Hannibal the Great. The other two are armored as a Gaul and an Iberian, the former sporting a beard that drapes to his feet. The four men face the Scipio dais, kicking and shoving each other until they form a straight line. They raise their wooden swords and bow.

Scipio rises amidst the crowd's eager laughter, grinning broadly. "I am honored to witness your combat, brave warriors." He holds his fist high. "Commence!" he shouts.

The dwarves charge at each other, clacking their wooden swords against their plate-sized shields. The Scipio performer runs behind the Hannibal dwarf and kicks him in the backside, prompting roars of laughter. He repeats the maneuver with the Iberian and Gallic warriors, chasing them about the sands. After several minutes of tumbling and wrestling, the Scipio dwarf stands triumphant over his three supine fellows, mimicking Scipio's victories in Iberia, Gaul, and Africa.

Scipio stands up and lowers his thumb in a mock death sentence. The Scipio dwarf runs to each victim and whacks his blade against his enemy's helmet, prompting them to twitch in exaggerated death throes. The horns sound. The performers dash into a nearby portal, applause ringing in their ears.

"And now for the event you have all been waiting for," Scipio shouts. "The beasts of Murmus versus the beasts of Capitolus!"

Prima leans in from behind Amelia. "I have to get ready. See you soon." She rises from her seat and hurries to a rear stairway, clutching the skirts of her gown.

Twenty gladiators march out from a portal near the entry. Five spear-wielding hoplomachi face off against five of Capitolus' thraex; Thracian-style fighters who fight with shield and short sword. The rest of Capitolus' men are trident-wielding retiarii, their nets draped over their shoulders. They stand against Murmus' five Gallic-style gladiators, men equipped with long sword and shield.

Scipio motions for Murmus and Capitolus to approach. The two elderly lanista stand next to him, basking in the crowd's cheers—their fighters are known for their artistry and fierceness.

"Murmus and Capitolus have brought their finest warriors to do honor to General Glabrio. In consideration of their efforts, the lanista with the most victors will receive this token of honor," Scipio holds up a gold crown etched with gladiators in combat. The lanista's eyes shine with greed.

Pairs of gladiators disperse about the racing track, each moving to their appointed combat point. Scipio nods to the trumpeters. The cornu blare the signal. The gladiators rush at each other.

The retiarii fling their nets high, hoping to snag their Gallic opponents and yank them off-balance. The Gallics lever up their shields to protect themselves, chopping at the net's tough fibers. A referee bustles about the darting gladiators. He uses his long staff to separate overzealous combatants, and poke reluctant ones into engagement.

Amelia stretches back in her linen-draped seat, her brow furrowed with concern. "Twenty gladiators? A golden crown? How much is all this costing us?"

"Our storehouse plunder is almost gone," Scipio murmurs. "Lucius and Laelius have to win this election."

"What if they don't? Do we use the money from our farms to fund the next election?"

"That is money for you and the children," Scipio says. He points to the whirling combatants. "I will fight down there before I touch any of that."

A hoplomachus bends low and stabs his spear into a thraex, cutting deep into his stomach. The gladiator falls onto his back, moaning. The referee rushes in and grabs the hoplomachus' spear arm before he can use it, raising his arm in victory. The crowd wildly cheers. The hoplomachus stands against the wall, a winning tally for the house of Murmus.

The match continues for another half an hour. The victors line the wall, while the wounded are helped toward the doctors inside the portal. Five of Murmus' gladiators stand near four of Capitolus' men. A lone hoplomachus and thraex fight on, their shields held low from exhaustion.

The hoplomachus suddenly leaps at the thraex, thrusting his spear at the thraex's exposed shoulder. The thraex angles his shield sideways, deflecting the thrust. He lunges upward and jabs his curved blade into the underside of his opponent's visored helmet. The blade plunges through the hoplomachus' throat and severs his spine.

The fighter's arms fall to his sides, twitching. He crumples face first to the earth, blood pouring from his helmet's apertures. The thraex stares at his fallen opponent, gasping for breath. The referee takes one look at the fallen gladiator, and waves toward a dark portal.

A stout man emerges from the portal, lugging a fist-sized hammer. His face is masked with the image of Pluto, god of the underworld.[cxlvi] Two slave boys walk behind him, dragging a rope tied to an iron hook.

The man turns the hoplomachus onto his back. He pounds his hammer upon the gladiator's chest. Seeing no reaction, he nods at the two slaves. The boys push their hook into the corpse's jaw and drag him into the Porta Libitina, the doorway to the death goddess.

The thraex walks over to join the rest of Murmus' men. The referee points his pole at the six gladiators, indicating victory for the House of Murmus.

Scipio hands the crown to the exultant lanista. He motions to Lucius and Laelius. "Go on, get down there."

The two candidates step down the stairs and approach the six gladiators. The fighters remove their helmets. Laelius takes a laurel wreath from a basket held by an attending slave. He places it atop the head of the first gladiator, drawing ecstatic cheers from the crowd. Lucius repeats the procedure with the next one, drawing more accolades. When all the victors are wreathed, Lucius and Laelius raise their arms to the crowd. Rome's citizens deluge them with applause.

Scipio leans toward Glabrio. "Hear that? They are going to be elected. Don't let me hear of you doing anything to subvert it."

The retiring consul gazes disdainfully into Scipio's eyes. "I'm returning to Greece until the new consul arrives. If it is Lucius, I swear he will not live to see a battle. He's not going to destroy one of our armies." He stomps away before Scipio can reply.

The cornu declare the finale of the day's events. A capital offender is to be executed by combat. Two guards lead in an elegantly coiffed patrician, his muscled swimmer's body clad in a simple black loincloth.

Scipio descends the steps until he is standing above the edge of the Circus wall, looking down upon the aristocrat. The man stares, a sneer on his lips.

"Senator Postus Novus, former commander of the fourth legion, former praetor to Sicily, you have been found guilty of treason. Treason is punishable by death. What say you?"

"I say go fuck yourself," Novus replies. "You set me up."

He shouts up at the senators, throwing his fist at them. "He arranged this with the censor. Aren't you going to do anything about it?"

The Hellenic senators whistle at him, jabbing down their thumbs. Cato leans toward Flaccus. "Novus may have committed treason, but I would wager Scipio had a heavy hand in getting him convicted of it."

"Let Scipio play his final gambit," Flaccus replies. "His star is fading." *Or I will dim it myself.*

Scipio raises his arms, and the crowd falls silent. "You are sentenced to death," he says. "As a former legate, you are given the honor of death by combat. You will fight until you die."

Four slaves march out. One carries a Roman shield, the other an unsheathed gladius, the third a new bronze cuirass. The fourth bears a visored officer's helmet, its red plume stripped from the crest. Novus dons the armor and weapons. He stands facing the Porta Libitina, slapping his blade against his thigh.

Prima strolls from the portal, wearing a white loincloth and breast strap. Without helmet or shield, the gladiatrix fights as a dimachaerus, holding a freshly-edged sword in each hand. Her oiled muscles ripple as she stalks across the sands, her red-dyed hair clasped into a shoulder-length ponytail.

Laelius' mouth drops open. "What's she doing?" he splutters at Scipio. She said she was going to be armored! She's practically naked!"

Scipio shakes his head. "In truth, I did not know this. She has given him every advantage. She must truly want to disgrace him."

"But he's a trained soldier, not some half-drunk Gaul," Laelius blurts. "Oh gods, I'm going to be sick."

Scipio squeezes Laelius' knee. "She was the champion of Capua, Brother. She knows what she's doing."

Prima halts in front of the glowering Novus, waiting for the call to engage. She stares into his helmet's eye-holes. "You are the cur that conspired with Flaccus. You are the ones who killed Pomponia, and tried to kill Amelia, aren't you? I will be glad to speed you to the underworld."

Novus snorts. "Try your best, woman. I'll cut out your cunt before this day is done."

"How crude," she says, wrinkling her nose. "Just for that, I'm going to give you the Four Count."

The cornu sounds. Prima steps within a sword thrust of Novus, warily circling him. Novus crouches low and follows her, jabbing with his blade.

Prima leaps at him, battering her right sword against his shield. Novus swoops his blade sideways, aiming for her liver. Prima's left blade clangs against his gladius. Her right blade darts in and cuts a deep furrow across the top of his forearm. "That's One Count," she says, as she skips backward.

Novus glances at his bleeding arm. He raises his shield to eye level and charges forward, his blade cocked.

Prima crosses her blades in front of her chest. She crouches with her left foot ahead of her right, balancing her weight. Novus shoves his shield at her body, chopping his sword at her head.

Prima spins off her left foot, whirling behind him. Her right sword flashes like a striking snake, its point slicing into his shoulder. Novus yells. He jabs behind his back, but cuts nothing but air. The crowd screams its excitement.

"That is Two," Prima declares. She stands back from Novus and rests her swords against her sides, mocking him.

Flaccus watches the duel unfold, his fist pressed into his mouth. *Come on, Novus, get rid of her. I can take care of the others.*

Four rows in front of Flaccus, Laelius grips Scipio's arm. "Just stay away from him!" he bellows at his wife. "Let him bleed out!"

"She won't do it," Scipio says. "She wants the kill."

Novus stands in front of Prima, willing himself to be calm. *You can't drag this out, you're losing blood. You have to surprise her.*

Novus strides in. He raises his arm as if he is striking at her head, but his eyes search the ground near her feet. He sees Prima shift her left foot forward, ready to counter his blow.

Novus ducks down and rams the edge of his shield into the top of her sandal, bashing her toes. Prima screams out her pain. She topples sideways, landing on her back.

Novus rushes in and bends over her. Prima rises on one elbow, but his shield bashes her to the ground.

Novus lunges his blade at her throat. Lying on her back, Prima's right blade flashes across her chest, catching Novus' sword arm in mid thrust. Her blade crunches into his wrist bone, just as the tip of his sword gashes across her upper chest.

The senator drops his sword. Prima rolls from beneath him and limps back several steps. A bright ribbon of blood blooms across her chest. Novus bends over and retrieves his sword, pressing his numbed fingers around it.

Prima grins at him through clenched teeth. "That's Three. And this is Four."

Prima charges in, hopping on one foot. Novus drops his shield and grabs his sword in his left hand. Prima drops to her hands and knees and kicks out with her injured foot, scooping Novus' left foot from under him. As he topples sideways, she clambers upright and springs upon him, both blades flashing down.

Prima's left blade blocks Novus' weak counterthrust, and her right sword darts in. The blade slices through Novus' larynx, pinioning his head to the bloody sands. Novus' head pitches back and forth, his neck gouting blood. He kicks, once, and lies still.

Prima yanks out her sword. Balancing herself on one foot, she raises her dripping blades to the sky. The crowd erupts. Their cheers drive droves of stadium pigeons into the sky.

Scipio walks up the steps and sidles in next to Flaccus. He puts his shoulder against him and leans into his ear, smiling as if sharing a humorous secret. "That's your man, Flaccus, and I'm the one that put him down there." He squeezes Flaccus' shoulder. The senator winces. "If I have the slightest hint, even a whiff, that you or your henchmen are working against my candidates, I'll get you down there, too!"

Scipio rises and returns to his place, waving happily at the glum Latin senators.

"What were you doing with that scum?" Laelius asks.

"Just doing a little reverse campaigning." He grins at Laelius' confused look. "I was just making sure nothing goes awry."

Laelius chuckles. "I am sure whatever you said was of great interest to him."

"We had best get going," Scipio says. "We have to get you and Lucius to the main entrance." The Scipio party hurries down the stone steps behind the dais, followed by a dozen of the city militia.

A man with a Jupiter mask rides out from a portal. He circles the race track, waving his staff to bestow blessings upon the departing crowd. As he circles the track, the pipers prance onto the grounds, playing dozens of sprightly tunes. The horns signal the end of the games, and the citizens file out.

Laelius and Lucius stand at the main entryway, shaking hands with the exiting patricians and plebs. Scipio and Amelia stand behind them, chatting with several senators.

"Don't forget the banquet at Scipio house," Lucius tells a portly Latin senator. "We'll have large plates of peacock tongues, and we'll be pouring the finest Falernians!"

"I would not miss it!" he declares, grinning broadly. He sees Cato approaching, and his smile vanishes. "Apologies. I must go now. See you tonight."

Cato barges past Lucius, ignoring his outstretched hand. He halts in front of Scipio, his fists on his hips. Scipio's well-wishers quickly disperse.

"You can fool them, but you can't fool me. I know where you got the money for all this. There will soon be a reckoning!"

"What I spent I gained as a servant to Rome," Scipio says, speaking as if to a child. "I have risked my life a dozen times to save our nation. Can you say the same about your mentor Flaccus? Where was he when our men were fighting in Thermopylae. Lost in the hills somewhere?"

"He is not at issue in this. And I am not he."

"No, and you are not Cato, either. You were but a humble farmer, known for your unimpeachable morals," Scipio says. "Can you say the same about yourself now?"

Cato's face darkens. "We all change as our power grows. We gain the capability to do a greater good via a lesser evil. But you, you have kept money that should have gone into the public coffers. And I will prove it."

"The only thing I have stolen is this election, stolen it from you and your Latin ass-kissers. The people's votes will prove it!"

Two weeks later, the Centuriate Assembly gathers at the Campus Martius. Each clan of one hundred citizens casts a majority vote for two consuls. As dusk approaches, Consul Glabrio looks at the piles of pebbles cast for each candidate, their marks face down to avoid detection. He points to the two largest piles. "This one, and that one," he says. An attending praetor plucks a pebble from each pile and shows him the mark on each of them. Glabrio reads the marks and nods.

He rises from his chair and faces the election officials, his mouth a line of resentment. "Gaius Laelius and Lucius Cornelius Scipio are the new consuls of Rome," he intones. As the crowd cheers and hisses, Glabrio hastens down the steps, intent on retreating to his country villa before he returns to Greece.

*Lucius Scipio is consul,* he thinks. *Gods help us all if he contests with Antiochus and Hannibal.*

EPHESUS, 190 BCE. "You have to make your move," Hannibal urges. "The Romans are completing their consular elections early. They will send an army to Greece as soon as possible."

"Do we really need a war with Rome?" says Seleucus, Antiochus' son. "We can make peace with them, and keep our gains in Thrace and Pergamum."

Hannibal shakes his head. "We cannot can make peace with Rome. If we just sit here, soon we will have to fight the Romans in Asia. Then you will be fighting for your own kingdom."[cxlvii]

"Maybe the Romans are be tired of war," Antiochus replies. "They have fought Carthage and Macedonia, with scarcely a year's respite. Their main man Scipio, he advocates alliances rather than conquests."

"He advocates alliances over those he *conquers*," Hannibal says, "but that is only because he knows Rome is not strong enough to rule far-flung dominions by simple force of arms."

Hannibal walks to Antiochus and grips the top of his forearm. "Listen to me! The Romans aim at having an empire all over the world. Unless you thwart them, they will come here and take your kingdom!"[cxlviii]

Antiochus places his bejeweled hand over Hannibal's. "I doubted you once, when I listened to Thoas. I swore then I would never do it again." He glances at his son. "I will keep my promise to you. We will prepare for war. I will send a call for my allies to meet me in Phyrgia."

"No, Father!" Seleucus blurts. "You're risking everything! These new consuls, they are friend and brother to Scipio himself! What if he comes here with one of them, leading their army?"

Antiochus arches his eyebrows. "I have Hannibal, the one general that can outwit him. And I have my own way to tame Scipio's aggression."

"How?" asks Hannibal. "Have you gotten the Egyptians to join forces with us?"

Antiochus laughs. "I am a king, not a god! No, the Egyptians still hate me—this is something better. Something Admiral Polyxenidas brought me from his raid on the Italia coast." He turns to an attendant standing near a side door. "Bring him in."

The attendant disappears inside. Minutes later, two guards march into the throne room, leading an auburn-haired boy in the navy blue tunic of the Roman marines. The young man's shoulder-length hair is unkempt and his clothes spotted with blood, yet he stares unblinking into

Antiochus' eyes.

Antiochus grins with delight. "Men, let me introduce you to Publius Scipio the Younger, son of Scipio Africanus."[cxlix]

MANSE OF GAIUS LAELIUS, ROME, 190 BCE. "You look magnificent," Scipio remarks good-naturedly. He rests his hands on Laelius' shoulders, gazing into his freshly oiled face.

Laelius raises the hem of his new toga, smiling as he looks at its wide purple border. "Look at that the size of that stripe! Everyone will know I'm a consul." He gapes wonderingly at Scipio. Tears well in his eyes. "I'm really a consul!"

"You are, and it is richly deserved," Scipio says, wiping the corners of his eyes. "You have come far from the back streets of Ostia. I am so proud of you."

"I came with your help. So much of your help." He grasps Scipio's face in both hands and kisses him deeply. "I love you, Brother."

Laelius draws back from Scipio, giving him a friendly shove. "Come on, Prima wants to say hello before you run back to your house."

"Just for a moment," Scipio replies. "We have a Senate meeting in a few hours."

The two childhood friends enter the palm-lined atrium of Laelius' new town house. Prima is over by the fishpond, scattering bread crumbs to the swarming carp. She crouches down and spreads her arms, her back to Scipio and Laelius.

"Who is that sneaking up behind me?" she barks. "Is it a couple of politicians? Someone fetch me my sword!" She turns and smiles broadly at them, her green eyes fixed on Scipio.

"Well, there's the old puppet-master!" She hurries over and kisses Scipio lingeringly upon his cheek. "Gratitude for all you have done for us. Our house is yours, now and forever."

"That is welcome news. After all the time I've spent on this election, Amelia has threatened to throw me out!" Scipio glances at the linen patch above the décolletage of Prima's flowing indigo gown. "Is that some new form of adornment?"

She wrinkles her nose. "A parting gift from that pig Novus, before I stuck it to him." She sighs. "And a reminder that I am not as quick as I used to be."

"That's right, "Laelius says, "you should quit the ring." He winks at Scipio. "Maybe I should take her with me to Greece. She can be part of my personal bodyguard!"

"You still want Greece, eh? Why not the assignment to North Italia? The Boii and Insubres have been quiet. It would be an uneventful time. You'd likely get a nice fat praetorship after you were done there."

Laelius flings up his arms. "That is the crux of it—nothing's going to happen there! If I go to Greece and defeat Antiochus, my name will be written in history. Me, the orphan from the docks—I'd be rich and famous!" His smile vanishes. "Besides, do you truly want Lucius to lead our men against the Syrian hordes?"

"Well, not by himself. I could join him."

"But you could join me, if I went," Laelius says. "We'd be unstoppable. Just like we were in Iberia and Africa."

"My husband's mind is set on it," Prima says. "He still thinks he has to prove himself. As if he wasn't the best man in Rome already!"

Laelius shakes his head. "It's just that I'm the best choice. If Lucius gets the Italia province, he will be tasked with repopulating the Placentia and Cremona garrisons.[cl] That is safer than leading our army against Antiochus' trained killers. Safer for him, and for our legions!"

"He is my brother, Laelius. I promised Mother I would help him make his way, and I fear he cannot do it on his own. This is his best chance for permanent fame and fortune." *And then I am shed of him.*

"What about me," Laelius snaps. "What about Rome? Would you sacrifice us for an oath to a dead person?"

"You, I am not worried about. Besides, the point is moot. You know you will draw lots. Fortuna will decide who goes to Greece."

Laelius shakes his head. "Not this time. This is too important to trust to luck. I think we should let the Senate decide this." His eyes grow cold. "*They* will understand the wisdom of my words."

"I see you will not be shaken on this," Scipio declares. He walks toward the vestibulum. "I won't oppose your recommendation, Laelius, but I will not advocate for it. I have to give Lucius a chance. It's the honorable thing to do."

Laelius turns his back. "You are thinking more about your precious honor than you are about Rome," he says over his shoulder. "Is that so very honorable? You had best hope the Senate listens to me. It would be best for all of us."

Scipio bites his bottom lip. "You may be right. I can only hope Fate makes the decision for me." Scipio walks out the front door and takes his mount's bridle from a house slave. He trots down the wide Via Sacra to the Scipio domus. He enters the atrium and finds it empty.

"Lucius? Amelia?" he says, his eyes searching the hallways. "Where is everyone?"

Amelia's voice rings out from the garden. "We are out here!" Scipio walks into the sun-washed garden room. And enters a celebration.

Lucius stands in front of the lush red roses that fill the center gardens, wearing his new consular toga. Amelia stands next to him, garbed in a ivory-colored gown. Cornelia stands next to her mother, holding a spray of pink oleanders that matches her dress. A tray of moon cakes and wine goblets rests on a marble pedestal next to a beaming Lucius. He waves his crystal chalice, beckoning Scipio inside.

"Come, Brother. Drink to my new office!" Lucius' slender fingers wrap around Scipio's wrist. He pulls him into the center of the garden.

Scipio forces a smile to his face. “I would be honored, Consul Lucius.”

Lucius grins mischievously. “I am a consul! Now my younger brother won’t be the only Scipio that Rome is talking about!”

The thought comes unbidden to Scipio: *But what will they be saying?* Scipio grabs a chalice of watered wine, and Amelia follows suit. She raises her shining goblet.

“To the new consul of Rome, General Lucius Cornelius Scipio!”

Lucius raises his goblet. “To the finest brother a man could have.” His eyes meet Scipio’s. “A man who has given me much, and asked for so little in return.”

Scipio drains his vessel. He claps his hands together, rubbing them energetically. “Well, now, should we go? You should not be late for your own swearing-in ceremony. It would anger the gods.”

Lucius smiles tightly. “Always looking out for me, aren’t you! You’d think I was the younger brother!” He pops a moon cake into his mouth. “You think Fortuna will gift me with Greece?” he says. “I could put old Philip in his place, and run the rest of Antiochus’ men back to Syria!”

“The bulk of Antiochus’ force is still in Syria,” Scipio replies. “I fear you’d have to go farther than that. He needs to be eliminated as a permanent threat.[cli] You’d need to cross into Asia.”

“Well, if that is what it takes, I’ll do it,” Lucius blithely replies. His eyes narrow. “And I’ll do it by myself.”

“As you say, Brother,” Scipio replies. *Gods helps us if that is true.*

Two hours later, Laelius and Lucius stand in the center of the Senate floor. Cyprian reads the oath of office from a weathered goatskin scroll, his reedy voice echoing through the chamber. Two hundred and eighty senators stand silent, listening to Laelius and Lucius repeat the Senate Leader’s words.

Tiberius Gracchus concludes the ceremony by offering a prayer to the gods, beseeching them to bless the new consuls with wisdom and safety. Lucius and Laelius walk to each side of Cyprian. They take their seats on their freshly carved four-legged stools, each one topped with a thick purple pad.

"I call this first meeting of the new year to order," Cyprian declares. "We begin with the allotment of provinces to our new consuls."

Laelius tugs at the Leader's yellowed toga. "I have a suggestion," he murmurs.

"What?" the elderly Cyprian barks. "Speak up! You have something to say, stand up and say it!" The senators grin at one another—Cyprian's deafness has been an object of humor for years.

Laelius stands up and takes a deep breath. "I think the province allotments are too important to be left to chance. I propose that the Senate decide who should go to Italia and Greece."[clii]

Scattered "yays" and "nays" welcome Laelius' suggestion, followed by dozens of arguments. The Senate Elder pounds his oak staff on the floor, and the senators quiet.

"This is very unconventional," Cyprian says, "but not without historical precedent. What say you, Lucius Scipio?"

Lucius gapes at the Senate Elder. "Uh, may I consult with my brother?"[cliii] he says.

The Leader points his staff to an empty side of the floor. "Talk there, beneath Jupiter's statue." Scipio rises from his front row seat and joins Lucius.

"What should I do?" Lucius blurts. "Will they give me a fair chance to get Greece? You have many enemies. What will Flaccus and Cato say?"

"Trust in the Senate vote,"[cliv] Scipio says, squeezing his brother's shoulder. "I know what will get you Greece." *Gods help me.*

Lucius walks back and stands to the right of Cyprian, who is sitting in his throne-like oak chair. "I agree with Gaius Laelius' proposition," Lucius says. "Let the Senate decide."

For the next hour, the ruling fathers listen to a score of senators testify for Laelius or Lucius, each presenting arguments why their favorite should be given the Greece assignment. Flaccus and Cato sit in the second row, avidly following the debate.

"I don't know whom I would prefer," Flaccus says. "Laelius is a born warrior and leader, so he gives Rome the best chance for victory. But Scipio's brother gives us the best chance of Latin Party electoral victories for years, after Antiochus humiliates him."

"You would endanger Rome for a political victory?" Cato growls.

"Psh! We have Glabrio, and Flamininus. They would drive the Syrians into the sea."

"After thousands die at the Syrians' hands," Cato snipes.

Scipio weighs to the senators' testimonies. *They are leaning toward Laelius,* he decides. *If they vote for him, there's nothing I can do about it. I did the best I could.*

Then the thought occurs to him, one that has lurked in the back of his mind. *You know what you can do. Have you kept your promise if you don't do it?*

With a heavy sigh, Scipio rises from his seat in the front row. He steps out onto the chamber floor. The senate quiets, waiting for Rome's greatest general to speak.

"Honored peers, I trust you will select the consul for Greece that is most likely to defeat King Antiochus. It is certainly a formidable task." He glances at Laelius and then at Lucius. They look expectantly at him. He swallows.

"If you decide that Greece will be my brother's province, I will accompany him as his subordinate."[clv]

The senate erupts into applause. Laelius stares at Scipio, his face changing from shock to anger. Lucius nods glumly, his face mirroring his resentment.

"Here now, let's have order," Cyprian shrills, futilely pounding his staff.

Flaccus' mind races, mulling the consequences of Scipio's words. *Scipio would likely prevent his brother from failing. But if Scipio leaves, I will be free of his persecutions for at least a year.*

He rises from his seat, sweeping his hand across his colleagues. "I must admit," Flaccus shouts, quieting the din from his colleagues, "I am intrigued at who would provide the more powerful support: the help given to Antiochus by the vanquished Hannibal, or that given to our consul and his legions by Hannibal's conqueror, Scipio Africanus!"[clvi] The senators murmur excitedly among themselves, recounting the battle between the two military geniuses.

Flaccus resumes his seat. *There! I bet they'll like nothing better than a rematch between those two.*

Cato leans toward Flaccus. "You chose Rome's welfare over your personal enmity for Scipio. That is most commendable."

"Gratitude," Flaccus replies. He smiles. *Ah, Cato! Your honor blinds you to intrigue. Such is your weakness.*

Hearing Flaccus' words, Scipio frowns with dismay. *Why is that wretch supporting me? Regardless, I had best capitalize on it.* He rises from his seat and steps out to again face the senators, bowing low.

"Whoever we send is not there just to drive Antiochus from Greece. That merely allows him to regroup his forces across the channel, only a day's sail from Greece. No, we must break his power."

He faces Lucius and Laelius. "We must drive Antiochus from western Asia, back over the towering Taurus mountains. That means we must face the beast in his lair, and cross the Hellespont into Syria!"[clvii]

Scores of senators flap their togas and snap their fingers, while a few hoot their disapproval.

Cato springs from his seat. "Have a care, Scipio Africanus! When Rome moves from Greece to Asia, we move from republic to empire, extending our reach beyond our grasp." He bares his calloused palms at the senators. "We are a nation of farmers, simple men of the earth. Do we really want to become a nation of conquerors?"

"I would hope not," interjects Scipio. "But we need garrisons in Pergamum and Syria—we need a protective zone in Asia, to prevent Syrian incursions into Greece—and Rome."[clviii]

He shakes his head at his peers. "Believe me, the last thing I want is a Roman Empire!"

The Senate Elder pounds his staff. "Enough debate! It is time for a vote. Those who support Lucius Cornelius Scipio taking the Greece province, stand up."

Laelius watches the senators rise in groups of two and three, his heart thumping with excitement. A minute later, his head slumps to his chin.

The Leader glances at the standing senators. "The vote is almost unanimous.[clix] Lucius Scipio is assigned the province of Greece. Gaius Laelius takes the province of North Italia."

Scipio stares entreatingly at Laelius. He avoids Scipio's gaze, his face a stone. Scipio looks at his brother, who is nervously kneading the sleeve of his toga. *Now that he's got it, he's afraid to have it. What have I done?*

The meeting moves on to the next topic, whether to formally forgive the Aetolians for siding with Antiochus. After deciding not to decide, the Senate adjourns for the day. Laelius strides for the open doors of the Curia Hostilia. Scipio hastens after him. He grasps Laelius by the elbow.

Laelius spins about and faces him. "Can you just leave me alone for a while? Can you just get the fuck away from me?"

"You must understand," Scipio says. "I am bound by chains of obligation. I tried to do the best I could for the both of you."

"You are bound by your determination to seem more virtuous than the rest of us, regardless of consequences," Laelius spits. "You are just another Cato, fighting for a different cause."

Laelius stalks down the Senate steps, embracing several of his supporters. The senators pat him on the back, smiling encouragingly as they walk to the Forum grounds.

"I didn't need your help," comes Lucius' voice behind him. "I'm perfectly capable of doing this campaign by myself!"

"No, you're not," Scipio growls, turning to face him. "You've never led an army into battle. Antiochus has a hundred thousand men at his disposal. I'm not trying to steal your glory, I only seek to offer you guidance. Follow it, and you just may win this war."

"Appreciated," Lucius stiffly replies. "But let us be clear. I am the general, and the consul. I make the final decisions."

"Of course," Scipio says tonelessly. "Now let's go home."

"You go. *I* have military matters to attend to!"

"As you say," Scipio replies. He takes a carriage back to his domus and hastens to the atrium, looking for Amelia.

"Where are you?" he shouts.

"Here, in the tablinum. Reviewing our farm accounts."

Scipio enters the carpeted study adjoining the atrium. He finds Amelia bent over a wax tablet of accounts, making tallies with her ivory stylus.

"How did the meeting proceed?" she asks. "Who's going to oppose Antiochus?"

"Lucius," Scipio says. "With my assistance. I volunteered, and it swayed the Senate."

Amelia slaps down her stylus. “You are going to war again? Doesn’t Rome have anyone else?”

Scipio shrugs. “I could not let Lucius fight alone, even though he resents my help. And now Laelius resents me siding with him.”

“You chose Lucius over Laelius? Was that wise?”

He laughs mirthlessly. “I must have made the right decision, because neither of them likes it!”

“Perhaps you can get Publius’ ship assigned to your naval contingent, so you can keep an eye on him.” She purses her lips. “You know, I am worried about him. We have not gotten a message from him for over a month.”

“He is probably somewhere far out to sea, so it will take him some time to reach us. But I will see if Lucius can arrange for him to join me.” He rolls his eyes at Amelia. “After all, Lucius is in charge of the army.”

“If he has any sense, he will listen to you.”

“And if he has too much pride, he will not.” Scipio plops onto a stool, his hands clasped over his knee. “I worry about facing Antiochus, and I fear Hannibal. But Lucius, sweet Lucius, he gives me the most concern. He is a born follower, thrust into the role of a leader—a leader who resents my advice.”

Amelia snorts. “This is a fine state of affairs. The Scipio brothers are going to war—with Antiochus, and with each other. You had best resolve one before undertaking the other.”

**Gladiatrix**

# VIII. CAT AND MOUSE

ANTIOCHIA, PHYRGIA,[clx] 191 BCE. Antiochus flings another grape at Zeus' head. The grape flies across the house-sized throne room and bounces off the statue's marble eyebrow. It rolls off the head and splats onto the marble tile floor. Antiochus rises from his eight-foot granite throne and jerks up his fist.

"That's four of six!" he crows at Zeuxis, his commander in chief. He pulls out a gold coin. "I wager I can make it five of seven!" Zeuxis does not respond. The hawk-faced king picks another grape from his attendant's silver tray.

Hannibal sits to the right of Antiochus, perched on a tufted maroon settee. He toys with a papyrus scroll that contains the king's waiting list. *His concentration is waning. He's getting bored from meeting with all these leaders.* He smirks. *This next one should interest him.*

"Who is next?" Antiochus asks Zeuxis. The grizzled warrior consults his papyrus scroll. "Judoc, chieftain of the Galatians."

"Send him in," Antiochus orders. The guards open the throne room's iron doors.

A red-haired giant stalks into the room, glowering at Antiochus' guards. The man's head is crowned with a domed silver helmet that sprouts twin bull's horns. His right hand clutches his favorite weapon, a short-handled pickaxe that he has found perfect for puncturing helmets.

The captain of the guard grabs Judoc's leg-sized forearm. "No weapons."

Judoc shoves him sideways. The guard stumbles backward. Blushing with embarrassment, the Syrian yanks out his curved sword. Judoc turns and faces him, his axe arm cocked. He grins, his left hand beckoning the guard.

"You going to stop me, little man?"

The guards swallows. He shuffles forward, eyeing the pickaxe.

"Here now, no bloodshed!" Zeuxis scurries over and interposes himself between the two men. "All visitors must leave their weapons in the hallway, Chief Judoc."

The Galatian's ham-sized fist tightens on his weapon. Hannibal smiles, enjoying the drama.

Zeuxis unstraps his sword belt and gives it to the guard. "Look, I give mine up, too!"

The red-bearded colossus eyes Zeuxis speculatively. He hands his pickaxe to Zeuxis. "You a chief, you keep for me." He jerks his thumb at the guard. "I kill that one, he touch me again."

Antiochus drums his fingers on his throne's gilded arm. *Galatians! They're as crazy as their Gallic cousins.* "Approach."

Judoc takes three steps and halts in front of Antiochus. The king steps down to him, extending his hand. Judoc grips the king's sinewy forearm, his hoary fingers completely encircling it. Antiochus gapes at the gigantic hand. *Gods, he is a man and a half! I hope he has a thousand more like himself.*

Judoc taps the top of his gold neck torus. "I come pledge men to you." He declares in his pidgin Greek. "I bring ten thousand: five sword and five horse." His blue eyes flare beneath his rust red brows. "We kill many for you."

Antiochus nods. "Good, good, that is good to hear. In return, I will give your tribes the highlands of Phyrgia. And a big share of all plunder." He points to the hallway. "Go and make your mark on the contract. That means we are allies."

"Contract!" Judoc sneers, tramping toward the entryway. He stops and extends his hand to Zeuxis. The commander walks over and gives him his pickaxe. "You give me shield?" Judoc asks, nodding toward the guards. Puzzled, Zeuxis grabs one of the guards' round iron shields and hands it to him.

The Gallic chieftain steps to the statue of Zeus. He tosses the shield into the air. As it falls, he swings his pickaxe. With a deafening clang, the pickaxe punctures the center of the shield, buckling it in the middle. Judoc raises his axe, the shield dangling from it. "See? We kill many. Crush their heads! That my contract." He kicks the shield off his axe and stalks from the throne room.

"Well, I'm glad we have *them* on our side," Hannibal says, blinking at the caved-in shield. "How many recruits does that make for us?"

Zeuxis consults his scroll. "King Darya pledges twelve hundred of his Dahae horse archers. We have three thousand Cretan light infantry now, and four thousand skirmishers from Phyrgia. The King of Mysia promises three thousand archers." He rolls up the papyrus and smiles at his king. "We'll soon be back up to a hundred thousand men. We can restock our garrisons and still field the largest army in the world!"

The Carthaginian nods approvingly. "What about the ships?" Hannibal asks.

Zeuxis shakes his head. "Polyxenidas lost twenty-three ships at Corcyrus. Eumenes of Pergamum and Livius of Rome captured thirteen more."[clxi] He rolls up his report and slaps it against his palm. "We need to rebuild our fleet."

Hannibal's pulse quickens. "I can go to Phoenicia and get us more ships," he says. "The Phoenicians are master shipbuilders. They supplied my fleet when I warred against Rome."

"We have to maintain control of the seas," Antiochus says. "It will keep Rome from crossing to invade us. Leave immediately."

"As you command," Hannibal says. He summons himself for what he will say next. "My King, I am well acquainted with the strengths and weaknesses of the Phoenician vessels. I would ask that you let me captain that part of your fleet."

"You no longer want to be my advisor?" Antiochus says peevishly.

"Not at all! I hope to be by your side in every battle. But we have to take the seas first. If we don't, the Romans will march across Greece and sail over here." He bows his head. "I simply want to serve you as best I can."

"I will make it so," Antiochus declares. He notices Zeuxis' worried look. "Of course, Admiral Polyxenidas will still be commander of the entire fleet."

"Of course," Hannibal says. He leans back on his settee. *Now I can show these fools how to win a battle*!

APOLLONIA, WESTERN GREECE, 190 BCE. "You go down first," Scipio says, poking his brother on the shoulder.

"I fully intended to," Lucius says. He airily waves his hand. "After all, I am the consul and you are my legate."

"Which you will never let me forget. Now go on down, the men are waiting for you."

Lucius pulls his purple cloak over his armor and steps down his flagship's gangplank. He pauses on the wide plank dock that leads to the Port of Apollonia, waiting for his brother. Scipio joins him, followed by Lucius' consular guard. The two stroll toward the dockside town that surrounds Apollonia's twelve landing docks, watching hundreds of legionnaires debark from the adjoining slips.

Scipio watches the Apollonia dock workers load grain sacks into the army supply wagons. "Everything seems to be proceeding well. Even the seas cooperated. Ask Tiberius Gracchus to offer a thanksgiving sacrifice to Neptune. Perhaps an ox."

"You think the seas were calm?" Lucius snaps. "Surely you jest. I was sick half the journey. All that rolling and pitching! If I offer an ox to anyone, it will be to Mars. I want our land wars to proceed successfully."

"Mars is a good idea, too," Scipio replies. "You can use all the help you can get."

"What do you mean by that?" Lucius bristles.

Scipio looks heavenward. "Nothing. Nothing at all. I just meant we should ensure we have the gods on our side. That's what I did in Iberia and Africa, remember?"

"That was you," Lucius says stiffly. "I have my own ways."

*That is what I most fear*. The two stride to the end of the dock. A dozen Greek cavalry amble out from a portside street, led by a regal-looking elder wearing a gold-hemmed amber cloak. As the party approaches, Lucius' guards rush forward and surround him.

"That is far enough," Scipio says, fetching a disapproving look from Lucius. The older man slides from his saddle blanket and walks toward the two Scipios. He raises his right hand.

"Salve, Scipio brothers! Greece welcomes your presence! I am Damen, emissary from King Eumenes of Pergamum!"

"Antiochus has taken half of Eumenes' kingdom," Scipio murmurs into Lucius' ear.

Lucius nods imperceptibly. "What is your business with us, noble Damen?"

"My king offers an alliance with you, to the purpose of driving Antiochus from all of Greece. And Pergamum!"

"That is welcome news, indeed," Scipio replies. "Perhaps we can meet the day after tomorrow, after we have finished unloading our ships."

"I am staying at our ambassador's house, near the Temple of Apollo. I await your summons." The elder springs onto his horse and trots away, his retinue following.

"You think an alliance with Eumenes is a good idea?" Lucius asks.

"Let us see," Scipio replies. "You have thirteen thousand Roman and allied infantry, and five hundred cavalry.[clxii] And the legion that Glabrio will turn over to you at Amphissa. That gives you less than twenty thousand men. Antiochus probably has eighty, maybe ninety thousand fighters. So yes, I'd consider an alliance."

Lucius scowls, clearly irritated at his brother's sarcasm. "I am glad you mentioned Amphissa. I need you to leave for there tomorrow. You can help Glabrio break his siege of it, and see if neighboring Hypata will surrender to us."[clxiii]

"You want me to head east to Aetolia tomorrow?" Scipio asks incredulously. "That's a week's ride. We just got here!"

"Don't act so surprised," Lucius replies peevishly. "We have to take Amphissa before we march through Thessaly and Macedonia." He grins at his brother. "We can't leave enemies at our back. Haven't you told me that before, Brother?"

"What about this Damen?"

Lucius flips his hand. "Oh, I am quite capable of handling him. Besides, Tiberius Gracchus is here to provide spiritual guidance. He can be quite persuasive—for a priest."

"Too persuasive. He has almost talked me into him marrying young Cornelia. He says the gods predict they will sire a great family." He chuckles. "He is the one who should run for consul!"

Lucius shrugs. "You on ahead of me and use your diplomatic prowess. I will be at Amphissa in two weeks."

Scipio bites his lip. *Let him learn to command. You may not live to see the end of this campaign.* "I will take Tribune Marcus Aemilius, unless you need him here. He is well versed in the mountain terrain."

"Granted, Legate," Lucius says officiously. He throws his arm about Scipio's shoulder. "I want my senior officer to have the best counsel with him."

"Gratitude," Scipio murmurs, his voice tinged with sarcasm.

A week later, Scipio halts his mount at the overlook to the widespread Amphissa Valley. He can see Amphissa's stout walls nestled against the round-shouldered mountains at the end of the valley. Two jagged pinnacles jut from the center of the garrison, their sheer sides topped with barracks and huts. Glabrio's legion rings the base of the outside walls. A string of catapults hurl rocks at the city. They bounce off harmlessly.

Marcus Aemilius draws his horse next to Scipio's. "Vulcan's balls, they turned those cliffs into a citadel! And look at those walls. The blocks they used are big as a man!"

"Aren't they magnificent?" Scipio says. "Those are the famous Cyclopean walls.[clxiv] They say that only the giant Cyclops could pile those massive stones on one another." He grins. "I suspect some cyclopean engineers are the real culprits!"

"No wonder Glabrio is stuck in his siege. What an impossible task!"

Scipio smiles at the young tribune. "Your father Marcus Silenus, he would agree that it is an impossible task. Then he would say, 'But I will take care of it.' And he would! Come on, let's get down there and help Glabrio take care of his 'impossible task.'"

Scipio trots down the looping trail to the grass-covered valley, followed by a squadron of equites. They find General Glabrio prowling among his siege engines, his face a mask of frustration.

"Get larger rocks! We've got to knock out more holes!" He yells. "We need breaches in those walls!"

"On my word, General. I think they can hear you up in Olympus!" Glabrio turns to the voice behind him. He sees that it is Scipio, and his inquisitive look turns cold.

"I heard you were coming here with your brother," he says flatly.

"And it is well I did, since you threatened to kill him if he came alone," Scipio replies.

"I said no such thing," Glabrio huffs. "I only said he would not get out alive. Which is likely, given his military capabilities." He crosses his arms. "What brings the *esteemed* Scipio Africanus here?"

"Why, I came to see if I could help!" Scipio says merrily.

"You can. Grab a ladder and get at those walls."

Scipio cocks his head. "Is that the way this is going to be between us?"

"This is my last battle before I return to Rome. I intend to win it myself," Glabrio replies icily. He marches back to his catapults, shouting orders at his men.

Scipio walks back to his cavalry squadron. He remounts his horse, taking the bridle from Marcus. "Glabrio's going to get a lot of men killed going at those walls," Scipio says to him. "We have to find a way to get inside."

"You want to sneak in there?" Marcus says.

"Yes, sneak in like a Carthaginian! We'll lose less men and time. You found a way at the Aous Gorge and at Thermopylae. Can you do it again?"

The tribune is silent, studying the foothills that climb about the citadel. "Give me a few days up there. I'll find something."

"Fine," Scipio replies. "I'll be back three days from now."

"Where are you going?"

"To Athens, to meet with our amici. I want them to talk to the Aetolians." He shrugs. "Lucius and Glabrio won't listen to me anymore. I might as well try our enemies!"

A week later, Lucius' army descends into the Amphissa Valley, a miles-long train snaking its way down a narrow, winding trail. Scipio sits on a boulder by the base of the trail, wearing only a gray army tunic. He waves happily as his brother rides over to him. Lucius dismounts, and the two clasp forearms.

"I trust your march was uneventful?"

"A few Aetolian raiders harassed our flanks. I caught a few and put them on the cross. We received little trouble after that. How goes the siege?"

"Little progress. Their walls are as thick as Carthage's! When they saw you coming, the soldiers and townspeople retreated into their impregnable citadel. There is little chance they will surrender."

Lucius flushes with anger. "Then we will bring the walls down around them, no matter what it takes!"

*And lose a thousand doing it,* Scipio thinks. "I think it would delay us too long. We have to march through Thessaly and Macedonia, then on to Thrace. If we don't move soon, we won't have time to stop Antiochus before winter sets in—before your consulship expires."

Lucius' lips pout in anger. He sets his chin. "I will send every man we have at Amphissa. I will not be denied my glory!"

*Patience,* Scipio tells himself. *Your visitors may arrive tonight.* "You've had a long trip," he says. "Why don't you sleep on this? We can discuss it in the morning."

"Sleep would be good," Lucius says, rubbing the back of his neck. "And a hot bath in that tub I brought along. Come to my tent for breakfast. Where are you at?"

"I am in Glabrio's camp for now. Sleep well, I will see you tomorrow."

Scipio returns to Glabrio's camp, entering his spacious tent near the west palisade. "Any visitors?" he asks one of his guards. The guard merely shakes his head.

*Pisspots!* "If anyone comes, notify me immediately." Scipio goes inside and stretches out on his sleeping pallet, his arm over his eyes. His camp attendant hobbles in, a former escalader who lost his lower leg at Zama.

Scipio hands him a parchment scrap. "Here's a list. I need five loaves of bread, a block of cheese, five stools, and two amphora of wine. Get that Helleniko wine I brought from Athens." The attendant clomps away on his bronze leg, its hinged knee creaking shrilly. Scipio lays back and heaves a deep sigh. *Come on. You men have to get here before Lucius does something stupid.*

As dusk descends, four middle-aged men ride into camp and halt before Scipio's tent. They are accompanied by a dozen Roman honor guards. Two of the envoys wear the forest green robes of Athenian officials. The other two have the hawk-crested amber tunics of the Aetolians.

Scipio welcomes them into his tent. Five stools surround a plate laden with food and wine.

"Take a seat please." He nods at the two Athenians. "Echedemus and Pigres, gratitude for interceding on Aetolia's behalf, as neutral parties."

"The idea was yours. We merely found favor with it," Echedemus replies. "There has been enough Greek blood shed already." He sweeps his hand toward the two men in amber. "These magistrates are the rulers of Aetolia's two major cities. The rest of the country will follow their lead.

"I am Polemion, chief magistrate of Amphissa," the tall man says. He fixes Scipio with a frosty glare. "I am responsible for the town you are assaulting."

A rotund man steps in front of him, grinning at Scipio. "It is an honor to meet the famous Scipio Africanus! I'm Tros, first cousin to Thoas." He smiles ingratiatingly. "I oversee Hypata, as best I can!"

"Gratitude to you all for coming," Scipio says. "The Athenians have heard my proposal, and doubtless told you about it. I want us to strike a truce between Aetolia and Rome—a cessation of hostilities. We can sign it and send it to Rome."

"That would be a waste of time," Polemion says. "Aetolia went to Rome with a peace proposal five months ago. They asked us to give them a thousand talents of silver,[clxv] which we found ridiculous. Why would it be any different now?"

Scipio smiles. "Because the consul is my brother. The two of us will make a joint proposal to Rome, waiving that indemnity of a thousand talents. We will cease all hostilities upon Amphissa and Hypata, upon Aetolia's promise not to ally itself with Syria."

"I think it is an excellent idea," Tros blurts. "Fighting for Syria was Thoas' idea, and now he's hiding over there in Syria! Besides, I do not want my city ravaged by a siege such as Amphissa endures."

The Amphissa magistrate sneers. "*I* do not fear the Romans. We know our citadel is impregnable.[clxvi] And so do they, unless they are fools."

Echedemus scowls at Polemion. "We brought you here in good faith, and now you say something like that!"

Scipio raises his hand. "I thought the 'impregnable' citadel might be an issue," he says calmly. He opens the tent flaps and sticks his head outside. "Marcus!"

Marcus Aemilius steps into the tent. He wears a worn forest green tunic, his face and legs blacked with charcoal. He salutes Scipio and nods toward the delegates.

"My tribune has been on a hike these last couple of days, haven't you?" Scipio says. He nods toward Polemion. "He took a hike up by your citadel."

"Actually, I was *in* the citadel." Marcus grins, his teeth blazing bright from his blackened face. "That statue of the Hydra is truly impressive. Did you request that?"

"How do you know about that?" Polemion sputters.

"Because I was in the room. I went in through the east gate in the northern pinnacle. You know, the one that is hidden from outside view?" He holds up a pottery figurine of Hera. "This was in the room. Do you recognize it?"

"How did you get that?" Polemion stammers.

Scipio edges closer to the Amphissa magistrate. "You see, Polemion, we know your citadel's weaknesses. And trust me, Marcus knows some that even your officers do not know. Once we attack your inner stronghold, we will spare no one, I can promise you that. Do you *really* want to trust in its impregnability?"

The next morning, Scipio joins the delegation inside Lucius' tent. Lucius listens to Echedemus outline their proposal for a cessation of hostilities. Before he can finish, Lucius is shaking his head.

"I cannot betray the Senate's earlier decision," he says, avoiding his brother's eyes.[clxvii]

"Will you please wait outside?" Scipio says to the delegates. They shuffle from Lucius' spacious tent.

Lucius shoves his palms toward Scipio. "No! Don't try to talk me into this. What would the Senate say if I subverted their demand of a thousand talents?"

"What would they say if you were mired here for another three months, losing your chance to confront Antiochus? We still have hundreds of miles to traverse, a dozen towns to take over, and yet here we sit!"

"I *have* to take Amphissa," Lucius says, his voice suddenly pleading. "I have to start my campaign with a victory."

"That citadel is impossible. It's built into two mountains. Do you hope to knock down two mountains? Glabrio hasn't done it, and he's been here three months!"

"I know. But it would be an important victory for me."

"Let peace be your victory. If you keep the Aetolians from joining Antiochus, Rome will rejoice." Scipio's voice softens. "It's your decision to make, Consul. But what do you think Father would do? Would he not seek peace before war?"

Lucius gazes at the tent exit. He hears the delegates talking among themselves, several of the voices becoming strident.

"They're going to leave. Make a decision," Scipio says.

"Bring them back in," Lucius mutters.

A week later, Glabrio stands at the valley overlook, flanked by Lucius and Scipio. He looks down at the open gates of Amphissa, watching the farmers' wagons trundle into the fortress.

"I wish I had taken it before you arrived," he says wistfully. "We had almost breached their outer walls."

Scipio resists an urge to laugh. "A good commander always wants to finish what he started. But now we have neutralized their garrisons, without loss of men."

Glabrio ignores him. "What will you do next?" he asks Lucius.

"We march north to Thessaly, then on to the Hellespont. There we cross to Antiochus' kingdom."

"You will have to go through Macedonia, then," Glabrio says, pursing his lips. "That means you must deal with Philip."

"Philip is a declared friend to Rome," Lucius says. "He should welcome us with open arms."

"Philip is a friend to Philip. He may welcome you with arms, but not the ones you are thinking of. You'd be wise to sail out from Thessaly, and avoid him altogether." Glabrio's voice becomes stern. "Be careful, Lucius. I think he has far more men than we think."

"Gratitude for the warning," Lucius says, his voice cold. "But he is now our problem, as is this war. You have been relieved of your duties."[clxviii]

"Yes I have," Glabrio says, looking at Lucius. "And now they are yours. May Fortuna bring you luck." *You will certainly need it.*

Glabrio strides past Scipio and mounts his horse. trotting away with a squadron of his personal guards. The Scipio brothers watch Glabrio's party break into a gallop, heading for the pine-covered foothills.

"I think Glabrio bears you ill will," Lucius says. "Why would that be? He wouldn't have become consul without you."

Scipio shrugs. "Who knows? Success does strange things to a person." He flings an arm over Lucius' shoulders. "We must get back to camp. We have to prepare for the march to Thessaly. Now that this cursed siege is over, you have a real war to win."

Lucius' shoulders tighten under Scipio's grasp. " I will win it, Brother. I am a Scipio, too."

EPHESUS, SYRIA, 190 BCE. Publius Scipio strides down Antiochus' spacious palace hallway, his steps heavily muffled by its thick red carpet. He admires the statues of Greek gods and goddesses that line each wall, reading the inscriptions beneath.

*Look at the detail on the faces, and the musculature! These are worthy of the finest Greek temples. And their rugs—so ornate! How can such an artistic people be so murderous? I hope Father does not have to destroy them.*

Publius fingers his lemon-colored tunic, scowling with distaste. *They dressed me so everyone would know I'm a captive. I'm a canary in a golden cage.* He eyes the four Syrian guards who stand at attention by the hall entryway, then examines the rafters over their heads. *At least canaries can fly away.*

A deep bass voice jolts him from his reverie. "What are you thinking about, young Scipio?" Publius turns around and stares into Hannibal's grinning countenance.

"You are not planning something, are you? Perhaps an untimely departure?"

"I was just admiring Antiochus' palace. There is nothing like this in Rome."

Hannibal chuckles. "You weren't plotting some type of escape, were you?"

Publius meets his eyes. "I am Scipio Africanus' son. Would you expect any less?"

"I would not. You would shame yourself if you didn't try." Hannibal's eye grows distant. "You and I are kindred souls. I know the burden of living up to lofty expectations. My father was Hamilcar Barca, known as the Thunderbolt.[clxix] I have spent my life trying to fulfill my promise to defeat Rome."

"My father wanted me to be anything but a soldier," Publius remarks. "You are more like him than me. He still carries the burden of his vow to protect Rome."

Hannibal laughs. "Him to protect it, and me to defeat it. Either way, we are both dancing in chains!"

He drapes his sinewy hand about Publius' narrow shoulders. "Let's go to the royal stables. There's a young stallion that needs riding. Just don't try to jump him over the wall!"

After depositing Publius with the local stablemaster, Hannibal hurries to Antiochus' throne room. Antiochus crouches over a rectangular iron table, studying a map of the Aegean coast. A papyrus scroll lies next to him, wadded into a ball. When he sees Hannibal, he juts his finger at the crumpled papyrus.

"That just came. The Scipios struck a cessation of hostilities with the Aetolians. We have lost them as allies, save for Thoas' men. And the Romans are marching north, toward Thessaly!"

"That was likely Scipio Africanus' doing," Hannibal says. "He was always good at striking a bargain with his enemies."

"Why should he bother?" Antiochus replies. "He could march straight through Macedonia. Philip's armies are greatly reduced. It was part of his treaty after Rome defeated him."

"You think he's followed that treaty?" Hannibal says. "That fool Glabrio allowed Philip to retake garrisons in the name of Rome. Philip has restocked them with his own men—thousands of them. I would not put it past him to attack the Romans." He grins. "And why not? Lucius is not the general his brother is."

"But Scipio is with him."

"Yes, but we have the means to control Scipio, don't we?" says Hannibal. "Just keep an eye on the boy—he has a wandering eye."

"If he escapes, I'll send Nicator after him," Antiochus replies. "He'll never try to escape again!" He looks back at the map, "So you think Philip poses a threat to the Romans?"

"Yes, if the Romans enter his kingdom. That means we should keep the Romans from launching at Thessaly, so they have to go through Macedonia and Thrace."

"Admiral Polyxenidas is already patrolling the Thessaly coast. He has a dozen quinqueremes."

Hannibal shakes his head. "Not nearly enough. The Roman admiral Livius has twice that many ships around there. We have to wipe him out."

"Do we send another dozen warships to Polyxenidas?"

"We send all our warships to Thessaly, including the ones I bought from the Phoenicians. Think of it! A hundred ships marauding the ports of the Pagasetic Gulf, the only place suitable for army transport.[clxx] That will drive the Romans north. And give us months to prepare for them."

Antiochus fingers his curled beard, his lips compressed in thought.

"The Romans have scores of ships in the Aegean," the king says. "And Eudamus of Rhodes is rumored to be joining them. He would have scores of ships, too."

"Let him join them!" Hannibal exclaims. "As your admiral, I have commissioned some special ships from the Phoenicians. We will have a little surprise for Admiral Livius, and this Eudamus."

"What kind of a surprise?"

Hannibal grins. "Let's just say we will be looking down on our Roman enemies—in more ways than one."

ROME. "Gods curse it, he has it hidden somewhere around here!" Cato fumes.

Cato stalks through the slum-filled Street of Merchants, peering at the storehouses that line the sides of the streets. "My informant told me Scipio's trove was hidden in a storehouse on the Aventine, near the statue of Libertas."

"Is this where they found his body?" asks Flaccus. Cato jerks his thumb toward an adjoining alleyway, where two red-lipped prostitutes lounge against a wall.

"Titus' body was in that alleyway over there. There was a boy there, too. Must have been the 'spy' Titus talked about."

"Look out down there!" comes a voice above them. Cato looks up. Two claw-like hands emerge from a third-floor window, clutching a wide, flat chamber pot. The hands tilt the clay vessel upside down. Its contents tumble toward the two patricians.

Cato grabs Flaccus' tunic and jerks him into the middle of the street. The pot's contents splash onto the brick-lined gutter. Flaccus stares at the yellow droplets dotting his freshly shaved legs. His eyes start in horror.

"Give fair warning up there!" Cato barks at the window.

A grizzled crone sticks her head from the window. Her seamed face breaks into a gap-toothed smile. "Oh, did my precious patricians get piss on their legs?" she cackles. "You don't like it, take your powdered asses back to the Capitoline. Come the people's revolt, you'll be sponging my cunt!"

"If you have a husband, send him down here," Cato growls, his thick fingers balled into fists. "I'll show you who has a powdered ass!"

Flaccus tugs at Cato's elbow. "Come on, let's get out of here. We have better things to do than dodging insults and shit."

"I can't. I have to figure out where he hid that plunder he stole!" Cato sweeps his hand at the field of storehouses that line the street grid. "It's in here somewhere. He may have left a sign. Or someone may have seen him."

Flaccus rolls his eyes. *He is such a child about espionage*. "Why don't you get someone to spy on the Scipios, like that dead boy did for Titus? Sooner or later, someone will sneak in here."

Cato shakes his head. "I don't think so. The Scipio brothers are in Greece. Laelius is in north Italia."

"Ah, but that bitch Amelia is still here. And that fop Marcus Nobilior is running for consul. She's sure to have her hand in his election. Elections need money—lots of money."

Cato grimaces. "Jupiter help us if Nobilior wins. He's the one always bringing Greek art into the city,[clxxi] as if we need any more of that crap. He'd have us lying around all day, eating grapes and talking about plays. Decadence will be the ruin of Rome, not a bunch of soft-handed Syrians!"

*Now, while he's suggestible.* "You know, if something happened to Amelia, it might pull Scipio back to Rome. And Lucius would be left to lead the army by himself. And our candidate would have a better chance to—"

Cato's face flushes. "Speak no more!" he commands, his tone both threatening and pleading. "I will be forced to turn you in to the censor!"

"Don't be so impetuous!" Flaccus snaps. "I was merely thinking out loud—musing, as the poets say."

"Poetry!" Cato spits. "Another waste of time! But your idea to spy on them, that is most appropriate. I'll talk to some people."

"Let me help. I know some of the Aventine's Unnamed, people who are good at this type of thing. You can arrange a meeting and talk to them by yourself." *So your actions cannot be traced back to me.*

Cato eyes Flaccus. "Let us be clear. I want someone who will watch Amelia. Nothing else."

"Of course. Just let me know whom you select, so I can tell you how much to pay them." *And I'll pay them extra for my own assignment.*

Cato grimaces. "All right. You do have more experience in these matters."

"Of course I do!" Flaccus exclaims. "You just leave it to me, I'll take care of everything!"

Two days later, Amelia meets with Prima at her domus. The women recline on two of the padded cement couches in Prima's triclinium. The spicy fragrance of cloves and basil wafts in from the kitchen archway.

"Ineni! Bring us some refreshment," Prima calls, eyeing the empty doorway.

An Egyptian slave patters out from the adjoining kitchen, clad in the bare-breasted linen sheath of her people. The young woman lays down a silver tray filled with small food plates. Amelia stretches her arm out and pops a handful of pomegranate seeds into her mouth. The ruby juice spurts from her mouth and dribbles down her chin. She claps her hand to her lips. "Apologies!" she giggles.

"Be as sloppy as you like, there are no husbands about," Prima says.

"Don't I know it," Amelia replies, grinning as she wipes her chin. "My loins remind me nightly how long it's been!"

"Psh, that is your own fault," Prima replies. She picks up a cucumber and waggles it at Amelia. "Here, try this on. It's almost as good as a man."

Amelia makes a face. "I don't want anything inside me that I eat!"

Prima's lips purse into a smile. "Oh? That's not what your husband tells me."

Amid their laughter, Amelia flings up her hand. "Enough, please! We have to figure out how to get Nobilior elected consul. It's all on us now, everyone else is out fighting wars. Time grows short."

"I know," Prima says. "It's only June, and the consular candidates are already making speeches in the Forum."

Amelia shakes her head. "It seems like the elections start earlier every year. Our finest minds spend all their time campaigning, listening to campaigns, or planning campaigns. Meanwhile, the roads lie unbuilt, and the citizens lie idle."

Prima chuckles. "Maybe we would be better off with a benevolent king, like Servius from the old days. At least we wouldn't have to put up with all this politicking!"

Amelia sighs. "Perhaps, perhaps. But that was then, and this is now. We have the curse of duty upon us. If the Latins regain power, we can abandon those plans for Rome's first library."

"So where do we start?" Prima asks.

"We start with money," Amelia replies. "We figure out how much we have, and how we're going to spend it. I have to see what's left in the warehouse."

Prima pushes herself upright. "You're going out to the Aventine tonight? Not without me you're not!"

"You have a newborn," Amelia says. "Besides, I can handle myself."

"But can you handle four men at once? The gods themselves cannot change my mind—I'm going with you!"

Amelia raises her chalice. "Then drink up, and go fetch your shabbiest clothes. We have to do some night-riding."

Three hours later, two cloaked figures ride out from the rear door of the Scipio manse, bouncing along on two swayback geldings. An assortment of wicker baskets dangle from the sides of their horses, the traveling merchandise of Rome's basket weavers.

"We'll take the Street of Merchants," Amelia tells Prima. "That's the route all the craftsmen take."

The riders clop down the main avenue toward the Aventine. They pull their horses aside when a noble's caravan streams past them, his slave-borne litter surrounded by attendants and guards. Seeking safety in numbers, the two women follow the city's torch lighters as they work toward the Aventine, maintaining enough distance to keep their faces in the shadows.

Amelia and Prima do not notice the ebony-skinned Nubian who slinks along behind them, sliding into darkened doorways whenever one of them turns around. The slim man sidles along the mud-brick walls of the insulae, his eyes never leaving their backs.

A half hour later, the pair turns into a side street. They tie their horses to a log postern in front of the Scipio storehouse.

"Watch the horses," Amelia says. She takes out a circlet of iron keys and unlocks the granary's battered oak door, then opens its inside door and closes it behind her. Fumbling for her kindling tools, she strikes iron to flint and kindles a wall torch. Amelia holds it above her head and surveys the storeroom.

The large room is empty, except for a mound of bagged Roman coins and a pile of gold neck torques. Dozens of emeralds and rubies are sprinkled about the chamber, signs that the piles from which they came were hastily removed.

Amelia bends over and scurries across the floor, grabbing the dusty jewels and stuffing them into her belt pouch. Fumbling in a dimly lit corner, her fingertips encounter two pebble-sized stones. She blows off the dirt and holds them up to the torchlight, rolling them in her fingers.

Two clear, multifaceted gems wink back at her, shimmering with the blazes of their inner fires. She rolls the stones between her thumb and forefinger, marveling at their crystal clarity. *These must be what they call diamonds, those stones from India! Gods, they are worth a fortune!*

Amelia hurries to the exit and peers out from the doorway. "Prima! Bring the wagon!" she hisses. Prima pulls the horses into a nearby stable. Unlocking a side gate, she pulls the two mounts next to a slat-sided wagon heaped with foul-smelling rags and castoff papyrus, the daily collection of a city rag-picker. After divesting the horses of their baskets, she draws the wagon next to the storehouse.

Amelia totters from the doorway, lugging a sack of coins. She shoves the rags aside and flops the sack onto the bottom of the wagon, gasping with the effort. Prima stumbles out from the room and pitches in another sack. Soon, the two women are shoving the last of the neck torques under the rags.

Amelia takes a last look at the storehouse that held Scipio's plunder from Africa, Iberia, and Gaul. "That's the last of it," she tells Prima. "The ransoms of a dozen kings, all spent to elect the best men for Rome."

Prima sniffs. "Men such as Nobilior? You could have retired in luxury to Liternum, far from this city madness. That would have been a better use of the money."

"Ah, but that would have made it stealing," Amelia mutters. Her eyes flare. "I will not see the last of this wasted—we will get that stump Nobilior elected." She fingers her pouch and smiles. "But I'm keeping two of those two stones for myself, I don't care what happens to him!"

They clamber onto the splintery pine slab that serves as the driver's seat. Prima whips the reins forward. The two swayback mares clop down the Avenue of Merchants, heading toward the Scipio domus.

As they rumble around the corner, the African steps out from the darkened doorway. He trots across the darkened street and halts before the storehouse. The African whips out a finger-sized piece of chalk and etches an "X" above the doorknob. He dashes down the street, already planning how he will spend his pay from the short and severe man who hired him—and the storklike man who paid him for another task.

The Nubian draws near the Avenue of Merchants. He turns into a side street and knocks on a narrow, weather-beaten door. The door cracks open. A pair of onyx eyes glare at him from beneath a dark brown cloak.

"Is it time?" the cloaked figure asks.

The Nubian nods. "They are coming this way," he says. The door slams shut in his face.

The wagon clops down the side street, the torches from the Street of Merchants flickering in the distance. Four men step into the street and grab the horses, their faces shadowed by their hoods.

"You got anything besides them rags?" A gruff voice asks.

"You really don't want to find out," Prima says, her voice heavy with threat.

The man's grin splits his face. He turns to his accomplices. "Oh ho! We have a woman here! No Vestal Virgin, I'd wager, but good enough for a poke in the ass, eh?"

"Please, just let us go on," Amelia says. She flips a small purse onto the street slabs. "Take this and be on your way."

"Another woman," a squat man declares happily. "And a fine lady, from the sound of her. Now what would two fine women be doing out at night, and dressed so poorly?"

Prima heaves a sigh. "I told you, you really don't want to know. Now be off with you!"

The leader grins. "Not without whatever you have in there. And a piece of you!" He yanks out a two-foot dagger. "Get off the wagon."

"Whatever you say," replies Prima. In one quick motion, she casts off her cloak and springs onto the street, whipping out her short sword.

The leader sees the flash of her steely blade. He jabs with his dagger, intent on skewering her sword arm. Prima's blade rings against the dagger hilt, deflecting his stab. She strikes back, aiming for his chest. The man catches her sword arm with his left hand, halting her thrust. He pulls her arm back, grinning malevolently.

"I'm going to cut your guts out," he spits, aiming his dagger for her stomach.

Prima twists sideways and kicks upward, planting her sandal squarely in his testicles. The leader doubles over, grunting with pain. Prima jerks up her knee and catches him on the jaw, knocking the stunned thug onto his back. She bends over him.

"Crassus!" his alarmed accomplice yells. He darts forward, pulling a knotted club from his cloak. "Fucking bitch!" he yells, cocking his arm to bash in her skull.

A knife squishes into his right eye socket. His left eye stares sideways at the steel hilt sticking next to it, his mouth working soundlessly. The man falls to the earth, whining piteously. The other two men stalk forward, daggers in hand. Amelia cocks her knife arm. They cower.

Prima shoves her sword into the center of the fallen leader's chest. His head jerks upward, eyes clenched in agony. Prima stares into his face, her teeth clenched. "You are going to cut *what* out of me?"

She plunges the blade deeper, twisting it. The man falls flat, his legs twitching spasmodically. Prima rises from her dying assailant, wiping her sword on his grimy thighs. Amelia steps next to her, a knife in each hand. They face the two remaining men.

Prima raises her bloody blade. "Fight or run," she tells them.

The men dash away, their sandals clapping furiously on the stones. Prima walks to the back of the wagon. She pulls out a rag and wipes her face and arms. "Well, these old things came in handy after all."

"Let's get home before some other fool tries to take advantage of us," Amelia says. She pulls her knife from the man's eye socket, wipes it on his tunic, and clambers onto the wagon seat.

With a snap of the reins, the friends guide their wagon into the torchlit Street of Merchants. They rumble past the dozens of morning fisherman strolling toward the Tiber River, their cane poles perched on their shoulders.

The next morning finds Cato standing in front of the Scipio storehouse, his gray eyes bright with excitement. A drowsy Flaccus stands next to him, accompanied by Marcus Tullius, one of Rome's two censors.

"This is Scipio's hiding place, Censor. We have only to break into it."

Tullius scowls. "Shouldn't we get him to open it?"

"Pah! You know he's in Greece, with his brother. And he wouldn't trust his keys to a woman. Here, I will take care of it."

Cato takes out a chisel and places it on the door lock, beneath the chalked "X" mark. Hammering furiously, he knocks the iron lock off the door and kicks it open. He does the same with the lock on the second door.

"Give me a torch," he says. Flaccus hands him a burning brand. Cato steps inside.

Cato stares into an empty room. He holds the torch over his head and waves it from left to right, searching for plunder. All he sees are sandal prints upon the dusty floor, accompanied by long, snakelike tracks.

Tullius steps into the room, blinking in bewilderment.

Flaccus steps in behind him. "Jupiter's balls, it's empty!"

Cato bends over and points at the tracks.

"See here? This is where they dragged the sacks! They took them away before we came!"

Tullius shrugs. "Those tracks could be from grain sacks, or sacks of feathers. Why does it have to be sacks of coins? Or gold?"

"Check the city register!" Cato sputters. "We will find Scipio's name as the renter!"

"You think he'd use his real name if he did this?" Flaccus says. He chuckles bitterly. "You'd be the only person honest—and stupid—enough to use their real name."

"You look the fool," the censor says. "Best you abandon this goose chase before you do further damage to your reputation. And before I bring charges against you for calumny!"

That night, Cato sits on the patio of his austere country villa, his head cupped in his hands. A beeswax candle flickers next him, his only light in this moonless night.

Cato recalls the nights he spent as Scipio's army accountant in Africa, his back aching as he bent over a candle and tabulated the spoils and expenses of Scipio's many victories. He remembers his arguments with Scipio about his wasteful spending, culminating in Cato's angry return to Rome. *I should have kept my accounting scrolls. They'd show the discrepancies between what he gathered and what he shipped home. Fool, you let anger take your sensibilities!*

He buries his face in his hands. Moments later, he jerks his head up, his eyes bright. *Felix! Felix succeeded me in Africa.*

Cato's heart thunders in his ears. *Scipio brought home shiploads of Carthaginian spoils. He must have stolen some for himself. If Felix recorded any discrepancies, it would be a matter of public record!*

Dawn breaks over the Sabine Hills. Cato gallops down the roadway toward Rome, seeking the residence of Felix Juvenius, retired army quaestor. After inquiring several of Scipio's former tribunes, Cato locates Felix's modest stone townhouse.

Cato pounds upon the varnished pine door. "Quaestor Juvenius! Are you in there?" A birdlike man opens the door, his cheeks puffed with food. He holds a rolled-up pancake in his hand, its inside dripping with honey.

"Senator Cato! What can I do for you?" He glances at the pancake and smiles sheepishly. "I was just finishing breakfast. Please come inside and join me!"

"I have not the time," Cato sputters. "I just need you to answer one question. You were the accountant for Scipio's Africa campaign. Did you keep a record of all the profits and expenditures? Of all the plunder, and what was sent to Rome?"

Felix shifts uncomfortably. "Of course. That was my duty."

Cato takes a deep breath. "Did you note any discrepancies?"

Felix's mouth tightens into a line. He rolls the pancake in his fingers. avoiding Cato's gaze. "Yes."

"Were they significant?"

The quaestor's mouth puckers. "Yes, large amounts of spoils were missing when we landed in Rome. Maybe three thousand talents' worth."

Cato locks the man's wrist in an iron grip. "Three thousand talents! Why didn't you report this?"

"Scipio had just defeated Hannibal. He saved Rome, and brought back a kingdom of wealth. It seemed petty—and dangerous."

Cato steps back from Felix, his face cold. "I see. Are the records still safe?"

"Of course. They are in the Hall of Records, on the left side of—"

Before he can finish, Cato is galloping toward the Forum. An hour later he is bent over a low stone table in the government Tabularium,[clxxii] carefully watched by of the Keeper of Records. Cato unrolls one scroll after another, pouring over Felix's accounts for the African campaign.

Dusk settles onto the city. Cato rises from the table and stretches his stiff shoulders. With a grateful nod to the Keeper, he returns the scrolls and marches from the hall, energetically swinging his arms. His eyes twinkle. *It is all there, my slippery friend. Your ending, writ large in ink. When you return I will spring my trap. I will do it when you are at your highest, so you can fall the farthest.*

As Cato rejoices in his discovery, Flaccus stretches out upon a wicker chaise lounge at his country villa, fuming over the news that his plot was foiled. *Those idiots messed up everything. They could have thrown spears into them, but no, they had to engage in a swordfight. After all that I paid them!*

He laces his fingers together and presses them to his lips. *Just have to bide my time. The way those women run around, they may give me another chance.*

CREMONA GARRISON, NORTH ITALIA, 190 BCE. Laelius leans over the garrison's stone block parapet, staring moodily south toward Rome. His scarlet cloak billows out behind him, wafted by the early autumn breeze.

*Wonder what Prima's doing now? Probably playing with the baby. Glad she gave up the gladiatorial matches. At least I don't have to worry any more about her getting a sword through her chest.*

For the hundredth time, Laelius paces around the city's two-mile walkway, watching the horizon for oncoming enemies. As always, he sees no billowing smoke from burning villages, no dust clouds from thundering hooves, no jagged black lines of approaching infantry. Nothing but peasants scattered among the serried rows of distant wheat fields, stuffing weeds into their wicker shoulder baskets.

*Auuugh, I'm going crazy! I'm the consul of a cemetery—nothing's happening here! Not even a skirmish to break the monotony. Where's a horde of Gauls when you need them?* Laelius turns to the open grounds beneath the camp gates.

The townspeople's children scramble about below him. They roll hoops and pitch balls, their voices bright birds of joy and excitement. He leans back against the parapet. *At least they are enjoying themselves. They don't need a fight to get excited. Maybe all this peace isn't so bad.* He turns back to the ramparts, looking toward Greece.

*Where are you, Scipio? What are you doing? The last messenger said you were in Thessaly.* He slams his fist against the travertine block. *We could have conquered Asia, you stupid bastard. Where's my glory here?*

Laelius pushes himself from the parapet and treads down the walkway. He weaves between the scurrying children, patting them on their heads. Laelius pauses to play several games of tic-tac-toe with an older child, using his dagger to make marks in the dirt.

"That's all I have time for," he tells the boy. "I have to go face my fate."

Laelius straightens his shoulders and marches to the bronze-covered doors of the city blockhouse. *Come on, get it over with.* After a moment's hesitation, he grabs the door handle, jerks it open, and strides inside. Fourteen townspeople sit around the wood slab banquet table, their faces severe.

Laelius forces a smile onto his face. "Good morrow, councilmen. What is today's business?" *What bullshit are you going to whine about today?*

An old man stands up, his bony frame doubled with age. He points a roll of soft vellum at Laelius as if it were a weapon. "We have a list of complaints here, Consul. The fullers say that someone is stealing the urine they collect—we suspect the thieves are selling it across the river in Placentia. Our fullers don't have enough to clean our togas!" Several councilmen bark out their assent.

"I will put several of my speculatores on it, they will track down these pissy thieves." Laelius rubs his eyes. "What else?"

The reedy little man takes on a look of outrage. "Several of your centurions have been luring our young men into dice games, and using crooked dice."

"How do you know the dice are crooked?" Laelius asks.

"The boys told us. They lost all their money!" The man replies.

*You think dice are nothing but luck? I could play the lot of you and leave you naked.* "I will look into it," he replies.

The elder nods solemnly. "Then there is the matter of toilet sponges. We need twenty denarii to buy extra sponges. Your men have been frequenting the town latrines, and the latrine attendants tell us they are wearing them out!" He glowers at Laelius. "Too much grain in their diet, you know."

Laelius stares at the ceiling. *Vulcan take me, just strike me dead*!

Four hours later, Laelius staggers from the meeting room, rubbing the small of his back. "I need a bath and a wrestle!" he says to himself. He returns to his spacious manse adjoining the town forum. A messenger stands in front of its double bronze doors, waiting for him with scroll in hand.

Laelius takes the scroll, noticing it has the bear's head seal of the Julia family. He unrolls the scroll and hastily reads it. His expression quickly changes from curiosity to rage. *Someone tried to kill them! This has the smell of Flaccus*!

"Will you have a response?" the messenger asks.

"Only one that I will deliver myself, when the time comes." The soldier salutes and marches toward the doorway. When the door closes, Laelius slams his foot into a nearby washstand, sending its bronze bowl clanging off the wall.

*I should have killed that bastard after Pomponia died. He must have had his hand in that.* Laelius scowls. *I should never have promised Scipio I'd wait until we knew for sure about Flaccus.*

Laelius dashes to the front door. "Come back!" he yells. The messenger returns, looking puzzled. "Wait. I have a consular order for you." he tells him.

The consul stoops over his writing desk, hastily inking an order upon a goatskin scroll. He rolls up the scroll and pours wax onto it, pressing in his consular seal.

"Get this to Cyprian, the Senate Elder, as soon as possible," Laelius says. He watches the legionnaire trot out the door, his eyes as cold as ice.

*There! Amelia and Prima will have guards about them night and day. That will do for now, but there will be a reckoning, friend Flaccus. I will see to you.*

**Roman Quinquereme with**

**Boarding Platform**

# IX. CALL TO ARMS

PORT OF AMALIAPOLIS, PAGASETIC GULF, THESSALY. Commander Gaius Augustus paces angrily across the foredeck of his flagship, his chapped hands clutched about a scroll. *Neptune's ass, the morning wind is blowing right into our faces! Livius just had to send us out early, curse him. At least the rowers are making good time.*

The quadrireme's curved prow delves through the three-foot seas. Its four banks of rowers dig deeply into the white-capped waves, beating their way through the swirling northeast breezes.

The ship's tribune plods toward Augustus, his ringed curls wiggling in the stiff wind. "It's a bad day for sailing, Commander. Unless you're heading back the way we came! Can't we wait until the winds shift?"

Augustus shakes his head. "My orders were quite clear, Remus." The navarchus slaps his scroll into Remus' leathery palm. The tribune unrolls it and reads the terse message.

"Isn't that just a pot of nonsense?" Augustus mutters. "Admiral Livius wanted us leave the port and patrol the coast for Syrians."

Remus scratches his head. "Our twelve ships can't cover the entire Thessaly coast. We'd be better off paying the damn fishermen to keep watch for us!"

Augustus shakes his head. "They are watching. Livius has spread the word across the coast. A verified sighting brings a purse of silver. They'll probably spot a ship before we do!" He stuffs the scroll into his belt pouch. "But orders are orders. We have to get out there and see for ourselves. Six of our ships to the north, and six to the south."

Remus nods. "I'll go check on the rowers. This wind must be a nightmare for them."

The tiny Roman fleet lurches toward the mouth of the Pagasetic Gulf, a two-mile gap enclosed by forested peninsulas. An hour later, the flagship's watchman shouts out a sighting. "Land ahead!"

Remus appears at Augustus' side, his face concerned. "The wind has picked up against us. Our men are tired from all the rowing."

Augustus spits over the lacquered side railing, his mouth tight with disappointment. "Shit! It seems like Neptune does not want us to get out to sea today!"

He examines the faint outlines of the two peninsulas. "When we reach the mouth, we'll turn to starboard and anchor at the leeward side of the south peninsula. Then we can give the rowers some food and rest. But only a few hours, Remus. I promised the admiral we'd be in the Aegean before sunset."

The quadriremes tack toward the narrow mouth of water that divides the two hilly fingers of land. Augustus points to the faint outline of a tree-lined cove on the south peninsula. "Take the ships over there. The hills will block the wind."

A sleek trireme edges into the mouth of the gulf, its square sails bowed from a stiff tailwind. Five more appear, then twelve, then another twelve, their three banks of rowers cutting deep into the waves. The thirty ships hurtle toward the oncoming Romans, their bronze rams shimmering in the late morning sun.

Augustus spies the lead ship's crescent moon flag. "Syrians!" he shouts to Aeneas. "Head for the cove, we'll set up a defensive formation!"

The weary Roman rowers bend to their oars, digging their long oars into the white-capped waves. Even so, the sleek triremes close the distance between them and the quadriremes.

Leaning over the prow of the lead trireme, Hannibal breaks into a feral grin. "Hard astern! Full speed from the rowers. I want everything they've got!"[clxxiii] The deck officers scramble down the ladder to the lower decks, screaming orders. Hannibal's trireme leaps ahead, angling for the side of the Roman flagship.

Augustus sees the lead trireme surging toward him. His heart sinks. "All men above decks! Prepare to board!"

The weary marines abandon their oars. They grab swords from the racks above their heads. Three hundred rowers scramble to the deck. They mass along the railings with the ship's seventy-five marines, ready for hand-to-hand combat.

"Get the corvus ready!" Remus shouts. Ten marines drag up a thirty-foot boarding platform and hold it near the railing, waiting to cast its spiked end onto the enemy deck.

Hannibal watches the marines massing above decks, ready to attack. *Oh no you don't! I'm not getting these Syrians into a sword fight with Romans!*

He grabs the captain by the shoulder strap of his breastplate. "Listen carefully! I want the men to act like we're going to board them. Then go hard to port, and ram into their side. Go!" The captain rushes below decks.

The Syrian ship eases sideways and closes upon the Roman vessel. As it draws closer, the ship abruptly turns straight for the side of the quadrireme.

"Prepare to be rammed!" Augustus yells. The marines grab railings, masts, anything that will keep them from being knocked overboard.

With an ear-splitting crash, the Syrians' beaked prow delves into the side of the Roman flagship, splintering its side timbers. Water gushes into the quadrireme's lower deck. The top deck marines raise the corvus high above the railing, ready to drop its spiked end upon the enemy deck.

"Don't let them get on board," Hannibal shouts. "Reverse, full speed!" The rowers push the ship backwards. As they row, dozens of Syrians rush to their ship's prow, lugging stout oak ramming poles. They shove the poles against the side of the Roman ship, pushing their vessel from the quadrireme's ruptured timbers.

As the Syrian ship withdraws from the Roman vessel, dozens of Syrian archers rush to the top deck railing. They dip their arrows into the ship's pitch pots and put torches to the arrowheads. Streams of flaming arrows descend upon the quadrireme, igniting man and ship.

"Abandon ship!" Augustus shouts. A flaming arrow thunks into his leather cuirass, setting him aflame. He unstraps his armor and dives into the unruly seas, joining his crewmen.

The outnumbered Roman ships are soon surrounded, rammed, and burned. Hundreds of Romans splash toward the forested peninsula, shouting encouragement to their fellow swimmers.

"Hunt them down," Hannibal orders. The Syrian ships drift by the escaping Romans. The Syrian archers line the sides of their ships, their bows cocked and ready.

"Loose!" Hannibal shouts. The archers flood their arrows into backs of the helpless swimmers, savoring the screams when their missiles strike home.

On board Hannibal's ship, several archers spy Augustus' red-bordered tunic. "Officer!" one of them declares. A dozen archers bunch up along the bow, loosing arrows at Augustus.

Swimming for the cove, Augustus hears a splash next to his right shoulder. Then two more. He turns his head sideways and sees a trireme bearing down on him, its archers bunched in the front with bows aimed at him. He dives under the waves, just as a half dozen arrows cut into the water where he swam.

The Syrian archers stare into the dark green waters, waiting for the commander to emerge. They see a red stain float up into the top water, spreading across the chop. Augustus surfaces, gasping, his arms slapping at the waters. An arrow juts from his right shoulder.

"There he is!" an archer shouts excitedly. As one, the archers release their shafts.

An arrow thunks into the side of Augustus' head, another into his throat. Augustus gasps with agony, rolling his eyes sideways to gape at his tormentors. Sea water pours into his mouth. After a few feeble splashes, he disappears under the waves.

Two hours later, Hannibal watches the sun set over the Pagasetic Gulf, its deep blue waters dotted with the flaming islands of burning quadriremes. He waves over Maxim, his Syrian commander.

"Send a messenger to Admiral Polyxenidas. Tell him I want forty more triremes over here. We're going to bottle up the bay. The Romans won't dare to sail for Syria from here."

"Won't that just send them north, where we have fewer ships?" the veteran sailor asks. "They might head for the Macedonian ports of Dion or Pydna."

"I hope they do. That means they will have to travel through Philip of Macedonia's territory."

"So? He is now a friend to Rome, is he not?" Maxim says.

Hannibal smirks. "The die is not yet cast on his loyalties."

A loud gurgling noise draws Hannibal's attention to his ship's starboard side. He watches a Roman quadrireme slowly disappear into the depths, its quenched embers hissing like a thousand snakes. "Let the Romans go to Macedonia. The Scipios may find that we are not their only enemy."

The sun creeps below the horizon. The Syrian triremes sail out from the mouth of the gulf, heading into the boundless Aegean. As his ship enters the sea, Hannibal studies the rest of his fleet, scores of ships moored near the Aegean side of the south peninsula. His gaze roves over the quadriremes and triremes, pausing upon his four hulking hexaremes. Dozens of archers stand along the top of each hexareme's two-story tower.

*Too bad the Romans didn't have enough vessels for me to use my fireships. If Baal blesses me, I'll have another opportunity soon.*

"I need a ship to sail me over to Ephesus," Hannibal tells Maxim. "I have to help Antiochus organize our ground forces."

The Carthaginian grins. "Besides, I'm looking forward to meeting my old friend Scipio. He owes me a victory, and I intend to get paid."

PELLA, MACEDONIA. Philip closes the thick door that leads in to his private courtyard, muffling the screams. Ares' cock, I thought Thracians were supposed to be tough. A few minutes in the fire, and he's screaming the name of his accomplice. Well, he'll soon have company.

Philip flicks a spot of dried blood off the emerald ring attached to his long, slender forefinger. *I'm going to wear gloves next time. No sense making this more unpleasant than it has to be.* The king ambles down his palace's statue-lined hallway, his ermine robe trailing behind him. He enters his throne room.

Two macaques scramble across the throne room floor, racing to be the first to greet their master. The small, gold-collared apes tug at Philip's thick robe, chirping with excitement.

"Did my little loves miss me?" Philip coos. The monkeys blink their beady black eyes, their wizened faces expectant. He reaches toward his belt purse, and the beasts begin to leap about. Philip smiles. "First, a tune," he says, extracting a tiny flute. He hands it to the largest macaque, a dusky brown ape with the face of an aged woman.

The ape grabs the flute and blows a cacophonous tune, scrambling about with his partner as he plays. Philip guffaws. "Here you are, my precious ones!" Philip pitches them a handful of grapes.

"Wine!" the king barks, his voice echoing in the vast empty chamber. He hears no response. *Lazy shits!* "Wine, boy!" he shouts. A slave boy hustles out between the room's rear curtains, lugging a chalice and a stoppered wine jug. He fills the chalice and hands it to Philip.

"You delay me again, it will be your balls in this cup," Philip growls.

A squat older man pads into the throne room, his pot belly pushing against the confines of his bare-shouldered summer chiton. He shows Philip a mud-stained sheaf of papyrus.

"What is it now, Boban?" Philip moans. "Another plague in the north?"

"Amaxenes came in last night," the minister says to Philip. "He rode all the way from Thessaly."

Philip's eyes light up. "And what does my favorite spy have to say?" he asks, steepling his bejeweled fingers.

"His message is brief but important," Boban replies. The diminutive Macedonian hands the sheaf to Philip.

"He reports that the Syrians now control the seas about Thessaly," Boban says. "Lucius Scipio's army cannot cross there. They are marching north."

"North toward us," Philip replies cheerily.

Boban nods. "I would expect so. They will want to cross through Macedonia, that they may access the Hellespont from Thrace."

"But they do not know about the roads and bridges I have built since our war with them,[clxxiv] do they?" Philip says. "Their journey to the Hellespont could be difficult indeed, if they wander into the pathways wrecked from the war." The king's gaze grows distant. "They might even wander into some deep pass or canyon—rendering them vulnerable to attack."

Boban's eyes widen with alarm. "Rome still holds your son Demetrias as a treaty hostage."[clxxv]

Philip winks at his minister. "I am merely musing about possibilities. I wouldn't endanger Demetrias—unless I needed to."

The king taps a forefinger against his cheek. The throne room grows quiet. "How many men do we have?"

"Twenty thousand, if we count the ones in the garrisons that you took over for Consul Glabrio."

"Many more than the Romans know about, I am sure," A slight smile plays about his lips. "Yes, let them come. We will prepare a grand reception for them."

AMPHISSA, THESSALY, 190 BCE. "We can't trust him," Scipio says, pacing about Lucius' command tent. "We can't just march into Pella and expect him to welcome us with open arms!"

"Philip has disavowed Antiochus, and we have a signed treaty with him," Lucius says. "He will have to help us."

"Like he helped General Glabrio last year? Where was he when Glabrio fought at Thermopylae? I'll tell you where he was—home in his palace, waiting to side with the winner!"

"But what other choice do we have?" Lucius pleads. "The Syrians have blockaded the ports of Thessaly. We have to go through Macedonia to get to the Hellespont."

"My advice is that we first test the king's intentions. We'll send an emissary to him, but we won't let Philip know he's coming! He must take Philip by surprise, in public. Then cannot give one of his rehearsed performances."[clxxvi]

Lucius shrugs, bewildered. "What good would all that do, if we cannot trust him?"

"Philip is a proud man," Scipio says. "If he renews his promises in public, he will not renege on them and be thought a liar." He grins. "Especially if his oath is given to a priest. His people would fear the wrath of the gods!"

"We should send Tiberius Gracchus?"

"Just so, Brother. Who better than the high priest of Rome? He can catch Philip when he is at some public function. The full moon rises in three days—there's sure to be some festivities in Pella for the Nemoralia."[clxxvii]

"I don't know," Lucius says, his voice trailing off.

Scipio shrugs. "It is your decision to make. Just don't wait too long. Gracchus will have to cover over two hundred miles to get there in time for the festival." Scipio walks out, a slight smile upon his face. "I'll leave it to you," he says over his shoulder.

Lucius stares at Scipio's back, kneading his fingers.

The next day dawns upon a drizzling sky. Tiberius Gracchus is mounting his horse in front of stables, preparing for his run to Thessaly. He carries a small bag of dried bread and cheese and a large saddle sack of his best dress armor.

Scipio hurries over, lugging a thick cotton bag. He hands it up to Gracchus. "You need a gift for Philip. Take this."

The handsome young priest peers into the sack. He gazes wonderingly at Scipio. "You want to give this to him? Are you sure?"

Scipio sighs. "We need to touch his heart. What better way than giving him my most prized possession?"

"All honor to you, Scipio Africanus," Gracchus says, wiping the corner of his eye. "I will get there on time, I swear. Somnus will not conquer me—I will stay awake and through the night."

"Switch horses at the towns," Scipio advises.

"Every chance I get," Gracchus replies. He digs his heels into his white stallion's side. The beast hurtles for the camp gates, heading north for Pella.

As dusk sets on the third day of his ride, a dust-covered Gracchus trots through the gates of Pella.[clxxviii] He halts before an armored spearman and brandishes his spread-eagle truce staff.

"I bear urgent news for King Philip. Where is he?"

"In the palace's main banquet hall, celebrating the full moon. Not that the festival matters to us on guard duty—we'll be here all night."

"How unfortunate for you," Gracchus replies dryly, studying the carefully tended streets and houses. "I'll bring you back an egg."

Gracchus trots through Pella's torchlight streets, halting at the white marble columns that front Philip's three-story palace. As he walks up the palace steps he is intercepted by two of Philip's royal guard.

"I have an urgent message from the consul of Rome," Gracchus tells them.

"The king is taking his leisure at a banquet," the lead guard says. "You will have to wait until tomorrow."

Gracchus' mind races. He seizes upon a lie. "King Philip has been waiting for this. He demanded it as soon as possible."

"Come with us, then." The guard says. "But do not expect too much from him. The celebration has been going on for hours."

*All the better,* Gracchus thinks. "Just a minute." He throws off his dusty cloak and gropes into one of his saddle bags. He pulls out a gleaming silver cuirass, its breasts decorated with gold eagle heads. He dons the cuirass, followed by silver greaves and a flowing scarlet cape. He grabs the bulging sack that Scipio gave him. "I'm ready."

The three tread up the wide stone steps to the palace entry. The guards push open the doors. Gracchus steps into a hall the size of a mansion. A riot of sights, smells, and sounds bursts upon him.

A dozen lyre players roam among hordes of robed and masked revelers. Scores of nude maidens pirouette behind them, their faces covered by gilded masks of Selene, the moon goddess. A tall platform on each side of Philip holds a man and woman engaged in sexual congress, glistening with the gold paint that covers their undulating bodies.

Dozens of slaves weave through the boisterous crowd, tilting their wine jugs to refill the guests' bronze goblets. Streams of fragrant incense drift among the celebrants, making it appear as if they are walking among clouds.

King Philip stands on the high dais that holds his throne, waving a phallus-shaped scepter. A flowing fur robe covers the king's lean, muscular body, naked except for a gold mesh loincloth.

*What a decadent mess*, the priest thinks. *Cato would fall dead at the sight of this.* He studies Philip, noting his bleary eyes. *He is full of wine.*[clxxix] *Now is a propitious moment.*

Philip spies Gracchus standing in the doorway, holding his truce staff. "Who goes there?" Philip shouts, pointing his scepter at Gracchus. The music quiets. All eyes turn toward the door.

Gracchus takes a deep breath. He lifts up his chin and marches toward the king, his cape billowing behind him. Gracchus holds his staff in his right hand, and grasps the cotton sack in his left. He halts in front of Philip and genuflects.

"Honored king, I bear you greetings from Rome, your friend and ally. And from Lucius Cornelius Scipio and Scipio Africanus."

Philip eyes him warily. *What the fuck is he doing here at this hour?* He waves his scepter across the crowd. "We of Macedonia are honored to receive you." He burps wetly, prompting scattered laughs.

"On behalf of the Senate of Rome, I have come to ask you an important question. If you would give me your answer, I will depart and relay it to the Scipios."

Phillip plunks onto his throne, his chin in his hand. "State your piece."

Gracchus walks to the bottom of the dais. He gently lowers his bag onto the marble tiles. "Rome wants to know if you will welcome Consul Lucius Scipio and his consular army within your borders, as per your agreement in the treaty."

Philip's face flushes. *Impertinent dolt!* His bleary eyes light with malice. *I'll let you in. Then I'll let you pricks find your own way over to Thrace.* "What's in the sack?" Philip mutters, reaching for a wine goblet.

Gracchus bends over and reaches into the bag. "A gift from Scipio Africanus. A token of his esteem for you."

The priest extracts a worn tribune's helmet, its battered surface gleaming from a fresh polish. Grasping it with both hands, Gracchus reverently extends it to King Philip, his head bowed.

"This is the helmet of Marcus Silenus, Rome's greatest warrior. He was friend, confidant, and brother in arms to Scipio Africanus, the world's greatest general." He raises his head. "It is Scipio's most prized possession," he says softly.

Philip rises, dumbfounded. *Marcus Silenus, the undefeated!* He gingerly lifts the helmet from Gracchus' hands. Philip traces his finger over the sword dents that dapple its crown. A lump grows in his throat. He glances at the hundreds of revelers watching him.

"Go back to the Scipios," Philip says, his slurred voice echoing through the chamber. "Tell them I welcome them as friends to Macedonia. My people are here to bear witness."

Gracchus bows. "Gratitude for those words, my King." He rubs his eyes. "I have made a long journey in a short time. If you could give me a bed for the night, I would be most appreciative."

"You will have a room adjoining my own," Philip gushes. "But stay awhile, and celebrate the rising of the moon goddess!"

Tiberius' eyes roam across the throngs of drunken, half-naked guests, many staring hostilely at him. "I think it best I get some sleep. It would be better for my health."

Two weeks later, the Roman army enters the wide plain that fronts the walled city of Pella. Lucius and Scipio lead the cavalry vanguard, searching the terrain for ambushes. As they approach the high-walled city, a small army of Macedonians marches out to meet them, their bronze shields shining like a flowing wave of copper.

Lucius grabs Scipio's arm. "Here they come! Sound the horns for battle formation!"

Scipio pulls Lucius' hand away. He gives him a playful shove. "Look closer. No swords or spears. They are not the threat they seem to be." He grins. "That, or Philip is even trickier than Hannibal himself."

"Battle formation," Lucius shouts, ignoring Scipio.

The Roman army halts. Their marching columns stream out to the side and form into maniples. They plant the edge of their shields into the ground in front of them and hold their javelins upright, ready for battle.

Philip of Macedonia rides in on a silver-bridled black stallion, leading two phalanxes of Macedonians. He halts his men and rides alone to meet the Scipios.

"Welcome consul. Welcome, Scipio Africanus. I trust your journey was uneventful?"

"A few raiding parties near Dion," Lucius replies, "but our cavalry soon dispersed them."

Philip sweeps his arm across the plain, taking in the rounded mountains that lie behind it. "You are now in my kingdom. My Companions[clxxx] and I will personally escort you through Macedonia and Thrace, and on to the ports of the Hellespont. [clxxxi] No one will dare bother you, not even those pestiferous Thracians."

"Good," replies Scipio. "We will have battles enough when we meet Antiochus."

Philip's face takes on a look of regret. "I would love to take my men and fight beside you, but I only have a few thousand of them, as per the terms of our treaty with Rome."

"I am sure you would," Scipio says, with ill-concealed sarcasm. "Fear not. Eumenes of Pergamum is joining us. His troops should more than suffice."

"Good," Philip says. "But watch out for him, he cannot be trusted." Scipio resists the urge to laugh.

"Can you tell us the best way to cross your kingdom?" Lucius says. "We had heard that the old roads were destroyed."

Philip lifts his chin. "They were, but *I* have built new passages. You will make the Hellespont by late autumn. Stay here for a week, and we will provide you with all the supplies you will need."

"Excellent," Lucius replies. "Now we can engage Antiochus before my year expires." He looks across the plain. "Do we have your leave to establish our camp here? Over by that lovely lake?"

"Of course! And tonight we feast in my palace. I will make the preparations." Philip wheels his horse about and walks it back toward his men.

Scipio trots out and draws up beside him. "I am curious. What did you do with Marcus Silenus' helmet?" Scipio asks.

"It sits on a marble pedestal in my bedroom, between two of my own war helmets," Philip smiles. "I could not put it among my crowns. It somehow seemed inappropriate, like a lion among lambs."

"He was a lion, in every sense of the word," Scipio replies.

Philip grasps Scipio's shoulder. "That was very clever, sending Gracchus to surprise me in public. Even so, I was truly humbled by your gift. Know that I call you friend, now and forever."

Scipio places his hand over the king's and squeezes it firmly. "I hope we will keep that bond. Now and forever."

Scipio rides back to Lucius, who is convening with the tribunes. *Thank you Marcus, for your one last service*. Scipio thinks. He smiles sadly. *Even from the underworld, you have served Rome well.*

"My command tent will be up within the hour," Lucius tells Scipio. "Yours will shortly follow." He peers into Scipio's face. "You look very tired, Brother. I fear for your health. Perhaps you should rest as soon as your tent is finished. I will get Marcus Aemilius and Tiberius Gracchus to help me prepare the camp."

Scipio rubs his brow. “In truth, I am feeling a bit weary. I think I will go sit by the lake. I have some writing to do.” He turns to Consus, his favorite attendant.

“Bring my writing tools.” The camp slave rushes toward one of the oncoming baggage wagons, trotting back with a goatskin satchel and a large square plank. “Follow me,” Scipio orders.

Scipio strolls toward the aquamarine waters of Lake Ostrovo.[clxxxii] He folds up his purple-bordered cloak and lays it upon its reed-lined shore. He eases himself onto the cloak, his legs stretched in front of him.

His lanky young attendant hands him his tools. Scipio nods his thanks. “Return in two hours, Consus.” The slave trots back toward the campsite.

Scipio turns back to the lake. He lays the oak plank in his lap and flattens a papyrus scroll upon it. *I have just made a friend of one king. Time to recover a friendship with another.*

Scipio pulls the stopper from the octopus ink bottle. Dipping his stylus into the pot, he inks out a message in his florid handwriting.

*To Masinissa, Rightful King of Numidia:*

*I call on you to honor your promise, and join me in battle. Hannibal and Antiochus loom before us, with overwhelming numbers of cavalry. Your peerless riders are sorely needed. Again.*

*The Syrians do not pose an immediate threat to Numidia. Should they conquer Greece and Italia, however, Hannibal will surely lead them into Africa. And you will be left alone to combat them.*

*Come to the Hellespont, old friend. Let us battle together, one more time, against our common enemy.*

*Your brother in arms.*<br>
*Publius Cornelius Scipio Africanus*

Scipio rolls up the papyrus and ties a string around it. He pulls out another scroll and begins a letter to Paullus Julianus, the praetor of Sicily.

After finishing the message, he wraps his arms about his knees. Scipio watches the giant white pelicans fly low across the lake, their webbed feet skimming its mirrored surface. A fever tremor shakes him, then another. He ignores them.

Consus returns. He gathers the writing accessories into the satchel, holding the plank under his arm. Scipio follows him to camp and walks into his newly-raised tent. He seals the two messages with the owl's head seal of the Scipio family, and writes the recipients' names upon the scrolls. "Bring me a messenger," he tell Consus.

A rider soon appears at Scipio's tent. "Take these to Apollonnia," he says. "See that they go out on the next ship to Numidia." The messenger dashes from the tent.

Scipio throws himself on his sleeping pallet, and is soon fast asleep. Dusk approaches. Scipio stumbles from his tent, still drowsy. He walks over to the consular tent, where he finds Lucius in the midst of a conference with his legion commanders. Lucius and the officers look up from his map table. Lucius raises his right hand. The conversation halts.

"Yes?" Lucius says icily.

"Stop by my tent when you are done," Scipio says. An hour later, Lucius enters his brother's tent.

"I sent a messenger to Masinissa, requesting he send cavalry to us," Scipio says.

"What! You had no right! I am the consul, I determine who is part of my army. I wouldn't have done that."

"Which is exactly why I didn't ask you," Scipio replies. "Antiochus may have ten thousand cavalry in his army. We need more riders, and the Numidians are the finest on earth."

"Don't ever do that again!" Lucius splutters. "I'm the one Rome elected as consul!"

"And I'm the one who got you elected," Scipio calmly replies. "You'd do well to remember that."

"You think I can't do anything without you! I'll show you how wrong you are!" Lucius blazes. He slaps open the tent flaps and strides from Scipio's tent.

MACRIS ISLAND,[clxxxiii] AEGEAN SEA, 190 BCE. "This is our best chance to destroy them, Juval," Admiral Polyxenidas declares. He jabs his finger into his camelskin map of Teos Bay. "When the Romans sail into Teos Bay, we'll trap them like rats in a jug!"

"What makes you sure they'll enter the harbor?" Captain Juval asks.

Polyxenidas grins. "Teos is known for its fine wine. They are Romans—they'll want to go there to restock."

"If they see us coming into the bay, they'll attack us," Captain Juval notes. "And they've got Eudamus of Rhodes with them. His ships are very fast. He'll be on us in the blink of an eye."

"Not if they don't see us," the admiral replies. "We'll enter Teos Bay at night, and put our ships on the inside of the two peninsulas.[clxxxiv] We'll moor them as close to the shore as possible. Half along the Myonessus Peninsula, the others on Corycum."

Juval nods. "That would leave only the mouth of the bay open. It's barely wide enough for two ships to get out."

"Exactly." Polyxenidas runs his finger along the outline of the Myonessus Peninsula. "We will moor our triremes near the front of the peninsulas, with the hexaremes behind them. We want to attack the port as swiftly as possible, so we can trap them at the docks."

"We can burn most of them before they even raise their sails!" Juval exclaims.

"And destroy the rest inside the bay, because they can't escape," adds Polyxenidas, rubbing his pudgy hands together. "We'll wait until they are all docked, with their men in roaming about the town. Then we sneak in during the night."

"The seas will be ours," Juval declares. A worried look crosses his face. "But they do have to enter the bay for that wine."

Two days later, the Roman and Rhodian ships sail into Teos Bay. Admiral Aemilius Regillus leads his eighty ships into Teos Harbor, docking his one-hundred-fifty-foot flagship alongside the citadel's main pier.

Florus peers over the lacquered oak railing. The captain watches the Roman warships pull into the adjoining docks. "We'll have them all docked within two hours," he comments.

"Make sure Eudamus has room to land his ships," Regillus orders. The slender young patrician trots down the quinquereme's gangplank, eager to explore the famous seaport. *Now to see if their wines are as good as I hear!*

"I am going to scout out the town," he shouts up to Florus. "Eudamus can meet me there." He grins at his weathered old captain. "I await his pleasure at the nearest wine bar."

An half hour later, Eudamus' slim trireme docks behind Regillus' vessel. The stern, white-haired commander steps onto the pier, his green eyes examining every local man and building. He stares back toward the Aegean, frowning at the two peninsulas that enclose the quiescent bay. *Too damn easy to get trapped in here.*

As Eudamus contemplates the harbor, a Roman marine approaches. He points to a weather-beaten wine bar that fronts the dockside avenue.

"Admiral Regillus awaits you."

"I'll be there after I affirm that all my ships are here," Commander Eudamus replies, his lips tight with irritation. *This pup Regillus is the replacement for Admiral Livius? Livius would see to his men before taking refreshment. Why these Romans switch commanders every year, I will never know.*

When the last of his fleet ties up on the far side docks, Eudamus marches to the wine bar. He spies Regillus at a corner table, his bare feet stretched out in front of him. A bronze pitcher and goblet rests next to a plate of bread and cheese. He waves cheerily at Eudamus.

"Come sit with me, and have some bread. And some of this excellent wine! I'm going to have a thousand amphorae brought into my ships, as a reward to the men. Should I fetch some for your vessels?"

"We are fine," the Rhodian replies coldly. "We do not require any more drink."

Regillus shrugs. "As you wish, but there's plenty for all." He grins. "Back in Rome, we'd always open an amphora or two after our sailing races. Win or lose, we'd always celebrate!"

"Is that where you gained your experience?" Eudamus says, fighting to keep the sarcasm from his voice. "In sailing races?"

"Oh yes. I raced biremes. My crew captured a number of laurel wreaths. No one could beat us."

The older man stares at the threadbare naval flags flapping from the wine bar's ceiling. *Poseidon save me! A patrician dandy is leading the fleet!* "I am sure you were quite accomplished."

Regillus' lean lips curl into a smirk, acknowledging the sarcasm. "That was not the only sailing I've done. I had served as a junior officer for three years, one with our dear Admiral Livius, who now has left for Rome." He sniffs. "He did the best he could here, but you know how Romans are! More interested in boarding and fighting than in outmaneuvering a foe. We are more like a floating army than a navy."

"Livius was a good man," Eudamus replies evenly. He peers out the open doorway, at the walls of ships that line the inner harbor. "I would hope we can depart by the morrow," he says. "It's too easy to be trapped in here."

Regillus blinks. "Depart? We just landed. I gave the men three days' leave. They're already out in the town!"[clxxxv]

Eudamus rises from his stool and strolls to the doorway. He sees hundreds of rowers and marines roaming along the dockside streets, tilting jugs of wine to their mouths. He quickly returns to Regillus' table, his eyes smoldering with rage.

"Do you realize that we are only a day's sail from Antiochus' kingdom? That Polyxenidas' fleet is out there searching for us?"

Regillus tilts his goblet to his lips. "I hear you, it's dangerous to be here. I will send out some scout ships as soon as I finish."

He cuts his eyes sideways at Eudamus. "Really, Commander. If the Syrian's fleet was around here, we would have seen them."

A small, sun-browned man appears in the doorway, nervously twisting the hem of his stained green tunic. "Is this where I get my reward?" he mutters, his eyes wide with apprehension.

"Here now, be off with you," barks a guard. The peasant retreats into the street, dodging a pack of boisterous Romans. He sets his chin and steps back in. "I hear Romans pay for information."

The guard places his hand on the pommel of his sword. The peasant edges back into the street, but his face remains hopeful.

"Wait a minute, Cassius," Regillus says to his guard. He waves in the peasant. "And just what information do you have for us?" He winks at Eudamus. "Do you know where the best brothel is, is that what you want to tell me?"

The little man stares at his feet. He vigorously shakes his head. "Ships. I saw lots of ships. Syrian ships."

Eudamus rises from his stool, his eyes staring. "You saw ships where?"

The peasant looks up at the frightening figure, and quickly glances down. "I fish on Macris Island. Yesterday I sail to windward. See scores of ships in harbor. They hidden from sight. Big ships, purple flags with moons!"[clxxxvi] He points to a Syrian flag dangling from the ceiling. "Flags like that."

Regillus vaults from his seat, his face ashen. Eudamus grasps his wrist. "We have to get out of the bay before we are trapped!"

"I know I know," Regillus blurts. "Get your ships to follow me!" He turns to his guards. "Sound the recall! You hear me, recall everyone at once!" Regillus and Eudamus rush from the wine bar, followed by the Roman guards.

"What about my money?" the peasant shouts at the empty doorway. He hears no response. "Come back!" he yells, but receives no reply.

The peasant walks to Regillus' table and draws up a stool.

The portly bar owner approaches, his pig eyes burning with disdain. "What are you doing? Get your bony ass out of here!"

The fisherman draws out his filleting knife and places it on the table. "I think I stay and finish." The owner eyes the keen blade. With a shrug, he walks into his kitchen.

The peasant pours himself a goblet of the admiral's wine and drinks deeply, smacking his lips. He bites a chunk off the pie-shaped barley bread lying next to him. He chews slowly, eyeing the empty doorway. "Fucking Romans," he mutters.

Regillus rushes back to his ship, shouting orders as he runs up the gangplank. Soon, dozens of Roman hornsmen rush through the seaport streets, madly blowing their calls to return to ship.[clxxxvii] The sailors dash for the docks. Some stagger drunkenly toward their vessels, others run while hastily knotting up their loincloths. The piers swarm with frantic marines and rowers, but still the horns echo throughout the town.

Regillus stands at the foot of his gangplank, frantically waving his men into his flagship. "Come on, come on, we have to be the first out of here!" The last marine jumps onto the deck. The ship casts off for the mouth of the harbor, drawing out the rest of the Roman fleet.

Eudamus strides over to his ship, ignoring the Romans who stampede past him. He strides up to the prow of his flagship, watching Regillus' ship ease out from its mooring.

"Should we launch and follow them?" asks Faustus, his deck captain.

Eudamus watches the careening Roman ships bump into one another, their captains cursing at each other across the railings. "Wait until the confusion dies down. For once, we will bring up the rear."

By day's end, the Roman fleet has sailed past the peninsulas and is out into the Aegean, drawn up in a line. The ships anchor there, while the Roman scout ships sail toward Macris Island.

Morning finds a fully armored Regillus pacing about the deck, his mind whirling with plans to defend against a Syrian attack. The young admiral strides to his ship's stern and looks off to his right. Far astern, he sees the trim Rhodian triremes at anchor in an attack wedge, their lowered sails flapping against the masts. Eudamus' snake-faced flagship floats at the head of the wedge, the sun glinting off its brass ramming head.

*You're waiting to see what I will do if they attack, aren't you?* Regillus thinks. *I know you don't trust me, old man.*

A Roman bireme surges in under full sail, its twin banks of oars plowing furiously. The scout ship glides toward Regillus' quinquereme and slows. Regillus leans over the railing, his eyes wide with excitement.

"What news?" Regillus shouts down to it. The bireme's captain rushes to the middle of his narrow deck and cups his hands to his mouth. "The Syrians are coming, hard in from the northeast! Fourscore ships, or more!"

Regillus feels his stomach churn. "Sound the battle horns!" he yells. The ship's trumpeter grabs his cornu and blares three short blasts. The call echoes across the water, relayed from ship to ship. Florus raises the ship's red battle flag to the top of the main mast.

"For Rome and the Republic," Regillus yells. "Attack!"

The ships raise their sails and surge forward. Regillus' keen-eyed lookout leans over the bow, searching for signs of the enemy.

Aboard the Syrian flagship, Polyxenidas stomps about in a fit of rage. "Gods damn them, those Roman scout ships found us! No sneaking into the harbor, we've got to meet them head on."

"We outnumber them," Captain Juval says. "And our triremes are faster than their lumbering quinqueremes. We've should try to outflank them."

"Agreed," the admiral replies. "We'll pick on the weakest side."

The Syrians approach the Roman line of battle, their eighty-nine ships riding two deep across the sea. Polyxenidas notices that the Roman vessels are bunched closer together than his flotilla, with the Rhodian fleet miles behind, to his right. *The left side will be their weak side*, he decides. He beckons his captain.

"Juval, we're going to lead our rear triremes on a sweep to our left, so we can outflank them. Bring our big ships to the center, behind our triremes. Tell the fire archers to get ready."

The Syrian flagship close-hauls its sails and turns its rudder to port side. Polyxenidas' vessel curls in behind his front ships and surges toward the Roman's right flank. The admiral's flagman runs to the side rail, signaling the rear ships to follow. The dagger-shaped triremes slice through the Aegean chop, and begin a wide turn around the Roman flank.[clxxxviii]

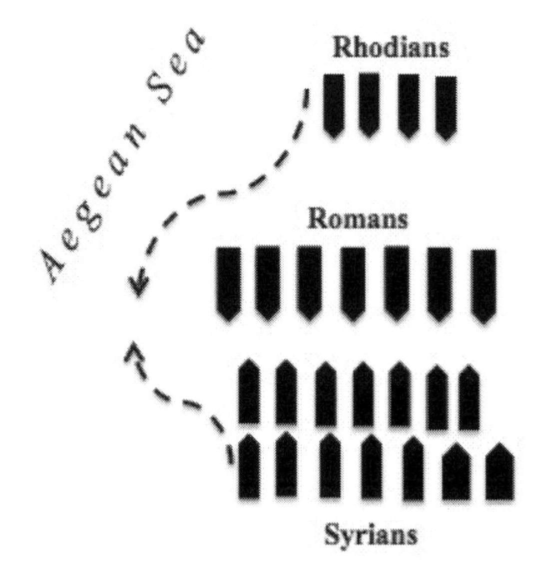


**Battle of Myonessus**
**191 BCE**

While the Syrians initiate a flanking maneuver, Eudamus' ships close in behind the Roman vessels. Standing in the prow of his trireme, the Rhodian watches in alarm as Polyxenidas' rear ships sail out toward the Roman right, their bronzed prows aimed at the open sea. *They're going to encircle Livius' flank!*

Eudamus glances at the Roman center, affirming that they are still moving straight ahead. *That boy Regillus is too stupid or scared to do anything about it.* "Full speed east, oars double time," Eudamus tells his captain.

The Rhodian triremes surge to their left, powered by banks of sturdy oarsmen. Admiral Eudamus spies the purple flag upon Polyxenidas' vessel.

"Aim for the flagship," he tells his captain. "We take him out, the rest may lose their spirit." The Rhodian flagship veers farther to the left, slashing toward Polyxenidas' vessel.

Regillus watches helplessly as the Syrian ships race to outflank him, knowing his quinqueremes cannot catch them. He sees the Rhodian fleet surge out to meet them, their side oars beating like the legs of a maddened centipede.

"Full speed ahead, Florus, we'll break into their front," Regillus says, his heart pounding in his ears.

Regillus watches the sleek Syrian triremes arrow toward him. *They might be faster, but we are better deck fighters*, he decides. He beckons Florus to his side. "Signal our ships—we're going to ram and board."

The young admiral gazes into the Aegean's dark green depths. "Oh sea gods, I pray you, let me have this battle. I promise I will build a temple in your honor."[clxxxix]

The Syrian ships draw within two spear casts of the Romans. They turn abruptly, aiming for the sides of the quinqueremes. A Syrian ship crashes its beaked ram through the side of one Roman vessel, caving in its timbers at the waterline.

The Roman craft rows off toward the rear of the fleet, slowly sinking. Another quinquereme draws alongside the crippled ship. It drops its corvus onto the deck of the foundering vessel. The sinking ship's marines and rowers race across the boarding platform, lugging their weapons and possessions.

A second trireme rams a Roman ship. The quinquereme limps from the battle line, slowly drawing water. After a half hour of ships attacking and dodging, a Roman ship manages to grapple a Syrian vessel. The marines throw down their boarding platform and stream across it.

With no room for organization or movement, the deck becomes a freewheeling swordfight between the Roman marines and the Syrian sailors. Battling in close quarters, the Romans' short swords and discipline begin to tell. The Syrians soon surrender, throwing their swords and spears into the sea.

The victorious Romans rope the rowers and soldiers together. They strip the trireme of its sails and rope it to the quinquereme's stern, towing their captive to the rear of their fleet. Over the next two hours, four more Syrian ships are captured and removed. A dozen more row out from the battle, their sides wrecked by Roman rams.

Delirious with the prospect of victory, Regillus dashes about the deck, searching for a ship to assault. "Sails to starboard!" he yells. "Aim for that bastard over there!" The quinquereme veers around and plunges toward a nearby trireme.

Regillus studies the trireme's angle of sail, plotting the shortest route to cut it off. A hand tugs at Regillus' tunic sleeve. "What is it Florus?"

His wide-eyed captain points to the stern. "Three monsters behind us!"

Three enormous hexaremes sail into the swarming sea battle. Each carries two thirty-foot towers upon its deck, towers commissioned by Hannibal when Phoenicians built the new ships for him. The hexaremes turn toward the Romans nearest them, their oars delving deep into the choppy Aegean waters.

A tower ship closes on the quinquereme nearest to Regillus. The admiral sees the Roman ship's marines lining the deck railing, preparing to board the Syrians' craft. *My marines will slaughter them. What a prize that big bastard will make!*

The hexareme's towers release a withering fire of flame arrows. The shafts penetrate man and deck alike, setting them aflame. Scores of burning marines dash madly across the deck, screaming for help. Dozens more dive into the sea, mad to escape their agony.

The quinquereme's top deck bursts into flame. The ship's rowers run from below decks and pitch themselves into the sea, trusting they will be succored by the other ships.

The hexareme turns toward Regillus' ship, its towers spitting arrows.

A flaming shaft thunks into the deck near Regillus, then another. "Throw some sand on these!" Regillus yells, "and get us out of here!"

The quinquereme strokes away from the hexareme's line of fire.

Regillus watches his ships surge aimlessly about the scene of battle, chased by the relentless Syrians. Off to his left, another quinquereme bursts into flames, ignited by a hexareme's flaming onslaught.

The admiral's face becomes grim. "Florus, take us about. We're heading back in."

"Back to where?" Florus asks.

Regillus points at the nearby hexareme. "Back into the side of that oversized puke bucket. Triple-time rowing. We're going to break it." The flagship rows toward the hexareme, its sails stiff with wind.

"Get every marine armed and onto the deck," Regillus commands. The ship's eighty marines crowd onto the top. They stand facing the enemy ship, swords drawn and waiting.

Arrows rain down from the hexareme's towers, arching toward the flagship's deck. "Testudo!" Regillus yells, raising his own shield. The marines square up and raise their rectangular shields. The arrows stab into the shields and the deck. A handful of marines scurry across the deck, their gloved hands yanking out the shafts.

Regillus scrambles below decks. He faces his half-naked, sweat-soaked oarsmen. "Lean your backs into it!" he shouts. "Twenty more strokes and we have them!" The banks of oars delve into the sea, surging the quinquereme forward.

Regillus' flagship crashes its armored prow into the hexareme, lurching it sideways. The young admiral stumbles drunkenly, grabbing a deck ladder to right himself. "Port rows hard, starboard rests!" he shouts, clambering to the top deck.

The Roman ship scrapes against the side of the hexareme. Scores of Syrians shove poles against the quinquereme, but the Roman rowers shove the ship closer. After several tries, the marines drop their corvus onto the enemy deck. Dozens of Syrians grab the sides of the corvus, trying to throw it overboard. The marines rush across the platform and cut them down.

While scores of marines beat back the deckside Syrians, dozens of Romans break into the towers. They run up the stairs, swords bared, and stab down the unarmored archers.

Watching Regillus' ship board the hexareme, the Roman ships emulate their admiral's assault tactics. They board dozens of the enemy triremes. Others attack the two hexaremes in groups of three, ramming them until they sink.

While Regillus' ships duel with the Syrians' center fleet, Eudamus of Rhodes charges his twenty-three triremes around the outside of the Roman battle line, seeking the forty triremes led by Polyxenidas. The Syrian admiral sees the Rhodian fleet approaching, but he remains unperturbed.

"They're coming on fast," Juval observes.

Polyxenidas shrugs. "We outnumber them two to one. While they occupy themselves with one of us, another will ram into them, then another. We'll sink all of them before nightfall."

Eudamus stands in the prow of his ship, the stiff breeze ruffling his white mane of hair. His eyes follow Polyxenidas' gorgon-headed flagship, its bronze prow aimed directly at him.

Captain Faustus joins Eudamus. "Here they come," the Rhodian exclaims. "There looks to be two score of them. They'll try to double up on us, and ram our sides."

The aged Rhodian's gaze does not waver. "Get the pots lined up on the deck. We're going to need them."

The Syrian triremes close upon their Rhodian counterparts. As they approach, the Syrian ships edge apart from each other, seeking more room to maneuver. The Rhodians sail on, maintaining their wedge formation, with Eudamus' flagship in the lead.

The two flagships close upon one another. Eudamus turns toward

Faustus, who stands in the center of the trireme's narrow deck. The Rhodian admiral throws down his right hand. Faustus spins around and repeats the gesture to his helmsman. The helmsman shoves the rudder sideways while the sailors pull the trireme's two sails to the opposite side of the craft.

The Rhodian ship veers abruptly to the left and slides past the Syrian's flagship, dodging its attack. Eudamus sees Polyxenidas standing at the railing, glowering at him. The Rhodian admiral's seamed face breaks into a grin. He raises his middle finger and jabs it at the Syrian, emulating a dagger thrust.

"Hard about to port side," Eudamus tells Faustus. "Let's go back and get him." He grins. "Signal the other ships. Tell them to use the pots."

The two fleets surge into one another, angling for the best fighting position. The Syrian ships aim their prows at the sides of the Rhodians, intending to bash them in. The Rhodian vessels slow, waiting for them to approach. The Rhodians turn their vessels sideways, drawing close to the sides of their attackers.

Pairs of Rhodian sailors rush to their ships' side rails. Each pair carries a forty-foot pole with an iron pot attached to the end. They halt at the railing and stab torches into the resin-filled pots. Fires roar from the containers, flames fueled by unquenchable Sea Fire, the nightmare of every sailor.[cxc]

Bracing their long poles against the top of their railings, the Rhodians slide the pots across the gap between the two ships, hovering them over the Syrian decks. With a twist of the wrist, they dump the pots' contents onto the triremes.

Sea Fire streams across the Syrian decks, burning everything it touches. The Rhodians rush out with more pots. They pour the burning resin down the sides of the enemy triremes, igniting the oars and hulls.

A dozen Syrian ships turn into burning barges of death, their occupants diving into the sea. A score of them row from the battle, fleeing the unquenchable fires.[cxci]

Polyxenidas watches his assault fleet break apart, his victory dissolving before his eyes. He sees Eudamus' flagship heading toward him, backed by three Rhodian triremes.

"Run for Ephesus," he yells to Juval. "Quick, while we still have the wind at our back."

The Syrian flagship flees the battle. The rest of the demoralized fleet soon follows him, capitalizing upon the winds at their backs.[cxcii]

"Get after them!" Eudamus bellows. "Full speed!" The swift Rhodian ships angle into the escaping triremes, cutting the fleet in half. Regillus' ships close in from behind, completing an encirclement. One by one, the captive ships lower their sails.

Regillus leans over the prow of his ship, watching the enemy sailors pitch their arms into the sea. He sobs with joy.

"You've won," Florus tell him, grinning from ear to ear.

A look of dismay crosses Regillus' face. "Gods curse me, now I've got to fulfill my promise, and build a temple to the Lares!" He smiles. "There'd better be plenty of plunder on those ships, Florus, or I'll be out begging in the streets!"

"For a while there, I thought they had us," Florus says. "Those fire towers were fearsome!"

Regillus nods. "How many ships did we capture?"

"Thirteen. Another forty of them are at the bottom of the sea. A half dozen of ours are badly damaged, but they sunk only two."[cxciii]

*Two too many. That's hundreds of men lost.* "Tie their ships together and tow them into Teos. We'll sell their crews to the slavers. Keep the officers, we can ransom them. Four days' rest, then we go out again."

Regillus' hands shake. He feels a rush of elated weariness. "Head to port as quickly as possible. I need to rest—and repay a debt."

The next afternoon finds a solemn Regillus sitting at the battered wine bar he first visited, a watered wine jug resting next to a plate of quail eggs and asparagus. Eudamus steps into the open doorway, clad in the simple green tunic of a Rhodian sailor. He nods at the young admiral.

"I thought you would be here."

Regillus grins, embarrassed. "I never rewarded the fisherman for his information. I thought he might come back here." He chuckles. "The owner says he ate my food and drank my wine. At least he had some recompense."

"He deserved far more. We would have been destroyed without him," Eudamus says. "A simple man who changed history, and will forever remain nameless."

"Well, we won. That is what history will recount."

Eudamus eases his aching body onto a stool at Regillus' table. He steels himself for the words he must say. "You did…very well. Antiochus' navy is broken. The Scipios will be free to cross the Hellespont."

"There is still much to be done," Regillus replies. "Polyxenidas will have returned to Ephesus with the remnants of his fleet. I have to go there and blockade the harbor, so he cannot escape. And we've got to give the Scipios some ships for their crossing into Asia." [cxciv] I'm not sure we have enough craft to accomplish all of that."

"We can staff the captured triremes. They are good ships," Eudamus says, his tone implying Regillus should have thought of that. "And your new Roman ships will help you, too."

Regillus blinks at him. "What new ships?"

"Why, there are a score of Roman quinqueremes coming in from the south, according to my scouts."

"More ships? I know nothing of this."

Eudamus chuckles, enjoying Regillus' discomfiture. "They are an escort. They're leading a fleet of African transports."

The older man tears off a piece of barley bread and wags it at Regillus. "Get ready for a show, Regillus. The Numidians are joining the war."

PORT OF EPHESUS, SYRIA, 190 BCE. "Don't put fir planks in that hull, they need oak!" fumes Juval. He tugs the plank from the stocky shipbuilder's hands.

The craftsman waves his arm across the shipyard docks. "You find any oak out there, I'll eat it! It's fir or nothing. It'll take me two months to rebuild this ship as it is!"

"Fir! Bah!" Juval throws up his hands in frustration. He stalks toward the dock authority building that fronts the piers, heading for the two men that stand watching him, arms crossed.

Hannibal and Antiochus survey the ruins of Antiochus' once-proud fleet, their faces grim. Dozens of burned and wrecked ships lie at anchor along the shallows, waiting to be pulled to the overloaded repair docks.

"How many functional ships do you have?" says Hannibal.

Antiochus' lips pucker. "Fifteen, maybe twenty. And a handful of scout ships."

"That means the Romans control the seas," Hannibal says.

"It's worse than that," sputters Antiochus. "My scout biremes came in this morning. They say that Regillus is bringing his fleet toward us. And the Rhodians are coming with him."

"Which is just what I would do," replies Hannibal. "He'll bottle up the harbor."

Antiochus rubs his eyes. "Then there's no way to stop the Romans from crossing the Hellespont. They'll be in my kingdom within the month. Ah, gods! You shit on me again!"

"The gods have nothing to do with it. You still have time to reinforce your Lysimachia stronghold. The Romans can't pass into Asia without taking it. Laying siege to it would take them many months, now that winter is coming."

"With my navy weakened, I cannot defend my outlying possessions. It's too risky, I could lose more men."[cxcv]

Hannibal leans toward the king. "Keep Lysimachia—it will stall them in Greece. It's almost October. Lucius Scipio's consulship will expire in a few months. Scipio Africanus will be gone, with some lesser general in his place. And your navy would be rebuilt."

The Syrian king shakes his head, his shoulders slumped. "I am sending Nicator to withdraw the last of our troops from Lysimachia and Colophon. They can help me protect our homeland from the Romans."

"You are going to attack the Scipios when they invade Syria?" Hannibal says, his voice hopeful.

"I will sue for peace, but prepare for war."

Hannibal's heart sinks. *Peace! Cursed fucking peace!* "So be it. But I will help you prepare for battle, so we are not caught unawares."

The king's eyes flare. "I know you want to me to fight them, and I trust your counsel. But I have my nation's welfare to consider. If we have to fight, we will fight. But I will explore every option until then."

"Then heed my words," Hannibal says. "Pick a battle site that is favorable to your horses and chariots. No more holing up in narrow passes such as Thermopylae."

"I will. This time there will be no Tiny Army fighting the Romans. This time, tens of thousands will face the Scipios, warriors from a dozen nations. This time, one of us will not depart."

ROME. "Come on, Prima, pull me in!"

Amelia turns her back to her friend, dangling the straps of her emerald green gown. "Pull these tight and knot them. Our consular candidate will soon be here!"

Prima grabs the velvety strands. "You want them tight? Your breasts stick out any more, you'll have to get a cuirass to cover them! Are we planning an election, or a seduction?"

Amelia wags her finger. "Do not take that attitude. We have to get Marcus Fulvius Nobilior elected—to do that we have to make him more…compliant." She gasps as Prima yanks in the cords that cross her breasts. "Did you have to pull so hard?" Amelia snaps.

Prima shrugs, the hint of a smile on her face. "You said you wanted to impress him. He'll see your tits before he sees your face—if he ever sees it at all."

"Be serious. Nobilior is our best chance to get Rome civilized before it turns into a war machine. The Latins have their way, we'll be melting our bronze statuary to turn them into weapons."

"I like it not," Prima says. "Nobilior's a pumpkin-head! Someone else should represent the Hellenic party."

"It is not our decision to make," Amelia says. "The elections magistrate has declared him the patrician candidate for consul.[cxcvi] He'll run against Auos Messina, that Latin Party shill."

"But why did we pick Nobilior?" Prima fumes. "Laelius told me he never reads any of the Senate policy scrolls! He's just another dullard with money!"

"All you have to know is that Cato hates him,"[cxcvii] Amelia replies. "That 'dullard' believes that Rome can become another Athens, a city of arts and learning. That drives Cato and the Latins insane."

"But he is such an odd duck," Prima says. "Did you hear? He's going to take that poet Ennius with him on campaign,[cxcviii] so he can write odes about Nobilior's victories. What kind of general does that?"

"He will likely achieve some victories," Amelia says. "He might be unsavory, but he is a warrior born. Remember when he was praetor of Iberia? He quelled the Celtiberian rebellion with little loss of life. They said that my husband could not have done any better."

"Why couldn't the Senators pick someone such as Postumius Pulcher?" Prima says. "He's a learned, fair-minded man."

Amelia hoots with laughter. "Pulcher? He is almost sixty years old! He's waiting for the undertakers to come and throw him on his funeral pyre! Besides, Nobilior is one of the Fulvia. He has the money to support his election."

"How impressive," Prima snipes. "Another fool who thinks money makes him special."

"Money is important, more now than earlier. Scipio and I no longer have funds for a candidate—we spent the last of it on Lucius." She crooks an eyebrow at her friend. "And Laelius."

"And we both are grateful," Prima says. "But Laelius would have made the better general for Syria, you know that."

*That again!* Amelia sits upon one of the atrium's six-foot dining couches. She pats the space next to her. Prima joins her. Amelia takes Prima's hand. "Lucius needed it more, Sister. You and Laelius are willful and strong—you will always succeed. Lucius is weak—he needs a triumph to secure his life."

Prima waves her hand. "Pft! Scipio endangered Rome to keep his promise to his mother! To keep his precious honor."

"I do not think he endangered Rome. He accompanied Lucius, there is no better guarantee that Lucius will win." She glares at the gladiatrix. "As to his honor, he has compromised himself a dozen times, all for the sake of Rome. For once, it can compromise itself for him!"

Prima crosses her arms, her stare distant. Amelia reaches out and squeezes her friend's forearm. "Laelius is where he is. We now have to consider the future."

After a minute, Prima nods. "I hear you. We will get Nobilior elected. But I am not happy with doing it. There are rumors has beaten his wife. That makes him a coward, no matter his military victories!"

"There are rumors he did," Amelia says. "We know no more than that. And Flaccus is an expert at planting rumors."

Prima's eyes harden. "Nobilior would know my husband Laelius is sequestered in North Italia. Perhaps I can lure him in to trying something with me. Then I could teach him a lesson. Nothing permanent, just a few broken fingers."

"Easy, girl." Amelia says. "We know nothing for sure."

The gladiatrix springs to her feet. She turns slowly in front of Amelia, pressing her amber gown against the front her lithe, muscular body. "You think I can lure him into trying something?"

"Hah!" Amelia laughs. "He's seen you fight in the games. He'd worry that you'd cut off his manhood—or bite it off! " She walks toward the rear of the house. "Help me get some stools into the tablinum. I think an office meeting is best, so he will take us seriously."

"The only thing he'll take seriously is your chest," Prima replies.

An hour later, a handsome, elegantly dressed man strides to the front doors of the Scipio manse, his tanned arms bulging from his silver-bordered toga.

Rufus, the elderly house slave, is there to meet him. He holds out his stout oak staff, topped with the owl's head symbol of the Scipio clan. "Welcome, honored Nobilior," Rufus quavers, bowing low.

"Take me inside, old one," Nobilior orders. "I've got to meet with some beautiful women!" Rufus shuffles through the vestibule, leading the patrician into the sun-washed atrium. Nobilior sees two women waiting for him.

Nobilior gives them his best smile. "Amelia! Prima! You are goddesses come to earth!" Nobilior rushes forward to embrace them.

Amelia wraps her arms about him, pressing herself against his chest. Nobilior feels himself harden.

"Welcome to Scipio House," Amelia purrs, gently disengaging from him. "We hope your visit will be profitable."

"I am sure it will!" Nobilior gushes, pulling at the bottom of his tunic. "Praetor Scaevola sings your praises. He says you could get a Carthaginian elected consul!"

He turns to Prima. "Ah, the Amazon herself!" he steps forward to embrace her.

"Welcome, Fulvius Nobilior," Prima mutters. She extends her right hand and grips his forearm. Her sinewy fingers bite deep into his muscles. Nobilior's eyes bulge in surprise. He grasps her arm and forces a grin through his pain. Prima tightens her grip, boring into Nobilior's eyes. The general clamps tighter onto her arm, slowly twisting it sideways. Prima's expression does not change.

Amelia pulls them apart. "Yes, well, enough greetings! We have many plans to discuss. Why don't you come into the office, Senator? It's much more private."

"Alone with two gorgeous women? What else could I ask for?" he says, resisting the urge to rub his forearm. "It's time to mount our assault on Rome!"

"Your wife should have joined us," Prima snaps. "I hear she is experienced in assaults, too."

"What are you implying?" Nobilior sputters.

"Nothing at all," Amelia says. She pushes Prima toward the tablinium. "Come on. Let's get down to business."

The three enter the office and sit at its round marble table. "Let me show you our campaign plan," Amelia says.

Amelia takes a linen bag from a nearby shelf and pulls out four wooden figurines. She places a carving of a prancing piper in the center of the table.

"The first step is the banquet. It will be held here and sponsored by Scipio House, though you will pay for it. We'll have pipers, flautists, a water organ, and pantomime players. The main courses will be hare, roast pheasant, oysters, pomegranates, and sow's udders."

"Pomegranates! Sow's udders! You must think I'm rich as Croesus!" Nobilior exclaims.

"You can recoup your losses when you are a consul," Amelia replies calmly. "If you wage a successful campaign in Greece or Gaul, you will have wagonloads of plunder."

"If you don't get killed," Prima adds cheerily. Nobilior gapes at her.

"If I'm paying for the feast, I should have my name attached to it," he declares.

Prima shakes her head. "If the Scipios sponsor it, you can circumvent the election laws that limit the amount of banquets you can personally host."[cxcix]

"That seems to be bending the law quite a bit," Nobilior replies.

Amelia shrugs. "Senator Flaccus has done this for the last six elections. We can decry his behavior—to little effect—or emulate him and win. It is your choice."

Nobilior chuckles. "Then I would be delighted for you to hold the banquet! But I pick the wines."

*Let him have his victory*, Amelia decides. She places another figurine into the center of the table, a pole with a waving flag upon it. "Starting tomorrow, we drape the city with pennants, and paint slogans upon our supporters' townhouses."

Nobilior places his palm upon his chest and strikes a noble pose. "Ones that will extoll my virtues and victories?"

"Not really," Amelia replies. "Your most effective banners will be the ones that support your rival, Auos Messina."

"You say what?" Nobilior blurts. "Has the goddess Rabies taken your senses?"

"In the banners," Prima says, "your opponent will be supported by groups our senators despise,[cc] such as the late night drinkers, or those touting you to be Rome's next king."

"Of course, you will also have your own propaganda," Amelia adds. "It will extol all your virtues."

"Such as they are," Prima mutters. Nobilior flushes, but he pretends to ignore her.

Amelia places a third figurine in the table center. It depicts Janus, the two-faced god of transitions.

"This is simple. When you meet Senators Tuditanus, Piso, and Ligo, I want you to wax rhapasodic about the glory of early Rome; about your desire to return to a simpler time devoid of wasteful art and culture."

"But I do not support that!" Nobilior exclaims.

Amelia places her hand over his, a wry smile upon her face. "In elections, dear, there is a saying: 'People will prefer that you give them a gracious lie than an outright refusal.'[cci] And when you meet all the Hellenic senators, tell them about your poet Ennius. They will eat that up!"

"I don't want to get caught in a lie," Nobilior says.

"You won't," Amelia says. "Those senators don't talk to each other. And if they did, they wouldn't believe each other anyway!"

Amelia lays down the final figurine, an eagle with outspread wings. "The biggest boost to your campaign may occur abroad. If Consul Lucius Scipio defeats Antiochus, it will be a tremendous victory for the Hellenic party. You election would be almost assured."

"So? I can't do anything about that," the senator replies.

Amelia looks sideways at Prima. She nods.

"You have to demonstrate that you are behind our men in Greece," Prima says. "When you speak to the plebs in the Forum, talk up your support for the Scipios, remind the people of our recent victories at sea and on the land. Tell the plebs that victory is guaranteed, that a new age will come to Rome when it happens. That Rome will be the mightiest empire on the earth!"

Nobilior frowns. "But who knows what will happen over there? With my luck, Lucius will arrange a peace treaty with the Syrians, and there won't be a battle!"

"Yes, how very unfortunate that would be," Amelia replies sarcastically, rapping the eagle upon the table. "But I doubt that will happen. When two men fight with dreams of glory, the hope for peace is the first to fall."

Two hours later, Prima and Amelia lounge on atrium couches, reviewing their meeting with Nobilior. They pluck sweetmeats from the silver tray in front of them, washing them down with heavily watered wine.

"Domina, Domina! You have a messenger!"

Rufus ambles into the atrium, followed by Philo, the one-armed messenger. The old war veteran somberly hands Amelia a scroll with the wax owl's head seal of the Scipios. Amelia cradles it in her hands. She looks up at Philo.

"This is from my husband?" What is it about?

Philo's face is as expressionless as a stone. "It is about your son," he says flatly. "That is all I know." He spins on his heel and marches out, determined to be gone before she reads it.

Amelia unrolls the message and hastily scans it. The scroll drops from her hands.

"What is it?" Prima says anxiously.

Amelia stares at her, her eyes wide with terror and tears. "They've taken him! They've taken Publius! The Syrians have him!" She collapses upon the floor, wailing. "Oh, the gods are punishing me for what I did to that boy!"

Prima drops to her knees. She wraps her arms about Amelia, hugging her close as she sobs out her grief. "Do not be afraid, Sister." Prima murmurs, fighting back her own tears. "Publius is safe. Antiochus knows what would happen if he harmed him."

"I know," Amelia says, dabbing at her eyes. She picks up the scroll and folds it backward, showing the last lines her husband wrote to her. She holds it out to Prima.

*Do not fear, Antiochus knows his fate if he harms him.*

*I will bring Publius home, or die in the trying.*

*S*

LYSIMACHIA, THRACE, 190 BCE. The javelin hisses through the air, its shaft feathers fluttering in the soft morning sunlight. It sinks into the leathered back of a rangy Syrian rider. The cavalryman yelps, once, and topples sideways from his saddle.

"Ramsin! What is it?" His companion looks back over his horse—just in time to see a bronze-headed spear hurtling at him.

The javelin lances into his throat. He grapples feebly at the spear handle, coughing clots of blood. The Syrian slides off his horse and thumps into the bushes, joining his friend's corpse. The riderless horses wander to the side of the roadway. They pause there, placidly chewing on the pale winter grass.

Thrax scrabbles down the rubbled hillside, his sheathed sword slapping against his bare thigh. After retrieving his spears, he watches the fading outline of the Syrian baggage train, the drovers oblivious to the fate of its two rear guards.

A score of Thrax's men descend from the hillside, casting off their shrubbery crowns. “What next, Thrax?” asks the bearlike Burbix. “Do we get the rest of the men and go after them?”

Thrax spits into the dusty road. “No, curse it. They’ll be at the Port of Gallipolis by the time we’re ready. Best to gather our men and go back to Lysimachia. If that was the last of them, we can retake the city.”

The chief gestures toward the hills that surround the roadway. “Burbix, take six men and watch the road. See if any more Syrians come through. Meet me at Lysimachia, two days hence.”

The rest of the Thracians hike to the hilltop and retrieve their horses. After hours of traversing mountain passes, they arrive at their mountain hideaway. Thrax immediately calls a meeting of his chiefs.

“Send messengers to your tribes. Tell them I want every able-bodied man at Lysimachia within five days. No more hiding, we are going to war. “

The next morning, two of Thrax’s men return from the Gallipolis roadway, their faces grim. They tie their exhausted horses to a pine tree and march toward the camp caves. One lugs a bulging wool sack over his shoulder, its bottom darkly stained.

Thrax sits by his cooking campfire, gnawing on a chunk of roast venison. When he sees the expression on his men’s faces, he drops the meat into the dirt. “What is it?”

The Thracian upends his sack. Five heads tumble to the ground in front of Thrax, each face horribly disfigured.

“They must have come upon them in the night, while we were scattered along the upper trails. I didn’t find any bodies. Just their heads, stuck on the hilts of their swords.”

The warrior blinks back his tears. “Why did they have to do this to their faces.” He points to a lipless, noseless head. “I couldn’t hardly recognize Burbix. Look at him!”

“There was no ‘they’ that did this,” Thrax says. “This was Nicator. On a final hunt before he left." Thrax's sandaled toe reaches out and turns one of the heads upright. Its vacant eye sockets peer back at him.

"Get the men over here," Thrax says, his eyes never leaving the head.

Soon, hundreds of warriors ring their leader, staring at the heads of their companions. Thrax stands before them, his chest heaving with anger.

"The Syrians have killed our men, looted our cities, and raped our women." He lifts Burbix's head by its blood-darkened hair. "And look, they violate our dead!"

He lays Burbix's head down and stands up, hands on his hips. "The Syrians are abandoning Thrace, but we will not allow them to escape. We will join the Romans and destroy these monsters. Not for honor, or plunder, or glory. We fight for revenge!"

The Thracians' voices rise to the sky, roaring their agreement. They men exult, knowing they will never hide in caves again. Now they will fight as warriors, on an open plain of battle.

The next morning, Lucius and Publius Scipio enter the broad plain that sprawls to the west of Lysimachia, riding in the vanguard with King Philip of Macedonia. The three ride slowly, accommodating the pace of their road-weary infantry.

Scipio weaves in his saddle, faint and woozy from lack of sleep. Last night, the fevers came upon him as he lay in his tent. And with the fevers, the dream—the dream he always dreads. Visions of Lucius and his men being overcome by the Syrians, as Scipio watches helplessly.

Scipio shakes his head, trying to fling out the memory. He looks over at Lucius, who nods a greeting at him. *You put him here, he is your responsibility. And so are his men.*

Philip draws up next to Scipio, a jaunty smile upon his face. "Look at the sea channel behind Lysimachia. Can you see the ships? Those are Roman and Rhodian vessels. They must have taken over Lysimachia's port!"

Philip slaps Scipio on the back, almost knocking him from his saddle. "The city is yours! The waters are yours! You can cross over to Syria!"

"None of it is mine," Scipio replies. He nods toward his brother. "You should tell Lucius. He is the consul."

Philip snorts. "Yes, he is. But we know who runs this army, don't we?"

The miles-long army train draws nearer to Lysimachia. As Scipio watches, the city's twenty-foot gates swing open. A dozen town elders shuffle through the gateway. They halt in front of the oncoming vanguard, waiting.

"Here come the magistrates," Philip says. He turns his horse toward the rear columns. "I had best not be seen with you. Thrace and I have a long history of disagreements."

Scipio and Lucius trot slowly toward the officials, followed by a squadron of Lucius' elite equites. The two dismount and approach the magistrates, cradling their helmets in their arms.

A skeletal elder totters out from his fellows, a gold embroidered cloak draped over his knee-length tunic. He raises his ebony staff.

"I am Dion, the leader of our group." He glances over his shoulder, pointing his staff at the gates. "The Syrians are gone. We surrender the city to you."

Lucius shifts about uneasily. Scipio leans in next to him. "Go shake his arm, it will seal the agreement," Scipio mutters.

"I know that!" Lucius snaps.

Lucius strides forward and grasps Dion's forearm. "We accept your surrender," he intones. "Your city is now under the protection of Rome."

"The town awaits you, Consul." The town elders snap their fingers, applauding the agreement. The elders return to the city.

The Scipios remount. With their guards leading the way, they enter Lysimachia. Throngs of Thracians line the town square, waving brightly colored scraps of cloth. The Scipios nod and wave, savoring the accolades. They halt at the end of the square, where the five-story Temple of Apollo looms before them.

Dion stands on the temple's top steps, flanked by its treelike marble columns. He waves his staff to the right, taking in several squat stone buildings. "Those are the granaries. Avail yourself of whatever you need."

"Gratitude, Magistrate," Lucius replies. "We would like to camp outside here for several days, to let the rest of our baggage train catch up to us. And to rest from our weary march."[ccii]

"Whatever you wish," the magistrate replies. "Now, Generals, let me show you what else we can provide."

After following Dion on a tour of the city facilities, Lucius and Scipio ride back to their developing camp, leaving a dozen equites to explore the rest of the city. King Philip and his retinue await them in front of the camp's newly-erected palisades. He rides out to meet the two of them, leaving his men behind.

"I have led you to the passage into Asia," Philip says. "My work is done. It is time for me to return to my kingdom."

*And retake more towns while we are away*, Scipio thinks. "It is just as well," Scipio replies, a wry grin on his face. "We wouldn't want you near your old partner Hannibal. You might not know whose side you were on."

"Why, whoever's winning!" Philip replies merrily. He beckons to his cavalry. "Come on, men. I want to go home and see my monkeys."

He grasps Scipio's forearm. "Fare you well, Scipio Africanus." He nods at Lucius. "Good fortune, General. But I hope you won't need it."

With a final wink at Scipio, the King of Macedonia rides away from the budding Roman camp, heading west toward his palace.

"I appreciated his guidance and company," Lucius says, "but I am so glad to be rid of him."

Scipio chuckles. "For once, we agree."

After an evening conference with the army's legates and tribunes, Scipio gratefully collapses onto his straw pallet. Somnus quickly descends on him, cloaking him in dreamless sleep.

The buccina calls the first watch of the day. Scipio is shaken awake by Tribune Marcus Aemilius. "Pardon, Imperator. Lucius has requested that you and I join him—there are barbarians at the gates!"

Scipio pulls on a purple-bordered tunic and marches to the front gates. Lucius is there with two maniples of legionnaires, pacing nervously in front of them. "Come up and take a look at this," he tells them.

Lucius climbs up a wooden ladder by the guard tower. Scipio and Marcus join him, Scipio's aging knees protesting every step he takes.

"What do you make of that?" Lucius says, leaning over the edge of the palisade. Hundreds of armed barbarians stand outside. A man covered with blue tattoos stands in front them, clutching a battered Thracian polearm.

"Who are those men?" Lucius asks, wrinkling his nose. "They look like they've been living in a cave."

"Which they likely have," Marcus replies. "Those are Thracian warriors. They've been fighting the Syrians since they invaded here." He chuckles. "They must have driven Antiochus crazy!"

"They do look crazy," Lucius says.

"Let's go, Lucius," Scipio says.

"Let's go where?"

"We have to go down and meet them. On foot, as equals."

Lucius blinks. "You're joking. They're wilder than a bunch of drunk

Celtiberians!"

"Thracians live to fight, but they have a strict code of honor," Marcus says. "They won't attack without formally declaring you an enemy. You are safe. Just be careful what you say."

The blue tattooed leader lays down his fearsome polearm. He approaches the Roman camp, leaving his men behind.

"That's Thrax," Marcus says excitedly. "I'd wager a month's pay on it!" He grins. "He's a very good fighter!"

"You seem to know him," Scipio says. "Maybe you can help us avoid a fight. Come along with us."

Scipio, Marcus, and Lucius climb down from the ladder.

"You men get right behind me," Lucius says to the maniples.

The threesome tread into the plain's scrabbly bushes. The Thracian chieftain strides out to meet them. He raises his right hand.

"I am Thrax, chieftain of southern Thrace. I fought with the Thirteenth Legion, against Mago Barca and his Gauls."[cciii]

"The slave legion," Scipio declares. "You were a slave."

Thrax raises his chin, his eyes glinting defiance. "I was a Roman slave, once. But I won my freedom."

"He's the one that killed Morcant, the Gallic chieftain,"[cciv] Marcus says.

"It is an honor." Scipio sweeps his arm toward his brother. "This is Lucius Scipio, and I am—"

"I know who you are, Scipio Africanus." Thrax replies. "You are why I am here."

Scipio sees Lucius flush with embarrassment. "I am merely the advisor to my brother Lucius. He is in charge of the army."

Thrax turns to Lucius, his face a stone. "I come to ally our forces with you, in combat against King Antiochus."

Lucius nods. "How many men do you bring?"

"Three, maybe four thousand," Thrax replies. "They are still coming."

"That is all?" Lucius says.

Scipio winces. He puts his hand on Lucius' shoulder and leans close to him. "Go easy, now."

Lucius shrugs off his hand.

A grim smile comes to Thrax's face. "We are not many, but each of us is worth ten of yours."

"I've seen them, General," Marcus says softly. "They are lions on the field!"

"And we need every sword we can get," Scipio declares.

Lucius bites his lower lip. He sighs loudly. "We welcome you as one of our allies, Thrax. We will apportion some of our plunder to you and your men."

"I only want one thing," Thrax says, rubbing his fist with his hand.

"Which is?" asks Lucius.

"The chance to kill the one called Nicator. He has been the scourge of my people."

Marcus Aemilius grins. "Well, now. We do have one thing in common! I seek his head, too. He got away from me once, but it won't happen again!"

Thrax glares at him. "Do not get in the way of my revenge, little man."

"You had best not get in *my* way," Marcus replies. The two glower at one another.

"We are not beginning our alliance with a quarrel!" Scipio declares, glaring at the both of them. "Fortuna will decide who has a chance at him, let us leave it at that."

"We are still organizing camp," Lucius says to Thrax. "After we finish the camp and move our headquarters into the city, we will meet there and celebrate our new alliance."

Thrax nods. "I will return in three days, with the rest of my men."

A week later, the Roman army decamps from Lysimachia and marches south toward the port at Gallipolis, seeking to take it from the Syrians. Thrax and his three thousand Thracians march in the rear, following the Romans' Italia allies.

Lucius' lead scout gallops in from Gallipolis, accompanied by two unfamiliar Romans. He halts in front of Lucius and salutes, a broad smile covering his face.

"What news, Quintus?" says Lucius.

Quintus points to the two riders behind him. "This is Tiberius Juvenius and Atticus Fulvius," he says. They are marines from Admiral Regillus' fleet."

Scipio crooks an eyebrow at him. "Are you saying what I think you are saying, Quintus?"

The scout nods. "Our fleet has taken the port. The Numidians are there, too, with an escort from Sicily."

Scipio's heart pounds. "Who leads them?"

Quintus looks at the two scouts. They shake their heads. "We know not," Quintus answers.

Lucius breaks into one of his rare smiles. "Well, that saves us a siege and a battle!" He rises straight in his saddle. "Double the march. Tell the men that we own the port. That should lend a spring to their step!"

"Let's go ahead of them," Scipio says, his mind on Masinissa.

Lucius and Scipio lope toward Gallipolis. An hour later, they emerge from the hilly forest that fronts the port city. One glance at Gallipolis, and they realize why it was named the Beautiful City.[ccv]

The Scipios face a hilltop city crested with gleaming white temples, its stone walls shining like polished eggs. Colorful pennants flap from the twenty-foot ramparts, which are lined with legionnaires. The azure bay glistens before them, with the dark blue Aegean peeking out on the east side of the city.

"Thank Jupiter the Syrians didn't burn it," Lucius says.

"They must think they're going to take it back," Scipio says. "We've got to be ready for a surprise attack."

The brothers trot across the thirty-foot bridge that spans the city's deep moat. They tether their horses at a squat basalt building that flies a blood-red flag with SPQR stitched in golden thread.

The Scipios declare themselves to the two legionnaires standing guard outside the doors. The soldiers disappear inside. Admiral Regillus steps out to meet them, beaming with excitement.

"You made it here already, that is such good news! The weather has been good—we can cross the strait anytime." He grins. "You can have breakfast in Thrace and a late lunch in Syria!"

"It is good to see you," Lucius says. "We heard of your victory at Myonessus."

The young admiral throws out his arms, smiling. "Isn't this a beautiful city! When we got here, there was nothing more than a hundred of Antiochus' men, and they surrendered immediately." He steps into the marble tile hallway. "Come in and sit with me, tell me about your journey."

"I will join you later," Scipio says, looking around the tapestried hall. "Where are the Numidians?"

"Masinissa and his men are camped along the seaside. They wanted to be near their horses," Regillus replies. He grins. "They race up and down the beach, doing all sorts of horse tricks!"

*He's here!* "Apologies. I must go see the King."

Regillus bows. "Whatever you say, Africanus. There is no hurry, the wine will keep!"

Soon, Scipio is riding into a village of sand-colored camelskin tents, centered by a black tent the size of a small mansion. Scipio sees a tall, lean, gray-haired man standing in front of it, wearing nothing but a leopard skin loincloth. He is conversing angrily with a young man who looks to be his double.

*It's Masinissa. And Sophon!* Scipio walks his horse toward the two, his heart thundering. Masinissa glances sideways, noticing his approach. Recognition dawns on his face. He turns from his son and fixes his eyes upon Scipio.

Scipio slides from his saddle, dropping the reins from his hand. He strides forward, extending his arm.

Masinissa walks slowly toward Scipio. He halts, forcing Scipio to complete the final steps. He pushes Scipio's handshake aside. "I am here, as final payment of my debt to Rome—and you—for helping me to liberate my kingdom." He gazes icily at Scipio. "Though some debts can never be repaid."

Scipio pulls in his arm, his face red with embarrassment. "Debts that were never owed, need not be repaid," he replies.

Sophon steps in front of Masinissa. He warmly embraces Scipio. "I am so glad to see you again! Forgive my father, he is a bit distant today."

"My heart rejoices at seeing you, Sophon. I hope your journey was pleasant."

Sophon points to the scores of riders racing along the beach. "As you can see, our horses traveled well on your ships. Some of our men caught the rolling sickness, but now they are ready to fight."

"You will not have long to wait," Scipio says. "It's a day's crossing to Asia from here. We will leave in a few days, when these early winter winds calm themselves."

"That is good," Sophon says. "I do not like these chill northern climes. A good horse fight would warm me up!"

"And you?" Scipio asks Masinissa, who stands impassive.

The king gazes into Scipio's face, his eyes opaque. "I await the settlement of my debt to Rome, be it in Greece or Asia." He turns on his heel and strides back to the frolicking riders, head held high.

Sophon grasps Scipio's forearm. "Do not fret. My father still loves you. He thinks he cannot show it, and that grieves him the most."

Scipio nods his thanks, his eyes closed. "You are a good man, Sophon. We tamed the Gauls together—now it's time to do it to the Syrians."

Scipio returns to town, his heart heavy with regret. "Where has Consul Lucius gone?" He asks the gate sentries. They direct him to a small, open-air temple on the side of the town square. The temple is fronted by two gigantic ivory statues of a stern Grecian warrior, naked save for his visored helmet and the curved sword. *Ares!* Scipio thinks. *What's Lucius doing in the war god's temple?*

Scipio trots up the temple's travertine steps and strides into the main room. Lucius sits on a stool at a twelve-foot marble slab, flanked by Admirals Regillus and Eudamus. The table is blanketed with sea maps and ship's figurines.

"Come in, Brother," Lucius says, his voice echoing through the vast inner hall. "We are organizing the fleet's departure. Now that King Eumenes of Pergamum has brought the last of his infantry to me, I am ready to confront Antiochus."

He leans his head toward the young Roman admiral. "Regellus says we can leave in three days, as soon as all the beasts and men are loaded onto the transports." He beams at his brother. "Just think of it! When we land, we will be the first Roman army to set foot in Asia!"[ccvi]

*He needs to lead the army over there without me, so the men will look to him as their leader.* "That is momentous news," Scipio replies. "But you will have to go ahead without me."

"Are you sick?" Eudamus asks. "Have the fevers come upon you again?"

"No more than they always do." He looks at Lucius, an embarrassed smile upon his face. "You remember when I was fourteen? I became one of the Salian priests that danced to celebrate Mars.[ccvii] The end of the war season is being celebrated in Rome. As one of the priests, I have to remain where I am until the end of this month. To do otherwise would be impious."[ccviii]

The three commanders look at each other. "Perhaps I should wait?" Lucius asks half-heartedly.

*He's glad I have to stay behind.* "I think you should go, Lucius. Neptune has blessed you with favorable seas. I will cross as soon as the new month starts."

Three days later, the Roman and Rhodian ships transport Lucius' army across the strait. They land near Abydos, a port fortification recently abandoned by Antiochus. Lucius trots down his flagship's gangplank as soon as it clacks onto the docks, anxious to be the first to set foot on foreign soil. Marcus Aemilius follows, carrying Lucius' helmet and breastplate.

"General, I beg you, please put on the rest of your armor. Some of Antiochus' men might still be out there."

"Let them come," Lucius declares, his voice filled with bravado. "I fear no Syrians!"

*That is what I am afraid of,* Marcus thinks. He studies the long rows of Syrian barracks that border the ancient dock. "Where shall we arrange camp?" he asks Lucius.

"Outside the city walls. We'll march on Antiochus as soon as my brother arrives. November is coming. Soon a new consul will come to replace me. I must move quickly, if I am going to remove the Syrian threat."

"Very well. I will tell the officers. I take it we will meet tonight?"

"Tonight, after the eighth hour. At the city magistrate's house." Lucius chuckles. "He doesn't know it, but he's going to give it over to me while we're here. No more camp tents for me!"

"I will notify the officers. They will be eager to hear our plans."

"Our plan is for glory," Lucius says. "Glory to Rome, and to the House of Scipio."

He gazes at the dockside statue of the Syrian king Seleceus I, conqueror of Asia and India. "Soon there will be a Scipio Africanus, and a Scipio Asiaticus!"

SARDIS,[ccix] SYRIAN EMPIRE, 190 BCE. "You see?" Antiochus crows. "The Roman army lingers at Abydos, instead of marching here to battle. They could be waiting for me to make peace with them!"[ccx]

"If they wanted peace, they would have stayed in Lysimachia." Hannibal says. "There must be some other reason."

"Perhaps not. Perhaps they thought they had to invade my kingdom, to make their point. Surely, they would not want to fight Syria if they did not have to. We vastly outnumber them."

"Scipio Africanus conquered Africa with two legions," Hannibal replies. "He will not shy from overwhelming numbers."

"Then I will make my proposal to Lucius Scipio." Antiochus replies. "I hear he does not have the spine of his brother."

Hannibal rubs his chin. "This Lucius is mercurial and indecisive. Who knows what he will do? But Scipio, he has always been ready to make peace with those he defeated, and give them generous terms." He smirks. "I should know."

"True," Antiochus says. "And we have another inducement for him to be agreeable." He turns to his attendants. "Bring in the boy."

The attendant slips through a side door. Moments later, a burly guard drags Scipio's son into the throne room. He shoves the boy toward Antiochus.

"Take your hands off me!" Publius spits. He kicks the guard in his armored midriff, sending him stumbling. Hannibal grins.

"You should learn to act like a prisoner," Antiochus says. "I could burn you alive for your insolence."

Publius glares at him. "Hah! You know what my father would do if you did. There's no place on earth you could hide."

The hawk-faced king flushes. "You insolent whelp, I'll—"

"How would you like to go home?" Hannibal interjects.

Publius looks sideways at him, his eyes slitted. "Under what conditions?"

Antiochus motions to his attendant. The man approaches Publius with a writing table that holds a square of parchment, and ink pot, and a stylus.

"You merely have to write a short note and sign it," The king says. "Tell your father you are ill. Tell him you want to come home."

Publius shakes his head vigorously. "Father won't betray Rome for me. And I'm not going to betray my honor!"

Antiochus walks to his fireplace. He grabs a half-burned ember from the fire and stalks back to Publius. He holds the glowing wood under his nose.

Publius cranes his head back, his eyes glassy.

"I'm tired of coddling you. You will sign it or I'll burn your nose off!"

Publius clamps his eyes shut. He mutely shakes his head.

"Let him go," Hannibal says, easing himself between the two. "Scipio knows you have him, that is enough."

"I should burn his fucking eyes out!" Antiochus mutters.

"He is but a silly boy, my King." Hannibal says. "We have much more important things to do. Look, if you want a treaty with Rome, we should work on the peace terms we'd give to Scipio."

"I have already considered that," Antiochus says. "I will offer him riches that will change his life."

Hannibal looks over at Publius. He sees the boy's lips tremble with efforts to stifle his sobs. "Riches are fine, but why don't you give him what he wants most?"

ABYDOS. Scipio walks through the bustling Abydos marketplace, in search of gifts for Amelia and Cornelia. He had arrived at Abydos the day before. and immediately fell into sleep. Now that he is rested, he is eager to send gifts to his family, to ease their pain at Publius' capture.

A silver-haired Greek approaches him, elegantly dressed in a black silk tunic. Scipio's two guards step out to confront him. The elderly man halts and spreads his knobby hands, the trace of a smile playing about his face.

"Two Romans to fight an old Spartan? I'd say those are fair odds."

"Assassinations are easier to win than battles," Scipio replies. "And they can come from the unlikeliest sources."

The Greek holds out a camelskin scroll, pointing at the crescent moon imprint upon its wax seal. "I am Heraclides, messenger to Antiochus III. I have a message from him. A peace proposal."

Scipio looks at him, puzzled. “You have a peace proposal? Shouldn’t you make this to the consul, Lucius Scipio?”

“My orders were to approach you privately,”[ccxi] the messenger calmly replies. “That is why I came to you here, while you are away from camp. He glances around him. “Can we talk without Roman ears about us?”

Scipio glances around him. He spies an open-air taberna, filled with mushroom-shaped tables and stools. “That place to the right, by the candle shop.”

The two men stroll across the field-sized town square, dodging the merchants’ wagons that rumble past them. Scipio and Heraclides pull up seats underneath the taberna’s dark green canopy.

The apron-clad proprietor appears instantly, beaming at his well-dressed customers. “Welcome, welcome! It is an honor to serve you! Can I tell you what foods we have today?”

Scipio runs his eyes over the owner’s stained wool apron. “I think I can tell just by looking at you. What drinks do you recommend?”

“We have an excellent Lesbos white, and a red from Antiochus’ Mount Bargylus vineyards,” the owner replies. “But our best drink is our Ebla beer. They’ve been making it there for thousands of years!”[ccxii]

“Camel’s milk for me,” the old man replies. He places a gaunt hand over his pot belly, smiling. “I have some dark spirits in my stomach. Milk helps to quiet them.”

“I’ll take a small jug of this beer you talk about,” Scipio replies. The proprietor bustles away. Heraclides chuckles. “A Roman drinking beer?”

“When in Syria, do as the Syrians do,” Scipio remarks. “Besides, it’s good to act like a barbarian, every now and then.”

The owner returns with a small terracotta jug and two bronze goblets.

He hands Heraclides a goblet brimming with a tan liquid. With a great flourish, the owner uncorks his jug and cascades beer into Scipio's cup, wiping off the top foam with his finger. "Enjoy!" he chirps, and bustles to another table.

Scipio sips the beer. He grimaces. "This tastes like turtle piss! I don't know how those Gauls can drink this stuff!" He eyes Heraclides. "Which brings us to our topic. What does your barbarian king propose?"

Heraclides flaps his hands. "Oh, he is far from a barbarian, you know. He has treated your son with the utmost gentility!"

Scipio sits bolt upright. "That is good—for Antiochus," he says. "Now what do you want?"

Heraclides slaps the scroll on the table and taps it with his finger. "It's all in there. In return for a Roman withdrawal from Syria, Antiochus pledges to renounce all claim to Lysimachia, Lampascus, and Zymrna, even though he perceives these as part of his rightful claims in Greece."

The envoy studies Scipio's face, but sees no expression.

"And...?" Scipio says.

The envoy grimaces. "Antiochus agrees to pay half, an entire half, of Rome's war expenses!"[ccxiii] He slaps his hands on the table. "A most equitable arrangement, I would say!"

"You would say that," Scipio replies. "Basically, he proposes to give up the stolen lands that we have already taken back from him, and pay us half of what we have spent to reclaim them! It is not enough. He will pay for all costs we have encumbered."

Heraclides' face wrinkles with disappointment. "In the interest of peace and concord, King Antiochus is prepared to overlook your Roman greed, and pay for all of it. He will also give up some select regions of Asia."[ccxiv] He taps the scroll. "That is not in there, but I am authorized to offer it."

Scipio stares into his beer cup. *Hm. Lucius would gain the honor of striking a very remunerative peace with Syria. But Antiochus would still be near the coast of Greece, waiting to strike.*

He looks back at the envoy. The man pushes the scroll closer to Scipio. *We have to fix it so Antiochus will not ever be a threat to us.*[ccxv]

"Antiochus must renounce all claims to the land this side of the Taurus Mountains," Scipio declares.

Heraclides' mouth drops open. "What? Are you joking?"

"And he must withdraw all his men to the east side of those mountains."

The envoy throws up his hands. "Do you know how far that is? That's over a hundred miles from here! You ask him to give up an entire country!"

"I know it is far enough to remove Syria as an immediate threat to Rome's amici. And to us," Scipio replies levelly. He takes another sip of his beer, and grimaces.

"Might I remind you, he has your son." Heraclides ventures. "The king is prepared to return him to you, if Lucius signs the agreement." He leans toward Scipio, grinning slyly. "Great wealth will be yours, too—more than you ever dreamed possible."

Scipio closes his eyes. *Gods, I could certainly use the coins. No one would know—but me.* He feels his right hand start to shake, and grabs it. *Your body gives you the answer.*

"Tell the king that he is very generous. Of all his offers, I accept the greatest—the return of my son. As for the rest, I pray heaven that my fortune will never need them." He smiles forlornly. "My soul, at any rate, will never need them."[ccxvi]

"Surely you would not forsake a king's ransom in wealth?" Heraclides wheedles. "It is yours for nothing: land, money, slaves—whatever you want."

Scipio watches two dice throwers at the adjoining table. The dice clack onto the table. One curses with disappointment while the other cackles with glee, scooping the coins from the table. "Money comes and goes, but dishonor remains. You have my counterproposal—full payment and relocation beyond the Taurus Mountains. I will recommend nothing else to my brother."

"But—" Heraclides begins.

Scipio waves him away. "Words serve no further purpose," he says. He turns to watch the dice players, his face expressionless.

Heraclides rises from the table, his jowls trembling with repressed anger. "I will relay your *proposal* to Antiochus," he says acidly. "I am sure he will give you a quick response to it."

"He had best not wait long," Scipio says. "I'm coming to get my son, regardless of what he decides."

Two days later, Lucius' army departs Abydos. Thirty thousand men march south along the Asian coastal road, heading for a confrontation with Antiochus' army. Scipio and Lucius ride in the vanguard, accompanied by Eumenes of Pergamum.

The staunch legionnaires are wrapped in scarves, cloaks, socks, and woolen leggings, anything to protect themselves from the crisp winter weather. Scipio however, wears only a tunic and cloak, his body flush with heat. *Are the fevers coming upon me?* he wonders. His right hand begins to tremble. *Not now. Not when Lucius needs me the most.*

SARDIS, 190 BCE. Antiochus, Hannibal, and Commander Zeuxis stand in front of a fireplace in the king's private meeting room, warming their backs.

Heraclides stands in front of the powerful trio, nervously relaying his message from Scipio. The envoy is well aware of the old saying, *bad news, kill the messenger.*

"He wants me to move beyond the Taurus Mountains?" Antiochus splutters. His hands ball into fists. "The temerity of him!"

"I see his viewpoint," Hannibal says. "He doesn't want to simply win a battle, he wants your empire as far away from Rome as possible. He is concerned for its long-term security."[ccxvii]

Antiochus crooks his head at Heraclides. "Get out of here!" The old man scuttles into the palace hallway. Antiochus shakes his head. "Full repayment of their war expenses! He acts like he has defeated me in battle. Me, the king of the Syrian empire!"

"Why, those are terms for a conquered nation!" Hannibal says.

Antiochus rubs his eyes. "I had hoped it would not come to this, but you were right about Rome's lust for war. In my fifty years upon this earth, I have never heard of such an absurd proposal."

"What should we do, King?" Commander Zeuxis asks.

"As Hannibal said, the Romans give me the same terms for peace as if they had conquered me in a war. We have nothing to lose by fighting them."[ccxviii]

*Only thousands of men,* Hannibal thinks. "We go to battle, then?"

Antiochus pushes himself from his throne, his face suddenly animated. "Yes, we fight. And we fight with an army such as the Romans have never seen!"

The king grabs Zeuxis by the shoulder. "Send messengers to every part of my empire. I want all our allied commanders to join me. They are to bring every available man with them. Get the Dahae, the Galatians, the Arabs, and the Cretans. Everyone!"

"You want them here, at Sardis?" Zeuxis asks.

"Not here. I'll take the army north, to the plains of Magnesia. It's big enough to accommodate my hordes. There's wide, flat ground there, perfect for a chariot assault."[ccxix]

"Excellent," Hannibal says. "Make the terrain your ally."

"The terrain will be my ally, as well as the men of a hundred nations,"

Antiochus declares. "Scipio will regret the day he rejected my offer."

ELAEA, PERGAMUM, 189 BCE. Six days after leaving Abydos, the army draws into the port town of Elaea. The Romans pitch camp outside the low-walled city, waiting for Eumenes' grain ships to bring their supplies.

The infantrymen stake down their tents and gather branches for their cooking fires, grateful for the respite from marching. Many rush to the vendors who have already set up stalls on the outskirts of camp, anticipating the Romans' arrival. The soldiers buy expensive cuts of meat, pricey bottles of wine, and quick tumbles in the prostitutes' tents. They know this is their last stop before battle, and that money has little value to those too dead to spend it.

As soon as a contubernium of soldiers erects Scipio's tent, he rushes inside and collapses upon its straw mattress, his brow bathed in sweat. Instantly, he is asleep.

A hand shakes Scipio awake. He rubs his bleary eyes and looks up. Lucius looms over him, garbed from head to toe in his shining consular armor.

"Awake, brother. I will be leaving soon." He smiles. "I just wanted to say goodbye."

"Wh-what? We are leaving? How long have I been asleep?"

"It is almost midday. The supply ships arrived last night." He gently pushes Scipio back onto his mattress. "You must stay here."

Scipio rises to a sitting position. "I promised the Senate I would accompany you!" he declares, his voice raspy.

"And so you have, and your help has been invaluable." Lucius says. "But now it is time for me to lead my men into battle. I do not want them—or me—looking to you for guidance. I will make my own fate."

"Let me go, I will not interfere," Scipio says. He levers himself upright, wobbling on his feet. Lucius eases him down.

"Look at you. Your mattress is soaked in sweat. Your face is red as Cato's hair. You are sick, Brother. All the more reason for you to stay here."[ccxx] He grins. "I'll be back in a few weeks with a vast load of plunder—I promise you'll get half!"

"No, no, let me come. I just want you to win. I want you to have your triumph!"

Lucius' face becomes stern. "As consul, I command you to remain here. As your brother, I beg you to respect my words."

Lucius bends over and kisses his brother on both cheeks. He strides from the tent, wiping at the corners of his eyes.

*At least he is learning to take command,* Scipio thinks, his brain whirling. He lays back down and covers his eyes with his arm.

The camp medicus appears that evening, accompanied by two centurions. "We have a comfortable house for you in town," the doctor says. "You can heal better there. Your carriage awaits." Scipio shuffles into the carriage and falls onto its thinly padded seat, too weak to protest.

That night, fevers burn upon Scipio. He tosses in his feathered bed, sweat pouring from his body. The dream comes to him, again.

*Lucius stands on the plain, frozen with indecision. The Syrian chariots and infantry pour over the hills, rampaging toward the immobile legions. He pivots his head to each side, frozen in panic by what he sees. Finally, he turns behind him and looks entreatingly toward Scipio.*

*The chariots cut through the Roman maniples. Hundreds of legionnaires fall like new mown hay. Scipio urges himself to move, but he cannot. He tries to shout, but he cannot. Lucius gazes at him, tears filling his eyes. He falls to the pitiless chariots.*

Scipio lurches awake, his heart thundering in his ears. He scans the room for enemies, his body tensed for battle. He sees nothing but the wispy curtains that frame his ornate oak bed. *I cannot ignore my soul's voice any longer. Lucius needs me, though he thinks he doesn't. And my son is out there, waiting for me.*

He places his palm on his forehead. *Febris is gone, but she has left her message. I've got to leave soon.*

Scipio calls for an attendant. "Bring me meat and bread, and lots of fruit. Prepare a carriage to take me to the baths."

Two days later, Scipio sits on a marble bench in his temporary home's garden. He admires the sun-colored teardrops of the garden's winter crocuses, interspersed among its cherry-red tulips. His portly Greek medicus hovers over him, searching for signs of fever.

One of Scipio's guardians enters the garden, a young patrician from the wealthy Valerian family. "There is a messenger here from King Antiochus," the boy announces in his thin, reedy voice. "His name is Heraclides."

Scipio rolls his eyes. "Gratitude, Gnaeus. Show him in."

Heraclides steps into the garden archway, handing his black riding cloak to Gnaeus. "Take care of this for me," the aged messenger orders.

Gnaeus blushes with anger. He flips the cloak over a pedestaled statue of Hestia, goddess of households.

"Heraclides! Have you brought me another peace proposal?"

Heraclides forlornly shakes his head. "I am afraid the days of treaties are past. I brought you a gift from the king." The aged messenger presses his fingers to his lips and whistles shrilly.

Scipio hears the house doors being opened. He hears leather sandals slapping lightly across the stone tile floor.

Publius steps into the atrium.

Scipio blinks, not believing his eyes. "Ah, my gods!" He springs from his chair and runs to his son. The two wrap their arms around each other, merging into one.

"I wondered if I would ever see you on this earth again," Scipio says, choking out his words. He smiles crookedly. "You look bigger. You must like that Syrian food!"

"Nothing like our good bread and cheese, but I was treated well enough," Publius says, smiling through his tears. He bows his head. "I am sorry, Father. I tried to escape, but Hannibal caught me."

Scipio laughs. "He is a wily old fox. He probably had someone following you everywhere you went."

"He was good to me. I think he convinced Antiochus to let me go," Publius says. He smirks. "Not a bad sort, for a Carthaginian."

Heraclides clears his throat. "Your son is a gift from the king. He expects no concessions, knowing you would give none."

Scipio takes a deep breath. "I have a present for your king. It is my advice. Tell him not to go out to battle until he hears I have returned to Lucius' camp."[ccxxi]

Publius stares at his father. "You are leaving me, right after I got here? Aren't you too sick to travel?"

"Not so sick that I will forsake my destiny," Scipio tells his son. He turns a stern face to Heraclides.

"Go back to your king. Tell him I will see him in battle. Whether I be bane or blessing, Fortuna will decide."

Cataphract

# X. MAGNESIA

PLAINS OF HYRCANIUS, MAGNESIA,[ccxxii] 190 BCE. They ride in from the north, hurtling down from the mountains that border their arid desert kingdom. The Dahae horse archers thunder across the Hyrcanius Plains, the frost-limned sage crackling beneath their rangy steeds' hooves. They ride without reins or saddle, twelve hundred men in olive green tunics and leggings, their knees expertly guiding their mounts.

The Dahae splash across the wide River Phyrgus, heedless of the swift current's pull. They run past the tall walls of Magnesia city, urged on by their leader, the ruthless King Darya.

"Get them moving!" Darya yells to his captain, who rides next to him. "If I don't make the meeting, he'll have my head!" Darya barks out a command. The riders bend to their horses' necks and put heels to their sides. The horses race across the plains.

The cavalrymen soon slow to a trot, daunted by what they see before them. Antiochus' vast camp sprawls across the scrublands, ringed by a trench eighteen feet wide and nine feet deep. A staked palisade encircles the inner side of the trench, lined with fifteen-foot towers.

Thousands of soldiers bustle about the trench, constructing an inner palisade. Bare chested Galatians lug piles of sharpened stakes on their shoulders, oblivious to the chilling winter breeze. Cloaked Syrians push the stakes into a shallow wall of trench dirt. Their compatriots stand on platforms, using their mallets to drive the stakes home.[ccxxiii]

Darya gapes at the elaborate fortifications. *This place could repel giants! He must really fear the Romans*. "Keep our men on the plains," he tells his captain. "They can pitch camp by the river." The king trots across a rude bridge of roped logs, his eyes fixed on an enormous ruby-colored tent in the center of camp.

Darya dismounts in front of the tent. Two sentries beckon him inside. Darya enters a room filled with the commanders of Antiochus' tribal armies. The king stands over a low, wide map table, backed by his son Seleucus and Zeuxis, his commander in chief. Hannibal stands to the right of the king, with Nicator on his left.

"There you are," Antiochus says, frowning at Darya. "I was going to send Seleucus out with his cavalry, just to see where you were."

He sweeps his hand across the crowded tent. "Men, this is King Darya, leader of the peerless Dahae. Darya, you know most of those here, but let me introduce you to those you may not recognize."

Antiochus points toward a red-bearded giant covered in furs. He stands next to a man who is equally large, his hairless head snaked with black tattoos. "This is Judoc, chief of the Galatians, and his brother Artagam. Their infantry and riders will be our shock troops."

"We look forward to fighting these cocky little Romans," Judoc says, "and bringing their heads back to camp!"

The king gestures toward a dark, mustachioed Arab that looms behind him, his lanky frame covered in a tan wool robe. "You have heard of Duha, the Morning Warrior? He has brought hundreds of his camel riders to camp. These Romans have never fought camels, they won't know how to handle them!" Duha nods solemnly.

A husky, turbaned man leans on the table, his eyes luminescent in his charcoal gray skin. "Philipus here is my new captain of elephants. He has sixty-four elephants ready to fight."

"They are Indian elephants," he declares proudly. "Brought them from my home country and trained them myself! They are much larger and fiercer than the Romans' elephants, they'll run them off the field!"

"I assume you know the rest of my officers from our last campaign," Antiochus says. "The Pamphilians, Lydians, Psidians, and so on, they are all back. We have over eighty thousand men here!"

*Divided into a hundred groups*, Hannibal thinks, looking around at the scores of tribal officers.

Darya bows slightly. "It is good to see you all." He nods toward Nicator. "Even you, Nicator!" he says, provoking scattered laughs.

Nicator faces him, saying nothing. Darya stirs uncomfortably.

Antiochus puts his arm around his infantry captain. "Nicator says he has a debt to settle. There is a Thracian called Thrax, and a tribune name Marcus Aemilius. He has vowed to kill them both."

"Not if I get to them first," declares Judoc.

"Do not try," comes a voice inside the mask, "or you will be the third."

The Galatian flushes. "You little dung fly, you think you could withstand my axe? I'd—"

Antiochus spreads his hands. "Be of common purpose, my friends. There are more than enough to kill."

"I saw a camp in the distance," Darya says. "From the looks of its arrangement, I assume it is the Romans, They are only a few miles away."

"All the better for us," Antiochus replies. "We can fight near our fort. It will lend the men some confidence."

Judoc stomps his feet. "When we fight?" Antiochus nods at Hannibal. "Tell them."

"Two days hence, we march out in front of the fort and display ourselves for battle. The Romans will decline, but it gives us a chance to see their formations. Then we can prepare our attack accordingly."

"How do you know they won't change formations the next time?" asks Leuzus, the Parthian commander.

"Lucius Scipio is in command," Hannibal says. "He is not as, let us say, imaginative as his brother." He smirks. "I expect the standard

Roman arrangement: legions in the center and allies on the flanks."

"Scipio may be there." Darya interjects.

Hannibal shakes his head. "Our camp spies say they have not seen him. Besides, I hear his brother is determined to be his own man. He would not welcome Scipio telling him what to do."

Antiochus bites his lip. *Scipio said not to go to battle until he was there. Maybe he will arrive soon, and be willing to broker a peace.* "It makes sense to draw them out so we can study them," Antiochus says. "We'll try it three or four times, and see if Lucius changes his formations."

"Three or four times?" Hannibal says, incredulous.

Antiochus glares imperiously at him.

"As you command," Hannibal says, shrugging. *You are stalling for time. What do you expect to happen?*

TENT OF LUCIUS SCIPIO, MAGNESIA. "What are they doing over there?" Lucius fumes. "They march out like they are ready for battle, but they won't leave the front of their ramparts!"

Lucius paces about his oak plank map table, hands clasped behind his back. His legates and senior tribunes watch silently, waiting for him to recover his composure.

Scipio stands in the rear of the tent, doing his best to be invisible. His unexpected appearance at camp yesterday raised a furor of enthusiasm among the Romans and allies. It took him hours of conversation with Lucius—and several cups of wine—to convince him that he would not interfere with Lucius' decisions.

"That's the fourth day in row they've done that,"[ccxxiv] adds Gnaeus Domitius, Lucius' senior legate. "They just line up and stand in front of the camp, as if they are ready to run back inside."

Lucius paces around his map table, his hand clasped behind his back. "We can't wait much longer. The winter rains are coming. We'll soon have to withdraw to Greece and set up winter quarters. He'll get away!"

"My legion is ready," says Tiberius Gracchus, the other legate. "They have no fear of the Syrian mob. They're ready to cross the trenches and climb over the ramparts to get at them!"[ccxxv]

"That's it, then," Lucius blurts. "We attack them tomorrow, no matter where they are. We're not going home empty-handed."

"Very well," Domitius replies. "I will prepare the men for battle—again."

*Too early. I can't let him do this*, Scipio decides. He steps into the torchlight.

"I suggest you wait until the rains come." "The Syrians have twenty thousand slingers and bowmen,[ccxxvi] far more than we do. The dampness will loosen their leather bowstrings, slings, and javelin thongs. It will also be difficult for them to see.[ccxxvii] They will be less effective."

"You want us to fight in the rain?" Lucius says.

'I see his point," Gnaeus Domitius interjects. "It would help neutralize one of his army's largest components."

"If we wait too long, the winter will drive us back to Greece," Lucius replies testily. "We go at them tomorrow!"

"You are right," Scipio says, nodding slowly. "If we wait too long, we risk losing the purpose of our campaign. But dark clouds are gathering in the west. We may soon have another damp, foggy day."

He juts a forefinger into the air, as if an idea has just occurred to him. "Say, what if we attack the day after tomorrow, no matter what the weather is? Can we wait just one more day?"

Tiberius Gracchus starts to speak. Scipio locks eyes with him, and imperceptibly shakes his head. Tiberius closes his mouth.

"Didn't you hear? The men are tired of doing nothing," Lucius snaps.

"It's making us look weak."

King Eumenes of Pergamum steps in next to Lucius. The elder warrior king places his three-fingered hand on Lucius' shoulder. "Actually, Consul, I could use another day. I need to coordinate the Roman cavalry and Italia allies that I'm leading. They are confused about the timing of our wave attack."

"I am willing to wait another day," Masinissa adds. "Wet or dry, my men will ride rings around them," Scipio steps back into the tent's shadows, his face expectant.

Lucius stares down at the map table. He jerks up his head, his lips set into a tight line. "We attack the day after tomorrow, no matter the weather. Return tomorrow after the third watch." The Roman and allied commanders file out from Lucius' command tent.

Eumenes stands to one side of the exit, waiting for Gracchus and Domitius to push their way through the tent flaps. He looks over his shoulder and gives Scipio a quick wink. He slips through the flaps, leaving Lucius and Scipio alone.

Lucius whirls upon him. "Why did you undermine me? I said I wanted to attack tomorrow!"

"My intention was not to undermine you, Brother. I just mentioned another consideration that would delay us for a day. You were the one who made the decision."

"After you all started ganging up on me!" Lucius blazes. "I have developed our attack strategy. I should be able to direct it without interference."

"And so you shall," Scipio says. "You have an effective arrangement of forces."

He scans the battle figurines on the map table, halting at the figure of a lone horse placed by the river. "Who is guarding our left flank, over by the river?"

"I have a hundred and twenty of my equites over there,"[ccxxviii] Lucius replies. "And a thousand light infantry near them."

"Is that enough? They are the last line of defense between the enemy and our camp."

"More than enough," Lucius snaps. "The river is there to protect us from being outflanked."

Scipio bites his lip. "Of course, of course." He holds up his finger and grins, looking like a mischievous child. "One last suggestion?"

"What?" Lucius says, crossing his arms.

"Marcus Amelius and Thrax have both vowed to kill Nicator, Antiochus' assassin. They are fanatic about it, to the point of threatening each other. I question how rational they will be in this battle."

"You think they should be disciplined?" Lucius asks. "The Thracians are crazy enough as it is, without me belittling their leader."

"That's just it, they are too crazy to be trusted," Scipio says. "Just as Marcus Amelius has become." Scipio shrugs. "I don't know, I think they might be best left in camp, as a last line of defense. Then they couldn't mess up your plans."

"Marcus *is* a bit too independent for a tribune," Lucius says. "He thinks he's better than the rest of us because his father was Marcus Silenus. It wouldn't hurt to put him in his place. He can stay there with the Thracians."

"Good. That will keep them out of the way," Scipio says. *Now we'll have some of our best fighters to defend the camp.* Scipio stretches his arms and yawns. "I had best get some sleep. The sickness has not yet left me."

"Get your rest," Lucius says. "We are soon going to fight them, whether they decline battle or not."

SYRIAN CAMP, MAGNESIA. King Antiochus III stands outside the front gates of his imposing camp fortress, surrounded by scores of tribal commanders. He points his ebony scepter at the vast plain in front of him, indicating tomorrow's battle formations. "Our men have grown restless from inaction. There is talk that we are afraid to combat the Romans. The time for action has come."

The commanders clap and whistle. Zeuxis steps out from the crowd and faces the captains. He raises his fist. "Now, *now* is the time of our glory! When we defeat the Romans, the world will know we are the greatest fighters in the world!" The commanders cheer.

Antiochus' heart thumps with excitement. *There is no turning back now.* He steps forward to stand next to Zeuxis.

"We have seen Lucius Scipio's army arrayed for battle. It is always the same. The standard Roman formation of legions in the center, allies on the flanks, cavalry on the edges. We will arrange ourselves into three points of attack, each led by a separate faction."

Antiochus gestures to the right, pointing his scepter toward the wide Phyrgius River. "Hannibal, Nicator, and I will direct the right flank, along with Judoc and his Galatians. Darya, your horse archers will back us up."

He sweeps his scepter to the center of the plain, pointing at the faint outline of the Roman camp. "Zeuxis will lead our Syrian phalanxes in the attack center, with Philipus and his elephants stationed between each of our ten phalanxes."[ccxxix]

The king points to the far left, near the round-shouldered hills. "My son Seleucus directs our cavalry and chariots on the left flank, joined by Duha's camel riders and Artagam's Galatians."

"We will initiate the attack with our twenty thousand skirmishers, a veritable army of slingers, archers, and spearmen. After we have opened gaps in their defenses, we'll send in the chariots and camels on our left flank."[ccxxx]

A wolfish grin crosses his face. "We will send the chariots out after the skirmishers have withdrawn. Woe betide any man or animal who gets in their way!"

"What of our camp?" Darya says. "If the Romans take it, we lose all our supplies and weaponry."

"They won't," says Antiochus. "The fort is impregnable. We have thousands of our allies there, with two thousand of my Syrians. That will still give us a field force of over seventy thousand men."

For the next two hours, Antiochus' officers review strategy and tactics. The commanders disperse to their respective tribes, with several groups lingering to confer one last time. Hannibal and Antiochus stand alone, surveying the vast plain before them.

"What do you think?" Antiochus says, his voice ringing with pride. "Do I have enough warriors for these Romans?"

Hannibal turns around. He surveys the sea of tents. "Quite enough for these Romans, however greedy they are."[ccxxxi]

"You jest? Or are you serious?" Antiochus bristles. "I have carefully prepared all this."

Hannibal clamps shut his eye. "Yes, I jest," he finally replies. "Sometimes I see humor where others do not."

"Obviously," Antiochus snipes. "Let's get back to camp. We still have many preparations. There is a long night ahead for the both of us." He rubs the back of his shoulder. "You know, I am fifty years old now, and you are fifty-seven. We are becoming too old for all of this!"

Hannibal nods somberly. "Very true, my King. Very true." He gazes across the plain, watching a pack of gray wolves lope through the low-lying scrub, closing in on a limping deer. "Then again, I have a feeling this will be the last battle for the both of us."

**Battle of Magnesia**

# XI. MASTERS OF THE WORLD

PLAINS OF MAGNESIA, 190 BCE. The day of battle dawns grayly, laden with the weight of early winter mist. Thousands of legionnaires wake to the clanks and curses of their compatriots donning weapons and armor. Men who woke hours earlier, hearts pounding, wondering if this is the day of their death.

The Roman patrols trot toward the closed gates, two dozen men intent on identifying every soldier and formation in the enemy army. The sentries pull open the gates and wave them out into the morning fog. The camp buccinae sound the call to rise, their notes muffled by the misty air.

Scipio pokes his head between the flaps of Lucius' command tent. He finds his brother lacing on his silver-plated shin greaves, his hands shaking. "I'll be back soon," Scipio says to Lucius, "Do not lead them out without me." Lucius nods, not trusting himself to speak. Scipio's head disappears.

Lucius shuffles to the tall stool that serves as his improvised altar, his armor clanking about him. He kneels before the figurine of Victoria, his hands clasped in front of him. "Goddess of Victory, make this my day," he murmurs. "I promise to sacrifice four oxen at your temple."

He pinches his eyes tight. A tear trickles from the corner of one eye. "It is not for me, I swear. I just want to make Mother and Father proud. And my brother proud. Just this once, let me do right."

Lucius rises from the altar and wipes his eyes. He raises his chin high. His tear-glazed eyes become clearer, glinting with the green fire of determination. He pokes his head outside his tent. "Abraxos! Bring me my stallion. It's time to go to war!"

As Lucius mounts his horse, Scipio trots from the camp gates, arriving at a mist-shrouded field of auburn tents. Masinissa and Sophon stand in front of the Numidian king's tent, stuffing spears into their horses' leather saddle slings. Scipio dismounts next to them.

"The fog is lightening. Lucius and I will start the march in a few minutes. I wanted to wish you both good fortune today." He steps forward and extends his hand to Masinissa. "Here's hoping we have us another victory."

Masinissa slowly unfolds his arms. He lightly grasps Scipio's forearm. His icy stare melts momentarily. "May your gods follow you today." He turns on his heel and strides back to his tent.

Sophon beams at Scipio. "This is so exciting! My first battle on Asian soil! Is it true Antiochus has elephants the size of temples?"

Scipio smiles. "Well, not quite that large, but they make your African elephants look like mules!" His smile fades. "Be careful today, Prince. This is not like us fighting that Gallic mob in Italia. There are all types of beasts and warriors out there!"

Disdain glints in Sophon's eyes. "I am not worried. I have seen those armored riders of theirs, what they call cataphractii. They lumber about like pregnant oxen. We will ride circles around them."

"I believe you. That's why I asked your riders to come here." After a final embrace, Scipio slides onto his horse and returns to camp. He arrives in time to join Lucius at the front gates.

Lucius smiles nervously at Scipio. He fingers his purple consular cape. "Look at this, my cloak's already getting damp. Perhaps I should break tradition and leave this behind. I'm an easy target with this on."

"I know what you mean!" Scipio says with a smile. "But it makes it easy for your officers to find you."

Lucius snorts. "That's just it, Brother. It makes it easy for *everyone* to find me!"

Scipio chuckles. "You are cursed with visibility, consul!" He waggles his dull green cloak at Lucius. "Now me, I must remain inconspicuous. That way I can be your messenger, riding back and forth through the lines. That will give me something to do!"

Lucius leans across his white stallion and grasps Scipio's shoulder. "Apologies if it seems I abandoned you at Elaea. You *were* sick, and I needed to stand on my own."

"And so you have," Scipio says. He thinks of Lucius' decision to leave his left flank exposed near the river. *For better or for worse.*

Scipio places his hand over his brother's. "And now it's time to fight. Your men are waiting for you."

Lucius takes a deep breath. He raises his right arm, willing it not to shake, and jerks it down. The battle horns sound. The equites and legionnaires cheer.

The Scipio brothers ride through the gates, leading a ten-wide column of fifth legion veterans. The hastati lead the advance, followed by the veteran principes. The senior warriors of the triarii follow them, their long spears pointing at the sky. The stern-faced centurions march alongside the Roman columns, yelling at any who stray out of line.

The light infantry bring up the rear, youths armed only with sword, helmet, and shield. The velites' slings carry double loads of spears, the better to cope with their enemy's overwhelming numbers.

The five thousand legionnaires of the fifth tramp out onto the rain-dampened plains of Magnesia, followed by the battle-hardened cohorts of the sixth. The soldiers wear their wool sagum as proof against the cold, their rust-colored cloaks contrasting with their tribunes' scarlet capes.

The Italia legions follow the Romans, similarly armored and arranged. Barrel-chested Tarquin leads out the socii, singing a centuries-old Etruscan battle hymn. Nicknamed the Yellow Elephant by his men, the blonde-haired commander trots about his columns, sharing jokes and exhortations.

"This is the day that will make my life!" Tarquin exclaims to Larth, his grizzled Etruscan captain. He knows history will be made this day, and he rejoices to be part of it. Tarquin intends to kill many enemies, hoping for Antiochus himself.

The Italia allies are followed by the riders of Pergamum, mortal enemies of Antiochus and his Syrians. Stately King Eumenes rides in the vanguard of two thousand swift cavalry, their blue plumes flowing from their polished bronze helmets. Eumenes' men have forsaken their shields in favor of the twelve-foot thrusting spears used by the Macedonians, relying on their bronze cuirasses and helmets for protection.

Four thousand Cretan infantry follow them through the fading morning drizzle, lightly armored men with a flat oval shield and a short, thick thrusting spear. The mountain men tread quickly and lightly, easily keeping pace with the horses in front of them. They are quick-striking soldiers, famed for their swiftness of foot.

Masinissa's two thousand Numidians follow the Cretans. The bareback riders wear wool tunics and pants as protection against the northern cold. The Africans laugh and joke as if they are riding to a celebration, prancing about on their swift mountain ponies. Masinissa's face is stern, but his eyes shine with excitement. He tugs at the lion's head that covers his domed helmet, rearranging its fangs so they do not interfere with his vision. Sophon laughs at his father's fussiness, glad his leopard's head has smaller teeth.

Sixteen elephants complete the battle train. At Scipio's urging, the elephants will be deployed behind the legions. Though they are smaller than Antiochus' massive beasts, he knows they can become deadly weapons, when loosed among enemy infantry.

Marcus Aemilius and Thrax the Thracian lean out from the front gates' guard tower, glumly watching the army leave for battle. Though they are left to guard the camp, they are fully armored and weaponed. Both know that in the chaos of battle, enemies appear in unexpected places.

When the army columns are halfway across the plain, Lucius calls them to a halt. The buccina sound the call to formation. The Romans and their allies spread across the plain, the legions in the center and the allied legions on their flanks. The Roman and allied cavalry line up behind them. The Roman army stands at formation under the lightening morning sky, waiting for the Syrians to appear. They do not have long to wait.

The legionnaires hear their enemy before they see them, their presence announced by the pounding thrum of a thousand drums. The Galatians appear emerge from the misty veil, two throngs of enormous bearded warriors, separated by a half-mile space. Artagam's Galatians halt in front of the men of Pergamum and Crete. On the other flank, Judoc's warriors line up against the Etruscans.

Slavering for battle and plunder, the Gauls slap their clubs and swords against their long oblong shields. Several dash into the clearing between them and their enemies, waggling their bare backsides.

A rumbling sound begins in the gap between the Galatian flanks, growing ever louder. Scores of scythed chariots burst out from the murk, trundling toward the Roman lines. The chariots turn to their left and spread out across the right flank of the Roman army. They halt several spear casts across from the Roman and allied legions, their drivers and archers staring at them. Hundreds of Duha's Arabian camel riders trot in behind the chariots, brandishing their thin, six-foot stabbing swords.

Lucius and Scipio watch the chariots and camel cavalry enter the scene of battle. Lucius gapes in amazement. "What are the chariots doing out there on the right? They never came out there before?" His eyes roam across his army. He bites his lip. "Should I bring up the cavalry? They are way behind me."

Scipio grasps his brother's wrist. "Don't do anything until we see who's in the center. They might have—" Scipio halts in mid sentence, gaping at the plains in front of him.

Antiochus' ten phalanxes appear in the middle void, rectangles of sixteen hundred men, each square bristling with eighteen-foot spears. The phalanxes march in as they have the previous four times, five in the front and five in the back. But this time they have brought some allies.

Eight gigantic Indian elephants lumber between each pair of phalanxes. The elephants wear a bronze frontlet over their massive foreheads, a long-nosed helmet the size a bathtub. A pair of Syrian archers lean over the wicker towers strapped to the elephants' backs, their barbed arrows cocked and ready. The elephants' sides are draped with blood red chain mail, adding to their nightmarish appearance.

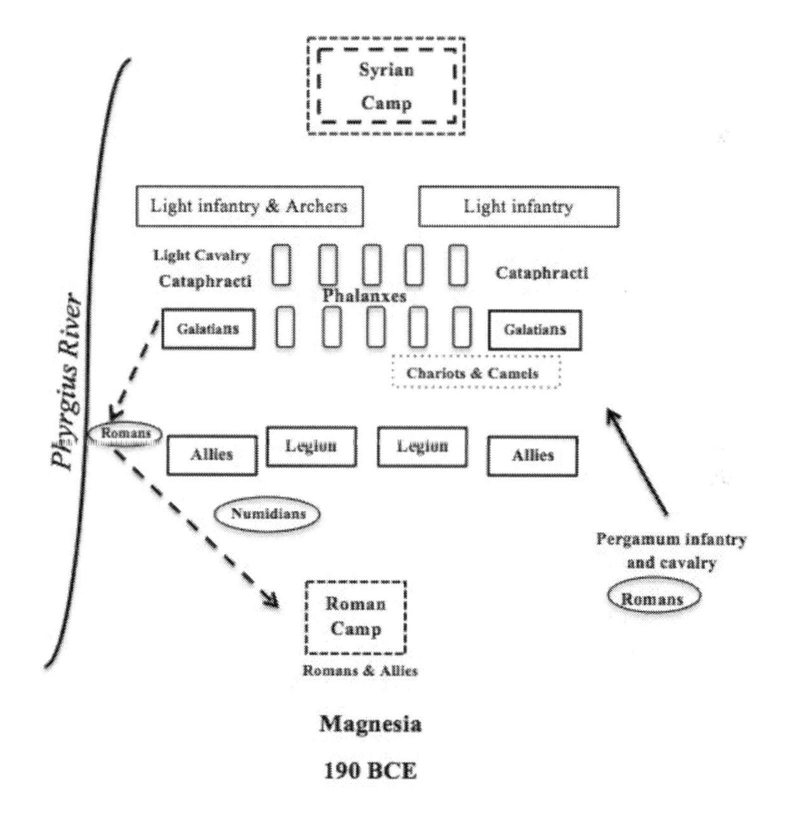


**Magnesia**

**190 BCE**

"They've changed their formations there, too," Lucius declares. "Vulcan's balls, I hadn't planned on elephants!"

“This is Hannibal’s doing,” Scipio says. “He loves the element of surprise.” Scipio watches hundreds of heavily armored riders ease in behind the Galatians to his left, their horses covered in shimmering ring mail. A tall man in silver armor leads them, his black cape flowing to his unarmored stallion’s haunches.

“There’s Antiochus!” Scipio tells Lucius. “He’ll lead his cataphractii around the flank near the river, I’d bet my son on it.” Scipio peers at Antiochus’ accompanying cataphracti. “Hannibal must somewhere over there. Watch out for him, he’ll have some trick in mind.”

More chariots rumble into the opening between the armies, lining up to charge. Scipio’s dream flashes to his mind. He recalls the vision of Lucius, paralyzed by indecision, standing immobile as his men are hewed under the chariots’ wheels.

“Lucius! I have to go talk to Eumenes. Don’t do anything yet!”

Lucius gapes at the two-mile line of enemies. “What should we do about those phalanxes and elephants?” he says, staring at the center phalanxes. “They’re monstrous!”

“Tell Tiberius and Domitius to hold the line at all costs. Help is coming!” Scipio races away.

Lucius summons his two legates. “You have to hold formation!” he barks, his face flush with excitement. “Don’t let the phalanxes break you!”

Tiberius studies Lucius’ moist, glazed eyes. *He’s scared shitless!*

Domitius snaps out his right palm and salutes. “We hear and obey, General.” The two legates return to their legions, bawling orders to their tribunes.

Scipio races behind the allied cohorts on his right, searching for King Eumenes. He finds him in front of his cavalry, poised behind the right wing of the Italia infantry. The Cretan infantrymen stand behind his riders, ready to follow them into battle.

"Eumenes! There are chariots massing in front of you. We have to get to them before they break the infantry."

"I can run my cavalry at them," Eumenes replies, "But those chariots are difficult to stop. One misstep, and you are chopped to bits by those wheels!"

"We don't need to stop them," Scipio says, "we just need to redirect them! We can turn them into a weapon for us, like I did with Hannibal's elephants at Zama. Herd the chariots into those Galatians behind them!"

Scipio pulls out his sword and sweeps it in front of him, as if he is shooing flies. "Your riders should attack the chariot's horses; poke at them from all sides. Scatter your Cretans among them, they can use their spears. Get your men to scream like madmen, that will sow confusion among the beasts."

"I remember that tactic," Eumenes says. "Alexander used it to great effect."

"As did I," Scipio replies. He grasps Eumenes' forearm. "Fare you well, King."

Scipio gallops back toward Lucius. He looks over his shoulder to check on the Pergamum cavalry. Eumenes and his riders are already looping around the allied cohorts, racing toward the center of the Syrian battle line. The swift Cretan infantrymen trot behind them.

As Scipio races to rejoin his brother, King Antiochus watches the last of his phalanxes march into the center of his battle line. "We're ready," he tells Hannibal. "Our center will keep their legions occupied, while the chariots break into their right flank. Judoc's Galatians will take over the left flank."

Hannibal nods. "If Judoc can keep the Etruscans occupied, we can attack the Romans by the river. Once we get past them, we can get at their camp and their rear lines."

Antiochus gestures to his hornsman. "Sound the attack."

Lucius hears the Syrians' attack call. "Send out the skirmishers!" he yells, his voice quavering. The cornicen blare three short blasts, and repeat them.

The velites trot out in front of the Roman legions. They arrange themselves into a three-deep staggered line, their left feet planted in front of them.

"Loose!" shouts their lead tribune.

The velites hurl their javelins into the phalanxes, eliciting scores of anguished cries. Dozens of the javelins clank off the elephants' armor. The beasts are unperturbed.

The young infantrymen hurl another volley. As they ready their third onslaught, cries of anguish erupt from their right flank.

The Syrian chariots crash into the right wing of the velites, cutting through the lightly armored troops. The chariots' archers loose hundreds of arrows into the scattering velites, lining the ground with their dead and wounded.

The death wagons steer toward the fleeing velites, carefully aiming their wheels' spinning blades. The blades strike home. Gore sprays from the wheels, accompanied by heart-rending screams. The velites dash for the safety of the legionary lines.

The front-line Romans watch hundreds of their compatriots crawl toward them, wailing with the agony of mangled arms and legs. They see men they have gambled with, whored with, fought with, lying with their intestines strewn across the field. The legionary ranks fill with the stench of voided bowels and bladders.

Tiberius Gracchus gallops across the front lines of the hastati, seemingly oblivious to the carnage around him. "Hold your place!" the warrior priest bellows. "Hold for Rome and family!" Tears stream down the faces of the battle-tested hastati and principes, but none move from their spot. Hundreds clench their javelins, shaking with the urge to revenge their young colleagues. They stay, and wait, knowing they will soon have their chance.

The chariots wheel around. They begin another grisly pass through the prone velites, searching for any sign of movement. The nearby Galatians howl and cheer, thoroughly enjoying the murderous spectacle in front of them.

A brass trumpet sounds, followed by the thunder of thousands of hooves. Eumenes' cavalry stampede into the field, led by the Eumenes himself. The riders races past the allied and Roman front, spreading out in front of the chariots.

When the lead cavalrymen reach the far end of the chariots, they whirl about and race toward them. The riders behind them follow their lead. A solid line of attackers gallops at the Syrians.

"At them!" yells the chariot commander, waving his command pennant at the Pergamum riders. The chariots rumble forward, their scythed wheels spinning.

Eumenes' cavalrymen close on the chariots. When they draw within a spear's cast, they break formation and dash madly in all directions.

"Get after the horses!" Eumenes shouts.

The cavalry fling their lances at the chariot horses, ignoring their drivers. Dozens of javelins strike the steeds' necks and shoulders.

The chariot horses rear in pain, shafts dangling from their bodies. They run from the tormenting lances, heedless of their drivers' commands. Scores of chariots bash into their fellows, flinging out the occupants. The Pergamum cavalry gallop into the openings, charging into the center of the Syrian wagons.

The Cretan infantry enter the fray, trotting into the maelstrom of horses and riders. Following Eumenes' command, they break ranks and disperse, attacking whatever chariot is nearest to them.[ccxxxii]

Dodging between the charging chariots, the Cretans fling their thick spears into the horses, following with hails of river stones. The Cretans scream at the top of their lungs, adding to the fearful clamor.[ccxxxiii] Dozens of chariot horses stampede aimlessly through the fight, dragging their drivers and archers.

Perched atop a rise, Chief Duha watches the chariot attack disintegrate. "Get at them!" the Arab commander yells. He tugs on his camel's bridle and surges forward. The camel riders lurch down to the chariot fight, their beasts running as fast as a horse.

The Arabs close upon the swirling cavalry and infantry, keeping a careful eye on the chariots' deadly scythes. They sheathe their long swords and pull out their short, curved bows.

"Shoot!" Duha yells over his shoulder. Hundreds of arrows fly down into the fight.

A Cretan infantryman plummets onto his face, an arrow jutting through his throat. Another stumbles to the earth, yanking at an arrow in his thigh. Scores follow them, groveling upon the ground. One, two, then ten Pergamum cavalrymen drop from their horses, pierced by the Arab's long, barbed arrows. The vengeful charioteers steer their chariots over Eumenes' fallen men, blood spraying from their wheels.

Eumenes trots through the battlesite, his eyes taking in everything. "Herd them, herd them back at the camels!" he shouts, pointing at the fleeing chariots. His cavalry captains echo his refrain.

Stabbing and screaming, the Pergamites and Cretans drive the chariots into the camels. The cruel scythes cut into the dromedary's stem-like legs. Dozens of camels honk in agony, panicking their fellows. Hundreds of camels and chariots careen away from the assault, heading toward their Galatian allies.

Chieftain Artagam watches with horrored amazement. "Get out of their way!" the Galatian screams at his men."

The words have no sooner left his mouth than four chariots crash into the Galatian front. The drivers yank their horses' reins, trying desperately to slow their wagons. The chariots tumble sideways, cartwheeling into the fleeing Galatians. Howls of anguish erupt from the Gauls. A dozen more chariots trundle madly into the Galatians, followed by scores of fleeing camels. The Gauls scatter in all directions.

"Get those fucking chariots out of here!" Artagam yells, insane with anger. He leaps onto the platform of a passing chariot and throws out its archer and driver. He yanks the horses to a halt. He waves for his men to emulate him.

The Gauls swarm over the chariots and camels, striking down any beast within arm's reach. Infuriated, the chariot and camel drivers retaliate with their swords and bows. The Galatians retaliate, chopping into heads and torsos. The Galatian front becomes an internecine battle between Syrians, Arabs, and Gauls.

Eumenes' cavalry delve into the midst of the bedlam, jabbing their lances at the distracted Gauls. The Cretan infantry dash in behind them, flinging spears into the compacted mass of enemies. Scores of Galatians fall, and scores more soon join them. The Gauls flee into the rear lines, dissolving into the mist.

"Get back here!" Artagam rages, watching his men run past him. He grabs a fleeing Galatian and flings him to the earth. He throws down another. "Stay here and fight, or I'll bash in your brains!"

A Cretan spear crunches into the middle of his broad chest, quivering like an oversized arrow. Roaring with anger, the huge barbarian yanks out the spear and flings it at a knot of oncoming Cretans.

"Come on, women, try me!" he bellows, raising up his club. The Cretans see two of their fellows lying near Artagam's feet, their helmets bashed into their skulls. They halt.

The eldest Cretan looks at his fellows. "Spread out. You know what to do." The Cretans spread out into a semicircle. "All together now," the elder warrior says, raising his spear. "One, two, three!"

The six Cretans fling their weapons at Artagam. The huge Galatian catches one shaft with his shield, and agilely ducks under another. A third lands crunches into the grainy soil between his feet.

A fourth cuts into his thigh, and another delves into the side of his stomach. The sixth buries itself in his chest. Artagam crumples to his knees, grappling at the javelin in his intestines. The Cretans swarm over the fallen giant like a pack of dogs, stabbing with spear and sword. Minutes later, Artagam's head dances on the end of a spear.

Word spreads like wildfire of Artagam's fall. The last of his Galatians dash from the battle, fleeing in all directions. Many hasten to Antiochus' camp, chased by Eumenes' vengeful cavalry and infantry.

A quarter mile behind Artagam's Galatians, hundreds of cataphractii wait on top of a hillock, anticipating Seleucus' orders to charge. They hear the sounds of battle emanating from the morning mist below them, though they can only see shadowy shapes surging within it.

"Get ready," says Antiochus' son. "We'll get the order to attack soon. Take no prisoners, however much they beg."

The clamor of voices rises. A driverless chariot careens past them, then several riderless camels. The Galatians explode from the fog, hundreds of fearful faces screaming that the Romans are coming. They weave through the amazed Syrians, casting off their shields and swords.

The cataphractii watch them flee headlong toward Antiochus' camp. Seleucus' riders stir restlessly, looking anxiously back toward the escaping Gauls. "Hold," Seleucus barks, pointing his six-foot lance at his men. "I'll kill the first one of you that turns your back on me!"

King Eumenes' riders surge out from the haze, followed by waves of the tireless Cretans. Seleucus' eyes start from his head. "Wedge formation!" he screams. "Get ready to charge!" His orders come too late.

The rear cataphractii break and run, following the Galatians. Before the slow moving riders can organize, Eumenes' cavalry are upon them, swarming over their outnumbered opponents. The Pergamum riders jab spears into the cataphractii's armor from every angle, searching for an opening. Dozens of Syrians sprawl across the battlefield, bleeding from multiple wounds.

The Cretans soon join the cavalry. They jab their blades into the horses' withers and haunches, prompting them to throw off their riders. Weighted down with heavy armor, the grounded cataphractii are easy targets for the Cretan swords and spears.

After mounds of their kin lie dead upon the ground, the surviving cataphractii pitch down their weapons and take off their helmets.

Eumenes draws his horse near Prince Seleucus. The Syrian prince removes his gold-wreathed helmet and drops it to the ground.

*He's even younger than I am,* Eumenes marvels. *Thanks the gods I didn't have to kill him!*

Seleucus wipes the corners of his eyes. He draws his sword and cradles its blade with both hands, presenting it to Eumenes. "I am Seleucus, son of Antiochus," he declares. His reedy voice quavers with fear.

Eumenes nods somberly. "Prince Seleucus, you will face a fine ransom. Be assured you will come to no harm."

Eumenes' soldiers rope the prisoners together, divesting them of their armor. The king waves over his brother-in-law Attalus, a diminutive man with an oversized ego. "Tell the men to rest for a bit, and take their breath," Eumenes says. He gazes toward the center of Antiochus' battle line. "We may have to go back on the attack."

"Good," Attalus says. He hoists up his studded leather skirt and begins pissing on a fallen cataphract. "I'm ready to take down some elephants!"

Eumenes winces with distaste. *Why did I let my wife talk me into taking him?*

While Eumenes rounds up his prisoners, a messenger hurtles in to Antiochus, bearing news of the Galatians' demise. "Gods damn them all!" Antiochus splutters to Hannibal. "Artagam's Galatians broke and ran!"

"Initiate the center attack," Hannibal urges. "Quick, before the Romans destroy your flank!"

"They won't break my phalanxes!" says Antiochus. "I've taken over half of Asia with them!"

The Syrian horns sound the attack. The phalanxes tramp toward the legions, their Indian elephants lumbering along between them. The phalangites lower their eighteen-foot sarissas, presenting the hastati with an impenetrable thicket of spears.

Scipio draws his horse next to Lucius. His brother stares across the battlefield, transfixed by the specter of the phalanxes and their gigantic elephants. Scipio squeezes Lucius' shoulder.

"Go ahead, brother, send out our infantry. There are lots of my veterans in our legions, men who fought with us at Zama.[ccxxxiv] They know what to do with phalanxes and elephants."

"Yes, we handled them that day, didn't we?" Lucius exclaims, his eyes alight with renewed determination.

"And you will do it again," Scipio replies.

"Legions forward!" Lucius barks to his cornicen.

The trumpeters sound the advance. Lucius and Scipio trot their horses toward the front, moving past the rearguard triarii.

The legions close upon the oncoming spear wall. The front cohorts are five-hundred-man rectangles of veteran fighters. Their stern centurions stride alongside them, searching for attack points in the oncoming phalanxes. The legionnaires raise their spears as Scipio passes by them, buoyed by the sight of their former commander.

As the two Roman legions advance in the center, the Italia legion treads out from left flank, heading for Judoc's stationary Galatians. The chief paces in front of his Galatian tribesmen, slapping his pickaxe against his broad, leathered palm.

"What is that Syrian pisspot waiting for?" Judoc fumes to one of his commanders. "We're standing around like a bunch of fucking sheep!" He sticks his pickaxe under his captain's nose. "I don't care what that Syrian pissant told me, I'm going to attack those bastards!!"

While Judoc fumes, Antiochus and Hannibal carefully monitor the Italians advancing in front of them. "They're close enough for Judoc's men to charge them," Antiochus says to Hannibal.

"Then send them!" Hannibal says peevishly. "What are you waiting for? If we break the allied flank, your cataphractii and horse archers can attack his legions from the rear."

Antiochus shakes his head. "I will stick with our original plan. While Judoc's men occupy the Italians, I'm going to attack their cavalry by the river. When they are out of the way, we have a clear path to the Roman camp." The king waves over his trumpeter. "Sound the Galatian charge."

Judoc hears Antiochus' trumpeter blaring two shorts and a long. His red-bearded face splits into a wide, bloodthirsty grin. *At last! Those Italian bastards were going to crawl up our ass while we just stood here!*

"Come on! Time to take some heads!" Judoc leaps out into the clearing, waving his pickaxe. He hits the ground running, screaming as he charges at the stone-faced Italians.

Two thousand Galatians spring to life, rushing to catch up to their leader. They hold their oblong shields high, fending off the stones flung from the socii's rear-line slingers.

The Gauls crash full speed into the allied cohorts, ignoring the spears that jab into their bodies. They leap upon the steadfast Samnites and Etruscans, hewing at them with their long swords and axes. The allied infantrymen counter with quick stabs from their short swords, puncturing the bodies of any Gaul who draws within arm's length. The Galatians persist, enduring the slashes for an opportunity to hack open an enemy's head.

The allied battle line is soon littered with Galatian bodies. The barbarians continue their assault, undeterred by the sight of their fallen comrades. The socii retreat a pace, then retreat again.

Judoc rages in the center of his battle line. He delves the point of his pickaxe into the helmet of an unwary Etruscan, smiling when the blood flows down his enemy's forehead. The Etruscan falls to his knees. Judoc kicks him out of the way and steps into the gap, battering at the next man in line.

"Come on, you shits!" he shouts over his shoulder. He whirls his pickaxe at two Italians standing in front of him, driving them back. A dozen Galatians charge into the opening, widening the split in the socii's front line. Scores of allies fall to the attackers. Judoc's Galatians batter the socii backward, leaving a trail of corpses to mark their progress.

"Now!" Antiochus declares. He gallops to his right, heading toward the banks of the Phyrgius River. His cataphractii and light infantry follow.[ccxxxv]

Hannibal gallops behind Antiochus' men, riding with King Darya and his Dahae horse archers. In the distance, Hannibal can see Antiochus' black cape flapping at the front of his heavily armored cavalry. *The man does not hide from battle, I will give him that. Perhaps he can win this, after all.*

As Antiochus leads his men toward the river, the center phalangites clash with the Roman cohorts. The Syrians shove their spears into the Roman front, their small round shields strapped across their left forearms.[ccxxxvi]

Crouched behind their scuta, the staunch legionnaires draw their swords and hack at the sarissas pushing against them. The phalangites persist, pushing inexorably forward. The Romans step backwards, following their centurions' shouted commands.

Antiochus' elephants lumber into the fray. The tower archers rain arrows into the principes and triarii who are stationed behind the hastati, felling scores of them. The phalanxes again step forward, and the legions again retreat.

As the center legions retreat, their left flank allies begin to break apart. Their lines disintegrate under the relentless hammering of Judoc's battle-mad Galatians.

With growing horror, Lucius watches his men retreat. "We're losing the front!" he cries. "They're caving in our center!"

Scipio points to his right. "All is not lost, Brother. Looks like Antiochus' men are attacking each other!"

Dozens of Artagam's retreating Galatians burst into the left flank of the phalanxes, madly fleeing Eumenes' assault force. Scores more follow, then hundreds. The huge barbarians jam themselves into the Syrians' orderly ranks, forcing gaps into the spear wall. [ccxxxvii]

Zeuxis rides along the front line of the phalangites, cursing the breaks in his formation. "Hold the advance," the Syrian commander tells Philipus, his captain. "Those Gauls have crowded our columns. Our men can't move!"

The midday sun rises, burning off the last of the mist. Stationed behind the front-line cohorts, Scipio and Lucius watch the Magnesia battlescape clear. Scipio notices the myriad gaps in the phalanxes' front wall. He looks to his left and sees Antiochus' cavalry disappearing around the left flank, heading toward the river.

He grabs Lucius by the forearm. "The phalanxes don't have any cavalry protecting their sides. It's our turn to strike!"

"With our legions?" Lucius says, confused. "They can't handle them."

"No, not the hastati. Send the velites at their front. Blanket those phalangites with every spear we have. I will rejoin you in a bit." Scipio turns his horse toward the rear ranks.

"Where are you going?" Lucius demands. Scipio halts his horse.

"I am going to summon our equites. And Masinissa's Numidians." He sees Lucius' face flush. "With your permission," he adds.

Lucius chuckles bitterly. "I am not so much of an ass that I don't recognize your tactical genius, Brother. Bring them out to the flanks. I will unleash hell upon their front."

Scipio hustles across the shrubby expanse that separates the sixth legion from its cavalry. He halts in front of Glaucus Justinius, the rangy young commander of the sixth legion's three hundred riders. Tiberius bows his head and salutes.

"Imperator! It is an honor! Is it our time? We languish here, without plunder or glory!"

"You will soon have plenty of both," Scipio replies. "The consul orders you to attack the east flank of the phalanxes. Harass them with your javelins. But don't try to break into them, you'll lose all your men."

"I should go now?" the young man says, his face flush with confused excitement.

"Are you waiting for Mars to join you? Yes! Go!"

Scipio wheels his horse about and races to the west flank of the army. Looking over his shoulder, he sees Glaucus' riders thundering toward the right side of the legion, heading out to harry the phalanxes.

The Numidians sit mounted in an open space behind the fifth legion, calmly watching the carnage unfold in front of them. Scipio sees Masinissa standing next to his horse, talking to his son Sophon. Scipio pulls his horse next to the Numidian king.

"You are ready for us?" Masinissa says.

"It's time," Scipio replies. "You and I need to break the phalanxes. Our legions cannot do it."

"You and I?" says Masinissa, his voice edged with resentment.

Scipio takes a deep breath. "I am going with you. One last battle, my King. Together."

"Excellent!" Sophon exclaims, before his father can reply. "This will be the honor of my life!"

He turns to his father, his eyes pleading. "Come on, Father. You told me about all your victories together. Do not deny me the chance to fight with the both of you!"

The ghost of a smile crosses Masinissa's face. "You have your mother's persistence. And wiles."

He nods at Scipio, and extends his forearm. "One last time, Publius Cornelius Scipio. For all the other times." Scipio solemnly grasps Masinissa's forearm.

Scipio throws off his drab army cloak. "We need to rain death upon the phalangites. Give me two slings of javelins." Scipio straps the rawhide slings across the back of his black stallion and clambers onto it. He reaches into his pouch and grasps the wood figurine of Nike that his son carved for him.

"I am ready."

Masinissa and Sophon strap on their helmets. Masinissa trots out and faces two thousand of the finest riders in the world. "Do not charge their spears—you will die," he tells them. "We attack with spear throws. Follow my lead."

The three gallop toward the left flank of the fifth legion. They ride across the open field, sprinting past the battling Galatians and Italians.

The Numidians hurtle past the front lines of the fifth legion, and rush into the phalanxes. Masinissa, Scipio, and Sophon run their horses along the side of the phalanx, close enough to see the eyes of the grim Syrians who stare at them.

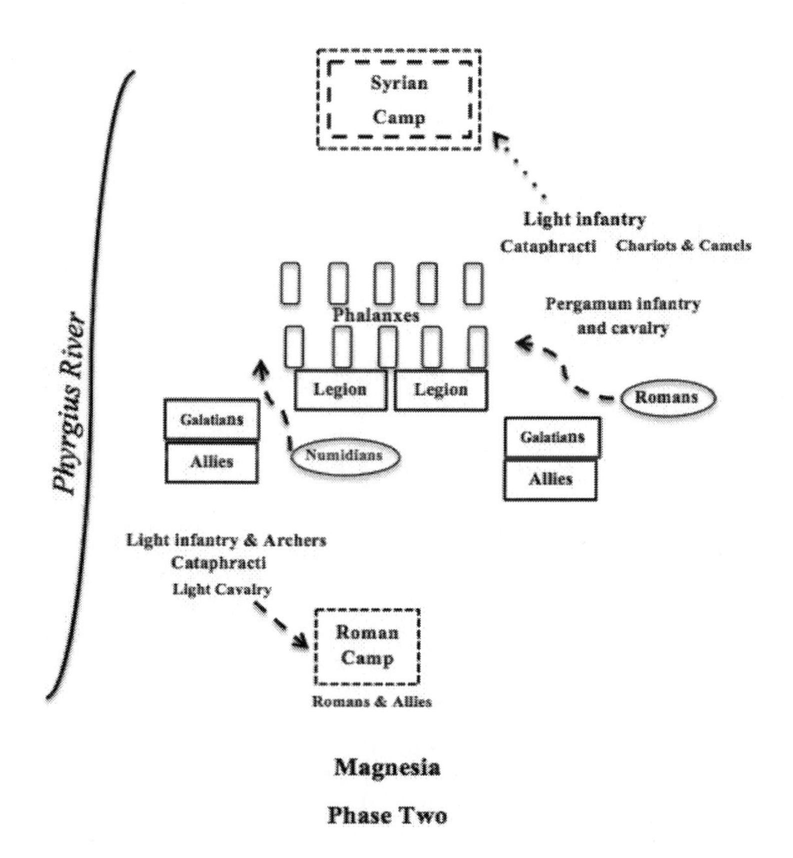


**Magnesia**

**Phase Two**

Masinissa hurls his javelin into the center of first phalanx. A scream erupts. The king smiles. Scipio and Sophon hurl their spears as they gallop past, followed by hundreds from the riders behind them. The Syrians, Galatians, and Arabs are so tightly packed that few spears miss their mark. The phalanx fills with cries of agony.

The Numidians race past the first rows of phalanxes and resume their attack on the five rows behind them, keeping their distance from the jabbing sarissas.

Masinissa pulls up next to Scipio. "Your men are on the other side!" He points to the far side of the phalanxes. Scipio looks across and spies Glaucus' scarlet pennant jogging past the forest of sarissas. Javelins fly out behind it, darting into the Syrian formation. "That's Glaucus and the sixth legion cavalry," he tells Masinissa. "They've got the other side covered."

The king nods. "Then we will go back the way we came, and kill some more."

Beset on both sides, the phalanxes withdraw to regroup. As the Syrians retreat, the legions' velites trot into the space they have vacated, eager to revenge the chariots' slaughter of their compatriots. They pause in front of the exhausted hastati, waiting for their signal.

The army horns sound. Fifteen hundred velites dash forward and hurl their spears with all of their might, raining them down upon the shieldless phalangites. They grab another of their seven javelins and repeat the process, sending a steady stream of spears into the enemy's front. Hundreds of Syrians and Galatians fall, rolling between the legs of the tightly packed phalangites. The phalangites stumble over them, dropping their spears.[ccxxxviii] More gaps appear in the wall.

Gnaeus Domitius races his horse to Tiberius Gracchus, his fellow legate. "There are breaks in the line!" he shouts excitedly. "We have to attack now! Use the principes—they fought at Zama."

As soon as Tiberius nods his assent, Domitius races across the open battlefield and faces his cohorts. He raises his gladius high over his head. "Death or victory awaits us, there is no other choice!" He chops down his sword. All across the half-mile front, the battle horns sound the legionnaires' advance.

The fifth and sixth legions' principes march forward, backed by the hastati. The Syrian phalanxes move out to counter them. The elephants follow, arrows flying from their saddle towers.

The centurions grab their battle whistles and screech out the charge command. As one, the principes hurl their spears and tramp forward, swords drawn. They turn their shields sideways and edge into the phalanx gaps, striking down dozens of unprotected phalangites. Scores of terrified Syrians drop the unwieldy spears and grab their swords, creating more openings. The principes stream into the new openings, stabbing down hundreds of Syrians and Gauls.

Captain Philipus gapes in dismay at the destruction of his front phalanxes. "Bring in the elephants! Trample those bastards!" he screams at his captains. Minutes later, sixteen gargantuan elephants lumber forward, their drivers aiming at the oncoming legions.

Domitius trots back to one of his rear cohorts. "Any of you men who fought elephants at Zama, get out there!" A hundred principes rush past the front cohorts and surge into the gaps between the phalanxes, heading straight for the gigantic beasts. Using the tactics they learned fighting Hannibal's elephants at Zama, the brave veterans rush in and jab their spears into the beasts' sides and underarms,[ccxxxix] herding them sideways.

Trumpeting with pain and anger, the elephants lumber away from the offending spears, bashing into the sides of the phalanxes. The nearby phalangites scatter, and the once-impenetrable spear wall disintegrates. With their formations broken, the Syrians become easy prey for the relentless principes. Hundreds fall quickly to the stabbing Roman swords.

After attacking the rear phalanx nearest to them, Scipio, Masinissa, and Sophon ride back toward the Roman front, flinging their remaining spears at the Syrians. Scipio spies ten elephants lined behind the front phalanxes. He waves over Masinissa.

"Call your men to a halt!" Scipio says. The king reins in his horse. The Numidians circle around him, waiting for orders.

"We can break their inner lines if we stampede their elephants," Scipio says, pointing at the ten beasts between the front and rear phalanxes.

Sophon grins. "They may be bigger than our elephants, but they are still elephants. We know how to handle them!"

The Africans stream into the gap between the front and rear phalanxes, flowing around the waiting elephants. Dozens of Numidians fall to the archers in the elephant towers, but still they ride on. The

Africans swoop in and spear the elephants' backsides, driving them forward. The monstrous beasts careen through the rear of the front phalanxes, destroying the last vestiges of their formations.

Beset by Roman and elephant, the proud phalangites run toward camp, setting the rear phalanxes into a panic of retreat. Thousands of Syrians and Gauls swarm up the gentle rise that leads toward Antiochus' camp, seeking shelter within its fortress-like fortifications. The army's rearmost infantry and cavalry join in the flight, panicked at the sight of their army stampeding toward them.

Domitius' Roman equites ride in from the left flank, joined by Eumenes' Pergamum cavalry. They hunt down the fleeing remnants of Antiochus' center forces, lancing down hundreds.

An elated Lucius Scipio trots in behind advancing principes. He watches his victory unfold before him. *We've broken their center!* he marvels. *I did it!*

"Get my legates over here," Lucius tells his messenger. Minutes later, Gracchus and Domitius appear at his side.

"I want their camp!" he blurts. "Don't let up until we have it!"

The legions march double-time through the field abandoned by the phalanxes, pausing only to stab down the enemy wounded. They tramp up the rise toward the tall palisades of Antiochus' camp, knowing they have one final, gruesome task.

Having driven off the elephants, Scipio and the Numidians regroup on the flank of the advancing legions, waving their arms at the triumphant legionnaires. Scipio sees Lucius' purple cape flapping in the center of the marching cohorts.

*Let him lead them in without you*, Scipio decides. *His men will say that he led them to victory*. He looks across the field, where the Italians are still engaged with the Galatians. *I had best check on the allies, they appear to be having a rough time of it.*

"Let's head over there." Scipio points to his right, and turns his horse toward the river. Masinissa nods, waving for his men to follow him. Scipio, Masinissa, and Sophon gallops towards the sound of battle. As they draw near, Scipio raises his right arm, calling the riders to a halt. He surveys the battle scene before him. His face twists with dismay.

Hundreds of Italian corpses are strewn along a half mile length of battlefield, a charnel record of the Galatian's relentless advance. A five-deep row of Galatians hammer against a compacted line of Italian infantrymen, the lone survivors of Judoc's unrelenting assault.

Scipio notes there are no cavalry behind the Gauls. *Where are Antiochus' cataphractii and Dahae? They were in formation behind the Galatians, they should be backing them up.*

His blood freezes. *He took them by the river!* He turns to Masinissa.

"We have to turn the tide of this battle, and do it quickly," he says to the king. "We are needed by the river." He points to the center of the Gallic line. "Take out that big, red-bearded one. He looks like he's the chief."

"Make sure every man has a spear," Masinissa tells Sophon. "We are going to ride right through them."

Nineteen hundred Africans hurtle across the plain, their braided locks fluttering from their helmets. The Africans flare out into a wide attack wedge, with Masinissa and Sophon riding at the point. Scipio gallops a spear's cast behind them, his stallion laboring to keep pace with the Numidian ponies.

The Galatians feel the ground tremble. They hear the thunder of hooves. They turn from the Italians, staring at the dark horde descending upon them.

"Blocking formation!" yells a chieftain. The order echoes among the Gauls. The barbarians dig in their feet and plant their oblong shields into the ground. They cock their sword arms, ready to cut into any horse that attacks them. Then the Numidians are upon them.

The Africans wheel their horses sideways and batter against the Gallic shields, stabbing their lances into the torsos of those who lose their cover. The Africans churn through the scattered clumps of Galatians, dodging and thrusting, then spin about for another attack. The Gauls scatter across the plain, some dodging the relentless Numidians, others raging after them. The Galatians turn in every direction, unsure where their next attack will come from.

The Italian allies gape at the whirling Numidian attack, as amazed as if the gods descended to help them. "At them!" screams an Etruscan centurion, the legion's highest surviving officer.

The Etruscans and Samnites sprint across the field, roaring their ancient battle cries. They attack like madmen, chopping at any exposed body part their short swords can reach, their vengeful lust blinding them to any danger. The battle becomes a swirling confusion of screams and shouts. The outnumbered Gauls fight like trapped animals. Scores of Italians and Africans pile at their feet.

Sophon steers his horse through the melee, his eyes fixed on the red-bearded giant. *That's the one Scipio talked about. If I kill him, I'll be the hero.* The battle suddenly parts in front of Judoc. Sophon spurs his horse at him.

As Sophon plunges forward, Judoc delves the point of his pickaxe into the top of an Etruscan tribune's helmet. The hapless officer falls to his knees, dead before he hits the ground. Judoc yanks out his axe and kicks the body sideways. He spies the young Numidian charging at him, his lance leveled at Judoc's chest.

The chieftain sneers. *Fool! I will jam that stick up your ass!* Judoc raises his shield, as if to take the brunt of the lance's force. He lays his pickaxe alongside his leg, freeing his right hand.

Sophon leans over the neck of his horse and thrusts his lance at Judoc's shield. The Galatian angles his shield sideways, and the spear scratches across it. Judoc leaps in and grabs Sophon by the back of his loincloth. He jerks him off his horse and hurls him to the ground.

The chieftain grabs his pickaxe and stalks over to his stunned foe.

Sophon struggles to his feet. Judoc's shield bashes him back to the ground. He arcs down his pickaxe.

A black stallion crashes into the side of Judoc, catapulting him sideways. Judoc quickly clambers to his feet, groaning from the pain of two cracked ribs. He retrieves his mud-grimed pickaxe and cocks it back for a strike, searching for the man who interrupted his kill.

Scipio's riderless stallion trots off. Scipio staggers upright, still woozy from his tumble. He bends over and grabs his small round cavalry shield, sliding its straps across his left forearm.

"Roman dog!" Judoc bellows. He lurches toward Scipio, his face a rictus of rage. Scipio pulls out his gladius and crouches low, his eyes fixed on the charging giant's heart.

*He's injured*, Scipio thinks, noticing how Judoc leans to his right. Judoc leaps upon him, swinging his axe blade at Scipio's head.

Scipio shoves out his small shield. The pickaxe crunches into it, buckling it in the middle. Scipio grabs his arm, his face contorted into a rictus of pain. He drops his ruined shield and scrambles backward, waving his sword in front of him.

Judoc's teeth bare in a yellowed, gap-toothed grin. He tramps forward, his pickaxe held low. *Block his sword and chop into his guts*, Judoc tells himself. *He can watch you kill the boy while he dies.*

Scipio scrabbles sideways around Judoc, forcing the chieftain to follow him. The Galatian chieftain grimaces as he turns, stooping sideways to favor his broken ribs.

Scipio circles faster, watching as Judoc's face twists in agony. Judoc charges repeatedly, but each time Scipio retreats and circles him. The chieftain's charges grow slower, and his breathing grows heavy. He pauses to wipe the sweat from his axe grip.

Scipio darts in and slices into Judoc's kidneys. The chieftain's mouth gapes, his eyes wide with shock and pain. He swipes his pickaxe backwards, but Scipio has already leaped out of range. Judoc turns and faces Scipio, readying himself for a final charge. Scipio raises his blade, his broken arm dangling at his side.

An ebony spear plunges into Judoc's chest, its white shaft feathers blooming from his breast. Another plunges into his abdomen. The pickaxe falls from Judoc's hand. He staggers, drunkenly swiping his axe hand about him.

Scipio rushes in, his cleaver-like gladius poised. With one swipe of his steel blade, he strikes off Judoc's head.

Scipio steps back, watching the gouting corpse crumple to the earth. He jabs his blade into the spear-studded body, gasping with effort.

"You can stop now, he's dead," says a voice behind him.

"May he rot in whatever hell his gods have for him," says another.

Sophon stands behind Scipio, his chest heaving. Masinissa stands next to his son, a black spear clenched in his fist. A dozen of Masinissa's guard stand behind their king, hooting their approval of the three men's kill.

Scipio grins dazedly. He sheathes his sword and stumbles toward them. He falls onto his back, grasping at his arm.

Masinissa and Sophon rush in and kneel over him. "Do not try to get up," Masinissa says, gently pushing him flat. "The Gauls have fled. My men are hunting them down." He grins. "My tribe will have many stories to tell about the campfire tonight, thanks to you."

"Thanks to you, I still have life," Sophon adds. "I will never forget that."

Masinissa squeezes Scipio's shoulder. "Nor will I."

"I have to get to our camp!" Scipio rasps. He tries to rise, and collapses.

"My men and I will ride to the river and follow Antiochus' path. But you are going back with Sophon and some of my men."

Masinissa rises. He points to Scipio and barks out several orders. The king springs onto his horse and gallops toward the river, followed by twelve hundred of his men.

One of Masinissa's men pulls several linen strips from his satchel and expertly bandages Scipio's arm. They lift Scipio onto the back of Sophon's horse and rope him against the prince. The prince and his riders trot slowly toward the Roman camp.

*We should go faster, they may be in danger,* Scipio thinks blearily. *Antiochus may be there already*. His head falls onto Sophon's shoulder. He feels sleep descending upon him.

*Marcus and Thrax are there,* he says to himself. *They will hold them off until Masinissa arrives.*

While the battle rages across the fields of Magnesia, Marcus and Thrax observe it from the camp ramparts, leaning their heads between its sharpened stakes.

"Can you tell if we are winning?" Marcus asks.

"All I know is we'd have a better chance for victory if my men were out there," he grouses. He spits over the wall. "That's what I think about that cursed Scipio sticking us back here."

"I don't like it any better than you do," snaps Marcus, "but he must have had a good reason, or we wouldn't be here."

"A good reason to hide two thousand Thracian warriors, and two thousand legionnaires? I'd say he's as dumb as his fucking brother!" Then Thrax falls silent, staring off to his left. "Look over there, by the river. There's riders coming at us."

Marcus closes one eye, squinting into the scrublands. "Are those Antiochus' men?"

"Who knows? They're either running to attack us, or running from something that attacked them. We'd best prepare for the worst."

Thrax clambers down a palisade ladder. "Get our tribesmen out here," he orders one of his chieftains. "Every one of them!"

Marcus calls out the order to assemble. Within minutes, four thousand seasoned warriors are pressed about the camp gates, waiting for them to open.

Marcus and Thrax scramble back to the wall, standing near a guard tower that looms over the gates. "What do you see?" Marcus asks a tower sentry.

"Give me a minute, I can't be sure."

The two men pace along the palisade, staring at the dark line of approaching figures. "There's infantry, and horses," the sentry says. "And a larger force behind them. Chasing them."

"Gods curse you, who's in the front?" Thrax yells at the Roman.

"I'll handle it, Thracian," Marcus growls.

The two tower sentries mumble to each other. One leans over the side of the tower, looking down at Marcus Aemilius. "They are Romans! It's our men who are running toward us. Cavalry and velites!"

"Our men are running from a fight?" Marcus shouts, not believing his ears. The sentry shrugs. "I tell you what I see."

"The Syrians must be coming," Thrax says, his voice rising with excitement. "They're coming after the camp!"

"We're not going to hide inside here!" Marcus declares. He beckons over one of his tribunes. "Get our men ready. We're going out to confront those cowards, and wreck whoever is chasing them!"

"Thanks the gods," Thrax exclaims. "My men are ready for good fight!" His eyes gleam. "Maybe that Nicator bastard is out there."

"That would not be disappointing," Marcus says, balling his hands into fists.

The guards open the camp gates. Four cohorts of legionnaires double-time their way onto the plain. They line up in battle formation, several spear casts from camp. Thrax and his Thracians pace out behind them, arranging themselves into ten blocks of two hundred men.

A wide swath of riders gallop toward them. The soldiers shift about uneasily, wondering if they will be trampled.

Marcus faces his cohorts. "Those men are deserting the battle. Do not allow them to pass!" His eyes grow cold. "I order you to kill them if they try!"[ccxl]

Marcus pulls out his battered gladius and rests it against his thigh. Soon, a Roman decurion gallops in from the right side of the field, his eyes wide with fear.

"Get back to the fort!" the decurion exclaims. "The Syrians are coming. Thousands of them!"

The officer's riders approach, halting behind their leader. The equite glares down at Marcus. "Let us pass, Tribune. We've got to get inside the camp!"

*These are the men who were commissioned to guard the river,* Marcus realizes. "What is your name?" Marcus demands.

"Aureolus, from the house of Junia," says the young decurion.

"Well, Aureolus Junia, you ran from your post!" he glares at him. "Now you turn your ass around and get ready to fight! We're not hiding inside our camp!"

Hundreds of velites rush across the plain, devoid of arms and armor. *They dropped their weapons to run faster* Marcus thinks, disgusted.

"The cataphractii are coming!" shouts an infantryman. He halts in front of Marcus and flaps his arms at him. "They're right behind us, we have to get into camp!" He shoulders his way past the tribune.

Marcus clubs the man with the pommel of his sword, crashing him to the ground.[ccxli] As the velite lies stunned at his feet, Marcus grabs Aureolus and drags him from his saddle, pressing his sword tip against his throat. "I'll kill the next man who tries to cross our lines!" he yells. "I don't care who you are!"

He glowers at the frightened velites, his eyes burning with rage. "Get a javelin from the men behind you, Romans, and line up in front of me. You are going to reclaim your honor."

The abashed young infantrymen fetch spears and line up in front of the hastati. Marcus sends the cavalrymen onto his flanks, with orders to strike the attackers' rear lines. The Romans and Thracians wait, eyeing the horizon.

A silver strand glimmers above the distant scrublands. The strand takes on the jagged outline of a horde of armored riders. Antiochus' cataphractii thunder toward the waiting Romans, their mailed horses gleaming in the late afternoon sun.

The velites peer nervously over their shoulders, trying to see if Marcus Aemilius has changed his mind. "Get ready," the tribune shouts at them.

Thrax appears at Marcus' side. "Let us go at them first, Marcus. My men know how to handle cataphractii, we've fought them before." He grins malevolently. "We have a special surprise for them."

Marcus says nothing, pondering his choices. Thrax grasps Marcus' bicep. "They destroyed our homeland! Let us have them."

Marcus nods. "Go at them, then. May your Ares be by your side."

"He is always with us," Thrax replies with a grin. "We are the war god's children!" He nods toward Marcus' cohorts. "You take care of whatever infantry is coming."

Thrax trots back to his tribesmen. He puts his fingers to his lips and whistles three sharp, penetrating notes. The Thracians spring to life, lining up in the spaces between the cohorts. Each unarmored warrior lugs two javelins and an eight-foot spear with a hooked end.

The cataphractii close upon the front line velites, aiming their twelve-foot lances at the velites' unprotected bodies.

*This won't do us a shit's worth of good, but those boys have to be men,* Marcus thinks. "Loose!" he bellows, shouting at the top of his lungs.

The young Romans hurl their spears at the cataphractii. The javelins fly into the oncoming warriors, clacking harmlessly off their armor. A few spears find their way into the horses' shoulders. The horses whinny and rear, tumbling their riders to the ground. The hastati and principes cheer.

"Retreat!" Marcus bellows. His hornsman trumpets Marcus' command. The relieved velites dash for the cohorts.

Marcus turns around and waves at Thrax. The chieftain nods. He whistles twice, and repeats the command. Two thousand Thracians trot toward the cataphractii. Thrax runs in the lead, his wolfskin cape flapping against his shoulders.

The lumbering Syrian cavalry tilt their lances toward the chests of their ancient enemies, aiming for a quick kill. The cataphractii close upon them. The Thracians spin sideways, holding their crescent shields tight against their bodies. As their opponents thunder past, the Thracians' barbed spears snare the wire underpinnings that support the cataphract's scaly armor.[ccxlii]

The Thracians yank the cavalrymen sideways, toppling them from their horses. Weighted by ninety pounds of armor, the Syrians crash heavily to the earth. Stunned and encumbered, the Syrian noblemen are easy prey for the merciless Thracian swords.

Hundreds of cataphractii fall along the front. The Syrian attack line becomes filled with bloodthirsty Thracians stooping over fallen Syrians, jabbing into their throats, armpits, and intestines—anywhere they find a gap in their armor.

The front line cataphractii wheel about to attack the Thracians. Hundreds of Thrax's men fall, but still they persist. Many leap onto the backs of the Syrians, pulling their heads back until they fall off their horses. The rear lines of cataphractii rush into the battlefront, lancing down more Thracians.

Marcus Aemilius watches with growing dismay. *There's too many of them. They'll wipe out Thrax's men.* He summons his four senior centurions, and the decurion of the fleeing cavalry. "Forget formation and discipline, that's a mob scene we're entering. I want your men are to attack at will. Aim for the hands and feet!"

Marcus grasps the decurion's wrist in a viselike grip. "As soon as you see me run across that field, I want your men attacking the flanks. You hear me? If I see even one of your men run for camp, I'll kill the both of you!" Aureolus nods mutely.

The centurions rush back to their respective cohorts. Marcus walks ten paces out in front of his men, his back to the battle raging a mere spear's cast away. He raises his blade high.

"For Rome and the Republic!" he shouts. The cry echoes across the line. Marcus strides slowly toward the battle, then breaks into a run. The hastati and principes follow, yelling at the top of their lungs. They Romans attack like a mob of crazed Gauls.

Aureolus sees Marcus plunge toward the battle, running ahead of his men. "At them!" he yells to his men. The Roman cavalry loop toward the flanks of the battle.

Marcus' soldiers crash into the front line of cataphractii, hewing at them from every angle. The battle lines fill with screams as the Romans jab into the Syrians' exposed feet and hands. Hundreds of cataphractii whirl about in circles, beset from every angle. Dozens of Romans and Thracians fall to the cruel lances, but hundreds of cavalry lie by them. The Thracians vault onto the riderless horses, attacking the cataphractii with their own lances.

The Romans move into the rear of the enemy cavalry, blocking the lance assaults with their sturdy curved shields. The Syrian riders begin to retreat, dismayed by the relentless swarm of their enemies.

Aureolus' cavalry plunge into the sides of the Syrians, weaving through their slower opponents like antelope through cattle. Scores of cataphractii race for the river.

Thrax dashes back and forth through the swirling melee, shouting commands to his troops. Having left his spear in the back of a Syrian captain, he fights on with his beloved polearm. Thrax slashes into the legs of a passing rider, his sickle blade gouging through the stiff rawhide wrappings.

A flash of black catches his eye, swirling behind the rear line of cataphractii. He sees a black plume nodding above a black cape. *Antiochus! He's there behind his men!*

The world narrows for Thrax. He sees nothing but the bobbing black helmet in front of him. The Thracian chieftain crouches low, praying he will not be seen. He slinks through the milling cataphractii, studiously avoiding any combat.

Antiochus looms less than a spear cast away. Thrax eyes the six guards that surround the king. He summons himself for a final charge.

A silver-masked warrior steps into the space. He points his curved sword at Thrax and beckons him forward.

*It's Nicator!* Thrax realizes, his heart hammering with excitement. *At last!*

The Thracian stalks forward, his eyes fixed on Nicator's chest. The Syrian commander widens his stance and balances on his toes, his curved blade poised by his side. He steps toward Thrax.

"Where are you going?" Antiochus cries. "I need you here!"

"I will return soon, my King," says Nicator. "There is someone I promised to meet."

Thrax slows as he closes upon Nicator, studying the assassin's stance. The Thracian lowers his shield, covering his legs. With an ear splitting cry, he sprints toward Nicator, his polearm cocked for a killing thrust.

Thrax swoops his blade at Nicator's head. The Syrian leaps sideways, readying his counterthrust. Thrax alters his cut in mid-strike, curving it downward to the spot he anticipated Nicator would move to. The blade slices across the back of Nicator's calf, drawing a bright ribbon of blood.

Nicator leaps backward. He glances at his bleeding leg. "For that I will carve out your intestines while you watch." Nicator stalks toward Thrax.

Thrax stabs out with his polearm. Nicator slaps the thrust away and springs next to Thrax's chest. The Syrian rams his silver mask into Thrax's face, splitting his nose and forehead.

Thrax staggers backward. His polearm drops from his hand. Nicator pivots on his left foot and scoops Thrax's feet with his right, dropping him onto his back.

The Syrian is instantly upon him. He plunges his sword into Thrax's chest.

The Thracian gasps. Nicator pushes the blade deeper, slowly twisting it. "You thought you would kill me, Thracian hog? How does that feel?" Thrax's face contorts in a rictus of agony. He glares into Nicator's shadowed eyes.

"See how *this* feels," Thrax growls.

The Thracian's left hand grabs Nicator's sword arm. His right hand flashes to his belt, yanking out his dagger. He chops it into Nicator's side.

Nicator gasps. He yanks out his blade and pushes it toward Thrax's face, intent on shoving it into his forehead. Thrax's iron hand pushes back Nicator's sword arm, his knuckles whitening with the effort. He plunges his three-inch blade into Nicator's side, the blade slapping wetly through muscle and intestine.

The Syrian batters his shield against the side of Thrax's helmet. Thrax's dagger strikes again, slicing into the Syrian's stomach.

Nicator cries out in pain and rage. He slams his shield into the Thracian's face. Thrax's hand falls from Nicator's sword arm.

"You stupid fucking puke," Nicator spits. He eases the point of his blade into the space between Thrax's glassy eyes, watching the blood trickle down his nose.

Marcus Aemilius slams into Nicator, knocking him flying. The Syrian rolls over and springs to his knees, but his attacker is already upon him, throwing him onto his back as if he were a doll.

In one furious motion, Marcus Aemilius grabs the sides of Nicator's helmet and slams his head into the hard winter ground. The Syrian's face plate flies off.

Marcus gasps, momentarily, transfixed by Nicator's scarred and pustulent visage. "Monster!" he blurts. He grabs Nicator by the ears and rams his head into the ground, again and again. The Syrian's red-rimmed eyes roll up into his forehead. Marcus releases his grip.

"Watch out, Roman!" a gruff voice bellows. Twenty Thracians dash past Marcus Aemilius. The mountain men swarm over the six cataphractii galloping toward Marcus. Six Thracians leap onto the riders' backs, while the rest hook into the Syrians' mail. Within seconds, all six are upon the ground, spasming out their life.

Marcus drops the unconscious Syrian's head onto the ground. He locks his rock-hard forearm around the Syrian's lower jaw, and grabs the top of his head. With a mighty twist, he breaks Nicator's neck.

The tribune rises from the convulsing corpse, his chest heaving. He staggers over to Thrax. The Thracian leans on one elbow, coughing dark blood. Marcus' eyes well with tears, but he forces a smile. "That monstrosity's dead. I got him."

Thrax bares bloodstained teeth. "*You* got him? I softened him up for you. If you hadn't got in the way, I'd have his head right now!"

The somber Thracians encircle their fallen leader. Marcus kneels over Thrax. He puts his hand behind the Thracian's neck, supporting his sweaty head. "Apologies, Chief. I did not mean to interfere with your kill."

Thrax's chest wracks with a hacking cough. Clots of blood fly from his mouth. "It does not matter. He is dead. And I will join him."

An elephantine Thracian bends over Thrax, tears trickling from his eyes. He starts to wrap a strip of his tunic about Thrax's red-stained chest. The chieftain waves him off.

"You have more important things to do, Gravlix," Thrax rasps. He looks around. "Where is my polearm? Give me my polearm!"

Gravlix hands Thrax his weapon. He shoves it against Gravlix's chest.

"Put his head on this." Thrax tells Gravlix. "Show it to the Syrians. That will do more good than bandaging a dead man."

His men shuffle their feet, reluctant to leave him. "Gods damn you, do what I say!" Thrax barks, spitting out more blood.

Gravlix draws his sica and bends over Nicator. There is a wet, crunching sound. He lifts up Nicator's bloody head and jams it onto the curved point of Thrax's polearm, twisting it back and forth to secure it. The enormous Thracian lifts the polearm high. His tribesmen cheer.

Thrax grins, his eyes squinted with agony. "Go. Show them all. Show them our victory."

Thrax falls upon his back. He closes his eyes, and shudders. His eyelids open. Thrax stares sightlessly into the heavens.

Marcus waves over a group of his legionnaires. He points at Nicator's head. "Come on, we're joining the Thracians. We're going to show this to Antiochus."

Scores of Thracians join them. The small army tramps toward Antiochus and his guards, attacking any who dare stand in their way.

Antiochus does not notice the attack party. He stares over his shoulder, back toward the plain he had raced across mere hours ago, when victory seemed so close. *Where are my infantry? And King Darya's archers? Where is Hannibal? What the fuck is going on?*

The sound of clashing weapons becomes more audible. A dozen of his guards abruptly gallop toward the battlefront. Antiochus turns to see where they have gone.

He sees Nicator's ghastly visage staring at him, bobbing from the top of a Thracian polearm. Scores of Romans and Thracians stalk toward him, with dozens more battling Antiochus' guards. A diminutive Roman marches in front of them all, with murder upon his face. His yellow-green eyes are fixed on Antiochus.

"Sound the call!" Antiochus shouts to his entourage. "Back, back to camp!" His bugler sounds two long, plaintive notes. Antiochus gallops toward the river, with the rest of his cataphractii following.

"They're retreating!" cries Marcus, and his men take up the call. The Romans and Thracians erupt with cheers. Thirty-four hundred voices unite in celebration of victory, and life for another day.

Marcus does not cheer. He returns to stand vigil over his fallen comrade's body, his head bowed in silence while the fierce Thracians kneel and weep.

Moments later, Marcus lays his hand on Gravlix's ham-sized shoulder. "Apologies, but we have to return to camp. We have left it unguarded."

The Thracians gather a dozen javelins and lace them into an improvised litter. They lift Thrax onto it, placing Nicator's mask in the crook of his arm. The Romans fall into formation and march back to camp, followed by Thrax's solemn tribesmen.

While the Romans return to camp, Antiochus bolts across a rise and descends into the Phyrgius River lowlands. The plain below him is mottled with moving black dots. As he draws nearer the dots become ravens, hordes of ravens pecking at the bodies of the dead.

Hundreds of Dahae horse archers sprawl across the plain, their bodies streaked with lance cuts. Dozens of Masinissa's Numidians lie among them, feathered shafts jutting from their torsos. The Dahae horses wander about the edge of the bodies, as if waiting for their riders to mount them.

King Darya lies in the middle of the field, ringed by the bodies of his royal guard. He is totally naked, mute testament to the riches of his plundered raiment and weaponry.

*Scipio's fucking Numidians*, Antiochus decides. The king summons a handful of his nearby riders. "See if Hannibal is out there. He was riding with them when I left." The cataphractii wander through the field. They return shortly, shaking their heads.

"Very well," Antiochus replies. "Keep looking. He must be somewhere."

Antiochus' Syrians continue their flight, galloping past the corpses of the Roman cavalry and infantry they destroyed near the river. Seeing the plain devoid of enemy, Antiochus directs his men to the right, on a path toward his camp. *We'll reorganize and mount a counterattack. I've still got more men than they do.*

A large body of camel riders appears on the horizon, loping toward Antiochus. *Those are Duha's men.* His heart leaps to his throat. *They're supposed to be with my son Seleucus.* The lead camel rider waves his lance back and forth.

"Where is my son?" Antiochus blurts.

"Captured," the Arab replies. "Eumenes' men led him away."

Antiochus purples with anger. "They are not taking my son! Get your men and follow me. We will go to camp and organize a counterattack!"

"Do not go that way," the camel rider replies. "The Romans have taken the camp."

"What? How did they get across the trench?"

The rangy, beak-nosed captain shakes his head. "You would not believe it. They heaped corpses into the trench until they could cross it, and yanked down the walls."

"What of my rear guard, and the men inside the camp? The Parthians and Galatians, and my light infantry?"

The captain spits disdainfully over the side of his dromedary. "The Romans slaughtered everyone inside. There are more dead about the camp than on the battlefield."[ccxliii]

Antiochus sits silent, numb with shock. The camel rider starts to trot away. "Where are you going?" Antiochus manages to say. "Where's Duha, your commander?"

The Arab looks back toward his men and jerks his head. An Arab leads out a camel with a man strapped face down upon it. A dark red stain fills the body's purple-bordered cloak.

"Eumenes and his men. They drove the chariots into us. Our king was cut to pieces."

He raises his chin high, a challenge in his eyes. "We are going home now. Home to bury our king." The captain waves his men forward. The camel warriors gallop toward the Phyrgius River, their sand-colored cloaks billowing behind them.

*It's all gone*, Antiochus realizes. *Everything's turned to shit.* He trots a few paces out from his men and turns his horse to face them, his head held high. "We are going to Sardis. With luck we will be here by midnight. Divest yourself and your horses of armor. It serves no purpose now."

Antiochus' small army gallops northeast to his main city. As they approach the foothills, hundreds of stragglers drift out of the trees, riding and running to join their king. Commander Zeuxis rides in with a cadre of his guards, his face haunted. At the sight of his friend and commander, Antiochus manages a weary smile.

"Thank Zeus, at least you are still alive!" He looks over Zeuxis' shoulder, peering into the trees. "Where are the phalangites?"

"Gone." Zeuxis spits. "Cut down by Romans. Trampled by our elephants. Rounded together and roped up like cattle. All that's left are a few hundred scattered to the winds."

The king stifles a sob. *My indestructible phalanxes.* "Come on, then, we must make Sardis and regroup. Then I have a task for you."

"You want me to muster our forces for another engagement?" Zeuxis says hopefully. "We have twenty thousand men in the garrisons around here. If we recruit more Galatians, we could—"

Antiochus cuts him off with a wave of his hand. "The time for war is past. Now we fight for peace, a fair peace from the Romans. You will go to them, and plead our case."

Zeuxis bows his head. "As you command, my King. But this Lucius, he now has his first taste of victory. He may seek more conquests." He eyes Antiochus. "Maybe your kingdom."

"That is so. And that is why you are going to Scipio Africanus first. He is known for his just treatment of Carthage and Iberia. He knows that a fair peace is part of a lasting victory."

"Are you sure?" I have heard about him destroying entire cities.

Antiochus is quiet for a long moment. "Scipio said I was not to fight until he was there at the battle. I think he intended to reward me for returning his son to him." He smiles forlornly. "At least, that is what I must hope."

"I will go to him, but I wish we had another chance to fight. This time we wouldn't have so many different nations to manage. Hannibal was right, they got in each other's way."

"Have you seen him?" Antiochus says animatedly. "He was riding behind me, with the Dahae. They were massacred, but his body was not among them."

Zeuxis shrugs. "Only the gods know. Perhaps the Romans captured him. Perhaps he lies under a pile of bodies." He grins tightly. "But I would wager he found a way out. He is that kind of man."

As Antiochus' remnants retreat toward Sardis, Hannibal gallops southwest from the Magnesia battlefield. He rides alone, heading for the friendly port town of Ephesus, seventy miles away. Hannibal wears no soldierly raiment or armor, his guise is that of a common merchant. His saddle bags faintly jingle with the gold coins he stored for what he expected would happen: Antiochus' defeat at the hands of the relentless Romans.

Hannibal weaves in his saddle, exhausted from his fight with the Numidians who assaulted his Dahae escort. *Just a little farther*, he tells himself. *You stop to rest and the Romans will find you. Or the Syrians.*

The sun edges into the horizon. The Carthaginian gallops through the Panayyr Mountains and descends to the fortress city of Ephesus. The Aegean sunset ignites the choppy waters of Ephesus Harbor, turning them into a field of dancing flames. His eye takes in the beautiful sunset and the placid city in front of him. *You wouldn't know there had been a massacre nearby*, he thinks. *This seems so far from it. Wish I could linger.*

Hannibal trots down to the mile-wide sprawl of the Ephesus docks. He dismounts at the first stable he finds and hands the reins to a boyish stablehand, plopping a thick silver coin in his palm. "Give him a brushing and some good feed," Hannibal says, knowing he will never see his prized stallion again.

The conqueror of nations wearily shuffles to a nearby tavern and books an upstairs compartment, throwing himself upon a flea-infested straw pallet. He is instantly asleep, his head resting on his cloaked saddle bags.

The next afternoon, Hannibal sails out on a merchant ship bound for distant Crete. He leans against the stern's railing and watches Asia fade away from sight. As the coastline dwindles, the weight of his defeat lightens. And his new plans begin.

*From Crete I can make it to King Prusias of Bythnia. He is fighting that cursed Eumenes, perhaps he can use a good general to help him.*[ccxliv] *The Romans want the Bythnians as allies, so they won't interfere with the dispute. I won't have to worry about Scipio being there.*

He spits over the railing, watching it disappear into the crest of a white cap. *If I was with him in Rome, or he was with me in Carthage, we'd own the world. The one man most like me is the one most against me. Truly, gods, you have a sense of humor.*

ROMAN CAMP, 190 BCE. "Put me out where I can see the flames," Scipio says. He grins at the concern on the medicus' face. "Don't worry, you old wine jug. I'm not going to let myself die after all this trouble. I still have to celebrate my brother's triumph!"

Two sturdy velites lift Scipio from his tent's sleeping pillows. They ease him into a stout wheelbarrow, its inside padded so that he remains in a sitting position. The velites wheel Scipio toward the camp gates, careful not to let his dangling legs brush against the ground. After they pass through the entry, Scipio jerks up his right hand. "That's far enough." The velites ease him down.

"What a beautiful blaze it is," Scipio says, watching the towering flames of Antiochus' camp. "All those staked walls he put in are burning beautifully, don't you think?"

The youngest velite gulps, nervous in the presence of his hero. "A magnificent spectacle, General. I wish I was there myself."

Scipio crooks an eyebrow at him. "You mean you want to be inside there, burning with all those corpses we piled into it?"

"No, no," he stammers, his mouth spraying spit. "I just meant that I wanted to be nearer, to, uh...You know what I mean!"

Scipio smiles mischievously. "Yes, I think so."

"Forgive him," says the other velite. "He fought at the Phyrgius River. He is still exhausted from running from Antiochus' cataphractii!"

"I didn't want to run!" the youth sputters. "Everyone took off, and I had no choice but to follow. But I fought with Marcus Aemilius' men. And I got me a Syrian!"

"You fought because he stopped you," the other velite says.

Scipio waggles his finger at the elder velite. "Be not so harsh on him, Glaucus. Fear and glory reside in the same man. A twist of fate turns one into the other."

Lucius strides in and stands beside his brother, looking every inch the conqueror. He wears a scarlet tunic with an embroidered gold border, his legs wrapped in new scarlet leggings. His right forearm bears a solid gold snake bracelet with ruby eyes, a memento from the mountain of plunder he harvested from the Syrian camp.[ccxlv]

Lucius bends next to his brother's head and stares at the conflagration. "What a beautiful site, eh? The flames of victory!"

"You did well," Scipio says, wincing as he bumps his bandaged arm against the wheelbarrow. "King Antiochus lost over fifty thousand men.[ccxlvi] He has likely had his fill of war."

"Rome will have to give me a triumph," Lucius says excitedly. "I will march down the same path you did! Perhaps I will get a name, too, like you did!" He straightens up and strikes a pose, his fists on his hips. "Scipio Asiaticus, conqueror of Asia!"

"Perhaps, perhaps, but let us see what fate brings us. Flaccus and Cato are still there. They will not be easy to sway."

"Can you help me with them?" Lucius says, lowering his voice. "You have squelched their intrigues before."

"And they have squelched mine," Scipio replies good-naturedly. "But we have Consul Nobilior on our side, according to Amelia's letters. Tiberius Gracchus will become a high priest and hero when he returns to Rome. They will both be powerful allies."

"I hope so," Lucius says. "I'm not going back without my triumph!"

*I was afraid you would say that*, Scipio thinks. *Now we have another war to win. With the Senate.*

The next morning, Scipio is taking breakfast in his tent, chewing on a piece of the local barley bread. He grimaces. *This crust is tough as a war sandal.* He dips the bread into his morning wine.

Tiberius Gracchus parts the flaps of Scipio's tent and enters, his face troubled. "You have visitors," he says. "Envoys from King Antiochus."

"Me? Shouldn't they see Lucius?"

"They asked for you specifically. They want to see you alone." He nods toward the tent exit. "I have not told Consul Lucius about it."

*Best you didn't.* "Very well, send them in."

Commander Zeuxis shoulders his way into the tent, accompanied by two Syrian elders. The three wear the black, ankle-length robes of Syrian envoys, their hands tucked inside the sleeves of their thick silk robes. Scipio rises to meet them, pulling the top of his tunic over his shoulder bandage.

"Greetings, Honorable Scipio Africanus. We come on behalf of King Antiochus the Great, Lord of Asia."

*Not any more*, Scipio thinks. "Welcome," Scipio says, waving to a corner of his hut-sized tent. "Please sit with me."

Scipio's guards grab four leather strap chairs and open them. "These are not very comfortable," Scipio says, easing down on one of them, "but you know how it is in a camp. You make do with what you have." The four men arrange themselves into a circle.

"Why have you come to me?" Scipio says. "You know I am not the consul."

Zeuxis bows his head. "With your great magnanimity, you have always pardoned conquered kings and peoples. And now, in your hour of victory, a victory that has made you masters of the world, we beg you to extend your consideration to us."[ccxlvii]

The Syrian commander stares at the tent wall, in the direction of Lucius' tent. "We know your words carry weight with your brother and your senate."

*Antiochus gave me my son, but Rome's safety is critical.* "That we are 'masters of the world,' as you call us, makes little difference. We Romans, our feelings remain unchanged in every kind of fortune. Before we engaged in battle, not knowing who would win, I offered you peace terms. Now I offer the same terms, as victor to the vanquished."

One of the elder envoys removes a wax tablet and stylus from his pouch. "What are the terms?" he says.

"The same," Scipio snaps irritably, ticking them off on his fingers. "You will abandon all of Greece. You will withdraw from Asia until you pass over to the Taurus Mountains. You will pay an indemnity to Rome of fifteen thousand talents." The envoy busily marks onto his wax tablet. Scipio waits until he is finished, hating himself for what he will say next.

"Is that all?" Zeuxis asks. Scipio takes a deep breath.

"You must surrender Hannibal to us," Scipio says. *Sorry, old friend. We would never have peace with you near them.*[ccxlviii]

Zeuxis shakes his head. "We don't know where he is. I swear upon my children's lives."

Scipio feels a wash of relief. "Then give us twenty hostages, which we will select. And the insurgent Thoas of Aetolia."[ccxlix] An envoy starts to speak, but Scipio raises his hand. "Do not protest, I know he's hiding under Antiochus' wing."

The three delegates shift about, not knowing what to say next. "We will need to confer about this," Zeuxis says, rising from his seat.

"Of course," Scipio replies. "But there is one thing you should know.

It is easier for us to simply conquer and take all from Antiochus than to worry through all these compromises. Rest assured of that."[ccl]

The Syrian commander's mouth tightens. "Give us a moment."

Scipio steps out of his tent, trying not to eavesdrop on the frantic murmurings within. He stretches his arms wide, gazing at the rising sun. *Gods, it feels good to be relevant again!*

"General Scipio?" comes Zeuxis' voice within the tent. Scipio enters, to find the envoys standing near the entry, their faces blank.

"On behalf of King Antiochus, we agree to your demands," Zeuxis says tonelessly.

"To *Rome's* demands," Scipio replies.

"As you say," Zeuxis replies. "What is next?"

"You will go to Rome and present the terms we have agreed upon. I will send a letter to them that Lucius and I approved them. Do this within the month."

The three men file out of Scipio's tent. He watches them leave, his hands on his hips. When the flap closes behind him, he lets out a whoosh of air. *We are taking over half of Asia! Rome is becoming an empire. Mars guide us, I hope we do not overreach.*

Scipio sheds his tunic and rebandages his arm. After washing his face in a basin of lemon water, he dons his best white tunic and hastens toward Lucius' command tent.

*Now for the hard part*, Scipio says, grinning to himself. *Convincing Lucius that this was all his idea!*

Two weeks later, the Scipio brothers lead the fifth legion toward winter quarters in Ephesus, accompanied by Tiberius Gracchus and King Masinissa. The sixth legion remains at camp, waiting for the new consul to assume command.[ccli]

Lucius rides upright and proud on his white Syrian stallion, his persona that of a world conqueror. Scipio rejoices at the change in his brother. *I have fulfilled my promise to you, Mother. I have helped him make his way.*

Scipio mops at his brow as he rides, fighting off the fevers that have returned to plague him. *Febris have mercy, don't let me die over here*! He snorts a bitter laugh. *At least you won't give me that same old vision about Lucius now, will you?*

The Romans enter the gates of Ephesus, welcomed as liberators by its war-weary inhabitants. The Scipios immediately commandeer the mansion of an absent Syrian merchant, luxuriating in the blessings of a soft bed, hot food, and—most important of all—hot baths.

Masinissa's men camp out at the base of the foothills. The day after they arrive, the Africans are out on the Ephesus plains, racing around their improvised course, acting as if they had never been in a war.

The Sicilian transports soon arrive, ready to take the Africans home. The Numidians file into the stout-bodied ships, leading their horses below decks. Wagonloads of plunder follow them, loaded into separate ships.

Scipio and his brother stand at the head of the docks. The brothers wear their battle armor, a symbolic sendoff to their African allies.

A bronze-sheathed carriage trundles onto the front of the docks. King Masinissa emerges, his lean frame draped in a thick wolfskin robe. Lucius steps forward and grasps Masinissa's forearm.

"Gratitude for all your help, King. Know that you are forever a friend to Rome."

"I am the one who should be grateful," Masinissa says, looking past Lucius to Scipio. "I have been able to repay a debt that has long lingered on my conscience."

Lucius follows Masinissa's gaze. "I'll be at our carriage," he tells Scipio, walking toward his waiting entourage.

Scipio lifts his head. He smiles tightly, not knowing what to expect. "Gratitude for coming, King. It was good to fight alongside you, one more time."

Masinissa strides forward. He wraps his arms around Scipio and pulls him to his breast, kissing him on both cheeks. He steps back, his hands upon Scipio's shoulders. His eyes glisten with tears.

"You risked your life to save my son, for no other reason than he was mine. I know now, you would not have willingly endangered Sophonisba's life. Forgive me." He bows his head. "Forgive me."

Scipio exhales, feeling the world rise from his shoulders. He folds his man-killing hands over Masinissa's. "Your words have lifted my soul to the heavens. Thank the gods we are friends once again."

"Come and see me," Masinissa says. "My people would love to hear you tell of our battles against Carthage!"

"Only death could keep me from it," Scipio replies, smiling through his tears.

The king of Numidia strides toward the Sicilian flagship, his back as straight as a spear.

Sophon stands near the ship's gangplank. He waves merrily at Scipio, who energetically returns the gesture. The two Numidians walk up the gangplank and disappear below decks.

Scipio watches the Roman sailors pull in the gangplank and cast off the anchor. The quadrireme glides from the docks, its oarsmen slowly stroking. The sails rise, and bloom with wind. Scipio watches until the ship fades from sight.

Wiping his eyes, he marches back to the broad avenue that borders the docks. Four legionnaires await him, eager to help him onto his horse. Scipio waves them away.

"Take the horse back to the mansion," he says. "And two of you come with me. I feel like a visit to the local tavern!"

"A tavern?" a centurion says, eyeing the bustling crowds of fishermen and stevedores. "Here?"

"Oh yes!" Scipio chirps. "We'll go somewhere there's a fireplace, with people are gathered about it." He looks back to the disappearing Sicilian fleet. "Somewhere friends are together."

Two days later, the first winter snowflakes drift in upon Ephesus. Scipio reclines on a deerskin couch in his mansion's andron, a spacious drinking room. He sips a cup of warm, watered wine laced with spices.

A grime-streaked dock worker treads into the andron, his soiled gray tunic dotted with flakes of melting snow. Scipio raises his cup in welcome.

"What news, Brutus?" Scipio gestures toward a stoppered flagon. "Have some calda."

Scipio's spy grabs a pottery cup and fills it with spiced wine. "Gratitude. It's colder than Aquilo's dick out there," Brutus says, referring to the god of the north wind. He grins sheepishly. "I had better not sit on anything. I've been loading fish all morning."

Scipio sniffs theatrically. "I can tell! Anything to report?"

"Just a tidbit. A week before we arrived, a shabbily dressed man rode into town on a beautiful stallion. He left the expensive horse at the docks' stables, but never returned. The man paid in Syrian silver."

Scipio's eyes widen. A smile tugs at the corners of his mouth. "Was he wearing an eye patch? Go find out."

"Why, yes he was." Brutus remarks. His eyes light up. "You don't think it was him, do you?"

Scipio chuckles. "You have done well. Go see if you can find out where this stranger went."

As the spy exits, Scipio stretches onto his back and puts his hands behind his head. He stares at the ceiling fresco, smiling at its scene of

Zeus, in the form of a swan, escaping from the bedroom of Leda.

*You got away, didn't you? Are you going to bedevil Rome again? And me?*

Scipio laughs. *Ah, Fortuna, I wish I had your sense of humor!*

**Cato the Elder**

# XII. THE TRIALS OF SCIPIO

ROME, 189 BCE. The circular Senate benches are filled to capacity. Every senator in Rome is attending, along with Flamininus and Marcellus, this year's censors. The senators are here to pay homage to the Scipio brothers, the victors of the Syrian War.

Marcus Fulvius Nobilior and Gnaeus Manlius Vulso sit on the tall bronze stools that serve as their consular chairs, facing the senators. The new consuls are flush with excitement. This is an important meeting, and there is much to be decided today.

Nobilior turns to Vulso, an owlish member of the powerful Manlia family. "Do you want to address them?" Nobilior asks.

"You do it. You are the one who fought all those battles," Vulso mutters, clearly nervous to be in front of the packed chamber. Nobilior rises from his purple padded seat.

"Honored Senators, following the precedent set by Lucius Scipio and Gaius Laelius last year, we would like to declare our preferences for consular assignments."

"Hear, hear," Laelius replies. "Let us know your minds." As befits his rank as retiring consul, Laelius sits in the front row of the Senate benches.

"I hear you, Gaius Laelius," Nobilior replies. "Vulso and I are in agreement. I would take the assignment to Aetolia, to quell the last of Antiochus' allies there. Consul Vulso would resume Lucius Scipio's duties in Asia, and finalize our treaty with Antiochus."

Cyprian rises from his seat between the two consuls. "Are there any objections to this decision?" No one replies. "All who are in favor of Fulvius Nobilior assuming the Aetolian region, and Manlius Vulso that of Asia, please stand up!"

Large groups of Latins and Hellenics rise from their seats. Both parties are well aware that the fractious Aetolians are the more difficult assignment, and Nobilior is the more experienced soldier.

The aged leader squints across the rows of senators, moving his lips as he silently counts. "It is decided," Cyprian says. "Their motion passes."

His seamed face breaks into a relieved smile. "Now to the next order of business, our new censors' appointment of the next Princeps Senatus, the First Senator of Rome."

Flamininus and Marcellus step out from their seats and face their peers. The former generals and consuls grin at one another.

"In truth, the 'new' Princeps Senatus is in fact the old Princeps Senatus," Marcellus says, a broad grin splitting his face. "We grant another five-year appointment to Scipio Africanus as the First Man of Rome!"[cclii] Hundreds of senators stand, flapping their togas in approval. Scipio rises from his place in the front row and waves to them.

Cato and Flaccus recline in their seats, their faces glum with disappointment. Cato leans over to Flaccus. "You'd think our two morality officers could find someone of better character," he mutters.

"The censors think he's some big fucking war hero," Flaccus replies. "As if any of us couldn't have beaten the Carthaginians and Syrians! If you were thinking of pressing charges against Scipio, you had best wait until these censors are out of office, because you'll only get one chance!"

Cato slumps in his seat, his hands balled into fists. "I'm tired of waiting of justice! "He should be thrown in the Mammertine prison!

Flaccus nudges him. "Bide your time, and content yourself with small victories. We kept the Senate from giving Lucius Scipio a year's extension in Asia, did we not?"[ccliii] He slaps one of his bony knees. "Now the bastard's sitting on his hands in Ephesus, doing nothing!"

"That diminishes the Scipios' power, but it is not enough," Cato replies. He nods down at Scipio, who is shaking arms with the two censors. "You know what he's is going to ask now, don't you?"

Scipio raises his arms, quelling the applause. "Gratitude, Censors Flamininus and Marcellus. And gratitude to you, my fellow senators. I am humbled by your support. But I am not the one that should be honored today. There is another who awaits your approval, one who has saved our city from ruin and destruction."

He sweeps his arm across the rows of senators. "It is time to give Lucius Cornelius Scipio his triumph!" Amid shouts and jeers, Scipio resumes his seat.

Cato rises from his seat. He places his left hand over his heart and raises his right hand, extending his forefinger. "We are grateful for General Lucius Scipio's endeavors, of that there is no doubt. And his victory at Magnesia was momentous. But our triumphs are reserved for generals who have accomplished one single, decisive victory that defeated our enemy."

Cato nods at a scowling Scipio. "A victory such as Scipio Africanus won at Zama." At the mention of Zama, scores of senators cheer, applauding Rome's greatest victory.

Cato stands silently, letting the drama build. "Was there a single decisive victory against Antiochus? Yes, but it was not at Magnesia, when the king was already pleading for peace. It was at Thermopylae, my friends. At Thermopylae, Manius Glabrio broke the Syrian's army, and drove them from the mainland of Greece!"[ccliv]

Dozens of senators vault to their feet, their voices clashing in support and disagreement. They push and shout at one another, flush with anger.

"Enough!" Cyprian shouts, pounding his staff of office. He glowers at Cato. "Resume your seat. The Princeps Senatus has the floor."

"We all know you won that battle at Magnesia, Scipio," Flaccus jeers. His comments provoke further uproar.

"That is a lie!" Scipio spits. "I was there, but I only provided counsel, I had no command." He glares at his peers, fixing them with the same commanding stare he uses on his troops. "Permit me to remind you that General Glabrio defeated an expeditionary force of Antiochus' men, what we have jocularly called 'The Tiny Army.' But Lucius Scipio defeated a force eight times its size, an army with the force of a hundred nations behind it! Had we lost that battle, Antiochus and Hannibal would have stormed across Greece, and ventured on to Rome!"

For the next hours, the Senate hotly debates Lucius' request for a triumph, led by arguments from Scipio and Cato. Finally, Cyprian calls for a vote. The Hellenic and unaffiliated senators outnumber those opposed to it, and Lucius is granted his triumph.

Scipio stares at Cato until he catches his eye, and grins smugly. Cato jabs his middle finger at his rival. *Enjoy it while you can, you arrogant patrician prick. I have your army accountant's records.*

The senators hurry from the Curia Hostilia, anxious to prepare for the celebratory feast at Consul Nobilior's plush urban villa, a mile outside the Servian wall. Senators from both parties plan to attend, anxious not to offend the new consuls.

"Are you going tonight?" Scipio asks Laelius, as the two step down the chamber steps.

"Of course," Laelius replies. "I may not be a war hero like you are—no thanks to you—but I *am* a former consul. My presence is required."

Scipio shakes his head. "You won't let that go, will you? You know why I did it, and it worked. Lucius can stand on his own now."

"And what of me?" Laelius replies. "Am I to live off my wife's fortune, and the few bribes I gathered from the Northern chieftains? Where is my plunder? Where is my triumph?"

Scipio lowers his eyes. "It grieves me that this has tainted our friendship. But please be patient. The system has a way of working out, and we are not without powerful allies."

That night, Nobilior strolls through his house-sized dining room, conversing with the senators who recline on his dining couches. Amelia appears at his elbow, resplendent in a flowing gown of emerald green.

"Consul Nobilior! I wonder if I might have a word with you outside?" she says, smiling demurely.

Nobilior winks at the senator next to him. "Why, it would be unseemly to be seen alone with a beauty such as you. The censors might get after me for immoral conduct. I could be expelled from my consulship before I've even started!"

Amelia lays her hand on his shoulder, her scarlet nails like blood drops against his stark white toga. "Gods forbid that should happen, Consul. Fear not, my husband will join us." She waves Scipio over.

*I'm being set up for something*, Nobilior realizes, feeling helpless. *But she did help me get elected.* "Excuse me, Titus," he says to the senator.

Amelia, Scipio and Nobilior walk toward the entrance to the consul's formal gardens, dodging the lyre players wandering among the laden food tables.

Amelia strides first through the archway, looking to see if anyone is in the garden. "Over here, Consul. I feel the need to sit for a moment." She walks to a bench situated on the far side of the garden, nestled between two lush mulberry trees. Scipio and Nobilior follow her.

"Please, just for a moment," she says, patting the space next to her.

"Just for a moment," Nobilior echoes gruffly. He sits.

Amelia smiles sweetly. "You will be nominating the praetors for the provinces of Sicily, Iberia, and Sardinia, it that correct?"

"Yes, their magistrates are leaving," Nobilior warily replies. He rises. "I really must return to the feast, I have plans to discuss."

Amelia drapes her long fingers over his forearm, and squeezes it tightly. "Oh, just another moment," she says, her eyes hardening. With loud sigh, Nobilior resumes his seat.

"I think you should nominate Gaius Laelius for praetor of Sicily," Scipio says. "He is a former admiral, so he is well equipped to manage our fleet. Besides, it is customary to reward former consuls with praetorships."

"What!" Nobilior blurts. "That is a plum appointment! He did nothing to get me elected!"

"He didn't, but *I* did," Amelia says. "And his wife Prima. Do you want me to tell her that you refused to nominate her husband? She would not take it kindly. Not at all."

Nobilior swallows. "What about Consul Vulso? He will have his own thoughts on the matter."

"No he won't," Scipio says. "I have already talked to him." Scipio sees the doubt on Nobilior's face. "Don't worry, I have already garnered enough Senate votes for Laelius. If you don't recommend him, then you should worry—about me."

The consul rises. "I don't care what you two have done for me, I will not be coerced!"

"We simply think it is in all our best interests for you to place Laelius there," Amelia coos, leaning forward so he can see her breasts. "Will you do that for me?"

Nobilior turns away from her. "Numidians," Nobilior says to Scipio. "I want Numidians to join my army in Aetolia."

*He's trying to bargain, to save his pride*, Scipio thinks. "Granted. I will visit Masinissa myself."

Nobilior pushes himself upright. "Then I will nominate Laelius, but that is all you can expect from me," he says coldly.

The two solemnly watch the consul leave. When he merges with the crowd, Scipio and Amelia embrace gleefully. "Wonderful!" Scipio says. "You tell Prima. I will go find Laelius."

Scipio rises from the bench and starts for the archway entrance. He suddenly doubles over, wracked by a coughing fit.

"Husband, you are ill! We need to get you out of this night air!" Amelia pulls him toward the entryway.

"Not yet," Scipio replies, dabbing at his mouth. "I may be a bit sick, but I'm still hungry!"

They walk to the food tables centered in the middle of the room. After slurping down several raw oysters, Scipio wends his way toward Ennius, Nobilior's favorite poet.

Ennius is reciting one of his war odes, as a harpist strums behind him. Laelius stands in front of Ennius, listening to the old man singsong a poem of Cincinnatus' heroic victories. Scipio sidles in next to Laelius and tugs at his purple-bordered toga.

"Can we talk for a minute?" Scipio says.

"Go ahead, I'm listening," Laelius replies.

"Over here, away from the music," Scipio says, pointing at an empty couch. Laelius joins Scipio. "What is it," he growls, staring back at the poet. "You want me to help plan Lucius' triumph for you? Suffice to say, I am not interested."

Scipio rolls his eyes. "I have a different kind triumph in mind. Yours. I have heard that Consul Nobilior wants you to be praetor to Sicily. As you know, it is a very prestigious appointment. You'll return rich!"

Laelius stares, his expression a mixture of excitement and confusion. "I would love to be praetor there, but why would Nobilior want me? He is closer to Flamininus and Glabrio. They'd both want something like that."

"I heard he needs someone who can capably oversee the Sicilian fleet. Those other two are army men. They have never been admirals." Scipio winks. "And our wives had a strong hand in Nobilior's election. That may have had something to do with it."

Recognition dawns in Laelius' eyes. He smirks. "I have a feeling that there was another strong hand guiding his decision." He locks eyes with Scipio. "You owe me nothing. There is nothing to repay."

Scipio squeezes Laelius' wrist. "I owe you everything, for a life of your companionship. You are my beloved friend, Laelius. I would do anything to keep it so."

Laelius kisses Scipio on the cheek. "It is so, Brother, now and forever. Just give me time to love you again. I know you felt obligated to give Greece to your brother. But we could have fought together, like we did in Iberia and Africa. Fought together one more time."

The vision of it brings tears to Scipio's eyes. "That may yet happen. The theatre of war has shifted to Rome." He nods toward Cato, who is glaring at Ennius. "General Cato there is mustering his political forces. I anticipate there will be another confrontation between us, on the Senate battleground."

"It is not the battle I was hoping for, but I will be there for you," Laelius declares. "Wonderful! So, if Flaccus is our enemy, maybe I can justifiably kill him now?"

He sees Scipio frowning at him. He grins. "I know, I know! You want to be sure of the crimes we suspect of him. I just don't share that need. Just think of what's he done that we don't know about!"

Scipio shoves himself upright. "Enough about politics, this is a day of celebration. For Nobilior and for you! Have you tried the roast thrush, they are absolutely—" Scipio bends over, coughing violently into the sleeve of his toga.

Laelius drapes his arm around him. "We can't let the Latins see you like this. Straighten up and march out with me." Laelius summons an attendant to notify Prima and Amelia of their departure. The three surround Scipio and make their way to a waiting carriage.

Later that night, Amelia rises from the bedroom sleeping pallet, her body dewed with the passion of lovemaking. She slips her sleeping robe over her head and plops down next to Scipio, leaning over him. She trails her finger across his broad, sweaty, chest.

"I want us to get away from here, before Lucius returns for his triumph."

Scipio blinks at her. "You want a vacation? Where?"

"Not a vacation, an initiation. An initiation into our new life. I want to start building a retirement villa in Liternum. Let's get away from politics and fighting, and work on our dream house."

Scipio chuckles. "I fear it will be a small dream. I was only a counselor to Lucius, not a commander. My war share will be small."

Amelia she pulls a small mouse skin purse from the sleeve of her robe. "Maybe not so small," she says, upending the purse. Two large, brilliant diamonds plop onto Scipio's chest, glittering among his rough gray hairs. He gapes at Amelia, a question in his eyes.

"They were left in the dust of your plunder house, covered up in a corner." She shakes her head and smiles. "Men! They never take the time to clean up after themselves!"

"These are ours?" Scipio says, not believing his eyes. "I didn't know I'd brought any back. There were some small piles of jewels, but I didn't see any diamonds!"

"They are ours. For us. She closes her fist about the stones and shoves it under Scipio's nose. "And we're not going to spend them on candidates, or political feasts and games. We have done enough of that."

Amelia opens her hand and stares into the diamonds' faceted surfaces, the room's wavering torchlight setting fire to their depths. "These will bring us acres of olive groves, and a nice new winery. And a beautiful garden where you can sit and tutor students." *And recover your health.*

Scipio folds his hand over hers. "You hold our dreams in the palm of your hand," he replies. He throws his head back onto his reed-stuffed pillow and stares at the ceiling. "Let's go to Liternum, and build us a dream."

LITERNUM, 188 BCE. "Put that grape press in the room next to the winnowing area," Amelia says. "Right in the center, between the wine fermentation barrels."

The burly Galatians lug the wheel-handled press past the brick ovens of the bakery, dropping it in the center of a small room adjoining the open-air fermenting yard. The slaves return to Amelia and stand with heads bowed, their unkempt beards dangling down their broad, hairy chests.

"Hard to believe that six months ago those two were trying to destroy us at Magnesia," Scipio says, speaking as if they were not there. "They seem resigned to their fate now."

"And why not?" Amelia replies. "They could never find their way home, and now they will live in a beautiful country estate, with a kind and beautiful mistress! As I have reminded them, they could be fighting for their lives in the gladiatorial pits." She stares at them. "Which is still an option," she says loudly, "should they misbehave!"

"They may be satisfied with their lot," Scipio says, "but I wouldn't give them a mattock to use while I'm around. I'm pretty sure they know who I am!"

The world's greatest general is dressed like a humble farmer, clad in a worn gray tunic mottled with his summer work sweat. Only Scipio's hob-nailed sandals give him away as a former soldier, his caligae stitched with "SPQR" across the toe straps.

Scipio grabs the handles of his boxy wheelbarrow, intending to unload its river stones next to the unfinished wall of the herb garden. The family molossus leaps into the barrow, adding his two-hundred pounds to it. The wheelbarrow drops from Scipio's hands. "Ursus, get out!" he snaps, trying to sound threatening. The eleven-year-old dog leaps from the barrow and cavorts like a puppy, elated with his freedom in the open farmlands

Scipio grabs the handles of the wheelbarrow. "Off to work!"

"You don't have to do that," Amelia says. "We have slaves and freedmen enough. Why, a dozen of your veterans have came out yesterday and volunteered! I think they want to repay you for establishing their retirement colony here."

"That's an old soldier for you," says Scipio. "When the fighting's done, they want nothing more than a plot of land in a peaceful village. Just like me."

He hefts the wheelbarrow's handles to his midsection. "I appreciate their help, but I *want* to do this—to do simple, honest work in the fields. I'll take the stink of manure over the stench of politics, any day!" Scipio trundles his load toward the rear of their rising villa.

"Careful what you say, noble farmer," Amelia yells out. "You're beginning to sound like Cato!"

"Jupiter forbid!" Scipio returns, his voice tight with strain.

As dusk approaches, Scipio and Amelia sit on the L-shaped cobblestone patio that surrounds their infant estate. They share a flagon of the local red wine, admiring the rows of stubby olive trees that line the gently sloping hillside beneath them. The aging couple watches the faint dots of fishing boats bobbing along the Mediterranean, taking their day's catch home to the humble Liternum docks.

Scipio sighs. "I have to get back to Rome next month. The Senate is meeting again, and Lucius is returning for his triumph." He chuckles. "He has marched his entourage all the way from Port of Brundisium, stopping at every garrison along the way. He'll be fat as a sow from all the victory parties!"

"Let him have his day in the sun," Amelia says. "He has long dwelled in your shadow."

"I hope he can stay in that sun without getting burned," Scipio says, sipping on his wine. "There are advantages to being out of the light."

As Scipio and Amelia recline at their villa, Cato pours over a scroll at Rome's Hall of Records. Felix Juvenius, Scipio's old quaestor sits next to him. The keeper of the Tabularium stands behind Cato, impatiently jingling his iron door keys.

"We'll leave when we are good and ready," Cato snaps, not bothering to look up from his scrolls. "And not a minute sooner."

"Have a care," says the Keeper. He is a proud young man from the hallowed Valeria family, one of the few men who does not fear Cato's wrath. "Those precious ledgers of yours could disappear from the shelves."

Felix tugs on Cato's toga. "It's closing time. I have a massage waiting for me at the gymnasium." With a final glare, Cato ushers Felix onto the marble-tile entryway, facing the bustling Forum.

"You saw the scrolls," Cato says. "Are they written in your hand?"

"They are," affirms Scipio's former army accountant.

"Are you willing to testify to that, before the Senate?" Cato says, pressing him.

"Only if you fulfill your half of the bargain," Felix replies.

"You will get your money. And an appointment as curule aedile, in charge of public markets."

"Done." Felix says. "When do I testify?"

"When Scipio returns from Liternum, I will press charges against him. All you have to do is stay alive until then."

Felix's eyes grow cold. "Don't worry about me. You are the one with all the enemies." A*nd justly deserved,* he says to himself. The fox-faced older man spins on his heel and stalks down the steps.

*I'm taking shit from that scurrilous insect*, Cato thinks, watching the spindly little man, *And bribing him on top of it.* The former consul and general squats on the wide limestone steps, his senatorial toga draped over his sandals. *Gods in heavens, who should be on trial here?*

CAMPUS MARTIUS, ROME, 188 BCE. Scores of trumpets line the temples and buildings of the Forum. They blare out the joyous news: Lucius Cornelius Scipio's triumphal parade is approaching.

The senators are the first to enter the Forum area, parading along the flower-strewn Via Sacra. Flaccus and Cato march in the front row, as glum as if they were going to their own executions.

Dozens of pipers and lyre players prance in behind the senators, cheered by the throngs lining the sacred street. Four white sacrificial oxen follow the musicians, followed by scores of captured Syrians, Galatians, Parthians, and Arabs. The crowd hoots and jeers at the forlorn captives, but their boos soon turn to cheers of wonder—Lucius' Scipio's plunder wagons rumble into the street.

Forty wagons tow captured statuary, frescoes, paintings, and carvings. The best of them are destined for government temples and buildings—and several powerful senators' houses. Mounds of coinage follow, flanked by guards who glare at any who draw too near the money wagons.

Ten horse-drawn platforms trundle into the street, heaped with jewels and jewelry. Slave boys frolic among the priceless collections, grasping handfuls and brandishing them at the crowd. The Romans cheer wildly, excited at the sight of their favorite type of plunder. Women stretch out their arms, entreating the boys to pitch them a bauble. The boys smile and shake their heads—they are well aware of what would happen to them if they did.

Finally, Lucius Scipio rides in on a gilded four-horse chariot, drawn by a white gowned charioteer. Lucius is draped in the purple toga picta of a victorious general, his face painted scarlet. A slave holds Lucius' triumphal gold crown over Lucius' head, repeatedly whispering "you are only a man" to him.[cclv]

Lucius solemnly waves is ivory scepter at the delirious crowds, looking every inch a general. No one can tell that he trembles with excitement, overcome with both anxiety and elation.

Scipio walks along in the third row of senators, content to go unnoticed at his brother's triumph. The senators disband at the end of the Via Sacra, breaking up into conversation groups. Cato stalks toward Scipio. He is accompanied by Rome's two tribunes of the plebs, both of them former military tribunes. Scipio pinches his eyes shut, knowing what will come.

"You know these two men?" Cato barks.

Scipio scrutinizes them carefully, a mocking smile upon his face. "Why, I do believe it is Titus Regillus and Titus Regillus, the two men I talked to last month." He smiles pleasantly. "How odd you both have the same name and the same office, don't you think?[cclvi] Are you twins? If so, your parents lacked imagination in naming you."

"You know we are not," says one of them. The middle aged soldiers shift restlessly, avoiding Scipio's eyes. Cato glares at them. "Go on," he growls, taking a menacing step toward them.

The older Tribune clears his throat. "Publius Cornelius Scipio Africanus, we hereby accuse you of misappropriation of army plunder gained in the African campaign. You are to be tried on these charges before the Senate."

Scipio ignores the Tribune. He stares at Cato. "Though we have had our differences, I had always thought you incapable of calumny. What has led you to stoop to this?"

Cato flushes. "You heard them. The Tribunes have accused you of malfeasance. They demand a trial."

"Hmm," Scipio says, thinking. "As the Princeps Senatus, it is my duty to schedule Senate meetings and set their agendas, correct?"[cclvii]

"It is," Cato replies. "But your accusation is a matter of public record now. You cannot avoid a trial for it. You can only set the date."

"I will. The Senate trial is set for the first full moon of the new year. I will have it recorded in the Senate calendar."

"What! That is months from now! Why are you waiting? You're not going to escape your fate!"

"If I'm not going to escape my fate, you shouldn't be so impatient," Scipio replies. He grins. "I may look sickly, but I'm not going to die soon!"

"See that you don't," Cato says. "Or you'll be labeled a suicide." He stalks off from Scipio, followed by the two Tribunes.

"I would not give you that pleasure!" Scipio shouts after him. He feels his right arm start to twitch uncontrollably. He grasps it with his left hand. *Steady now, there's nothing to fear. You have the people on your side. Just figure out how to use them.*

A rumbling behind him attracts his attention. He sees Lucius' chariot easing into a space near the senators, its sides draped in rose garlands. *At least he's not involved in this mess.*

ROMAN FORUM, 187 BCE. The dried leaves crackle across the cobbled streets of Rome, whirled into circles by Rome's capricious winter winds. Save for the occasional wandering cur, the main streets are totally empty. Rome's citizenry have vacated their homes hours ago, heading to the Forum Square. Today is the trial of Scipio.

Amelia paces about in the family atrium, her face a mask of anxiety. "I can't believe they are doing this to you," she says, wringing her hands. "We'd all be Carthaginian slaves, if it weren't for you!"

"Don't exaggerate," Scipio says, sticking his head from the bedroom entry. "*Some* of us would be slaves. The rest of us would be murdered while they pillaged our streets!" He strolls from the bedroom, a smug smile upon his face.

"You are wearing *that*?" Amelia says, gaping at him. "You're going to your trial. It is customary to dress like a penitent."

"There will be no penitents today. I am the Princeps Senatus, the Imperator, the savior of Rome. Besides, I am *not* going to a trial, I am going to a celebration! You know what day this is."

"Yes, but I'm not sure they will remember." Amelia says.

Scipio twirls in front of Amelia. "That is why I dress like this. It is my duty to remind them!"

The morning edges toward afternoon. Ten Senate judges arrive in the Comitium, the Forum's open space meeting area. They sit on two long marble benches behind the rostra, a huge stone platform perched fifteen feet above the Comitium, facing the Curia Hostilia chambers. The gathered thousands buzz with excitement, knowing that Italia's most famous personage will soon be marching up the rostra steps, there to answer the charges brought against him.

"Make way!" shouts a cattle drover. "Make way for today's celebratory sacrifices!" He drives two snow-white oxen through the crowd, heading them toward the Capitoline temple. Time and again he repeats his message. The people stare at each other, confused.

Cato stands atop the rostra platform. He frowns down at the drover. "What are you doing, fool? This is a trial, not a festival."

"That is not what *I* was told," says the burly old farmer. "Someone paid me a lot of money to bring them here today!"

The Forum trumpets sound. A gang of hundreds of senators and commoners enters the Comitium. Lucius Scipio leads them, resplendent in his purple cape and polished bronze battle armor. Praetor Gaius Laelius marches arm in arm with Scipio's brother, his gold African victory wreath glistening among his dyed raven curls.

The supporters chant Scipio's name as they push their way into the crowd, surrounding the base of the rostra. The crowd takes up a chant. "Scipio, Scipio," echoes across the streets of Rome, reaching to the sentries of the Servian Wall.

Cyprian totters to the front of the rostra and raises his staff, signaling the approach of the accused. The crowd hushes. Scipio Africanus ascends the rostra steps. The Romans gape at what they see.

Breaking all tradition, the conqueror of Iberia and Africa wears his all-purple toga picta, the one given to him for his triumphal conquest of Carthage.[cclviii] Scipio skips up the steps, his laurel victory wreath bobbing upon his gray-streaked curls. He walks to the rostrum, a speaking platform shaped like the prow of an attack ship.

The two Tribunes of the Plebs approach the rostrum, followed by Cato and Felix Juvenius. Scipio ignores them. He waves jauntily at the crowd.

"Declare the charges," Cyprian says.

Cato sidles next to Scipio, facing the crowd. "The Tribunes of the Plebs accuse you of misappropriation of army plunder gained in the African campaign," he shouts. "What say you to that?"

Scipio grins. "I am glad you specified which campaign, because there have been so many I have waged on behalf of Rome! To fulfill my vow to protect Rome, I have conquered the northern Gauls—twice—and the savage Iberians. Then Syphax and his Numidians, before I finally removed the greatest threat to us in history, Hannibal the Great of Carthage!"[cclix] The crowd erupts in cheers. Scipio raises his arms, as if he has just won a contest.

"Bring me the ledger," Cato barks. Felix Juvenius hands him a bound roll of scrolls. Cato holds the scrolls high over his head. The crowd stares up at them.

"These are Scipio Africanus' income and expenditures for the African campaign. There were recorded by Felix Juvenius, who stands next to me. Quaestor Juvenius reports a discrepancy of plunder worth three thousand talents,[cclx] money missing that should be in Rome's treasury." He turns toward Scipio Africanus. "How do you explain these missing three thousand talents?"

"Why don't you ask me to explain the fifteen thousand talents that I brought into the treasury from that campaign?"[cclxi] Scipio quips, grinning at the crowd. "More money than Rome has ever seen."

"That is not an answer," Cato replies, unperturbed.

Scipio extends his hand. "Very well, let me see the ledgers." Cato hands him the three scrolls. Scipio unrolls them and carefully lays them on top of one another.

"This is my answer."

Scipio grasps the ledger rolls in the middle. With one mighty swipe, he rips the scrolls in half, and proceeds to tear them into pieces.[cclxii] The crowd watches, amazed and awed.

"Stop it!" Cato bellows. He rushes toward Scipio.

"Go suck a slave," Scipio retorts. He flings the pieces into the crowd. The people jump on the scraps, brandishing their trophies to their fellows.

Scipio steps away from the rostrum, walking to the edge of the platform. He spreads his arms wide, his eyes staring into the heavens. "On this very day, O citizens, we once celebrated. I won our greatest victory and laid at your feet Carthage, that has lately been such an object of terror to you. Now I am going up to the Capitol to offer my sacrifices for this appointed day."[cclxiii]

He looks down at his people, his face softening. "If you love your country, you will join me in this sacrifice, which I offer for your own good."[cclxiv]

Like a king descending his throne, Scipio walks down the rostra steps.

"Get back here!" Cato shouts. Scipio does not even deign to turn around. He merges with crowd and marches west toward the Capitol. Scores of hands reach out to touch him, and he grasps theirs in return.

"To the Capitol!" Laelius shouts. He hikes up the tail of his purple-bordered toga and follows Scipio.

"The Capitol!" Lucius echoes, following his brother. Slowly, by tens, then hundreds, then thousands, the people of Rome file toward the temple, emptying the Comitium grounds.[cclxv]

Cato stands on the platform, mouth agape, his hands dangling at his sides. He looks to his left and sees the Senate judges stepping down the platform, hurrying to join the crowd. "Don't toady to them," he yells futilely. "Get back here and try him!"

With a shrug and a nod, the two Tribunes of the Plebs follow the patricians, leaving Cato alone with Felix. The scrawny little quaestor waggles a finger under Cato's nose.

"I don't care what happened, I want my money!"

"Oh fuck you," Cato mutters. Felix stalks off, in search of the nearest taberna.

A forlorn Cato sits on the edge of the platform, dangling his legs over its edge. *He's too strong, too popular with the people. But there must be a way to get to him.*

He stares at the small round Temple of Venus across from him, the twin statues of its namesake ringed with garlands from the recent triumphal parade. Cato's eyes light with renewed enthusiasm.

*Lucius!*

TEMPLE OF BELLONA. It is evening. Scipio sits on a stone bench inside the temple's sacred oak grove, his ears fixed on the nightingales' sweet trills. His eyes wonder to the marble steps of the beautiful little temple, and he recalls the historic meetings he has had here. *This is where I met the Senate after my conquests in Iberia, and then Africa. Where I sent Flaccus packing to Sicily, to keep him from further mischief.* He sighs. *After tonight, will I ever get to come back here?*

A tall, regal, figure emerges silently from the trees, garbed in the green tunic and leggings of a common freedman. Senator Tiberius Sempronius Gracchus, former high priest of Rome, eases down next to Scipio. He crooks one knee over the other and clasps his hands across them, a grim smile on his face.

"I suppose you have heard about Cato's latest antics?" Gracchus says.

Scipio exhales deeply. "Oh yes. He got those two asshole tribunes to speak to the People's Assembly. They convinced the Assembly to press charges against Lucius for misappropriation of funds from his conquest of Antiochus. Now the Senate will have to investigate *another* of his accusations!"[cclxvi] He shakes his head. "He just won't quit. You'd think I'd murdered his father."

"You murdered his way of life, his dreams," Tiberius responds, idly kicking his foot. "He saw Rome as a nation of conquests, not alliances, with the ascetic moral code of our agrarian forebears. But you have championed all these "corrupting" Greek influences of art and culture. And you keep making friends of our former enemies!"

Tiberius chuckles. "From his viewpoint, can you blame him?"

"I suppose not, were it not for the fact that he has corrupted himself to achieve his ends." Scipio throws up his hands. "Then again, I suppose I have done the same, telling myself it was for a higher purpose."

"I heard he is going after you again. He's got Lucius Purpurio, that fluff of an ex-consul, to demand an investigation."

"I am not concerned with myself. But a Senate investigation could break Lucius, at a time when he has finally gotten some dignity and confidence. I can't allow that."

"But what can you do about it?" Gracchus asks.

"Two things," Scipio replies, "both of which are long overdue. I'm leaving Rome."

"Leaving?" Gracchus sputters. "You are the most honored man in Rome! There is talk of erecting a giant statue of you near the Temple of Jupiter."

"No statues!" Scipio blurts, "I have said that before! Statues are for gods. When we erect statues of men, we purport to make them their equals. You tell the Senate, if they build one, I will come back and knock it down!"

"Where are you going?" Gracchus asks.

"To Liternum," Scipio says, his voice calming. "I have spent my life fulfilling a military promise to my father. Now I will fulfill one to myself."

Silence falls between the two men. It is shattered when several grackles set up a cackling dispute. One drives the other from the tree, and silence returns.

"You mentioned two things," Tiberius says. "What is the other?"

"Tiberius, you are a priest, legate, and senator. No man is held in higher regard. I want you to speak out against Lucius' oppressors, when the issue comes before the Senate."

"I am not sure I can do that," Gracchus responds. "You tore up the ledgers that would confirm his innocence. I have no proof."

"Say what you can, then, and no more. I will not ask you to sully yourself." He glances sideways at Gracchus. "Are you still interested in marrying my daughter Cornelia?"

"I *have* to marry your daughter," Gracchus declares. "I have told you that for years! The auguries have foretold greatness for our family!"

"If you support Lucius, I will give you my daughter's hand,"[cclxvii] Scipio says. "You may marry when she comes of age."

Gracchus is silent. "I can only say what my soul allows," he finally says.

"I would ask no more of any man," Scipio says. He rises and extends his forearm. The two grasp arms, sealing the agreement.

"I had best return home now," Scipio says. "Amelia and I have a big day tomorrow. We have to pack our moving wagons, before we sell our manse and leave for Liternum."

"It sounds like you are very serious about leaving," Tiberius says.

"I am done with Rome. Should they nominate me for consul, I will not serve. Should they summon me to trial, I will not come. I will be buried at my new home, near the men who served with me."

"Then Rome will be much poorer because of that," Tiberius says. "And get what she deserved."

**Scipio Africanus**

# XIII. SCIPIO'S END

LITERNUM, 183 BCE. "So, Aristotle tells us that a virtuous man is one who commits virtuous acts. The question is: does he do so because he is virtuous by nature, or because he has learned to be virtuous?"[cclxviii]

Scipio stares expectantly at his students, urging them to respond.

"My father says our neighbor Livius was born mean. He says he's like a rabid weasel!" ventures twelve-year-old Plinius. His fellow students giggle.

*You always talk about what your pater familias says*, Scipio thinks, resisting the urge to roll his eyes. *Will you ever think for yourself?*

"If people acted good or bad because it was their nature, could we really blame them for anything they do bad, or praise them when they do good?" asks serious-minded Germana, the daughter of one of Scipio's fifth legion tribunes.

"Exactly!" Scipio exclaims. "The philosophers tell us that moral virtue is developed by our ethos, our habits. And habits are derived by our actions, not our intrinsic nature.[cclxix] And that is why we hold people responsible for their actions."

Tatius, a tousle-haired boy of thirteen, scratches his head. "I don't understand, Tutor. Some people have good teachers who teach them to be good. Others don't have anyone, like the poor people. Are they both responsible for their actions?"

Scipio's smiles. "I know what you mean. I had a very good tutor. His name was Asclepius. He taught me much about right and wrong. But still, I am responsible for all that I have done. He bears no fault my misdeeds, but deserves praise for helping me do good."

Scipio slaps his knees and rises. "Anyway, that is a topic for another day. Class dismissed!"

As one, Scipio's students dash down the cobbled walkway between the hedges, their blue tunics flapping against the backs of their knees. Scipio pauses, savoring their bright screams and laughter. *That Germana, she is a deep one*, he thinks. *She'd make a good philosopher, or playwright.*

Scipio hobbles down the garden pathway, his knees feeling every day of his fifty-three years. *Time to get my hands dirty*, he tells himself, smiling. He marches up the packed-earth trail to his private vegetable garden, his back straight as a centurion's. *Can't let Amelia catch me bent over and limping, I'll get another lecture about working in the garden.*

Scipio opens a low, slatted gate and steps into his garden's furrowed rows. He frowns at what he sees. A tall crop of weeds have sprung up on the side of his prized beet patch, the one that has won him two wreaths at the Liternum Farmers' Market. *The god of crops must be angry with me*, he muses. *I had best offer a chicken to Saturn tonight.*

"Now where did I put my mattock?" he mutters to himself. He spies it on the other side of the garden, lying against the side of the house. He hurries over and grabs it, hefting it in his hands. The memories flood back, and his hands tighten about it.

He is again on the misty battlefields of Magnesia. The gargantuan Judoc stalks toward him, hefting his oversized pickaxe. Scipio sees himself dodge the Galatian's deadly blade, his gladius slicing into the chieftain's back. He sees Judoc fall.

*Ah, that was the day,* he thinks. *We defeated Antiochus' gargantuan army. And Hannibal, too.*

He chops the mattock's hoe blade into the loamy soil, his mind far away from his farm. *Where are you now, Carthaginian? Hiding from the Romans, as I am? There was a time we two held the fate of the world in our hands. Now we are exiles from our ungrateful nations.*

He digs into a clump of tall weeds and yanks them out by the roots, dousing himself with slender brown seeds.

"Husband, what are you doing out there?"

Amelia leans out from the kitchen window above the garden, her gray-streaked auburn tresses cascading onto the artichoke bushes. "Why are you chopping weeds? We have slaves to do that!"

"I like doing this,"[cclxx] Scipios says, knowing she knows this. He flexes his arms. "Look, I'm still strong enough to lift an ox!"

Amelia laughs. "And still stubborn as one, too! If you must kill yourself, at least bring me a few beets for tonight's dinner."

"Of course." He summons his best smile. "Might I have one of your chickens?"

She glares with mock anger. "Another sacrifice? No, I won't have enough left for eggs!"

"Come on." He winks at her. "Cornelia's away seeing Tiberius Gracchus. I could give you a nice back rub tonight. With fresh pressed olive oil."

"Mmm, that is a worthy deal. But no hens—take a rooster!" She swirls back into the villa.

*Still so beautiful, after all these years!* Scipio thinks, leaning on his mattock. He looks across his twenty-acre estate, at the slaves and freedmen laboring in his lush olive groves and wheat fields. *After thirty years of war, I have earned this peace.*

Scipio chops down with his mattock's chiseled end, prying out a small buried boulder. *I swear, this ground must grow rocks!* He chops down again. The mattock scrapes against stone. He levers the chisel underneath it, and pulls.

*Mph! This is a big one!* Scipio wedges the mattock under the buried stone and tugs the handle toward him, straining with all his might. His face flushes.

His right hand shakes. A deep, sharp pain cuts into his heart, as if an invisible sword has pierced it.

Scipio collapses to his knees, clutching his chest. Gasping heavily, he falls onto his face. He rolls onto his back, staring at the white sea birds circling in the azure sky. An iron fist seizes his heart, and squeezes.

A final thought comes to him, of his parents Publius and Pomponia.

*I hope I did well for you.*

A gray warbler lands upon the cooling body. The tiny bird hops across the unmoving chest, picking at the weed seeds embedded in the tunic's curled wool strands. The bird's black-capped mate lands next to her. He trills out his high, sweet call. The female soon joins him, and the garden fills with song.

Molossus wanders into the garden, attracted by the open gate. He halts at Scipio's body. The dog reaches out a hand-sized paw and gently nudges it, whining. He sniffs the body once, twice, then begins his mournful howl.

LITERNUM. The eighth day has arrived, and with it the sorrow of a grieving town. By twos and threes, the Liternum residents gather around the dirt road entrance to the Scipio villa, waiting for the start of the processional. Hundreds of legionnaires and equites are there, garbed in the simple gray tunics of the Roman soldier.

The infantrymen and knights have arrived from every part of the nascent Roman Empire. They come to bid farewell to the man that led them to so many victories in Gaul, Iberia, Africa, and Asia.

The villa's gates slowly swing open. The pipers and tuba players step out onto the road, playing their sorrowful tunes. Scores of indigo-robed women follow them, wailing and crying. "Scipio, Scipio Africanus," the professional mourners chant. They grab each other and weep, tearing out strands of their hair.

Eight white-togaed men follow the mourners. Each holds a wax death mask of one of Scipio's ancestors in front of their faces. "My son, my son!" moans a man holding the mask of his father, Publius Scipio.

"He has joined us," declaims one with the mask of Grandfather Lucius Scipio the Elder. Each ancestor announces his role as consul or general to Rome, impressing the onlookers with the glory of the Cornelius Scipio line.

After the eight men pass, the onlooker's eyes fix anxiously on the villa entryway.

The body of Scipio Africanus emerges, borne on a shallow purple couch supported by two golden poles. The great man is garbed in his purple triumphal toga, his gold victory wreath sheathing his oiled gray curls. A silver obol gleams from Scipio's cold blue lips, Charon's fee for ferrying him across the Styx to Hades.

Lucius and Laelius carry the front poles on their shoulders, weeping unabashedly. Marcus Aemilius supports the center, flanked by Scipio's son Publius. All wear the dark brown togas of family mourners.

A solemn King Masinissa of Numidia carries one rear pole, his lion skin robe trailing behind him. King Philip of Macedonia shoulders the other, resplendent in a black silk robe and bejeweled gold crown. The former enemy of Rome looks straight ahead, avoiding the glares of the soldiers who once fought against him.

Amelia follows behind the bier. Her disheveled hair flows down the shoulders of her indigo robe. Prima accompanies her, similarly garbed. Tiberius Gracchus walks with young Cornelia Africana, holding tight onto her tiny hand.

Scores of consuls and senators follow the Scipio family, wearing the dark gray toga pulla of mourning. Generals Nobilior and Flamininus are there, paying tribute to the man who helped elect them to their consulships.

Cato follows in the rear line of the dignitaries, his seamed face twisted into a grimace of disapproval. His fellow senators glance warily at him, still puzzled that he chose to attend.

The funeral procession wends its way to the necropolis on the edge of town, halting in front of a six-foot log pyre. The pall bearers raise Scipio's bier onto the platform and line themselves in front of it, guarding his body from invading spirits. Tiberius Gracchus steps from the line. He places his left hand over his heart and reaches out to the mourners with his right.

"Scipio Africanus and I had our differences, as is customary between men of strong will and opinion. But I am here to testify that Rome treated him ill. In Iberia, this man routed and put to flight four of the most renowned Carthaginian commanders.[cclxxi] He captured King Syphax of Numidia, crushed Hannibal, made mighty Carthage our tributary, and banished King Antiochus beyond the Taurus Mountains. He had no equal."

Hearing Gracchus' words, Cato stares at the ground. *He has the truth of it, but that does not excuse the man's thievery. Still, I almost regret what I must do.*

Tiberius steps closer to the mourners, his voice low and angry. "Rome has treated him most disgracefully, as Carthage did to Hannibal, but *we* are the more disgraceful. The two greatest cities in the world have proved themselves, almost at the same time, ungrateful to their foremost men. But Rome is the more ungrateful of the two, for whilst Carthage after her defeat drove the defeated Hannibal into exile, Rome would banish the victorious Scipio in the hour of her victory."[cclxxii]

Gracchus fixes his eyes on the Liternum townspeople, ignoring the patricians about him. "He was the greatest of all of us. And I tell you now, as a priest of Rome, I have seen the future. His children, and his children's children, shall bear the gift of his concern for the people. Their glory shall follow his into history."

Cornelia's husband steps back into the line of pall bearers. Lucius Scipio walks over to Amelia and kisses her on both cheeks. "It is time to send him to our ancestors," he tells her. She nods mutely, her body wracked with sobs.

Lucius beckons for an indigo-cloaked torch bearer, who is one of the local undertakers. Lucius takes the man's flaming brand and walks around the pyre, touching it to the balls of resin embedded in the split logs. Curtains of flames leap around the edges, masking the body within.

With a wail that would stagger the gods, Amelia falls to her knees, her hands clawing into the dirt. The funeral party stands silent as she cries our her grief.

Prima bends over Amelia and places her hands on her shoulders. "Come, Sister. He has begun his journey."

Prima eases Amelia to her feet and leads her toward the villa, followed by Publius and Cornelia. The crowd begins to slowly disperse, many wandering over to visit the humble family tombs that dot the seaside landscape.

Marcus Aemilius strides toward the Scipio villa, wiping at the corners of his eyes. A strong hand locks upon his shoulder. "Wait," it commands.

Philip of Macedonia steps in front of the tribune. "I have something that belongs to you," he says.

The king waves over an attendant. The muscular young slave approaches, hefting a small oak chest fastened with a gleaming gold clasp. Philip pulls the peg from the clasp and opens it.

The helmet of Marcus Silenus rests inside, its battered surface immaculately polished. Philip cradles it in his strong, spiderlike fingers and lifts it from its repose. He extends it to Marcus Aemilius.

"I was tempted to put it on the pyre with Scipio, so that Rome's greatest general and would have its greatest soldier protecting him." He smiles. "But your father is already in Hades. I am sure he will protect Scipio when he joins him."

Marcus stares at the helmet, dumbfounded. His lips move, but no words emerge. "Gr-gratitude," he finally manages. "With all my heart, gratitude."

The aged king's lips curl into a smirk. "Scipio gave this to me as a gift, so touching me that I vowed to be a friend to him and Rome, even though I was drunk on my ass!" He chuckles. "A pity that people will only know about who he conquered, not who he won over."

With a swirl of his robes, the mighty king marches to his squadron of guards. He vaults onto his black stallion and gallops from Liternum, disdaining even a backward glance.

Lucius stands next to the granite block house that will serve as Scipio's tomb, holding the black marble urn that will hold Scipio's ashes. Cato draws up behind him, his lips pursed into one of his perpetual pouts. Lucius lays the urn at the tomb's doorstep.

"This might not be the most propitious moment, but I thought you should hear it from me," Cato declares. "I am reopening the inquiry into Scipio Africanus. I suspect Antiochus gave him monies that rightfully belonged to the state,[cclxxiii] and that he—"

Lucius' fist crashes into the side of Cato's head, sending him spinning to the earth. Cato sprawls face first into the earth, stunned by the force of Lucius' blow. Scipio's brother stands over him like an avenging god, his fist raised to strike.

"You could never break his spirit, so now you try to sully his memory! You, who was once the Wise and Noble Cato, who has whored himself to the Latins for fame and power. You are the greatest thief of all, for you have stolen your own honor!"

Lucius spits upon his prostrate foe. "Go ahead, take me to trial. Take my money, steal my house, do your worst. But if you try to slander him any further, I will kill you with my own hands!" Lucius storms back to the Scipio villa, leaving a stunned Cato to grovel in the dirt.

That night, Masinissa sits at a center table of the Scipio banquet room, an honored guest at the funeral feast. Laelius sits next to him, his face still masked with sorrow. Amelia strolls in, wearing a brown mourning gown. She sits on the couch and places her hand over Masinissa's.

"I am so grateful that you came here to see him off, my King. But I am more grateful that you two finally became friends again. He so valued your friendship. And its loss so pained him."

"I have been a bitter fool," Masinissa says, a lone tear trickling down his cheek. "He saved my son and saved my kingdom. Were it not for him, Hannibal and Carthage would probably rule all of Africa right now!"

Laelius chuckles. "A pity Hannibal could not be here. Wouldn't that have made old Cato's eyes pop!"

"And mine, too," adds Lucius.

Laelius frowns. "Scipio has protected Hannibal from capture. With him gone, I fear that the Latins will only redouble their efforts to bring him back and execute him."

Masinissa shakes his head. "You Romans might catch him, but you'll never execute him. He would never let that happen."

NICOMEDIA, BITHYNIA,[cclxxiv] 183 BCE. CA-RUNK! CA-RUNK! CA-RUNCH! The battering ram crashes through the splintered oak door, its ram's head jutting over the bent reinforcing bar.

"Hit it again," growls a gruff voice. The ram crashes again. The thick doors bow inward, succumbing to the relentless assault.

Two stories above the manse's vestibule, a regal old man sits in his throne-like mahogany chair, listening to the Romans pounding through his entrance.

*They could have prised out the hinges and saved themselves the trouble.* He smiles to himself. *Typical Romans. No imagination. All muscle and noise.* He shakes his head, still smiling. *I swear, Scipio must have been sired by a Greek—or a Carthaginian!*

The battering grows louder. Hannibal sighs deeply. *You knew this day was coming. They wouldn't quit until they found you.*

"You know what to do, Olivo," Hannibal says.

The Carthaginian attendant blinks back his tears. "Master, are you sure? You could write Scipio—he's helped you evade them before!"

"I don't know if he's even alive," Hannibal says. "And I'm tired of running and hiding. Bring the cup. And don't scrimp on the herb!"

The portly old man pads into the next room. He grabs the brass cup that has sat there for a week, placed there when Hannibal learned that the Roman Senate had sent men to fetch him.

Sobbing and snuffling, Olivo empties a light green powder into the cup. He adds white wine and stirs it with his finger.

Olivo eyes the remaining powder. *No. You are not worthy to have the same death as him.*

"Quick, they'll be through it any minute," Hannibal calls. His former captain hurries in with the brimming cup.

Without a moment's hesitation, Hannibal gulps down its contents. He smacks his lips.

"Hm. I thought it would be more bitter." He turns to Olivo. "Get the ropes. You know what to do. We'll have the last laugh on these fools."

The Romans labor at the bent reinforcing bars, finally prying them from their wall clamps. The splintered doors fly open. The legionnaires pour inside.

"Check the rooms!" orders Tribune Quintius Flavius, carrying a set of manacles in his hands. The six soldiers range through the luxurious kitchen and bedrooms. Quintius ascends the winding iron stairway to the second floor. He stops at a wide mahogany door, intricately carved with scenes of Romans and Carthaginians locked in combat.

"Get up here," Quintius barks. "He'll be inside here!" When his men join him, Quintius pushes open the door.

A glassy-eyed Hannibal stares at the intruders, his mouth twisted into the ghastly rictus of a smile. A bronze cup lies on the floor, dotted with the final drops of his Sardonicus poison.

A thin gold wreath frames Hannibal's tight gray curls. His hands, legs, and torso are roped to the chair, ensuring that he would sit regally when he meets his pursuers.

Olivo sprawls face down at his master's feet. A dagger point juts from the bloody circle that blooms in the back of his snow-white tunic. His right hand rests upon Hannibal's silver-sandaled foot.

Carthage's greatest general sits beneath the fresco he has prepared months ago for this occasion, his final joke upon the Roman military that he has tricked so often.

In the fresco, hundreds of legionnaires sprawl dead across the Cannae field of battle. Hannibal stands on a hillock above them, leaning on his sword as he surveys the field of carnage. His dreadnought elephant, Surus, stands behind him, surrounded by a crowd of exuberant Carthaginians.

Quinctius scowls. "Get some whitewash. Cover that thing up immediately." He spits in disgust, knowing that whatever he does to the fresco, Hannibal will have accomplished his aim—Quinctius' men will talk of what they found today, speaking of it in hushed tones at Rome's wine bars and trattorias.

"What should we do with this old dog?" asks a young soldier, nudging Hannibal's shin with his toe.

The tribune glares at him. "Last year, that 'old dog' guided those torpid Bythnians to three victories over our allies.[cclxxv] He deserves our respect." He walks to the corpse and gently eases down Hannibal's eyelid, rearranging the black eye patch that covers the other.

The tribunes stares at Hannibal's smirking face. "He was a man for the ages. Were it not for Scipio Africanus, he'd have ruled the world. Both of them are gone, and the world is poorer for it."

SABINA HILLS, ROME, 180 BCE. Marcus Valerius Flaccus stretches out his long, bare legs, enjoying the feel of the velvet summer breeze. His villa's lush olive trees whisper invitingly below him, backdropped by the furious buzz of the busy cicadas.

*I'm the First Man of Rome!* he says to himself. *The successor to that cursed Scipio.*[cclxxvi] *What poetic justice! As if 'justice' didn't cost me enough bribes to ransom a prince. It was worth it. I'm at the pinnacle, and there's no Scipio to stop me!*

Flaccus plucks the last cube of salted tuna from a nearby tray. He pops it into his mouth, chewing thoughtfully. *What to do first? I should block that proposal to limit a man's public land holdings to three hundred acres.*[cclxxvii] *I'll buy at least that much of our new lands in Syria. Got to block that stupid idea that soldiers don't have to pay farm taxes while they are fighting. They can't support their lands, give it to us who can.*

Flaccus reaches for another piece of tuna, and finds the tray empty. "Evan!" he shouts. "Bring me more tuna. And some of that ostrich meat."

There is no reply.

"Gods damn you to Tartarus, where are you!" Flaccus barks. "Get in here or I'll whip your ancient ass!" Flaccus drums his fingers on his inscribed silver tray, listening for the sound of Evan's footsteps. He heaves himself from his padded chaise.

"I warned you! Now it's your ass!"

"Evan isn't coming," declares a voice behind him.

Flaccus leaps away from his chair. An iron hand locks onto his shoulder and slams him back into his seat. Before Flaccus can react, a hood is pulled over his head. A thick rope drops over his shoulders, cinching his arms against his chest. Strong hands lift up his legs and wrap them in rope.

"What? What do you want?" Flaccus blurts. "My guards are coming!"

"They aren't coming," the voice replies. "It is just the two of us. I have been waiting for this."

Flaccus feels a blade pressed against his heart, its sharp point pricking his chest. The stench of his urine fills the cool night air. "Money, I have lots of money. I'll pay you ten times whatever you were promised!"

"It isn't about money, it's about a promise," the voice replies. "Tell me, do you think a man is obligated to keep a promise to a dead man?"

*He must have promised someone he'd kill me*, Flaccus thinks, his mind racing for answers.

"You make a promise to a *person*." Flaccus whispers hoarsely, his voice muffled by the hood. "When that person ceases to exist, the obligation ceases to exist. It's only common sense!"

Flaccus endures a long, agonizing silence, backdropped by the buzzing thrum of a thousand cicadas. Finally, the voice replies.

"I see your point. And I agree."

Flaccus feels the blade retracted from his chest. He hears the weapon being laid upon his silver tray. Relief washes over him. *He was just threatening me. Now he'll tell me what he really wants.*

Two hands untie him and effortlessly pull him to his feet. The hood is yanked off of Flaccus' head. He stares into Laelius' grimly smiling countenance.

*He has let me see his face*, Flaccus realizes.

Laelius pulls back the hood of his night-black tunic. His golden curls cascade onto his wide shoulders. "I promised Scipio that I would not kill you until I knew you were truly responsible for the murders and attempted murders you have perpetrated."

A wicked smile curls about his lips. "But now he is gone and, as you say, my obligation is dissolved."

Laelius' steely hand grips Flaccus throat. "That only leaves the promise I made to myself. That I would kill you for what you have done." He chuckles. " I aim to keep that promise, because I'm not dead!" His grip tightens. "But you are, bastard."

Flaccus' eyes bulge from his head.

"This is for Scipio's mother, Pomponia. I know you and Postus Novus plotted her assassination. Prima killed him, and now it's your turn. Your turn for attempting to kill my wife, and Amelia, and who knows how many more!"

"I didn't do any of that!" Flaccus chokes. "You have no proof!"

"I have no proof, but I have no doubt." Laelius tightens his long, sinewy fingers. Flaccus' head thrashes from side to side. His hands tug futilely at Laelius' cabled forearms.

Flaccus' face darkens. Spittle foams from his mouth. Laelius stares into Flaccus' bulging eyes.

Flaccus' body spasms. His sandals scratch furiously across his white marble tiles. The scraping slows, then stops.

The cicadas' buzzing again dominates the night. Laelius shakes the limp body like a dog with a rat, searching for signs of life. He lowers the corpse to the tiles. Laelius squats upon the chaise, shaking and panting.

*Finish it before someone comes.* Laelius rises. He drags the body into the shadows, giving it a final kick. "At last, we are rid of you!" he says to the darkened space.

Laelius trots down the rose marble steps that lead to the gardens, sliding between the hedge rows that masked his entrance. He pauses before a statue of Dionysus, the god of life after death.

"You bring that bastard back and I'll kill him again," he tells it.

Laelius slides through the iron gates and trots to the grove where his horse is tied. He is soon riding on the Appian Way back to Rome, canopied by the infinite stars of a warm, moonless night.

**Cornelia Africana with Sons Tiberius and Gaius Gracchus**

**The Gracchi Brothers**

# XIV. EPILOGUE

ROME, 156 BCE. Polybius stands in front of the manse's double green doors, willing himself to be calm. *Take a few deep breaths, boy. He's nothing but a man. He knows the truth behind the legend. You have to find it out.*

The slender Greek historian grabs the brass knocker and bangs it twice, increasing its force as he gains more nerve. The door swings open. A broad-shouldered septuagenarian grins at him, his green eyes twinkling with delight.

"Come in, come in!" Laelius says. "I am so looking forward to this!"

Prima sticks her head around his shoulder. "Please do. Let him bother someone else with all his war stories, I'm sick of them!"

Laelius winks at Polybius. "Ignore that old woman. She still thinks she's a gladiatrix, except now she does all her fighting with me!"

"I have heard your gladiator school is the envy of the other ludi," Polybius tells her. "That you have a gladiatrix as the Second Sword of all Rome's fighters!"

"And she would be First Sword, if that wouldn't make our men feel so threatened!" She nods her rose-wreathed head at Laelius. "I like this boy. You tell him want he wants."

"As you command!" Laelius says, bending over in mock supplication.

The elderly couple pad into the hut sized atrium of their lavish Roman town house, shooing out their four grandchildren. Laelius gestures toward a plush, gold trimmed couch. "Recline yourself, Polybius. We'll have some wine here in the blink of Cyclops's eye!"

"You don't need any wine," Prima says, heading for her office. "It's bad for you."

Laelius winks at Polybius. "I survived three wars, and now I'm supposed to be scared of a grape?" he says loudly. "I do not think so!" Prima waves a knobby fist at him, and disappears into her room.

Laelius plunks onto a stool in front of Polybius, his hands clasped between his knees. "So, I hear you are writing this big, important book, which you are going to call The Histories.[cclxxviii] That is excellent! And I am going to be in it, which is even more excellent! How can I help you?"

"Well, you can start with telling me about Scipio Africanus, and your friendship with him. People remember him as the man who conquered Hannibal the Great."

"You want to hear about Scipio? Oh, of course you do! No, don't be embarrassed, I don't mind. Rome has not seen his like, nor ever will they. What do you want to know?"

Polybius removes a vellum scroll and an ink stylus from his satchel, then a writing board and a pot of octopus ink. He dips his stylus into the pot and places it near the top of the scroll. "Tell me how it all started."

Laelius laughs softly. "It started with a promise, a promise that changed his life. You see, Scipio was a quiet, scholarly, boy. He wanted nothing more than to be a teacher. As you know, that is an unpopular undertaking for a patrician from a military family. His father, General Publius Scipio, made him promise to protect Rome from harm. That led him down a pathway he would never have pursued."

"You were there when Scipio made his promise?"

"Oh yes! Scipio, Amelia, and I were in a tutorial session with old Asclepius,[cclxxix] when his father called him to the family altar to make the vow. I remember it very well."

"Amelia was there, too?" Polybius asks, surprised.

"They were childhood friends before they became sweethearts," Laelius says. He chuckles. "Young Amelia fought with Scipio so much! You would never think they would have the love of the ages."

Laelius leans forward. "In fact, you had best save some room in your book for their daughter Cornelia. She is quite the legend around here. She refused to marry King Ptolemy and become Queen of Egypt. All just to stay here and raise her two boys![cclxxx] I hear they are going to erect a statue to her and put it in the Forum. Quite an achievement for a woman, wouldn't you say?"

"You would say that," Prima snipes, her voice coming from the adjoining room. She pads in and stands beside Laelius, resting her hands lightly upon his shoulders.

Laelius pats Prima's hands. "Such a wife! This woman can kill a man with those hands, or lift the aphids off a rose without moving the petals!"

"Best you remember that," Prima says, squeezing his shoulders.

Laelius laughs. "Woman, you distract me! My point was, Scipio is dead and buried, but his story continues through his children and grandchildren. Those two young boys of Cornelia's, they will make their mark upon the tablet, just you wait and see!"

Polybius inks in some notes upon his scroll. "I heard that their father, Tiberius Gracchus, insisted he must marry Cornelia because the gods predicted greatness for his family."

Laelius waves his hand. "Yes, yes, that is true. Old Tiberius was a bit crazy, even for a priest! But this time, young man, I think he just may be right."

ROME, 133 BCE. *It's him!* Agrippa hears the familiar bass voice, ringing through the streets like a brass trumpet sounding the call to battle. *He's started already, I have to get over there*!

# Epilogue

The retired centurion leans over his marble butcher's counter and scoops a mixture of pork and sage into a pig's small intestine, knotting it at the end. *There! A sausage fit for a workingman, if you can still find one around here.*

Agrippa unties his butcher's apron and hangs it on a whale bone hook. "You keep an eye on the shop," he tells Consus, his teen-aged son. "I'll be back in an hour. I want to hear Tiberius stick the shaft to those patricians."

The elderly man hurries through a side door in Rome's new indoor marketplace. He strides down the Argiletum Passage, turning right to enter the Comitium, the Forum's open air meeting space. His friend Postumus walks out from the rear of the crowd and joins him.

Agrippa squeezes Postumus' forearm stump. "I didn't expect you here today."

The retired tribune laughs. "I let my students out early so they could see this. Why teach history when you can see it being made?"

Agrippa watches Tiberius Gracchus the Younger step up to the speaking rostra, a platform twenty feet above his adoring public. The sturdily built man is flanked by his brother Gaius, a slender youth with bulging, excitable eyes.

As is his custom, the newly elected Tribune of the Plebs faces away from the Senate chambers, evidencing his well-known disdain for aristocrats. Thousands of plebs pack the Comitium, filling every step alcove that surrounds it.

Though Tiberius is a patrician, the veteran soldier eschews his patrician toga, wearing the plain gray tunic of a commoner. He spreads wide his muscular, battle-scarred arms.

"The time has come," he shouts, his voice echoing across the square. "Rome's citizens are calling in their loan. And who owes us, my people? The Optimates, those soft-handed aristocrats who have stolen our jobs and lands!" He pauses as the crowd roars their agreement, his green eyes staring into their upturned faces.

He slowly turns north to face the Senate chambers. "Today's leaders buy our citizens' farms while they are away fighting for us, adding poor men's land to their bloated estates. Then they stock the farms with slaves, the very men and women our soldiers bring to them from the war! And what is our soldier's reward for all this? They return home to find that they have neither lands nor jobs!"

Gaius shoulders his way in the front of his brother. "We, the Populares,[cclxxxi] will no longer accept this!" he shouts, his gray eyes flashing. "Tiberius and I will recover these lands and restore them to the citizenry. Our people will be victims no more!"

"No more!" Tiberius echoes. "The wild beasts that roam over Italy have their dens, each has a place of repose and refuge. But the men who fight and die for Italy enjoy nothing but the air and light; without house or home, they wander about with their wives and children!"[cclxxxii]

He stabs his finger at the Senate chambers. "Our citizens fight and die to protect the rich and luxurious lifestyle enjoyed by others. But you, the so-called masters of the earth, have not one clod to call your own!"[cclxxxiii]

As one, thousands of fists rise into the air, brandishing their affirmation. "Gracchus, Gracchus!" the citizens chant.

Agrippa leans to Postumus' ear, shouting to be heard over the din. "Was there ever such a pair of brothers? Tiberius and Gaius are the most gifted men in Rome.[cclxxxiv] They could have been patrician scions, but they have deigned to champion the common man's interests."

Postumus nods. "And their grandfather was Scipio Africanus! A world conqueror who championed arts and culture. Mankind will remember him as the greatest Roman of all!"

Agrippa shakes his head. "Men being men, they will only remember Scipio's victories. Who will testify to his peacetime achievements?"

"Do not despair," Postumus tells him. "Greatness has a way of being discovered. Maybe Scipio's tale will yet be told."

## About the Author

Martin Tessmer is a retired university professor of instructional design and technology. He has served as a training design consultant to the United States Navy, Coast Guard, and Air Force.

The author of thirteen nonfiction and fiction books, his most current endeavor is the Scipio Africanus Saga. It contains *Scipio Rising, The Three Generals, Scipio's Dream, Scipio Risen, Scipio Rules*, and *Scipio's End.*

A decades-long resident of Denver, Martin Tessmer lives with his fiancée Cheryl and their two Australian Cattle Dogs, Hector and Rita. His website is scipioafricanus.org.

# End Notes

---

[ii] https://en.wikipedia.org/wiki/Calisthenics
[iii]https://en.wikipedia.org/wiki/Tiberius_Sempronius_Longus_(consul_194_BC)
[iv] Livy, 24,46,182.
[v] Ibid.
[vi] For an excellent example of a Roman marching schedule, see Steven Kaye's article, *Observations on marching Roman legionaries: velocities, energy expenditure, column formations and distances.* http://www.bandaarcgeophysics.co.uk/arch/Roman_legionary_marchingV2.html#Example
[vii] Gabriel, Richard. *Scipio Africanus: Greater than Napoleon.* Dulles, Virginia: Potomac Books, 2008. pp. 138-140.
[viii] Livy, 34, 46, 182.
[ix] Ibid.
[x] http://www.huffingtonpost.com/2013/11/11/history-of-birthdays_n_4227366.html
[xi] https://www.forbes.com/sites/drsarahbond/2016/10/01/the-history-of-the-birthday-and-the-roman-calendar/#2760a1f77bdc
[xii] https://en.wikipedia.org/wiki/Seleucus_II_Callinicus
[xiii] Antiochus had declared himself to be such a champion. See https://en.wikipedia.org/wiki/Antiochus_III_the_Great
[xiv] http://www.livius.org/articles/battle/cynoscephalae-197-bce/?
[xv] Livy, 34, 46, 182
[xvi] Livy, 47, 46, 183.
[xvii] Livy, 35,5, 200.
[xviii] Livy, 34, 46, 183.
[xix] Ibid.
[xx] Livy, 34, 47, 184
[xxi] Livy, 34, 47, 184.
[xxii] Ibid.
[xxiii] After Hannibal's victory at Cannae, in which forty thousand Romans were killed, he refused to attack a vulnerable Rome. Maharbal, his cavalry commander, told Hannibal he knew how to win a victory, but not how to use it. https://en.wikipedia.org/wiki/Maharbal
[xxiv] Marcus Sergius had an iron hand fashioned for himself during the Second Punic War, https://en.wikipedia.org/wiki/Marcus_Sergius
[xxv] As mentioned in *Scipio Rising* and *The Three Generals*, by Martin Tessmer. A dictator with imperium has the power to appoint his own officers to whatever rank he chooses. Scipio chose Laelius as his admiral, and later as his cavalry commander.
[xxvi] https://en.wikipedia.org/wiki/Risus_sardonicus
[xxvii] Plutarch, *Moralia*, 241.
[xxviii] Livy, 35, 13, 207.
[xxix] According to Livy, Antiochus worried that his son would replace him when he became old. Livy, 35, 15, 209.
[xxx] https://en.wikipedia.org/wiki/Cato_the_Elder
[xxxi] https://en.wikipedia.org/wiki/Pythagoreanism
[xxxii] https://en.wikipedia.org/wiki/Twelve_Tables
[xxxiii] Livy, 35,12, 206
[xxxiv] Livy, 34, 49, 185.
[xxxv] Ibid.
[xxxvi] https://en.wikipedia.org/wiki/Brazen_bull

[xxxvii] This refers to Scipio's raid on the camps of Syphax and Hasdrubal Gisgo, as mentioned in Chapter IV of *Scipio Risen.* See also Nigel Bagnall's *The Punic Wars: Rome, Carthage, and the Struggle for the Mediterranean*, p. 279.
[xxxviii] Chapter VIII of *Scipio Rules. Book Five of the Scipio Africanus Saga.*
[xxxix] Present-day Tivoli.
[xl] Livy, 34,62,190.
[xli] Livy, 34,58,190.
[xlii] Livy, 34, 57, 189.
[xliii] Ibid.
[xliv] Livy, 34, 59, 191.
[xlv] Livy, 34, 62, 195.
[xlvi] Livy, 34, 60, 191.
[xlvii] https://en.wikipedia.org/wiki/Cato_the_Elder
[xlviii] https://en.wikipedia.org/wiki/Cato_the_Elder
[xlix] See " Philip's Match" in *Scipio Rules.*
[l] Livy, 35, 12, 206.
[li] Livy, 35, 12, 207
[lii] Livy, 35, 13, 207.
[liii] Livy, 34, 61, 192.
[liv] Ibid
[lv] Vermina was the son of King Syphax, Masinissa's mortal enemy. https://en.wikipedia.org/wiki/Vermina
[lvi] Livy, 34,62,195.
[lvii] Livy, 34, 62, 194.
[lviii] Ibid.
[lix] Livy, 34, 62,195.
[lx] Cato acted as Scipio's quaestor in the Carthaginian War, until Scipio sent him home.
[lxi] https://en.wikipedia.org/wiki/Ch%C3%A2teau_Bargylus
[lxii] A YouTube version of the 3400-year old song is available at https://www.youtube.com/watch?v=DBhB9gRnlHE
[lxiii] Livy, 35,15,209. No one knows who poisoned the king's son, but the king himself was suspect.
[lxiv] Livy, 35,15,209.
[lxv] Livy, 35,14,208.
[lxvi] Ibid
[lxvii] Livy, 35,26,210.
[lxviii] Livy, 35,18,212.
[lxix] Livy, 35,19,213.
[lxx] Ibid.
[lxxi] Ibid
[lxxii] Chapter XII, "Cato's Wars," in *Scipio Rules.*
[lxxiii] Livy, 35, 11, 204.
[lxxiv] These are variants of the actual political graffiti found in the preserved ruins of Pompeii. https://www.ancient.eu/article/467/pompeii-graffiti-signs--electoral-notices/
[lxxv] Livy, 34, 52, 187.
[lxxvi] In ancient Rome, it was common to call in favors and pander to the wealthy, presaging current campaign practices. https://en.wikipedia.org/wiki/Elections_in_the_Roman_Republic
[lxxvii] Livy, 35, 23, 214.
[lxxviii] Livy, 35, 10, 204.
[lxxix] Livy, 35, 23, 214

[lxxx] Livy, 35, 33, 218.
[lxxxi] Ibid.
[lxxxii] Livy, 35,33,218.
[lxxxiii] Gabriel, page 218.
[lxxxiv] Ibid.
[lxxxv] Richard Gabriel. *Scipio Africanus, Rome's Greatest General.* Dulles, Virginia: Potomac Books, 2008. As Gabriel (p. 218) notes, Lucius Scipio had primarily served in staff positions up to this point, and Glabrio's appointment was likely politically motivated.
[lxxxvi] The site of modern day Pteleos, in Thessaly.
[lxxxvii] www.reddit.com/r/AskHistorians/comments/1ijuzx/why_was_the_anchor_the_symbol_of_the_seleucid/
[lxxxviii] Livy, 35, 43,224.
[lxxxix] Livy, 35,44,225.
[xc] https://en.wikipedia.org/wiki/Philip_of_Megalopolis
[xci] Livy, 36,8,241.
[xcii] The Lex Oppia limited woman's jewelry and dress.
[xciii] https://en.wikipedia.org/wiki/Cosmetics_in_Ancient_Rome
[xciv] Livy, 36,6,241.
[xcv] Livy, 36,7,243.
[xcvi] Gabriel, p. 218.
[xcvii] Livy, 36, 9, 245.
[xcviii] After Philip lost the Second Macedonian war, Philip surrendered his son to Rome as part of his peace agreement.
[xcix] Livy, 36, 8, 244.
[c] https://en.wikipedia.org/wiki/Battle_of_Thermopylae_(191_BC)
[ci] https://en.wikipedia.org/wiki/Erotes#Eros
[cii] Livy, 36, 10, 246.
[ciii] Ibid.
[civ] Livy, 33, 47, 138.
[cv] https://en.wikipedia.org/wiki/Ancient_Greece_and_wine
[cvi] In Greek weddings, the groom gave presents to the bride's family, to provide for her in the event of his death. http://factsanddetails.com/world/cat56/sub367/item2024.html
[cvii] Livy, 36, 11, 247.
[cviii] Ibid.
[cix] https://en.wikipedia.org/wiki/Battle_of_Thermopylae
[cx] http://penelope.uchicago.edu/Thayer/e/gazetteer/periods/roman/topics/daily_life/children/bulla.html
[cxi] Livy, 36, 11, 247.
[cxii] Ibid.
[cxiii] Shuckburgh, Evelyn. A History of Rome to the Battle of Actium. The Pergamum Collection, 2013.
[cxiv] Livy, 36, 16, 251.
[cxv] Ibid.
[cxvi] Shuckburgh, Evelyn. *A History of Rome to the Battle of Actium.* The Pergamum Collection, 2013.
[cxvii] https://en.wikipedia.org/wiki/Marcus_Baebius_Tamphilus
[cxviii] http://www.home-remedies-for-you.com/facts/greek-medicines.html
[cxix] The Battle of the Aous Gorge, as described in the "Philip's Match" chapter of *Scipio Rules.*
[cxx] Ibid.
[cxxi] Present day Mount Kallidromo.

[cxxii] Livy, 36, 16, 253.
[cxxiii] https://explorable.com/aristotles-psychology
[cxxiv] Livy, 36, 18. 255.
[cxxv] Livy notes that Flaccus failed to reach his strategic points, although it is not clear why. Livy, 36, 18, 256.
[cxxvi] Ibid.
[cxxvii] Ibid.
[cxxviii] Ibid.
[cxxix] Ibid.
[cxxx] Livy, 36, 21, 258.
[cxxxi] Ibid.
[cxxxii] Ibid.
[cxxxiii] Ibid.
[cxxxiv] Livy, 36, 26, 262.
[cxxxv] Ibid.
[cxxxvi] Ibid.
[cxxxvii] Livy, 36, 19, 257.
[cxxxviii] Recent evidence indicates that some Greeks used their houses as both tavern and brothel. http://www.thehistoryblog.com/archives/1473
[cxxxix] Modern-day Nafpaktos, in the Aetolia-Arcania province of western Greece.
[cxl] Livy, 36, 35, 270.
[cxli] Ibid.
[cxlii] Livy, 36, 34, 269.
[cxliii] Ibid.
[cxliv] https://en.wikipedia.org/wiki/Thracian_warfare
[cxlv]https://en.wikipedia.org/wiki/Roman_roads#Construction_and_engineering
[cxlvi] http://www.vroma.org/~bmcmanus/arena.html
[cxlvii] Livy, 36, 41, 275.
[cxlviii] Ibid.
[cxlix] Livy, 37, 34.312-13. Scipio's son was captured by pirates, who gave him to Antiochus. The specific circumstances of that capture remain unclear.
[cl] https://en.wikipedia.org/wiki/Gaius_Laelius
[cli] Gabriel, p. 219.
[clii] Livy, 37, 2, 280.
[cliii] Livy, 37, 3, 281.
[cliv] Ibid.
[clv] Ibid.
[clvi] Ibid. Flaccus is not named *per se* by Livy. Livy notes that the Senate as a whole was "intrigued" by this notion. I have used Flaccus to voice the Senate's interests pitting Africanus against Hannibal.
[clvii] Gabriel, p. 219.
[clviii] Ibid.
[clix] Ibid.
[clx] Phyrgia is now part of west-central Turkey.
[clxi] Livy, 36, 45, 278.
[clxii] Livy, 37, 6, 282.
[clxiii] Ibid.
[clxiv] https://www.greeka.com/peloponnese/mycenae/mycenae-excursions/mycenae-cyclopean-walls.htm
[clxv] Livy, 37, 1, 280.
[clxvi] Livy, 37, 6, 283.
[clxvii] Ibid.
[clxviii] Livy, 37, 7, 284.

[clxix] https://en.wikipedia.org/wiki/Hamilcar_Barca
[clxx] https://en.wikipedia.org/wiki/Ancient_Thessaly
[clxxi] https://en.wikipedia.org/wiki/Marcus_Fulvius_Nobilior_(consul_189_BC)
[clxxii] The known Tabularium (Hall of Records) was not built until 78 BCE, but it is reasonable to suppose that the assiduous Romans had a version of it before then.
[clxxiii] Hannibal directed part of the Syrian fleet for at least one engagement (the Battle of Side), although he was not a skilled naval commander. Livy, 37, 23, 300.
[clxxiv] Appian, Chapter V. Delphi Complete Works of Appian. Hastings, East Sussex: United Kingdom.
[clxxv] Livy, 33, 30, 124.
[clxxvi] Livy, 37, 7, 284.
[clxxvii] The Nemoralia was celebrated by Romans in August at the rising of the full moon. There was likely an equivalent in Greece. https://en.wikipedia.org/wiki/Nemoralia
[clxxviii] Livy, 37, 7, 284.
[clxxix] Ibid.
[clxxx] King Philip's elite cavalry.
[clxxxi] Livy, 27, 7, 285.
[clxxxii] Lake Vegoritida. https://en.wikipedia.org/wiki/Lake_Vegoritida
[clxxxiii] Near modern day Teos, on the Ionian peninsula.
[clxxxiv] Livy, 37, 28. 306.
[clxxxv] Ibid.
[clxxxvi] Livy, 37, 29, 306.
[clxxxvii] Livy, 37, 29, 307.
[clxxxviii] Ibid.
[clxxxix] https://en.m.wikipedia.org/wiki/Lucius_Aemilius_Regillus. He offered his prayer to the lares permarini, the deities who protect seafarers.
[cxc] https://en.wikipedia.org/wiki/Greek_fire#History
[cxci] Livy, 27, 30, 308.
[cxcii] Ibid.
[cxciii] Ibid.
[cxciv] Livy, 37, 31, 309.
[cxcv] Ibid.
[cxcvi] https://en.wikipedia.org/wiki/Elections_in_the_Roman_Republic
[cxcvii] https://en.wikipedia.org/wiki/Marcus_Fulvius_Nobilior_(consul_189_BC).
[cxcviii] Ibid.
[cxcix] https://en.wikipedia.org/wiki/Elections_in_the_Roman_Republic
[cc] Ibid.
[cci] Ibid.
[ccii] Ibid.
[cciii] As described in *Scipio Risen.*
[cciv] Ibid.
[ccv] https://en.wikipedia.org/wiki/Gallipoli
[ccvi] Gabriel, p. 222.
[ccvii] https://en.wikipedia.org/wiki/Salii
[ccviii] See footnote 11 in Livy, 37, 33, 311.
[ccix] Near modern Sart, in western Turkey.
[ccx] Livy, 37, 34, 312.
[ccxi] Ibid.
[ccxii] https://en.wikipedia.org/wiki/Beer_in_Syria#Ancient_history. Beer recipes were found on tablets dated to 2500 BCE.
[ccxiii] Livy, 37, 35, 313.
[ccxiv] Ibid.
[ccxv] Gabriel, 224.

[ccxvi] Livy, 37, 36, 314.
[ccxvii] Gabriel, p. 224.
[ccxviii] Ibid.
[ccxix] Gabriel, 226.
[ccxx] Livy, 37, 37, 315.
[ccxxi] Ibid.
[ccxxii] Modern-day Manisa, Turkey.
[ccxxiii] Livy, 37, 37, 315.
[ccxxiv] Livy, 27, 38, 316.
[ccxxv] Livy, 27, 39, 316
[ccxxvi] Gabriel, 226.
[ccxxvii] Livy, 37, 41, 319.
[ccxxviii] Gabriel, p. 227.
[ccxxix] Livy, 38, 40, 318.
[ccxxx] Ibid.
[ccxxxi] https://en.wikipedia.org/wiki/Battle_of_Magnesia
[ccxxxii] Ibid.
[ccxxxiii] Livy, 37, 42, 320.
[ccxxxiv] Ibid.
[ccxxxv] Livy, 37, 42, 321.
[ccxxxvi] https://en.wikipedia.org/wiki/Phalanx#Pushing
[ccxxxvii] Livy, 37, 42, 320.
[ccxxxviii] Ibid.
[ccxxxix] Ibid.
[ccxl] Livy, 37, 43, 321.
[ccxli] Ibid.
[ccxlii] https://en.wikipedia.org/wiki/Cataphract
[ccxliii] Livy, 37, 43, 322.
[ccxliv] https://en.wikipedia.org/wiki/Hannibal
[ccxlv] Livy, 37, 43, 322.
[ccxlvi] Ibid.
[ccxlvii] Livy, 37, 45, 323.
[ccxlviii] Livy, 37, 47, 324.
[ccxlix] Ibid.
[ccl] Ibid.
[ccli] Ibid.
[cclii] https://en.wikipedia.org/wiki/Princeps_senatus
[ccliii] Gabriel, p. 230.
[ccliv] Ibid.
[cclv] https://www.ancient.eu/Roman_Triumph/
[cclvi] Livy, 38, 50, 385.
[cclvii] https://en.wikipedia.org/wiki/Princeps_senatus
[cclviii] Appian (Chapter VII, Book 40) attests that Scipio was festively garbed instead of wearing the drab clothing that trial victims customarily wore.
[cclix] Appian, Polybius, and Livy attest that Scipio did not directly answer the charges, but proceeded to outline his life and victories. See Livy, 38, 50, 385.
[cclx] Polybius, 23, 14.
[cclxi] Gabriel, 232.
[cclxii] Gabriel, p. 230, reports this incident happening in 185 BCE. The scene depicted in this book is a combination of Scipio's reactions to several different accusations.
[cclxiii] Appian, Chapter VII, Book 40.
[cclxiv] Ibid.
[cclxv] Livy, 38, 51, 387.

[cclxvi] Gabriel, 231.
[cclxvii] Livy, 38, 57, 393.
[cclxviii] Aristotle, *Nicomachean Ethics*. Translated by Martin Oswald. Indianapolis, IN: Library of Liberal Arts. Book II, p. 33.
[cclxix] Ibid, pp. 33-35.
[cclxx] Gabriel, p. 233.
[cclxxi] These words are an adaptation of the speech Tiberius Gracchus gave to the Senate, in defense of Scipio. See Livy, 38, 53, 388.
[cclxxii] Ibid.
[cclxxiii] Gabriel, 232.
[cclxxiv] Nicomedia was the capitol of Bythnia, a northwestern region of modern day Turkey.
[cclxxv] https://en.wikipedia.org/wiki/Hannibal#Death_.28183_to_181_BC.29
[cclxxvi] https://en.wikipedia.org/wiki/Lucius_Valerius_Flaccus_(consul_195_BC)
[cclxxvii] https://en.wikipedia.org/wiki/Ager_publicus
[cclxxviii] https://en.wikipedia.org/wiki/The_Histories_(Polybius)
[cclxxix] As described in *Scipio Rising*, Chapter One.
[cclxxx] https://en.wikipedia.org/wiki/Cornelia_Africana
[cclxxxi] https://www.britannica.com/topic/Optimates-and-Populares
[cclxxxii] https://en.wikipedia.org/wiki/Tiberius_Gracchus
[cclxxxiii] Plutarch, "Tiberius and Gaius Gracchus." *Roman Lives*, Book 9, p. 90.
[cclxxxiv] Plutarch, p. 83.

Manufactured by Amazon.ca
Bolton, ON